SPREE

J.A. Konrath and Ann Voss Peterson

Chandler

"During the execution of a mission, you may find yourself outnumbered and outgunned," the Instructor said. "It will be your call whether to continue the operation, or abandon it. Always retain a cool head, and keep personal feelings in check. Once you let emotion control your decisions, you're dead."

The handcuffs were Smith & Wesson, gunmetal black. One bracelet was locked around my left wrist, the other around the aluminum side railing of the hospital bed.

I was in bad shape.

Exhausted.

Hurting in a dozen places.

Emotionally, I felt like a broken piñata, empty, my guts spilling out.

I wanted to rest. I wanted it so badly.

But I had promises to keep.

I reached my free hand into the duffel bag on my lap, prying out a pair of my jeans. My fingers squeezed the bag's seams until I located the bump—a fifty-dollar bill, tightly rolled around a length of wire. I teased out the money, shoved it into the front pocket, and then used the wire to open the handcuffs.

It took me fifteen seconds to dress in the jeans, a black shirt, and a black pair of Nikes. The cop who had left me my clothing, a Chicago homicide lieutenant by the name of Jacqueline "Jack" Daniels, had also provided some socks and underwear from my apartment, but I didn't want to risk the extra time it would have taken to put them on. According to her, the place was crawling with people who wanted to keep me there. Highly trained government people, who worked for an agency that didn't exist.

Just like me.

Though they worked for the same team I did, they followed a different coach. I'd become a liability. Something to be debriefed and disposed of.

I had other plans.

Jack had the smarts to also pack a baseball cap and my Ray-Bans. I stuck the Cubs hat on my head, keeping the brim low, and eased the sunglasses onto my face to cover up the many bruises. I'd still be recognized by pros, but hopefully the disguise would allow me an extra half a second before they reacted.

In the spy business, half a second was a very long time.

The hospital had all the obvious sounds and smells. Nurses chatting at their station. Intercom calls. Various beeping and pinging machines. Soft-soled shoes padding along polished tile floors. Down the hall a television was tuned to news of an accidental and aborted nuclear strike on England, and I tried not to listen too closely to the countless "facts," ranging from inaccuracies to blatant lies. I smelled lemon bleach, antiseptic ointment, body odor, and a lingering stench of powdered eggs—I must have missed breakfast.

I peeked out into the hallway and didn't see any men in black or men in uniform. Apparently the ones controlling the game had thought handcuffs and sedation were enough to keep me at bay.

Their mistake.

I imagined I was there to visit a sick friend. Someone who was very ill. I'd been up with him all night, and there wasn't much hope he'd live. Once the character was in my head, I adopted her posture, her movements. Shoulders slumped, downtrodden gait, lips pursed to keep from crying. I kept my face pointed toward the floor and headed to the elevator, my eyes darting back and forth behind my sunglasses, checking my periphery. On my way

I passed a patient's room, caught the snoring, chanced a look, and saw a glass vase filled with assorted flowers. I ducked inside, hefted the arrangement. Satisfied by the weight, I took it with me to the elevator and hit the call button.

According to Jack, my sister was being held on the sixth floor.

No doubt they were interrogating her.

No doubt they weren't being nice.

I felt a flare of rage, then forced it down. My sister, whom I knew by her codename, Fleming, didn't have the use of her legs. I'd been talking to her for years but only met her face-to-face a few days ago, surprised not only that I had a sister but that there were seven of us, all identical.

I was also surprised to discover the depth of the feelings I had for Fleming.

The thought of them hurting her...

The rage kicked in again, and I made a fist so hard my nails cut into my palm.

Despite my strong feelings, I had to be realistic. Attempting to rescue Fleming was a fool's game. I'd be killed, or captured. No two ways about it.

My primary objective should be to get out of there, find safe ground. The odds were against me being able to do even that much. No doubt the exits were being watched, I had no clue as to enemy numbers, and the only weapon I had was a posy vase.

The elevator doors opened. I stepped into the empty lift, eyeing the buttons.

First floor.

Sixth floor.

One or six. Pick your battle, Chandler.

My finger hovered over the 1.

I hit 6.

Fleming

"The enemy has no mercy," the Instructor said. "Don't expect to get any. The only things you can expect are pain and death. If they require information from you, they'll get it eventually. It's only a matter of how long you'll be able to hold out."

Fleming was in a wheelchair, a generic hospital model rather than one of her custom rides. She wore a hospital gown smelling of lemon bleach, and there were thick Velcro straps around her waist, legs, and arms. The straps hardly seemed necessary. She couldn't run away. Less than an hour ago she'd come out of surgery after being shot four times in the thighs. But the reason for the wheelchair had nothing to do with her current injuries. Fleming's legs had been crippled years ago, while she was in service to her country.

Now agents from that same country were holding her prisoner, trying to get her to talk.

Talk? About what? Chandler and I just saved millions of lives. They should be giving me a medal.

"Who do you work for?" the agent asked, staring down at her. He had a long, chalky face, a pointy nose, a pointy widow's peak. Fleming smelled aftershave on him. Old Spice. He wore the typical black suit of a spook—or spy—and judging by the way the other three in the room regarded him, he was obviously top man on the scene.

"We're on the same side," Fleming answered. "But that question is on a need-to-know basis."

The agent rested his hand on Fleming's bandaged one—earlier they'd allowed a doctor in to splint her broken fingers.

They still hurt like hell.

"I need to know," he said. "Who?"

"I take orders from two people. One is the president."

"And the other?"

"The other one is not you." Fleming flashed a bright smile.

The man squeezed her hand. Even though the lidocaine hadn't fully worn off, the pain was instant and overpowering. Fleming gasped.

"You have no identification," the man said, maintaining his grip. "No fingerprints on file. No hits on our facial recognition software. As far as our government knows, you don't exist." He squeezed harder. "Since you don't exist, I can do anything I want."

"Anything?" she grunted.

"Anything."

"Then you might want to brush your teeth. Smells like you were licking Uncle Sam's ass."

The agent released Fleming.

For a few seconds, it took everything she had to control her breathing and separate herself from the pain. Since her accident, she'd been behind a desk, working operations from the intel side. But she'd secretly longed to be a field agent again. To be out in the world, where the action was.

Be careful what you wish for...

"The other woman. She's your sister, yes?"

Fleming forced cool. "Where is she?"

"She's talking to one of my colleagues. He plays a bit rougher than I do. Your sister is telling him everything."

Fleming didn't have to force the laughter. It came naturally. While everyone had a breaking point, they hadn't had Chandler nearly long enough to reach hers.

The agent frowned. "You think I'm being funny? We're going to take you, and your sister, someplace where you'll never see daylight again."

"Where no one will ever look?" Fleming asked.

"Exactly."

"Like in your underwear?" It was sophomoric, but the insult felt good.

His frown deepened. "Prepare her for transport," he told his men.

The other agents moved forward.

"Hold on," Fleming said. "What's your name?"

The agent hesitated, then answered, "Malcolm."

Fleming looked beyond him, to the other men in the room. "Does anyone here have a mint for Malcolm? Or some gum?"

No one chuckled. Tough crowd.

Then one of them produced a syringe.

This was bad.

Very bad.

Fleming understood Malcolm's threat all too well. The United States had dozens of secret prisons throughout the world. Since it was the last superpower standing, those in charge had decided to wipe their asses with the Constitution. No more due process. No more trials by peers. No trials at all, in fact. US citizens could be kidnapped, tortured, and executed by their own government, all on the hush-hush.

Fleming knew what went on at these black sites. She also knew no one made it out of them alive.

"The president will have your head if you take me anywhere," Fleming said.

"Right now the president is in the middle of a worldwide scandal. It's a PR nightmare. I really doubt he cares what happens to you."

Especially since he probably blames me for his recent problems, Fleming thought.

She and Chandler had saved millions. But that didn't mean much for the commander in chief's approval ratings.

"You're worried," Malcolm said. "I can tell. You have good reason to be. Are you sure you have nothing to say?"

Fleming stayed quiet.

"Who do you work for?"

"OK, I'll tell you. I work for M."

"M?"

"On Her Majesty's Secret Service. I'm Agent 007. My name is Bond." Fleming forced herself to smile. "James Bond."

"Sedate her," Malcolm ordered.

The needle went in hard, and the drug worked quickly.

Fleming knew this would likely be the last moment of peace she would ever have.

She was tough. But everybody breaks.

And now, Fleming realized with terrifying certainty, she was about to find out what her breaking point was.

The White House

The president of the United States hadn't slept. And he wondered, with complete seriousness, if he'd ever sleep again.

The day before, the unthinkable had happened. Someone had managed to override the country's formidable defenses and launch a nuclear missile.

Only two things saved this from being the biggest debacle in the history of the United States. First, the damn thing detonated before hitting its target, causing no damage, collateral or otherwise. Second, the target was a friendly nation. Britain's prime minister was pissed off, for sure, and demanding answers. But the fact that the nuke had been headed for London and not Pyongyang or Karachi had probably saved the world from an all-out nuclear war.

So while the fate of humanity was assured, at least for the moment, the president was going to have to explain what had happened to the voters, the citizens of the United Kingdom, and the entire world, assuring them it wouldn't happen again.

The problem was that the president had no idea what had gone wrong. He had his best people on it, and no one could figure out where the directive to launch had originated. No weapons sites had been compromised. No one credible had claimed responsibility. The codes had been encrypted and guaranteed impossible to crack, and all the equipment had been tested and retested five times by three separate teams and assured to be in perfect working order.

The most powerful man in the world felt powerless. Worse, he felt impotent. His advisers had come up with various scapegoats and ways to redirect the blame, but none of them rang true, and he wasn't about to lie to the people, only to be caught later. So instead, the most powerful man on the planet was forced to do something even more reprehensible in the eyes of the world: admit he didn't know.

With a year left in his second term, he could take the popularity hit. Hell, it would sell more copies of his eventual memoir. But unless this was properly spun, it spelled death for his party, and for his running mate's chances in the next election. All the policies he'd worked so hard to implement during the past seven years would be scrapped when the opposition took the White House. Much as he disagreed with his vice president on many key issues, he could at least be counted on to continue this administration's efforts both at home and abroad. But now the VP's approval rating was synced with his, and at an all-time low, according to CNN.

The president wiped a shaky hand across his face, extending the motion into rubbing his jaw. A few minutes earlier, he'd ordered everyone out of the Oval Office, including the First Lady. He told them he wanted to be alone to compose himself before the next press conference, but in reality he didn't want anyone to see him so vulnerable. This was the lowest point of his career. Hell, it was the lowest point of his entire life. And there didn't seem to be any way out.

His breast pocket vibrated, and the president's breath caught. It was his cell phone. Not the regular one. The special one, the one to which only a handful of people in the world had the number. He placed it to his ear.

"This is the president."

"Mr. President, we have a lead on the attack. Two operatives. They're currently in a hospital in Chicago."

"Who do they work for?"

"That's the thing, sir. They work for us."

Chandler

"You are highly trained," the Instructor said, "and not many people in the world are able to do all the things you can do. But you aren't bulletproof. Avoid what danger you can. Run from what you can't avoid. Fight as a last resort."

The elevator doors opened on the sixth floor. Orthopedics. I kept the floral arrangement at face level, my head still but my eyes sweeping the floor. Three nurses, two in the center island, one in the perpendicular walkway, none of them paying attention to me. A fat guy in jeans, a cast on his arm, stood near the nurse's station, talking to an elderly woman. Ten rooms to my left, eight to my right, some doors open and some shut. And at the far end of the floor—

—an orange traffic pylon in front of a blue plastic tarp stapled to the walls and blocking the hallway.

I headed for that, maintaining focus on it but keeping hyper-aware of my surroundings. I stopped, briefly, at a hospital floor plan on the wall, memorizing the emergency exits. It revealed that the cordoned-off section led to a storage area and a freight elevator. I checked the nurses, each still preoccupied, and bee-lined toward the tarp. There was a card-stock sign taped at eye level, featuring a smiling construction worker in a hard hat: PARDON OUR DUST.

The posy vase in front of me was the dominating smell, roses and baby's breath, but beyond it I didn't catch any scent of plaster powder, sawdust, paint, or other remodeling smells. I dropped to one knee, setting down the arrangement and fiddling with a shoelace, and then took a quick peek under the tarp.

At the end of the hallway I saw three men in black suits. One pushed a gurney, two flanked him. Strapped to that gurney…

Fleming.

Picking up the flowers, I slipped under the tarp and began moving toward them at a quick clip. The nearest agent saw me, immediately reaching into his jacket. But my clothing, and the posies, caused him to hesitate for half a second, long enough for me to pitch the arrangement at his face—a two-handed shove, as if I were tossing a medicine ball.

It hit him in the forehead, and I launched into a sprint, reaching him after the vase broke across his nose in an explosion of water and flowers and shattered glass. I grabbed his emerging gun with my left hand, tugging him by the tie with my right, using speed and momentum to spin him around while bending his pistol to the side. He was quick enough to have gotten his finger inside the trigger guard, which I'd been anticipating, and his index finger hyperextended from the leverage, firing the weapon as his knuckle bent the wrong way.

The other two men had sprung into action, one pushing Fleming around the corner, the other dropping to a knee in a shooting stance.

I flipped over my guy's shoulder, putting him between me and the shooter, yanking the gun off his broken finger and dropping to the floor between his legs.

Two shots into the center mass of the agent on his knee, two more aiming up into the groin of Vaseface, and then I was taking a running dive onto the waxed tile floor, sliding on my belly, coming up on my side, and aiming in the direction where

I'd last seen Fleming, just in time to witness the service elevator doors closing.

I scrambled to my feet, racing toward the lift, sighting the small hole in the door. Contrary to action movies starring Bruce Willis, it is damn near impossible to pull elevator doors open because they have a locking mechanism. Firefighters and those servicing the elevator use a drop key to disengage the lock. I didn't have one, but I did have a Glock, and I aimed the barrel a few inches below the keyhole and fired four times in a tight grouping, then dug the butt of the gun between the doors.

I was able to pry them open, and I immediately jumped into the shaft after the plummeting car. I fell about twenty feet, a potentially lethal drop, but since the elevator and I were moving in the same direction I didn't hit with fatal force. I bent my knees and let my heels bounce against my ass, absorbing the hard impact while also keeping my balance. Even though I'd set my jaw, my molars clacked together hard enough to rattle my fillings. I felt a stab of pain in the side of my tongue where I'd bitten it, and the taste of blood tinged my mouth.

It was too dark to see much of anything, but I'd been in a few elevator shafts in my life and knew my way around. Judging from the sound, I determined the counterweight was to my left, and under my right foot I could feel the edge of the ceiling hatch. I moved farther right, sensing the wall behind me rushing past as we descended.

The agent below had to have heard me land, but if he was experienced, he wouldn't fire. Shooting in public places draws attention, and bullets and elevator cables aren't a good match.

I held my breath for a moment, anticipating the shots. They didn't come.

The lift stopped, and the doors opened. I waited, listening for the sound of gurney wheels, opting not to poke my head inside and have it shot off. When I heard the squeak of Fleming's cart being pushed away, I palm-slapped the hatch open and took a quick look.

The agent had pushed Fleming into a group of people milling in the lobby. I dropped through the opening, easing myself down with one arm, the other bringing up the gun.

"Down!" I yelled.

A few people dropped down. A few screamed. Some ran after the agent, blocking my shot.

I slipped through the elevator doors as they were closing, having to hopscotch over the civilians on the floor, rushing toward the exit doors at least three seconds behind my quarry. But he might as well have had an hour's head start; I was soon flanked by two, make that three, men in black suits, hands in jackets as they fought the crowd to get to me.

Did they want me alive? Or was I expendable because they had my sister?

It didn't matter. Either way I was outnumbered and outgunned, and we were in a hospital lobby filled with innocent people. Whatever secret branch of government this was, if they had the power to lock down a hospital, they wouldn't care much about collateral damage.

Unless I got out of there, innocents were going to die.

I switched directions, leapfrogging a cowering woman, trying to keep Fleming in sight as the agents closed in. As the gurney went out the exit, two more men in black suits came in the same door, blocking my pursuit.

I'd done my share of shooting while running, and though I was better than most, I still missed more often than not—it was damn near impossible to keep a gun steady at a full sprint. The Glock I held was a Model 21, chambered for .45 ACP. Its capacity was thirteen rounds, and I'd fired eight. I couldn't afford to waste any of the five shots I had left. But I also couldn't afford to stop, giving the agents surrounding me a stationary target.

As the new arrivals drew their weapons, I noticed a young mother in my peripheral vision, holding her baby tight as she crouched behind a water fountain. The stroller in front of her was empty.

Time to switch directions.

I made for the fountain and belly-flopped onto the stroller. Riding it like a boogie board, speeding toward the exit at a good clip, I extended the gun.

Wheels were smoother than footsteps, and my aim was true. Two shots. Two hits. Both agents went down, and I rolled between their falling bodies, coasting into the parking lot.

I saw Fleming's gurney being shoved into the back of an ambulance, already beginning to pull away.

I also saw six more agents converging.

I shifted my body weight, trying to steer left, but the carriage overturned, sending me rolling onto the blacktop. I tucked my arms in, protecting my head, using my toes to skid to a stop, and then I was on my feet again, sprinting after the ambulance. Gunfire peppered the asphalt around me.

Three of the agents got between me and my sister, one of them bringing up—

—Jesus, a Mac-10? Who the hell were these guys?

The submachine gun burped, spitting nineteen rounds a second. I'd barely had time to slide beneath the barrage, one leg out in front and one behind me like an MLB base thief, tearing my jeans to shreds on the parking lot sidewalk as the bullets screamed inches above my head.

Apparently they didn't need me alive.

I thrust from a modified splits position back to both feet, keeping my head low. Noting I was completely surrounded, I watched Fleming's ambulance vanish into Chicago traffic.

No time to pause, I cut left onto the lawn. Sprinting alongside the hospital building, I took aim at the two agents cutting me off, each of them already firing.

I went John Woo, diving forward, making myself a smaller target while giving me a chance to aim without having to compensate for the beat of my own footfalls.

For two full seconds I was Supergirl, flying straight at them, both arms outstretched, pointing the barrel at one and firing, seeing the back of his neck blowing out, adjusting my aim, squeezing the trigger a second time as I slammed onto the grass, chin and chest first, followed by my lower body.

Gunfire blasted in my ears. I didn't know if I'd hit the second agent, but the sod around me was getting chewed up by bullets, and I had to press forward or die. Scrambling up to my feet, I felt the tug on my shoulder, then the accompanying burn, and realized I'd been shot. I sighted ahead of me, leading with the Glock. The second agent clutched his bleeding gut with one hand, still firing with the other.

I ran straight at him, not willing to risk my final bullet unless I was guaranteed a kill shot.

He continued to fire, missing over and over, until I got close enough to see his frustration morph into fear, and the fear become disbelief as a blood flower blossomed out of his forehead.

I should have paused to scoop up his gun as I ran past, but the bulletstorm behind me had become a Category 5 hurricane. I turned the corner, and window glass and bits of brick from the building rained down on me so heavily I had to put my hands in front of my eyes and peek through split fingers.

I'd reached the rear of the hospital. A train platform stretched one story above me, attached to the building so any sick or injured Chicagoan with a transit pass could ride the El to health and well-being. I considered running up the stairs and hopping the train, but quickly dismissed the idea, instead ducking through the automatic doors to the ER just as the bad guys caught up and began to shoot at me again.

Incredibly, there were no agents in the emergency room lobby. Recalling the floor plan, I raced for the stairs, glass crunching underfoot, gunfire and screams drowning out my ability to hear myself think. Once in the stairwell, I started for the second floor, knowing I'd made the clichéd horror-movie mistake of going up, where I would likely become trapped. But I didn't have a choice. Fleming was gone, and the only chance I had of finding her was getting my hands on one of these agents and making him talk. Then, and only then, would I worry about escaping.

Still burning adrenaline, I charged up six flights of stairs, back to Orthopedics. When I reached the floor, I paused to get my breathing under control and do a body inventory.

Legs OK, except for a skinned knee. Feet OK. Hands OK. I was still holding the empty Glock, which I tucked into the back of my pants. Arms OK. Shoulders—

My one shoulder burned. I took a quick look, probing the wound with my finger. Just a graze, already beginning to clot.

Torso OK. Head OK. I took a deep breath, and did a quick inventory of my internal organs, finding all of them still working properly.

It was a miracle that I'd gone through that barrage and only sustained a few superficial injuries. Adrenaline could be useful in dealing with life-or-death situations, but it could also be hard to control, causing agents who are crack shots under normal circumstances to miss wildly. As luck and intensive training would have it, I was better at controlling the adrenaline rush than the men who were after me.

Regulating my heart rate and breathing, I let myself tune in to the surroundings. No one seemed to be coming up the stairs after me—which made sense because only a fool would have gone up. There were also no unusual smells or sounds—no sounds at all—which made me wary.

I opened the door fast, entered the ward in a crouch. The place seemed deserted, nurses and patients gone. Made sense. After the gunshots, they'd been evacuated.

A man was sprawled on the floor in the center of the corridor, a pool of blood beneath him. I recognized his uniform as hospital security. His hand was on his utility belt, reaching for his nightstick. He hadn't even been able to draw it before someone shot him in the heart.

I took the baton and stayed low, creeping around the nurses' station, heading for the cordoned-off hallway.

When I got within three yards, I paused, listening.

There was grunting going on beyond the blue tarp. Male, with accompanying heavy breathing.

I pressed my back against the wall and peeked through the slight opening in the side. An agent was lifting up a body bag—no doubt one of the men I'd killed—and muscling it onto a gurney.

I poured through the opening like liquid, fast and silent. Nightstick raised, I cracked down on the man's knee before he even noticed I was there.

The agent cried out, and although he'd missed my approach, he had enough training to draw his weapon as he crumpled to the floor on his good knee. I swung the stick two-handed, connecting with his gun, hitting a line drive down to the end of the hall. Then I followed up with a knee to his nose, and a tight spin kick to the side of his head.

He fell onto his ass. I hit his broken kneecap with the baton once more, making him scream. Like the other agents I'd encountered, he was white, midthirties, enough scars on his face and hands to indicate combat experience.

"You know the drill. Tell me where they took her, I let you live. Don't, and I keep bashing."

"Fuck you," he said, teeth clenched.

I hit his bad leg again, twice in rapid succession. He screamed. "Where is she?"

He grunted something unintelligible.

I whacked him again. "Right now you're looking at six months physical therapy. I keep this up, you'll never walk again. Where is she?"

His face was a rictus of sweat, pain, and fear. "OK! OK! She's—"

Movement, behind me.

I spun just in time to get an elbow to the side of my face. I turned with it, and then backpedaled while raising the baton. I was stunned, not by just the blow, but by the fact someone had snuck up on me. I'm not an easy girl to surprise.

It was another agent in a black suit, with the broad shoulders of a bodybuilder. He had four inches on me, and at least seventy pounds. Bald, black, his tie tucked inside his button-down shirt just below the Windsor knot.

I noticed the bulge in his jacket, indicative of a shoulder holster, but his hands were empty. I was confused as to why he hadn't drawn on me, and then I noticed his face.

The man was smiling, eyes crinkled in obvious enjoyment.

Big mistake, fella.

I moved fast, stepping close and swinging the nightstick at his head using a hapkido *dan bong* technique.

He raised both arms, somehow catching the baton between his right hand and left elbow, and then dropped to one knee, pulling me down with him.

As I shifted weight, he skipped from one knee to another, keeping me off balance, and then spun on one knee, pulling my baton in close to his face—kissing my hand—and then bringing his other fist around and connecting with my chin.

I staggered back, releasing the baton, not sure what had just happened. I was familiar with many different martial arts, and had earned black belts in half a dozen, but had never seen someone move like that.

I fell into a tae kwon do back stance, feet perpendicular to each other, palms flat, on the defense. My jaw was aching, and my ears rang from the blow.

He kept bouncing from one knee to the other, tossed the baton behind him, and then began to move his hands and elbows so quickly he looked like he was break dancing.

I struck with a palm, and he nudged away the blow with his elbow, extending the arm and punching me in the ribs.

I pivoted my hips, bringing up a knee; but he leaned backward, and I missed.

His smile got wider.

I switched my stance to Wing Chun, finding my centerline, throwing a fast vertical punch and stepping into it.

But as I extended, throwing my body weight behind the blow, he thrust a forearm at my wrist and deflected it. Then he tucked both hands against his face, his smile never fading, and began to bob and weave in an erratic, exaggerated way, practically impossible to hit.

I switched to muay Thai, jumping up, aiming a cobra punch at the top of his moving skull. He again blocked with his hand and elbow, stopping my forward momentum, then extending his elbow and snapping it against my temple.

I fell backward onto my ass, motes swirling through my vision. As I regained the ability to focus, I saw that my opponent was slapping his own forearms, beating out a rhythm that increased in speed until it sounded like a room of people applauding.

It wasn't capoeira. It wasn't Krav Maga. It wasn't pradal serey or Choi Kwang Do or any type of kung fu I'd ever seen. But whatever it was, he was so confident in his ability he didn't even bother to draw his gun.

I'd killed bigger men than this one with my bare hands, and his arrogance pissed me off.

I kicked out a leg, and one of his hands slapped at my ankle, gripping it tightly. I saw a black tattoo across his knuckles—the three letters JHR—and then he was throwing me against the wall. I got up fast, keeping my hands on the floor and lashing out with my right heel in a *meia-lua de compasso*.

It should have been a knockout kick. Instead he tucked his head into his shoulders so my foot glanced off, and then he dropped a knee onto my waist, knocking the air out of me.

"The Instructor didn't teach you these moves, did he?" the man said with a big grin. His voice was deep, with an accent I'd peg as Caribbean.

He lifted up one palm, then brought it down hard against my cheek, then the other, then the first one again, increasing in speed until he was hitting me as quickly as he'd been slapping his own forearms.

I tucked my chin into my chest, then scissored my leg around his and went for the knee lock, but he had weight and leverage on me. The punishing blows had begun to draw blood from my nose and mouth, the taste overwhelming, my head dizzy, and they were coming so fast I couldn't grab hold of my thoughts.

I reached behind the small of my back, grabbing the Glock, bringing it around and giving him something to focus on other than beating me to death. As expected, he deflected the weapon with his elbow, and I made a fist and crunched it between his legs, arching my back, trying to put my whole body into it.

He rolled with the punch, keeping a grip on my gun hand, and I let him have the weapon. Making my free hand into a claw, I raked it across his eyes, then pulled away in the opposite direction and scrambled out from under him.

I crawled on all fours, disoriented from the slapping, and scurried away, slamming my head into the wall before regaining my bearings and scuttling down the hallway as fast as I could move.

"Awww, don' go, sweet thing. Ol' Rochester ain't done playing with you yet."

Yeah? Well, I was sure as hell done playing with Ol' Rochester. I rounded the corner, the tile hard on my skinned knee, and smacked at the call button for the service elevator. My head throbbed.

Behind me, a beat thumped the walls and echoed down the corridor, a distinct Latin rhythm, reminiscent of a Gloria Estefan song from the 1990s.

Following me. Coming closer. Growing louder.

"Here I come, sweet thing."

I checked the call lights. The elevator was stopped on the fourth floor.

The drumming grew faster and crescendoed as he neared, the pounding echoed by my too-quick pulse.

Whoever this guy was, he wasn't a standard operative material. Not some Blackwater independent contractor hired for wet work. Not some military spook. This was a specialist. And if he knew about the Instructor, I could guess the exact reason he was brought in.

Me.

His fighting style rendered mine useless.

He was here to neutralize me.

"Chandler, baby. Don' you run from me, girl." He stretched out the *girl* like he was singing calypso.

I checked the elevator. On four, moving up to five. I peered through the open doors, down the shaft. The car was still too far to jump.

The tapping stopped. I turned to face Rochester.

His head peered around the corner, his smile wide and teeth gleaming.

My palms grew clammy.

"You're afraid, aren't you, girl? I like that."

His hands slapped the wall, and despite my best efforts, I flinched.

"I heard you were such a little badass," he said, increasing the tempo. "You're disappointing me, Chandler."

I wanted to pull myself to my feet, to run, but I was still too dizzy to manage it.

"They told me, if I bring you in alive, I can spend some quality time with you as a bonus."

He took another step closer. I checked the elevator. Still too far.

"I like a little spice in my girls. They always die on me too quick."

I glanced back at Rochester. He was two meters away, his fists up alongside his head.

"Ain't no sweeter sound than a woman makin' love, after I break her legs and hips."

He took another step forward. I decided there would be no lovemaking between us, ever, especially with broken bones.

I tucked my knees into my body, letting myself drop down the elevator shaft face first into the darkness.

Hammett

"When operations fail," the Instructor said, "don't spend time licking your wounds. Begin planning your next move. A lost battle doesn't mean a lost war."

After ditching the boat at the marina in Chicago Harbor, Hammett had taken an expensive cab ride to a hole-in-the-wall bar on Roosevelt and Pulaski, which she'd scoped out weeks earlier. As far as Hammett knew, the bar had no name, and it was only identifiable by the faded Old Style sign hanging in the storefront—a trait shared by at least fifty other local taverns in the city. This one boasted cheap domestic beer (though Old Style was conspicuous in its absence), an assortment of regulars in various stages of inebriation depending on the time of day, and four television sets, including a forty-inch flat screen that was always tuned to CNN.

Her nerves still frayed from her near-death experience with her sister Chandler, she settled into a booth with a large gin and tonic and put out a silent *don't fuck with me* vibe as she watched TV, waiting for the inevitable news that London had been destroyed in a nuclear attack.

But instead of glorious high-definition pictures of mushroom clouds and burning babies, the vacuous talking heads spoke with great gravitas about a missile launch malfunction over London airspace and how the warhead had been safely disarmed prior to detonation.

Hammett wasn't sure what happened. While on the boat, she'd been responsible for launching a US Trident missile using a sophisticated encrypted device, which had then fallen overboard. Her do-gooder twin sisters, Chandler and the cripple Fleming, had jumped into Lake Michigan after the device, which both annoyed and amused Hammett. Annoyed her because she didn't have the chance to kill those bitches herself, and amused her because there was absolutely no way they'd be able to find the sinking transceiver and call off the strike.

Hammett was no longer amused. And her annoyance level was at an all-time high. She'd had plans to celebrate her success by taking her recently purchased Harley Softail up to Toronto, finding some biker boy toy along the route, and spending a few days drinking and fucking and living like a queen.

But London hadn't been destroyed. No glorious mushroom cloud. No one burning, babies or otherwise. Just talking head after talking head, some looking apologetic, some looking stern, not a single one of them suffering from severe radiation sickness.

It was enough to make a grown operative cry.

"This seat taken?"

Hammett pulled her eyes away from the screen long enough to size up the local standing next to her table. Flabby, unshaven, dirty fingernails suggesting some unappealing blue-collar job.

"Not on my drunkest day, or your luckiest," she said.

Her gaze flitted back to the TV, and she watched absently while her mind puzzled out what could have possibly gone wrong. Fail-safe switch? Satellite laser defense? An override she hadn't known about?

Or had her goddamn sisters actually saved the day?

"Don't be rude to me, you dumb skank. I'm just trying to—"

Hammett lashed out, jamming her stiff fingers into the lothario's neck, feeling a small measure of satisfaction when she heard the sharp *snap!* of his trachea breaking. He clutched his throat, unable to breathe, and then fell to his knees as Hammett tossed five dollars onto the table and left the bar.

The safe house was a few blocks away, on the northwest corner of Keeler and Fourteenth. Lawndale was among her least favorite neighborhoods in Chicago. She would have preferred lodging in Lincoln Park, or Bucktown, or Roscoe Village, or pretty much anywhere else. But this was the first landlord she'd been able to find who hadn't required a credit check, and Hammett only had two current fake identities and chose not to burn either of them on a rental that she hadn't ever planned to use.

But Plan A had gone to shit. Now she had to regroup and begin the B game.

Which meant she had to call her boss.

He wasn't going to be pleased.

She walked west on Roosevelt, feet pounding against a filthy, cracked sidewalk, anger coming off her like heat waves. Her jaw, chin, and nose still hurt from where Chandler had hit her, and she had a deep gash on her calf that she'd sloppily sealed with superglue prior to the cab ride. Hammett wanted two more drinks, some Demerol, and a long bubble bath, but instead she had to clean up this mess. A mess she'd no doubt be blamed for.

"Dammit, dog, piss already."

Ahead, an elderly man smoking a cigarette kicked a short-statured, off-white basset hound whose only apparent offense was sniffing the curb for too long. The dog yelped, and then limped away as far as the leash allowed. The man gave the lead a vicious tug, jerking the dog off its front legs.

"Hurry up, dog."

Another kick. Another yelp.

Hammett was on them in three long strides, letting her inner mean bubble to the surface.

"Ever hear that you need to be kind to dumb animals?"

The man scowled at her, not answering.

"Me, neither," she said, raising her foot and violently kicking the codger above his right knee. His leg bent sideways at an unhealthy angle, and he fell onto the sidewalk, screaming and clutching his injury.

"Can I trust you to treat your dog better?" Hammett asked, bending over him.

"You crazy bitch!" He moaned and wailed and rolled around in a very unmanly way.

"Yes or no?"

"I'm calling the police!"

"I'll take that as a no."

The guy was old, so it didn't take much effort to snap his neck. Just a firm two-handed grip under his chin, a foot on his back, and a solid yank.

Her anger momentarily sated, Hammett noticed a teenage girl at the bus stop across the street, staring slack-jawed at her. She scooped up the hound and marched over to the girl.

"You see what I did to that old guy?" Hammett said.

The girl nodded dumbly. Hammett handed her the dog, thrusting the squirming animal into the teenager's arms.

"Treat this dog right, or I'll do the same thing to you. Got it?"

Another quick nod.

"And don't call the police."

Quick nod.

"You have a boyfriend?"

Quick nod.

"He treat you good?"

Slower nod.

"If he doesn't, just wait until he's asleep. It's easy to break their necks while they're sleeping. Get a good grip first. Then use leverage and lean into it. Understand?"

Frantic nodding.

Hammett wondered how it had gotten to this point. After years as the top operative in the world, she'd been reduced to venting her frustration on dumb civilians and lecturing teens about boys and pet care. Pathetic, and monumentally inappropriate. It was reckless to kill people in public, and downright stupid to leave witnesses alive. Must be her foul mood. For a moment she considered eliminating the girl as well, which must have shown in her face because the teenager immediately slunk away, gripping the dog so tight its eyes bugged out. But the bus was approaching, and if Hammett killed the girl, she'd have to kill the driver, and then everyone riding, which might very well lead to her murdering the entire West Side. Better to quit now.

She stormed off, continuing west on Roosevelt until she reached Keeler, then went south. After a quick lap around the block to make sure she wasn't being followed, she approached the large oak tree on the front lawn of her rental house and dug the door key out of a hidden notch in the bark. Then she walked slowly up to the porch, letting her senses report.

No unusual sounds or smells. The tiny strip of transparent tape Hammett had stuck between the door and the jamb at foot level was still in place, indicating no one had entered. No signs of entry on the front windows. The mailbox was empty, probably due to the note she'd stuck on it:

MAILMAN: NO FUCKING ADS OR I'LL SHOOT YOU.

A full mailbox meant a vacant house, which in this unsavory neighborhood meant burglars or squatters. Though, with the mood she was in, Hammett wouldn't have minded if someone had broken into her home uninvited and was waiting inside. The blue-collar pig at the bar and the Humane Society reject had gotten her adrenaline up. Putting the hurt on some clueless jerk would have been pleasant.

Unfortunately, her house was as vacant as she'd left it. It was a split-level, enough room for a single family if they liked living cramped. Hammett hadn't done any furnishing, other than the basics: weapons, first-aid kit, sleeping bag, several changes of clothing, towels, toiletries, some communications gear, non-spoiling food. She locked the dead bolt behind her when she entered.

The lights in the kitchen, set with a timer, were already on. Hammett considered a shower, but knew checking in was the priority. An encrypted cell phone was charging on the counter. She opened the freezer and took out a chocolate bar, nibbling on that while she punched in the activation code. Then she called the memorized ten-digit number.

"Al's Plumbing," someone answered in a digitally disguised voice.

"The toilet is clogged," she said.

"No shit. You screwed up."

"Victor screwed up."

"Where is Victor now?"

Hammett frowned. "He's clogging his own toilets, in hell. You should have taken out Chandler when you had the chance."

"You said you could handle her."

"She was a bit more"—Hammett searched for the right word—"*determined* than I'd anticipated."

"She's also still a player."

Her sister was alive? Interesting. "Chandler won't be a problem."

"My sources also say another team has joined the party. They grabbed the transceiver."

"How did they get the transceiver? It went overboard."

"The ICU satellite feed. They were watching your little boating expedition. Sent in some frogmen and retrieved the device. But that's not the priority. They also have the cripple. If she shows them how to use it..."

Hammett rubbed her face, wincing at the pain. This wasn't good. "Where are they?"

"In transit. I believe they'll take her to the nearest black site."

"Cuba? Romania?"

"Wisconsin."

Hammett's frown deepened. She'd long since lost faith in her government, but operating a site on US soil was, well, egregiously unconstitutional. Even for duplicitous Uncle Sam.

"Do we have friends within the newcomer's organization?" she asked.

"Negative. They're NIC spooks. Can't tell if they're rogue or not. No one is claiming them."

The National Intelligence Commission was the secret branch of Homeland Security, operating outside the NSA, CIA, and FBI, and it didn't officially exist any more than did Hammett's old agency, Hydra.

"I'll need a team," she said.

"I'll see who's in town. I'll set up the meeting and call. Charlie foxtrot tango."

Hammett checked her watch.

The shower would have to wait.

Chandler

"Sometimes you'll be forced to make tough decisions," the Instructor said. "They may turn out in your favor. They may turn out badly. You can live, or die, by the choices you make. But luck always plays a part. You can anticipate every move and execute perfectly, and luck could still kill you. Or you can make huge mistakes, and luck could save your ass. Don't confuse having a plan with having control. Control doesn't exist."

I fell into darkness, anticipating five kinds of death.

I could break my neck on the elevator below me.

I could become caught in the counterweight and get dismembered, decapitated, or strangled.

I could bounce off the roof of the lift and fall down the shaft.

I could injure myself so badly I couldn't continue, and eventually get discovered.

I could get caught between the car and the wall and be crushed.

But instead I fell for only a fraction of a second, then immediately hit the car and began to rise. The elevator had been less than three feet below me.

I rolled to my knees, trying to get my bearings, trying to shake the fear and the disorientation, trying to formulate some sort of plan.

I'd injured, but not killed, the agent in the hallway. If I got out of here, I could pay him a visit later and finish my questioning.

But I had very little chance of getting out of here.

I had no idea who these agents were, or what team they played for. But they were experienced, and there were a lot more than I had anticipated. If I didn't escape from the hospital, they'd catch me.

I considered that option. I could give myself up, and they'd take me to Fleming. But I'd also be giving up the advantage freedom gave me. A shark in the ocean has more options than a shark in the tank.

The elevator stopped abruptly. Made sense, since I'd been the one who'd called it to the sixth floor. This hospital only had six floors, which meant the roof was directly above me. It was too dark to see; I reached into the blackness, groping for a handhold. I found a metal bar to grab, and brought up a knee to hook around it. There should be an access panel to the roof. I felt around, touching old grease and grime and kicking up enough dust to clog my nostrils.

Beneath me, the elevator jostled.

A second later, tapping sounded on the walls, growing in force and volume. It morphed into a rhythm that vibrated the panel beneath me, and I didn't have to guess who had entered the car.

My pulse was way beyond normal, but I continued to grope around for the roof access. I'd be damned if I'd give in to Rochester's mind games, although I couldn't deny he had me more than a little rattled. I'd fought for my life countless times—several in just the last few days—but I couldn't remember any encounter where I'd been so thoroughly bested...except years ago during Hydra training, sparring with the Instructor.

Rochester had used a martial arts style I'd never encountered before, and I had no idea how to beat it. He'd played with me, not even breaking a sweat, and that scared me in a way I hadn't felt in a long time.

To be at someone's mercy, utterly helpless and without hope—the feeling was akin to drowning. And there was nothing I hated more than drowning. If I had to face him again—

The elevator hatch sprang open. Rochester smiled up at me.

"Where you going, sweet thing?"

He reached up a tattooed hand, seeking my ankle.

My throat closed, making it impossible to breathe. For a split second I shrank away, not knowing where to go, what to do. Then I realized that the light from the car illuminated the shaft. Looking up, I spotted the roof access less than two meters above. I tugged the handle, then jumped out just as Rochester's thick fingers brushed my leg.

Pulling myself onto the hospital roof, I forced myself to think, to breathe, quickly getting my bearings. I was surrounded by a bed of tar paper, the edge of the building to the north, the El train rumbling past a few floors down, four aluminum mushroom-style vents to the east right in front of me. And beyond those—

A helicopter.

I could fly helicopters.

I sprinted toward it. Red-and-white fuselage, standard flying ambulance colors—the vehicle looked like an AStar B3 or equivalent. No one inside, and when I reached it, the door had been conveniently left open. So far, so good.

I sat in the cockpit, familiarizing myself with the controls, reaching for the battery switch and flipping it on.

Nothing happened.

I searched for the engine starter button, fearing the worst. Sure enough, the keyhole next to it was empty.

I did a quick, frantic search for keys, finding none, and then went into the cargo bay. It was also entirely lacking in keys, but my eyes locked onto a medevac gurney, complete with an attached lift harness. I scanned around and located the winch. Steel cable, maybe forty meters on the spool. Enough to get me to street level?

Only one way to find out.

I hit the release on the spool, attached the line to the eyehole on the cart, and opened the side door. My head was still throbbing, but my balance had returned. Still, I felt unsteady and overwhelmed. I had to get out of here before Rochester caught up.

Sweeping a glance in the direction of the elevator and stairs to make sure he wasn't sneaking up on me, I rolled the gurney onto the roof and to the edge of the building. Once I'd lifted the cart up two feet and balanced it on the brick ledge, I ran back to the helicopter and adjusted the spool to slowly play out line, then returned to the gurney.

Here went nothing.

I pushed it off the edge of the building. It banged against the side, found its center, and then began to lower itself a few inches per second. I sat on the ledge, swung my legs over, and dropped onto the gurney, momentum almost pitching me forward and onto the ground below.

I regained my balance and squatted on the rubber mattress, holding on to the handrails. The aluminum scraped against brick, but it was pretty smooth going. In ten seconds I'd dropped about a meter, and as long as there was enough cable, and as long as Rochester didn't figure out what I was doing, and as long as no agents thought to look up at me, I was home free.

Another elevated train passed beneath me, green and white and filthy, perhaps ten meters off the ground and three meters away from the side of the building. It squealed to a stop, and I watched some dude in a wheelchair exit the train and roll across the platform toward the hospital.

I continued my descent. Halfway down the building, and all was well. I was already beginning to formulate my plan for my return when the cable suddenly jerked to a stop, almost throwing me off.

I looked up, wondering if I'd misjudged the length. Then the gurney shook, and began to rise.

Rochester. He was reeling me back in.

I looked down. Still at least forty feet from the street below. But only twelve feet from the El tracks.

I didn't think. I jumped.

While in the air, I remembered how Chicago's elevated train system worked. It ran on electricity, transferred to the cars via a hot third rail, which delivered a deadly 600 volts. As I fell, I looked at the train tracks rushing up at me, brown wood and brown rust, spotting two of the rails but not the third.

Normally when I landed from a fall, I would roll to displace the force of impact. But rolling could mean brushing the third rail and a hot, jolting death. So I opened my ankles and turned my body so I fell between the rails, straddling one of them, which could have been the hot one.

I pitched forward, knees bending, spreading out my hands so I fell into a push-up position. But gravity and g-force were stronger than I was, and my chest bounced off the center rail.

It knocked the air out of me, but at least it didn't fry me like a pork rind.

I manipulated my diaphragm, forcing air back into my lungs, and then pushed away from the rail with my arms. But my left palm slipped on the old wood, my arm dropping through the space between the railroad ties, my body weight jamming my elbow in the middle of them.

I tried to pull back.

Wood scraped tender skin. Stuck.

Tried harder.

Still stuck.

My bony elbow jutted out more than my biceps, and it was wedged between the slats pretty good. The tarlike odor of creosote clogged my throat, hot and blanket heavy. I thought about scooting forward, getting my knees under me for leverage, but there were rails on either side, one of them the widowmaker. Adjusting my footing didn't seem wise.

"What you doin' down there, girl?"

I looked up, saw Rochester was at the roof's ledge, waving down at me.

The last thing I felt capable of was relaxation, but I forced myself to do it anyway. I closed my eyes. I slowed my heartbeat. Unbunched my muscles. Then slowly tried to turn my elbow to the side.

I turned until my humerus felt like it was going to splinter, until the skin felt like it was scraping off my bones, then tried to pull back again.

Still stuck.

"I'm coming for you, sweet thing."

I chanced a look, saw Rochester riding the gurney down the side of the building, standing up proudly like Caesar on his chariot.

My trapped hand was going tingly, the circulation being cut off. I focused on turning my arm the opposite way, twisting until my muscles and tendons threatened to snap.

Pulled, hard and steady.

My elbow wouldn't budge.

The tracks beneath me started to vibrate.

"Train is a-coming, girl," Rochester called.

Heat swept over me, and my pulse jumped despite my efforts at achieving calm. I yanked with everything I had.

My shoulder popped out, dislocating with a bursting sound and excruciating pain.

But my elbow remained trapped.

Vision going fuzzy, I carefully inched forward on my knees, avoiding the side rails. Besides feeling the train, I now also heard it, a low, steady grumble like an approaching storm.

"Better hurry," Rochester said. I didn't look at him, but he sounded close.

Blinking away tears, I gave my torso a violent jerk, snapping my shoulder back into place. Using the pain, I coughed up some congestion in my lungs, spat between the railroad ties onto my stuck elbow, and tried to work it up and down.

The El train was impossibly loud now, practically upon me.

I stretched my whole body backward, like a reverse mousetrap. My elbow slid, just a little, then a little more. The spit lubrication working, my arm came loose, inch by inch. The train's thunder grew deafening, the tracks shook as if tossed by an earthquake. I wasn't going to make it. Even as I pulled my arm free, I could feel the train bear down—

—and pass me by, on the other side of the tracks.

I lost control of my emotions for a moment, a hysterical laugh escaping my lips, amazed that I was free and not a train version of roadkill. Then I carefully climbed to my feet just as someone jumped onto the tracks in front of me.

"You goin' somewhere?"

I tried to raise my fists, but my left arm wouldn't cooperate.

"Ah…you can't use one arm. That's OK. Rochester wouldn't take advantage of such a pretty lady."

Rochester grinned wide, then held his left arm behind his back.

I really hated this asshole.

He moved in fast, feet nimble on the railroad slats, avoiding the rails. Bobbing his head, slapping his neck and chest with his right palm in that rhythm I'd grown to loathe, he got within striking distance and threw a jab at my head. I pulled away, but his punch was a feint, and he extended into an uppercut, catching me under the chin.

I staggered backward, losing my footing, falling to the left, my foot touching a rail—

No shock. I'd gotten lucky.

Even luckier, I now knew which rail was the hot one.

Shaking off the punch, I pulled in my arms and swiveled my hips, doing a tight spin kick. It would have connected, but Rochester blocked with his left hand.

So much for him not taking advantage.

He followed up with a rabbit punch, drilling it into my kidney, so hard I knew I'd be peeing blood later. I fell to all fours, which quickly became all threes because I couldn't put any pressure on my injured arm.

"This is such a letdown for me, Chandler. The Instructor told me you were one of the best he trained."

"He told me about you, too. He said you're a pervert who gets off on beating up little girls."

Rochester winked. "A man can't deny who he is. This indeed is most arousing to me."

He took a quick step forward, and I rolled away from the oncoming kick. But it was another feint on his part, and when I raised my head he gave me a slap that sent me sprawling—

—my face inches away from the third rail.

I stared right at death, and could actually feel the power of the current running through the metal, like a magnetic wave tickling my face. It could have been my imagination, but it seemed like I could hear the crackling electricity and smell the ozone. I'd heard stories of drunk men urinating on the third rail, dying badly as a result of their shortsighted bravado, and this thought spun through my mind while I watched, mesmerized, as a drip of sweat fell from my forehead and kissed the metal.

Nothing happened, of course. The sweat didn't complete a circuit, and the electricity had nowhere to flow. Like a bird on the high wire, it became charged—the same voltage as the wire—but no current flowed through it. If I touched the rail, however, my body would be grounded on the tracks, completing the circuit and causing the 600-volt boogie.

I crab-walked backward, getting to my feet, turning to face Rochester. He began to do that tapping thing on his head, forearms, and elbows, moving so quickly his hands were a blur, making it impossible for me to know where to hit him, or guess where his next strike came from.

I threw a punch anyway, aiming where I thought his chin would be. He blocked it with his palm and elbow, then snapped the elbow around. I had the foresight to lower my head. His blow glanced off the top of my skull, probably hurting him as much as me. Then I abandoned my martial arts training and went pure NFL, punting as hard as I could between his legs.

He caught my ankle between his thighs before I did any damage, then dropped to his knees, pinning me as well.

"So, should Ol' Rochester break your hips now? Or get you back to his place first?"

The whole structure began to rumble. And this time, the train was on our side of the tracks. I was sure, because I saw it coming up behind my attacker.

"I got a better idea," I said. "How about you bend over, because the Blue Line is about to make you its bitch."

He turned around to look.

I jackknifed at him, jeet kune do style, my right arm a ramrod and my body the piston driving it forward, punching Rochester in his muscled neck as hard as I've ever hit anyone.

His legs released me as he grabbed with both hands at his throat.

I turned and ran. Ahead of me, maybe twenty meters, was the El platform where the train stopped to pick up passengers. I noticed a few of them, standing on the edge and pointing my way.

Behind me there was a screech of brakes, metal on metal, and the piercing wail of a train whistle. I didn't bother to check if the El had done the world a favor and sent Rochester to hell, instead concentrating on running on the evenly spaced slats without tripping, and making it off the tracks without getting killed.

Luck was once again with me, and I made it to the platform, where three Good Samaritans held out their hands and helped lift me up. I grunted a thanks and fought through the throng of people casting questions at me, slipping through the one-way exit, and then took two flights of metal stairs down to street level.

Every cell in my body was shaking, but I couldn't let myself think about that now. Instead, I absorbed my surroundings. No agents behind me. No agents around me. Civilians everywhere, none of them looking out of place. I smelled car exhaust, sewage from a nearby curb drain, and French fries from a fast-food place a few doors down. I listened for gunshots or anything else out of the ordinary, but there were only familiar city sounds.

I jogged to the closest bus stop on trembling legs just as the vehicle pulled up, brakes hissing. After forcing the driver to break my fifty-dollar bill, I collapsed into one of the middle seats near the exit and tried to determine my next move.

But as much as I wished otherwise, my next move was obvious. I needed to find Fleming. And the only way to do that was to get back to the hospital and ask someone who knew where she was.

This time, however, I'd be much better prepared.

The White House

The president stared at his face in the mirror. He looked feminine, and even worse, clownish. He dabbed a pinkie into the corner of his mouth, removing a tiny dab of concealer. His makeup artist was terrific, and on television he looked like a movie star. But this close he felt more like a vaudeville comedian, painted in grotesque broad strokes. He wanted to wipe it off, but he'd already done two press conferences that day, and had another that night.

"So they used a remote device like the one I have?" he said into his encrypted cell phone, the very device he was describing.

"It appears that way, Mr. President," said the man on the other end of the line.

"I was assured this couldn't be copied or cloned."

"We're looking into it."

"And the two women?"

"One has, regrettably, escaped from our custody."

The president closed his eyes. When he spoke again, his voice was a low whisper.

"Are you kidding me?"

"No, Mr. President. These women are…formidable."

"How about the other one?"

"She's being taken to a safe location. We should have some information from her soon."

"Do whatever it takes."

"We shall, Mr. President. She'll tell us everything we want to know."

Hammett

The Harley Softail was a joy to ride, the vibrating engine so strong Hammett almost didn't feel the vibration of the cell phone in her front pocket. She pulled onto the shoulder of I-90 and answered.

"Meeting at oh-sixteen-hundred," her boss said. "Five men. CVs sent to your encrypted e-mail account."

"I just crossed into Wisconsin," Hammett said. "Where is the meeting?"

"There were no decent hotels with conference rooms available at such short notice. So I hope you don't have coulrophobia."

Her boss named the venue. Hammett frowned. "You're kidding."

"Have you known me to kid?"

Hammett wondered if this was on purpose, a form of punishment, or if the spy game had truly become a ridiculous parody of itself. Even though she didn't directly blame herself for how the operation had gone sour, Hammett knew that ultimately it was her responsibility. Her stepfather used to tell her, "Your life is your fault," and she hadn't ever truly understood what that meant until recently. We are each the sum of our decisions, and what happens to us is ultimately the result of our decisions. Even if something freakish happens, like being struck by lightning, that is a risk of being outdoors on a cloudy day. That is a potential price to pay. Like kicking your dog when there is a pissed-off assassin nearby.

"Are they competent?" Hammett asked.

"Their dossiers check out. But that's for you to judge. Did you at least pack a swimsuit?"

"You're an asshole," Hammett said, hanging up.

And she meant it. She didn't like swimming. And though she'd never admit it to anyone, Hammett did have a small touch of coulrophobia.

She peeled off the side of the road, going zero to a hundred in eight seconds, pissed off at the world and her place in it.

Chandler

"The enemy has expectations," the Instructor said. "Always try to defy those expectations. If they expect you to run, that's the best time to attack."

I sat on the toilet in the bathroom stall, my gym bag at my feet. I was at the Stretchers on Clybourn, a women-only gym I belonged to where I rented a locker. I had several lockers at several locations in the Chicago area and around the country, each stocked with supplies. Though I didn't have any ID on me, I'd given the receptionist the fake name I'd signed up with, and she matched it to my picture on her computer and let me in.

My gym bag had a getaway kit in it. Essentials like money, passport, weapons, first aid; all the requirements of a spy on the run. I unwrapped a syringe, filled it with Demerol, and then gave some to my shoulder and some to my elbow; enough to kill the pain without putting my arm to sleep. Then I dry swallowed some Adderall—I didn't have ADD but needed the amphetamine boost—and opened the box of Clairol Nice 'n Easy. I set up a hand mirror on the toilet paper dispenser, wielded some scissors, and cut my above-the-shoulder bob to a decidedly shorter pixie cut.

Hairdressing wasn't among the many lessons the Instructor had given me. But I'd taken a few classes on my own, knowing that one day I might have to do just what I was doing. After flushing the shorn locks down the toilet, I snapped on the plastic gloves from the hair dye kit and in a relatively short time went from a deep brunette to a medium golden blond.

I took a quick shower, hot as I could stand it, and then dressed in a neon green micro mini and a tube top, no bra. After spending ten minutes in front of the sink, putting on enough makeup to shame a Vegas showgirl, I slipped on some three-inch pumps, shouldered my bag, and left Stretchers to hail a cab.

As expected, no one wanted to pick up a cheap whore who looked like Sandy Duncan, until I stepped out in front of a cab waving a hundred-dollar bill.

"The hospital," I ordered once I'd folded myself into the back. The cab smelled like curry, cigarettes, and body odor, and the safety glass between me and the driver had cracks in it. His radio was tuned to a talk station, and some angry blowhard was yelling about the aborted nuclear strike on England and how it was the fault of gay people who wanted to marry.

Tuning out the idiocy, I dug my hands into my pack, out of view of the prying eyes of the cabbie, and made sure my Beretta Storm had one in the chamber. It was a 9mm, held sixteen rounds, and I had two extra mags. I stuck them in the side lining, so they wouldn't be noticed immediately if the bag was inspected, then located the empty syringe. I jabbed the needle in my forearm, several times, watching little beads of blood pop out.

"Hey! None of that in my cab."

"Mind your own fucking business and drive," I snarled. Sometimes the best counter to indignation was bigger indignation, and the driver didn't look at or speak to me again until we reached the hospital.

I tossed the money at him, didn't wait for my change, and exited the cab with the full syringe.

Showtime.

Needle still in hand, I began to hyperventilate, staggering up to the ER doors past two agents in black suits, smearing the blood on my forearm with my fingers. When I was sure a nurse was watching me, I fell to the floor.

"We've got an OD here!" she called.

Through fluttering eyelids I watched two orderlies lift me onto a gurney. The nurse took my pulse—fast because of the amphetamines—and I began to pant.

"Tracks on her arm. She's got a syringe."

It was taken from me. I peeked at the men in black, but they were only giving me casual attention.

"Can you hear me? What did you take? What's in the needle?"

"Chest hurts..." I moaned. "Hurts so bad..."

Then I pretended to pass out.

Like all hospitals, they had a protocol for dealing with patients called ESI, the Emergency Severity Index. Near the top of the list was drug overdose and chest pain. I was immediately buzzed through the security door and wheeled into the triage rooms. The orderlies pushed me into one at the end of the hall, through a hanging curtain, and then they left. The original nurse set up an IV while I looked for the requisite equipment cart, reaching out a hand to grab a packaged scalpel. I sat up, throwing my arm around the nurse and grabbing her mouth, my other hand pressing the scalpel to her throat.

"An hour ago. White man in a black suit with a shattered knee. Where is he?"

I gave her throat a tiny prick with the blade, then released her mouth.

"He's...I think he's going into surgery."

That was fast. Knee injuries weren't anywhere near the top of the ESI, but I guess I shouldn't be surprised that the men in black had some pull. "What room?"

"Operating room C. Down the hall to the right. Please don't hurt me."

"I need you to take your uniform off," I said, reaching into my gym pack and seeking out my gun.

Then the curtain drew open. I expected to see a doctor, or at worst, an agent.

But I didn't expect to see Chicago homicide lieutenant Jack Daniels. Even more surprisingly, she was holding a .38 in my face.

"Hand out of the bag. Slowly."

She wore the same suit she'd had on when I saw her earlier, except now her gold star was hanging around her neck. Her gun was a Colt Detective Special, and I noticed that its cylinder was full.

"You won't shoot me," I said.

"And you won't shoot me either. But I will break your nose with the butt of this gun."

A tremor shook my hand—something I hoped was the Adderall and not fear or exhaustion. "You aren't fast enough."

"You want to try me?"

I didn't. Though Jack was an ally of sorts, I had scrapped with her before, and she was pretty good. She was also correct. I wasn't going to shoot her, any more than I was going to kill the ER nurse for her outfit.

"You came back for the agent," Jack said. "The one whose leg you broke."

I nodded. My shaky fingers were still on the Beretta.

"He's guarded. Four men, all armed. You aren't going to shoot up this hospital to get to him. Now take your goddamn hand out of the bag and don't make me ask again."

I weighed my options, and noticed Jack's eyes narrowing. She was really going to make good on her threat. She was going to try to break my nose.

Maybe she would. Maybe she wouldn't. But the chance of her gun going off was too high. That would alert the agents, and then everything would go to shit.

I took my empty hand out of the bag, fingers splayed wide. "Now what?"

"Now you let go of the nurse, and you get what you deserve."

Her choice of words intrigued me. And her eyes showed a glimmer of relief.

"Do it," she said. But it was less like a command, more like a request.

Did she want to arrest me? Or was she asking me to trust her?

I dropped the scalpel, but still kept my grip on the nurse.

"Nurse Rosetta," Jack said, reading her nametag, "I'm a police officer. I'm going to escort this woman out of here. But I don't want to cause a panic. There's already been enough trouble at the hospital today, and we don't want to add to it. So I need you to calmly walk out of here, and ask hospital security to come by. Do you understand?"

The nurse nodded.

"Let her go," Jack told me.

I did.

"Slow and easy," Jack told her. "Don't panic. Don't make a scene."

She nodded, smoothed out her uniform, and left the room without resorting to hysterics. Jack threw me her black Smith & Wesson handcuffs, which I caught. The same pair I'd had on earlier.

"Put them on," she said.

"No way."

"No time to argue. If the nurse does what I told her, security will be here in under a minute. If she panics, those assholes in the black suits will come running instead."

"I might need my hands free."

Jack tossed me something else. The handcuff keys.

"You can't get to the guy," she said. "But I've got something almost as good. When he went into surgery, his personal effects vanished. Including his gun, which has his prints on it."

She glanced down at her oversized Gucci purse.

"Won't help," I said. "His ID will be fake. Clothes will be untraceable. And even if you do get a match, he'll either be listed as dead or the information about him will be false. These guys are ghosts, Jack."

"Well, we're going to use good old-fashioned police work and try."

"And if I disagree?"

"I know this is some deep shit, Chandler. I even tried to call in a favor—the mayor owes me—and his hands were tied. But I'm not going to let you shoot up a hospital."

I let out a slow breath. "You knew I'd come back."

She nodded. "It's what I would have done. Now I'm asking you to do it my way. If it doesn't work, you can always try this again. He'll be in surgery another three hours, minimum. You really messed him up."

I considered it. Could I actually find my sister by examining someone's stuff? Jack seemed to be a good cop, and she'd helped me twice before. There were worse people in the world to trust.

"Come on, Chandler. We're wasting time."

I handed my gym bag to Jack, palmed the keys, and put on the bracelets, letting Jack escort me out of the room. She kept a tight hand on my arm, and put her gun back in her shoulder holster, letting the butt peek through the lapel in a way that was so obvious it had to be on purpose.

We marched out of the triage center and back into the ER waiting room. This time I drew more attention from the agents in black, no doubt courtesy of the hysterical Nurse Rosetta, sobbing behind the check-in counter to two guys from hospital security. One of the agents stepped in front of Jack, blocking our path. Thirties, ex-military, scars on his chin and his knuckles.

"What happened?" he asked, making a question sound like an order.

"Little Janis Joplin here was trying to score some morphine."

He stared at me. I tried to look as high and as unappealing as possible.

"She's cute," he said.

"She's off the clock now, spook," Jack sneered into his reflective Ray-Bans. "Maybe you can find another crack whore tonight, when Uncle Sam lets you off the leash."

His demeanor slipped, and he stepped aside. Jack led me out the automatic doors. We headed for the parking lot at a brisk clip.

"I almost didn't recognize you," Jack said. "That's some outfit."

"Don't knock it until you've tried it."

"Oh, I've tried it."

"The world's oldest profession?" I tried to picture Jack in hooker clothes.

"Second oldest. Vice squad. I wore things that make your clothes look frumpy. So do blondes have more fun?"

"Absolutely. I'm having loads."

As we wove our way through the cars, I tried to guess which was Jack's. She certainly dressed well. No doubt her car would be equally impressive.

Which is why I was surprised when we stopped next to a 1987 Chevy Nova.

"Get in."

"Seriously? This is what you drive?"

"Do you know how much this purse was? Or these shoes? I can't afford a nice car."

I slid into the passenger seat, and it almost swallowed me, as if someone very heavy had been sitting there for a long time. I undid the cuffs, and traded them for my gym bag. Jack turned the ignition, and it started on the fourth try.

"Your car sucks," I said.

"This car is a classic. It's so popular it was even stolen a few months ago." She pulled into traffic. "Unfortunately, they brought it back."

"Even thieves have standards."

"Do spies?"

"Let's say I'm glad I'm in disguise. I really wouldn't want to be seen in this car."

We pulled into traffic with all the acceleration of an ox-drawn cart. "Hungry?" Jack asked.

Actually, I was. I couldn't remember the last time I'd eaten. "Yeah."

"Can you secret agent types do hotdogs? Or does it have to be pâté de foie gras, beluga caviar, and Bollinger '88?"

"A hot dog would be great."

"I know a place nearby. My partner swears by it. It's his day off, and I wouldn't be surprised if he's there right now."

"What's your plan?"

"I'm thinking two double dogs with the works, and we can split a fry."

"With tracing the clothes, Jack."

"We've got one of the best crime labs in the country, but the waiting time is unbearable, and we don't want to draw any attention. I don't want to be awakened in the middle of the night by men surrounding my house and trying to kill me."

"They probably wouldn't kill you. They'd take you someplace where the Geneva Convention doesn't exist, then take their time torturing you for information."

Which is what was no doubt being done to Fleming.

"Luckily I have a friend, of sorts, who is almost as well equipped as the CPD."

"Do you trust him?"

"Trust him? Yes. Like him? That's another story." Jack glanced at me, her eyes moving down my body. "But he'll like you, for sure. Especially in that getup. His name is Harry. Harry McGlade."

Harry McGlade? Why did that name sound so familiar?

Chandler

"This line of work makes for strange bedfellows," the Instructor said. "Just like you have to roll with the punches, you sometimes have to roll with the weirdos. Whether that roll is literal or figurative is up to you."

After a delicious hot dog and some French fries of dubious freshness, we drove to McGlade's office. Apparently he was Jack's old partner, now in the private sector. She parked in front of a fire hydrant, and when I'd extracted myself from her trench of a passenger seat, I fell into my regular habits and scanned the environment.

Ritzy neighborhood, nice cars on the streets, sidewalks well kept and trees tended to. The storefronts were dominated by jewelers and art galleries, with a few clothing boutiques and non-chain cafés sprinkled in. I smelled dark roast, and heard pigeons warbling from a nearby park.

"McGlade is a bit, um, abrasive," Jack said. "If he says something rude, you have to promise not to kill him."

I smiled. Jack didn't.

"I'm serious. Promise me."

"I promise. I don't kill people just because they're rude."

"Yeah, well, that's because you haven't met Harry yet."

She pressed the buzzer on an inauspicious security door next to a brass placard that read McGlade Investigations.

"Can I help you?" a female voice asked.

"Buzz me in, Harry. It's Jack."

"Jack who?"

"Jack who is going to shoot the lock off your door, then kick your ass if you don't open up."

"Do you have an appointment with Mr. McGlade?"

"And stop that ridiculous falsetto. You don't have a secretary."

"Well, maybe I got one," a male voice answered. "And maybe she's hot, and maybe we're doing stuff to each other right now. Sexy stuff."

"I'm pulling out my gun," Jack said. Then she did and waved it at the security camera above the door."Who's the skirt with you? She's stacked like a plateful of pancakes."

"I'm aiming at your lock," she said, and did.

"You're being quite aggressive, Jack. That's hot."

Jack cocked her .38. He buzzed us in.

McGlade's office was on the second floor. His door had an actual stencil of a magnifying glass on it, with an oversized eye peering through. Jack entered without knocking. I followed.

Harry McGlade was sitting behind an enormous desk. He was in his forties, out of shape, unshaven, and I realized where I'd heard his name before.

"I know you," I said. "You were in the Cook County Morgue the other day."

He put his feet up on his desk and crossed his legs. "Who? Me?"

"You were wearing your old police uniform. You hit on me and my sister."

"That doesn't sound familiar."

"I had longer hair. Brown. She was in a wheelchair."

His expression remained blank. "Not ringing any bells."

"You tried to blackmail us into going to see some sports game with you. You had box seats. Then you offered us two hundred bucks if we French kissed."

"Apparently you weren't very memorable, but I'll double that offer if you plant one on Jack right now. First you need to take your top off. And shake them like they're on fire."

On reflex I dug my hand into my gym bag, seeking my Beretta. Jack grabbed my arm and said, "You promised." Then she turned to McGlade. "I need your help."

"You can't afford me."

"I'm not paying you. We're going to trade favors, professional to professional."

McGlade nodded and winked. "I get it." Then he reached for his fly.

"You whip that out and I'll shoot it off," Jack said.

"Easy there, Lorena Bobbit. Just going in for the scratch."

"Resist the impulse," Jack ordered. "You help us, then I owe you one."

"So the next time I need help from the CPD," Harry said, folding his arms, "I can call you?"

"Yes."

"No questions asked?"

"Yes."

"And you'll come over and sex me up?"

"Those rude come-ons, do they ever actually work?" I asked.

"Not so far. But if the Wright Brothers ever gave up, think of the loss to humanity. I mean, where would we be without airline food?"

Jack placed the paper bag on his desk. "We need to analyze these, see if we could find out where they came from."

"Hmm, real crime fighter stuff, huh? OK, let's see."

Jack dumped out the contents of the bag. A wallet, gun and holster, two shoes, a jacket, pants, a tie, underwear, sunglasses, socks, a belt.

"Where's the guy these belong to?" Harry asked. "Did you shrink him?"

Jack sighed. "Yes, Harry. I shrunk him. You guessed it."

"You have a way of making guys shrink, Jack." Harry opened his desk and snapped on a pair of latex gloves. He reached for the pants first.

"Off the rack, not tailored. Label has been cut out. They aren't high quality. Jacket is cheap, too. Nothing in any pockets. Looks like spookwear, right down to the sunglasses. This guy work for our government in some unofficial capacity? Or did you get this off some nerd at a sci-fi convention cosplaying Will Smith?"

I shrugged. "If I had to guess, I'd say NIC."

Both Harry and Jack gave me blank stares.

"The National Intelligence Committee. They don't officially exist. They work for Homeland Security."

"Does this have something to do with London almost blowing up?"

Maybe McGlade wasn't as stupid as he let on.

"The less you know, the better."

He nodded. "Good. Because I know very little."

"No shit," Jack said.

McGlade didn't appear insulted. "Underwear are Hanes tighty-whities. Guy apparently didn't do a very good job wiping himself. Want me to analyze the skid mark, try to figure out what he recently ate? My guess is something Mexican."

"We need to know where he's from, Harry."

"Someplace they have Taco Bell, apparently. Let's look at the wallet."

McGlade unfolded it. "Leather. Cheap. Got a Florida driver's license that says, oh this is good, 'John Smith.' No doubt the address will be just as fake. And here's something I don't understand." He held up the ID to the light. "Look at how shitty that ghost image of the portrait is. A blind bouncer high on pot could spot this as a fake. All that money we pay in taxes, and our government can't get better fake IDs? Why should they even be fake? Shouldn't they be able to get the real ones? Incredible."

He took some money out of the wallet, three twenty-dollar bills. "Hmm. This is good."

"Something there?" Jack asked.

"Yes. Dinner and a movie for me later tonight." He put the money in his pocket.

"You aren't helping much, McGlade."

"I'm just getting started. Let's look at this belt." He stretched it out over the table. "Finally, we have something good."

"We do?" I asked.

"Yep. Ralph Lauren. Probably cost a few hundred bucks."

"Can it be traced?" Jack asked.

"No. But it's pretty nice. Too small for me, but I do good business on eBay."

He tucked the belt into his drawer. I was really starting to dislike this guy.

"Shoes also have the labels removed, but the stitching above the sole is obvious. Doc Martens. Available everywhere. He put his nose next to one. "Hmm. Smell this."

He held it out. Jack and I each gave it a sniff.

"Anything?" he asked.

"Just stinky foot odor," Jack said.

I agreed.

McGlade nodded. "That's what I figured. I wasn't going to smell it myself, because that's gross. I'm surprised you guys did."

I was about to go back on my promise and reach for my gun when Harry said, "Hold up. Got something for real this time." He took a black leather case out of his desk and removed a dental pick. "Jack, hand me a piece of paper from the printer there."

Jack complied, and McGlade used the pick to tease something out of the tread of the shoe. A small rock dropped onto the paper. It was opaque, with a faint purplish color.

"We may have something here, ladies." He checked the other shoe, and found two more of the stones. "I think this is a job for Mr. Mass Spec."

"Who?" I asked.

"A mass spectrometer," Jack said. "It's a machine that determines the chemical composition of things."

"Where are we going to get one of those?"

"Got one," Harry said. "It's in the back room, next to my Richter scale."

Jack shrugged. "Harry's rich."

"Come on," he said, folding up the paper. "Let's see where our boy has been."

I remained dubious. "So you're going to go all CSI on those and find out it has some rare mineral only found in one part of the world?"

"Yep. That's the plan."

"That's ridiculous."

"If you want, we could take a picture of the shoes and spend a year showing it to every employee of every store in the whole world that sells Dr. Martens, and hope one of them remembers who bought this pair."

I didn't have a response to that. I simply followed Jack and Harry to the back room, which was jam-packed with expensive-looking equipment stacked on tables and carts and bracketed to the walls.

"Why do you even have a Richter scale in the Midwest?" I asked.

"I like to hook it up to my bed. My best is a six point two." He waggled his eyebrows at me. "Want to see if you and I can beat that?"

"And you were really his partner?" I said to Jack.

"I'm still in therapy. How long will this take, Harry?"

"Long enough to peel off our skivvies and get familiar."

"In minutes, Harry."

"Just a few. The mass spec burns the sample at tens of thousands of degrees, then it identifies the ions using argon plasma, or something like that. Hell if I know how it works. The instruction booklet was four hundred pages long."

"Is it dangerous?" I asked.

"Naw. Probably not. I hope not. Do either of you women ever plan on having babies?"

"This thing can make you sterile?" I asked.

"No. That was just a personal question. I was going to volunteer."

I almost laughed at that, but didn't want to encourage him. Not that lack of reinforcement seemed to be slowing him down. Harry seemed to be happy enough just amusing Harry.

"OK, stand back," he said. "I'm about to do science."

He put the rocks in a tiny drawer in a beige machine that looked like an oversized copier, then pressed a few buttons.

Nothing happened.

"Hmm. How about that." He pressed the buttons again, then scratched his chin. "Jack, can you grab that thick manual on the table there and find the number for customer service?"

"Is it plugged in?" I asked.

Harry checked under the table. "Jack, can you plug it in? Outlet is over there."

"Have you actually used this before?"

I got another wink. "I know how to turn things on."

I really doubted that.

Harry punched the buttons again, and a bright green light spilled out the center of the machine, bright enough to make me squint.

"Oooooo," Harry said. "Look at all that science."

He walked over to a computer, tapped on the keyboard, and a window on the monitor winked on, showing a porn video.

"Old case," he said, tapping more buttons. "I was researching this pervert with a big butt fetish."

"I bet you beat him mercilessly," I said.

"Did I ever. Poor little guy was sore for a week. OK, here we go."

The booty porn was replaced by a white graph with spikes all over it. Harry pressed a few more buttons, and some paper came out of his printer.

"Aha," he said, handing me the paper.

I glanced at it, half expecting more porn. Instead I saw this:

$(Fe^{2+}{}_2Al)Al_6Si_6O_{18}(BO_3)_3(OH)_3(OH)$

"What does that mean?" I asked.

"Fuck if I know. Look at all those letters and numbers. Is that even English?"

Jack put her hands on her hips, looking as annoyed as I felt. "Well, what are we supposed to do with this, Harry?"

"We ask Google."

Harry entered the formula into his browser. A moment later several Web pages appeared as results. He scrolled through them.

"Looks like it's something called tourmaline, commonly found in something called Baraboo quartzite."

Baraboo?

Oh, no. If that meant what I thought it meant, we had found Fleming.

And there was no possible way I'd be able to save her.

Chandler

"If the mission seems impossible," the Instructor said, "then opt out. There's no glory in marching to certain death. That's not patriotism or bravery. That's stupidity."

"You OK?" Jack asked. "You just lost all color."

Harry put his hand on my shoulder. "Can I get you something? A drink? Some sexy underwear?"

"I think I know where this rock came from. The old Badger Ammo plant in Baraboo, Wisconsin. It closed down after the Vietnam War, but it's still owned by the government. I've heard unconfirmed rumors that it was being used again, for something else."

"For what?" Jack asked.

"A black site."

"You mean like Harlem?" Harry asked.

"Don't you watch the news, McGlade?" Jack asked. "A black site is a secret US prison. Prisoners get taken there without due process. Abu Ghraib in Iraq. The Salt Pit in Afghanistan. No trial. No lawyers. No Amnesty International or Red Cross."

"Just torture, death, and an unmarked grave," I said, my stomach becoming tight.

"There's a black site in Wisconsin?" Jack asked.

"Unconfirmed. But possible."

Harry frowned. "That's…deplorable. My country can't do that."

"This country does a lot of things it isn't supposed to," I said. I knew, because I was one of those things.

"We can get the media involved," Jack said. "Blow it wide open."

"Then they'll take my sister somewhere else."

"Your sister?" Harry said. "That cute chick in the wheelchair? She's at this black site?"

I needed to think. Even with firepower and a trained team behind me, I wouldn't be able to break into a secret prison.

"How can we help?" Jack asked.

"You can't."

Harry shook his head "Look, Jack and I might not seem like much, but we've done some shit, and we're not afraid of—"

I held up a hand to cut him off. "If they find out you're helping me, you'll disappear and never be heard from again. So will your friends, your families, even people you went to high school with who signed your yearbook. These guys don't play around. They are the baddest of the bad, and they have unlimited power and an unlimited budget. They start wars and kill millions. You don't want to get on their radar, and even if you wanted to, I wouldn't let you."

I walked out of the room, wondering what my next move was. Saving Fleming from a black site on US soil? It would be easier to go to Cuba and rescue her from Guantánamo Bay. I didn't have a chance, and neither did poor Fleming.

But it was worse than that. She would tell them what she knew. And what she knew made it possible to launch a nuclear strike anyplace in the world. Millions of people could die. Billions of people. And there was nothing I could do to stop it.

Jack caught up with me on the stairs.

"Harry and I still want to help," she said.

"I won't allow it."

"It's a free country. Maybe we'll take a little road trip to Baraboo."

I spun on her, one hand gripping her neck and slamming her against the wall, the other pressing my 9mm into her belly.

"And maybe if I see you, I'll put sniper rounds through both of your knees. Or maybe I'll just ease my conscience and do that now. Is that necessary?"

I saw the requisite fear in her eyes, and that made me feel even shittier.

"Look, Jack, I don't know about Harry, but you, you're a good person. There's no way you can come with me on this. It isn't just a question of them hurting you. You'd have to hurt them as well. Are you going to be OK with sneaking up on an unarmed man and slitting his throat from behind? Could you cut off someone's fingers to get information? Could you blow up a building with innocent women and children in it to take out a target?"

Jack's eyes became wide and she waited several seconds before whispering, "You do those things?"

"I do what's needed," I said through clenched teeth. "And I can't have someone watching my back who cares about her fellow man. If I see you, I will shoot you. And if you break this to the media and they move my sister..."

"I won't," Jack said. "You're right. I can't...I can't do those things you said. Neither could McGlade. And I wouldn't risk them taking your sister someplace else. But you can't do this alone, Chandler."

I let her go and put my gun away. "I don't have a choice."

"Do you have any contacts?"

I shook my head. "No." The only contacts I had were through Fleming.

"I know a guy. I guess you'd call him a merc. He's...well, he wouldn't have a problem doing those things you said."

"This is a lot more than most people can deal with, Jack."

"So is he."

"Military?"

"I don't think so. I've run into him a few times. He's a former gymnast. A while ago he took on the whole Chicago mob, and won. He's not crazy, and he's not a psycho, but he's unaffected by guilt or remorse and does what is needed."

I considered it. "Is he stable?"

"He's the best I've ever seen. Always in total control. A pure sociopath." Jack stared deep into my eyes. "Like you."

I kept myself from reacting, from letting her know how much that stung. And as much as I wanted to protest her characterization of me, I wasn't sure if it was inaccurate, or if I just wanted to fool myself into thinking it was. "What does he charge?"

"You'd have to discuss that with him."

This is what my life had come to? Working with complete strangers to fight a government I was supposed to be working for?

"Where do I find him?" I asked.

"I can set up a meeting."

"Jack..."

"Then I'll be out of it. You're right. I have a fiancé. An elderly mother. I don't want anything to happen to them. But let me call him, Chandler. He can help you. I'm sure of it."

"OK," I told her. "What's his name?"

"I know this may sound odd coming from someone named Jack Daniels, but his name is Tequila."

Fleming

"When captured by the enemy," the Instructor said, "your first priority is survival. If you tell them what they want to know, they'll no longer have any use for you, and they'll kill you. And if you give them the information they want, they'll use it to kill others. If you talk, everyone loses. But they will eventually make you talk. Everybody talks."

When Fleming regained consciousness, she was still wearing the backless hospital gown that smelled like lemon bleach, and straps still bound her arms, torso, and ankles to a wheelchair, though this was a newer model. The morphine drip she'd enjoyed after surgery was gone, leaving the nerves in her bullet-riddled legs screaming. A tremor seized the muscles in her arms and hands, and she shook for almost a minute before getting it under control.

A recessed light glared down at her from a ceiling of poured concrete, a steel grate shielding the bulb. Whitewashed cinder block walls, steel door, concrete floor. There were no windows in the room, and the air—its pressure, the humidity—felt like she was underground.

In one corner, a steel chair was bolted to the floor, its arms and legs outfitted with thick leather straps. A large drain marked the floor's center, and the smell of dampness, mildew, urine, and blood hung in the air like the thick calm before a thunderstorm.

The hum of voices reached her from somewhere out in the hall.

The door opened, and Malcolm stepped inside, carrying a tablet computer with a touch screen. He wore his black suit, but he'd removed his tie. A younger man followed, dressed in a gray prison guard uniform. His hair was cropped close in a high and tight that emphasized the angular shape of his head. He didn't spare Fleming a glance, simply took position behind her.

"You had to bring security?" she said, forcing bravado into her voice that she didn't feel. "Seeing as I can't move enough to scratch my nose, it makes me doubt you own a pair of balls."

Taking measured steps, he approached her chair, then bent close and stared into her soul. In the bright light, the skin surrounding one of Malcolm's eyes looked even chalkier than the rest of his complexion. The strange pallor extended up to his forehead.

"Remember our little chat, back at the hospital?" His breath smelled like wintergreen, and when he flashed his creepy smile, she could see the telltale darkness at his gum line, evidence his teeth had been capped. "Well, it got me thinking."

"Thinking? Good for you. There's a first time for everything."

He chuckled, a disturbing sound like a rasp across the mouth of a tin can, then pushed the tablet computer in front of her face.

An X-ray lit the screen, the ghostly images of a pelvis, a femur, and a knee. Bright white indicated the pins holding the bones together and four slugs lodged in the surrounding flesh.

"Do you recognize this?"

Fleming wanted to say no or fling a smart-assed comment at him. She couldn't manage either.

"The bullets are no longer there, of course. But I'm more interested in the pins. Hard to forget going through that much pain, I'll bet."

"You want to know about pain, Malcolm? Ask your parents about the weird little boy they raised. I bet they can't even stand to look at you."

He didn't so much as blink.

"I have a philosophy." He pulled an ASP Friction Loc from his belt. "The threat of force is often just as effective as the use of force."

Often used by cops, the telescoping steel folded to about nine inches long and unfurled to twenty-seven. Fleming had taken a glancing blow to the head from one years ago and had been carried away with a concussion. If she'd taken the full brunt of the strike, she would be dead.

Malcolm paced the width of the room, tapping the collapsed ASP against the palm of one hand, the soles of his shoes drumming the floor.

"Where's my sister?" Fleming demanded, trying not to stare at the steel baton.

"I'm surprised you haven't heard her screaming. But then, this is a rather large facility. Care to guess where you are?"

Fleming had no idea. By the fullness of her bladder, she couldn't have been out for more than a few hours. But she couldn't be sure.

"Not even a guess? OK, I'll tell you. You're in a secret prison. One that doesn't officially exist. I can do whatever I want to you, for as long as I want."

"I should thank you," Fleming forced herself to say.

"Thank me?" Malcolm appeared confused. "For what?"

"You took my advice about the mints. Your breath was worse than anything else you could possibly do to me."

This time he winced. But he recovered immediately. "It must have been tough. The injury. Those weeks and months and years after."

He had no idea.

The thought sprang into her mind before she could catch it. She was falling for his tricks, first making her fear for Chandler, now the memories of her accident. Emotions surged to the surface, vulnerabilities that would leave her wide open to his techniques.

She tried to push back concerns about her sister, and the thoughts of Milan—hanging outside the building, the snap of the support wire, the five-story fall.

"All the pain..." He kept pacing. "All the rehab you must have gone through...and to no avail. You're still a cripple."

Tap, tap, tap.

"Such a horror it would be to have to relive all that pain, all those operations."

Tap, tap, tap.

"The bones being set, and rebroken, and set again." He flicked the ASP in the air, and it telescoped to full length.

Chhhk-chhk.

Fleming could feel the sound scrape up her spine, a visceral sound of danger, like the racking of a pump-action shotgun. She couldn't stop herself from flinching.

Malcolm smiled. "Now I'll ask you again. Who do you work for?"

He reached out with the baton. Resting it at her ankles, then running it slowly up her shins, lifting her hospital gown with it.

While Fleming had lost the use of her legs, the nerves still functioned just fine.

He skimmed the baton over her knees, reaching her thighs, tenderly tracing the tip along the spiderweb network of scars, then probing her bandaged bullet wounds.

She focused on breathing, on controlling her heart rate, but sweat broke out over her skin.

"I know the bullet wounds must hurt, but do the old injuries? Do they ache during bad weather? Do they stiffen up first thing in the morning? How about those metal pins? Can you feel them?"

He checked the X-ray on the tablet, then moved the ASP.

"Here's one. Right here. Can you feel it?"

Fleming ground her molars together. She knew what he was going to do, whether she answered or not, and there was no way she could brace herself for it.

"Fine. I'll make you feel it."

When he hit her leg with the ASP, the pain was sudden and explosive and terrifyingly familiar. A sound somewhere between a groan and a scream crested her lips.

"So your voice does work. Good to know. I was missing your smart mouth. I'd like to hear a little more from you."

He moved the baton back down her legs, to her shins, this time putting pressure on it.

"Let me consult your chart. Ah, yes. There's another pin… right…about…*here*."

Another slap of the ASP. The sound breaking from her throat was a full-on scream this time. Tears swamped her eyes and ran down her cheeks. She tried to breathe through it, blowing out hard with each exhale, but the shattering agony refused to fade.

Fleming had a high pain threshold, and years of training had enabled her to hold out much longer than most. But her injuries had sapped her strength. Already she felt desperate. She wouldn't be able to last very long. No one could. The urge to mindlessly plead for relief pressed at her lips, struggling to get out. Eventually Fleming would say anything Malcolm wanted to hear just to make the agony stop.

"We've only just begun," he whispered, wintergreen breath on her neck. "We're going to give your legs a lot of attention. For hours. Days. Weeks. And when those nerves are finally dead, we're going to do to you what we're doing to your sister. Trust me. That's even worse."

She turned her neck and met his eyes. Sweat beaded along his hairline, and he brushed it away with the back of one hand. Again, she noticed the strange pallor of his skin, but now part of the chalkiness had been wiped away, the smallest hint of dull purple beneath.

Makeup. That's what the strange pallor was. He'd put makeup on his face to hide a discoloration. A port wine stain reaching from his cheekbone into his hairline.

Maybe he could dig into her pain, make her scream, but now she'd recognized his deficiencies, too, number one being a strange kind of vanity. And that gave her a certain amount of satisfaction.

"You should try the new L'Oréal foundation. It's designed to match your skin tone. No one will even know you're wearing makeup, Mr. Gorbachev."

Red poured into the rest of his face. Tendons stood out on his neck.

She stared him down, knowing she'd probably pay. Hoping he'd get so angry he'd lose control and kill her outright, before he could torture her into giving up the secrets she'd been directed to take to her grave.

Malcolm raised his wrist.

Then he stabbed the baton squarely into the side of the chair, making her shudder. The friction locking the steel into its extended form broke, and the parts collapsed.

Fleming hissed out a heavy breath.

As much as she wanted to think the worst was over, it had only just begun. Malcolm would escalate.

Raise the stakes.

Raise his demands.

Raise the level of pain.

"I have something. Something I'd very much like to hear your thoughts about." He crossed to the younger soldier behind her. When he returned to her field of vision, he held the transceiver in his hands. The transceiver she'd almost died trying to protect.

Another round of tears welled in her eyes. The last she knew, it was at the bottom of Lake Michigan. How in the hell had Malcolm come up with it?

"So you recognize this little phone? I figured you might. But it's more than just a phone, isn't it? Still seems to power on, even after all that time in the water."

He flicked the baton open.

Chhhk-chhk.

"Now, it seems the device is locked. And I'm guessing you can solve that problem for me."

"Sorry," Fleming managed. "I'm not very good with technology."

"If that's true, it would be unfortunate for you." He started at her ankles again. This time instead of caressing her legs, he flicked the steel bar, inching up her injured flesh.

When he reached the bullet wounds in her thighs, she didn't even try to hold back the screams.

"How long do you want me to do this?" To make his point, he finished the trek back down her legs, the pressure growing behind each strike.

Fleming's hospital gown was soaked with perspiration now, and blood had started to seep through her bandages.

"Suit yourself."

Malcolm raised the ASP high for a bone-shattering blow. He hadn't been lying about the agony she'd gone through. Breaking, setting, then long months of healing, only to have to endure them breaking the bones again. She'd been ready to give up. If not for the Instructor, she would have. She couldn't go through it all again.

There was only one thing she could do. One thing that would stop this.

Fleming didn't need to make her voice sound weak and defeated. It already did. "Please. No more. I'll help you."

"The unlock code."

She drew in a long breath. "Give the phone to me. I'll unlock it. Just no more. I can't handle it."

Fleming couldn't give him what he wanted, the activation code or access to the rest of her knowledge. There was too much at stake. The phone, if properly used, could launch a nuclear strike. She couldn't allow that. But she also couldn't bear the pain.

That only left one solution. She had to die.

And death was just a few inches away. The transceiver had a self-destruct code. There was enough PETN in that little phone to blow someone's head off.

Fleming wanted it to be her head.

The strength of her resolve, the finality of it, surprised her. But she'd made up her mind, and there was really no other acceptable choice. Even if she had two good legs, escape was impossible. Better to die quickly and save millions than die in agony and be responsible for World War III.

"Free one of my hands, and I'll unlock it."

For a moment he stared at her, as if he thought he could bore into her mind with willpower alone. "No. You give me the code."

She met his intensity. "It has to be me. It recognizes my bioelectric signature."

Fleming had pulled the phrase *bioelectric signature* out of her ass, and she hoped it didn't sound like the bullshit it actually was.

There was an awful, tension-filled moment, and then Malcolm said, "Untie her left hand."

If anyone had ever told Fleming that the greatest victory of her life would be to kill herself, she never would have believed it. But that was about to be the case. Her only regret was knowing Chandler was still in this hellhole. But Fleming was incapable of helping herself, let alone her sister. She'd have to settle for saving the world.

"Hold it," Malcolm ordered his guard.

Fleming's hopes sank.

"You're a bit too eager to get your hands on this phone. I can see it in your eyes."

Shit.

Malcolm brought down the baton, cracking it against Fleming's leg.

"What is it you want to do?" he demanded. "Punch in an erase code?"

Another strike.

"Tell me!"

After the third blow, the pain became so bad Fleming passed out.

***

A whiff of ammonia brought Fleming around again. Back to her world of pain. She recoiled from the smelling salts, the agony so intense, she threw up.

Malcolm stepped to the side, distaste apparent on his face. He pointed the ASP at her.

"Give me the unlock code. If it doesn't unlock the phone, I'll see how many pieces I can make out of your femur. In fact, I'll take it as a personal challenge."

"I swear, I have to be the one who—"

He raised the baton over her thighs. "The code!"

"I'll tell you! Whatever you want."

"Now."

Fleming had lost. Her death wouldn't come easy.

But she could still destroy the phone. And maybe take this arrogant asshole out as well.

She rattled off the first six numbers of the sequence.

Malcolm tucked the ASP under his armpit and punched them in.

Fleming told him the next six.

He hesitated, narrowing his eyes, makeup creasing in his crow's-feet.

"I can do it," Fleming said.

Malcolm motioned for the young soldier to take the transceiver. "Punch in the rest."

Fleming's throat grew tight. That bastard. Maybe he *could* read minds.

She glanced at the young spook. Probably not too long out of training. His whole life ahead of him. But what could she do? He'd made his choice. Malcolm had headed off her bid to kill herself and deflected her chance to kill him. The least she could do was take care of the transceiver.

Malcolm brought the baton down, the steel rod sending agony through her.

When the ringing in her ears cleared, she could hear his voice.

"Repeat the numbers."

Swallowing hard, she forced out the last digits.

The young guard, just following orders, tapped at the phone. He stopped with two digits left.

"What are you waiting for?"

"I don't remember the last numbers."

"Five and seven. Oh, just give it to me." Face as red as his port wine stain, Malcolm reached for the device just as the guard punched in the last two numbers.

The transceiver exploded, showering Fleming with blood and bone.

But, sadly, none of it was hers.

Chandler

"You should keep your friends close, and your enemies closer," the Instructor said. "But make sure you know the difference between the two."

I'd traded my hooker outfit for jeans and a black sweater and had been waiting for Tequila on the corner of Wabash and Twenty-Sixth for almost half an hour, standing under the scorched marquee of a burned-out liquor store. The area could be generously described as "underprivileged." A block south I'd actually seen some homeless guys huddling around a burning barrel, something I'd never thought existed outside of the movies. Earlier, two kids, each no more than twelve, tried to sell me meth. A pimp who couldn't even shave yet attempted to force his game on me, talking trash and flashing the butt of a gun sticking out of his saggy pants. I relieved the teen of his piece and two teeth, and then chased him off. Now I was growing increasingly paranoid that he would be coming back with reinforcements.

I caught sight of someone walking toward me, opposite side of the street, and wondered if yet another kid would try to shake me down. But on closer inspection I saw it wasn't a black youth, but a short white adult.

Jack had mentioned that Tequila was a gymnast, but she hadn't mentioned he was two inches shorter than me, and I'm no giant. He wore a Blackhawks Starter jacket, jeans, and boots, and approached casually, a small bounce in his step, hands at his sides. As he got closer, I noticed the wrinkles on his face. I put him in his late forties, maybe early fifties. Blond hair in a buzz cut. A completely neutral expression. If he'd had a cigarette and a cowboy hat, he would have looked exactly like the Marlboro Man, if the Marlboro Man had been a member of the Lollipop Guild.

My first impression was that Jack had slipped a gear in her brainbox, because there was no way this elderly midget would be any help. That pissed me off, because I'd wasted a lot of time waiting for him when I could have been on my way to Baraboo.

Tequila stopped a meter in front of me, hands at his sides. This close he looked even shorter.

"I get five k a day, plus expenses." He had a deep, scratchy voice, as if he didn't use it often.

I smirked—his figure was outrageous. "And what do you do to earn that five k?"

"Whatever it takes to get the job done."

"Former military?"

He shook his head.

"Done any freelance overseas?" I asked.

"I'm mostly local."

"Any training at all in espionage, counterespionage?"

"No. My experience is in beating people up and shooting them."

I managed to refrain from rolling my eyes. "I don't think you're right for this job. Sorry to waste your—"

And the next thing I knew I was on my ass.

I hadn't seen the guy move. Wasn't even sure how he hit me. His body was in the exact same position it had been when I was talking to him. Except now I was on the ground, trying to catch my breath from a sharp blow to the diaphragm.

"Jack said you needed help. The kind of help I'm good at giving. You want to test me. So test me."

He held out his hand. I took it, and it was like gripping a two-by-four. As I pulled up to my feet, I shifted my weight and spun behind him, throwing a reverse side kick at his head. He caught my foot with his other hand, dropped to a knee, and flipped me as if he were sparring with a practice dummy.

I rolled with the throw, coming up on the balls of my feet, twisting my hips, and following up with a spin kick. Tequila did a back handspring away from it, and then another handspring, and then a somersault, landing in a crouch. Somehow during the maneuver, two silver .45s had appeared in his hands, both aimed at me. Before I could react, he raised the guns above his head, firing so fast that it sounded like a machine gun. Then the Bo's Liquor sign was falling on me, the chains holding it up having been severed.

I rolled forward, narrowly avoiding being crushed, and Tequila was right there when I came to my feet, his guns back in his shoulder holsters and his hands empty.

"You're not as good as you think you are," he told me.

I shrugged off my backpack, tossing it behind me. "You're old and short."

He didn't react at all. I couldn't even tell if he was breathing.

"If you want my help, Chandler, you have ten seconds to impress me."

He didn't appear cocky or smug. He appeared certain, which was even more irritating, especially after the day I'd had. But it was also a challenge. He'd had two chances to seriously hurt me, and one chance to kill me, but he wasn't interested in that. If anything, he was acting like a pro, and I wasn't. Even if I chalked it up to stress, or exhaustion, I wasn't channeling my best.

"I apologize," I said. "It's been a tough few days."

"Five seconds," he said.

I nodded, bowed to show respect, and struck a *kyorugi joonbi*—a centered tae kwon do attacking stance. He did me the courtesy of bowing back, and then stood in a *moa sogi*, feet together and arms straight at his sides, awaiting my attack.

This time I gave him my best, leading with a front kick, following with a palm strike, spinning on my axis, and drilling my heel into his chest before he could block it. He jumped, surprisingly high, and did a spinning kick, which I got under, connecting my shin to his thigh. I followed up with another palm, coming up under his chin, pulling it so I didn't hurt him.

But I hadn't needed to pull it, because he had captured my blow between his elbow and palm.

A move identical to what Rochester had done to me.

I rolled away, ducking the follow-up elbow, my fists clenched hard.

"What was that?" I said.

He offered only the same maddening blank expression.

"The block with the hand and the elbow," I said.

"It's called skull and crossbones."

"What's its style?"

"Jailhouse Rock."

Jailhouse Rock. I thought back to the tattoo on Rochester's hand. *JHR.*

Tequila tapped his elbow, his chest, his neck, and then began to pick up speed, beating out that familiar rhythm.

"Five thousand a day, plus expenses," I said over the noise. "But you have to teach me that."

He stopped the beat and shook his head. "You haven't impressed me yet."

So that's how it was? Fine.

I switched to muay thai, jumping at him with a shin kick. He moved to block it, and I let him push me off balance while I reached down and tweaked his nose. We both knew I could have broken it, but I didn't rest on my laurels, instead twisting in the air and hitting the sidewalk on my bad shoulder, damning the pain, arching my back and kicking up to lock my feet around his neck. He made the mistake everyone makes with this move; he tried to pull me off. I allowed him to yank my legs, grabbing his heel as he did, letting him pull his own feet out from under him with me as the lever.

We ended up on the sidewalk, him on his back, his head between my thighs and my knees pinning his arms.

If I'd had a knife in hand, I could have gutted him from groin to clavicle. Instead I gave him a firm slap on his belly to let him know I was in control. It was like hitting concrete.

With one fluid move he bucked me off and skipped up to his feet, and as he spun with his hands digging into his jacket, I produced the Beretta from my waistband at the same time.

We each crouched there, pointing our weapons at each other, him looking blank and me smiling wide. A police siren wailed in the distance.

"I recognized the tae kwon do, the judo, and the muay thai," Tequila said, "but what was that last move with the legs on my neck?"

"That's one of my own."

He seemed to think it over, then said, "You kill people for the government."

"Yes."

"I don't trust the government."

"Neither do I."

Another short stretch of silence.

"Jack said something about breaking your sister out of a secret prison. This is personal to you."

I thought about lying, but decided against it. What was the point? "Yes."

The sirens got closer. I had no idea what he was thinking.

"My truck is parked a block over, on State," he eventually said. "I brought clothing and provisions for three days. If it takes longer than that, you pick up the expenses."

I didn't have to think it over. "Agreed."

"You're in charge, so you call the shots. But I reserve the right to challenge your authority if I disagree."

"Agreed."

"I'll take two days' pay in advance. Cash. And you pay me every two days, as long as I'm needed."

Cash wouldn't be a problem, at least at first. But that would run out, and if I accessed any of my accounts, I had no guarantee they couldn't be traced.

Then again, those with the proper equipment could trace me anyway.

"Agreed," I said.

He tucked away his guns and stood up, holding out his hand. I stood up and shook it. Tequila held my hand longer than he needed to, and I saw something flash in his eyes. Amusement? Respect?

Attraction?

"Any witnesses saw a man and a woman fighting," he said, releasing my hand. "I'll grab my truck, meet you on Twenty-eighth and State. It's a white SUV. See you in three minutes."

He turned and walked off, leaving me to wonder if I'd just improved my odds, or made an enormous mistake.

Fleming

"Once you are captured, your biggest battle is with yourself," the Instructor said. "The enemy has as many ways to beat down your spirit as they have to hurt your body. It's up to you to find ways to keep your mind strong, your hope intact, in the face of whatever they throw at you."

After the explosion, more guards had come rushing in. Malcolm had ordered Fleming sedated and left the room, clutching his mangled hand. They escorted him out, and removed the remains of the young man who'd punched in the destruction code.

She felt a stab of regret for him, but Nuremburg had shown that just following orders was a fool's game. He'd died, but the transceiver had died with him. She took solace in that.

Unable to fight against the straps holding her down, she felt the sting of the needle plunge into her arm, then dizziness, then nothing.

Fleming didn't know how long she'd been out, but when she awoke, she was alone in a tiny room. The wheelchair was gone, and she lay sprawled on a concrete floor, naked under a bright overhead light.

She forced herself up to one hip. Pain pulsed through her ruined legs. Her head felt light, and it took a few minutes for her to solidify her balance and survey the room. This space was smaller than the last, about ten by ten, but it had the same white cinder block walls, lack of windows, and concrete floor. It also had the same recessed light, and she did her best to blink back its glare. A black plastic bucket was the only thing in the room, no handle, probably meant to be her toilet.

Also like the room where she'd been interrogated, the air was cold and held the dampness found underground. Shivers shook her. She tried to cover herself with her arms, but even as she did, she knew it was no use.

Nakedness was a tactic, of course, intended to strip her of her identity, make her feel vulnerable, let her know she was defenseless against the forces controlling her life.

It also kept her from tearing the hospital gown into lengths that she could tie into a noose.

She'd hoped to kill herself and take her knowledge with her, but with the smooth walls, empty room, and lack of anything but the bucket, Malcolm had taken away even that escape. They'd stripped off the long bandages the hospital had used to wrap her legs, leaving nothing but gauze stuck to her flesh by blood.

A noise filtered into the room, a low keening, like the complaints of a wounded animal. It grew in volume, becoming a feminine scream.

"No…no…please…no…"

She quailed at the sound. Chandler? She couldn't tell.

Pulling in a breath, she forced herself to continue her observations, taking note of her surroundings, filing details away in case they became useful later. Performing her job, following her training…something she could control.

This room wasn't as clean as the last. The odor of mildew, dust, and mice droppings reached her, along with blood oozing from the wounds on her battered legs. She wasn't sure how long she'd been here, passed out on the floor, but her mouth was dry, and her throat felt swollen. Bladder was fuller than before. She'd have to use the bucket soon, an enormous indignity considering she wasn't able to squat.

The woman's screams wrapped around her mind, impossible to ignore.

"Stop...please, stop...I'll tell you whatever you want to know... just no more."

Fleming's chest constricted. Was that Chandler? She couldn't tell by the voice, but Fleming couldn't imagine Chandler begging.

Unless they'd broken her.

Could they have broken her that quickly?

What were they doing to that poor woman?

Fleming thought about calling out. She wanted to.

But no good could come of that. It would only weaken her.

Instead, Fleming leaned back against the whitewashed wall. She cleared her mind and focused on breathing.

In four counts. Hold four counts. Out four counts.

It took several reps before she could feel her airway start to relax, then, using her hands, she dragged herself to the door.

There was no knob, no way to open it from this side. A few shoves, and she could tell it was solid steel and likely secured with dead bolts.

She wasn't getting out of here unless Malcolm or his men came to get her. If they did, it meant he was ready to make good on his threats, to wring every last bit of useful information from Fleming's mind.

"Oh, God...no. I've told you all of it. I swear...just...please...don't..."

Until then, they'd keep her naked and cold, trapped underground, the echoes of another woman's anguish beating her down like a physical force.

"Please! I'm begging you...no!"

Fleming tried to block out the sounds.

She couldn't.

Chandler

"The difference between an enemy and an ally can be minimal," the Instructor said. "Sometimes the only line between the two is timing."

When I saw the white truck I immediately thought *Cop.* White with blue trim, tinted windows, a spotlight above the side mirror, multiple antennas on top. But then a window rolled down and Tequila leaned an arm over the driver's door. I hopped in, putting my bag at my feet.

"We have to stop at my apartment."

"You're hot," Tequila said.

"Thanks. I try to keep in shape."

He gave me a quick sideways glance that conveyed bottomless disapproval. "Hot. Too many people after you. They'll be watching your apartment."

"I need equipment."

"We'll get more equipment."

"Some of it is specialized." I wanted to add, *I also need to pick up more money to pay your outrageously expensive salary*, but I kept that bit to myself.

Tequila pulled a cell out of his jacket. Like mine, it was a TracFone—one of those disposable models you could buy at drugstores. Untraceable.

"Give me a list of what you need."

I began to rattle off items, which he typed into his phone using his thumb while also managing to successfully navigate Chicago traffic without killing us both.

After he hit send, he said, "Tell me about the mission."

There wasn't much to tell. We needed to locate the black site, infiltrate, and escape with Fleming.

"What do you know about the area?" he asked.

"Just that it was an old ammo production facility."

"It's about two hundred miles northwest of here," Tequila said. "It encompasses roughly thirty square kilometers, which equals about seventy-four hundred acres total. When it was built in 1942, it was the largest ammunition propellant plant in the world. At its peak, it employed over twelve thousand workers making smokeless powder, acid, oleum, rocket propellant, and mortar. The military ceased production after the Vietnam War and closed it down in 1997. Since then various companies have been dismantling, demolishing, and basically cleaning up the facility."

So he'd done a bit of research before taking the job. That's probably what took him so long.

"I'd guess the best point of entry is from the north, through Devil's Lake State Park. There's a perimeter fence, and no doubt cameras. Depending on where the prison is located in the facility, and depending on what kind of shape your sister is in when we get her, we may need to bring a vehicle."

"My sister is in a wheelchair. She doesn't have the use of her legs."

Tequila went silent. We merged onto the expressway. I yawned, needing sleep even though I'd only been awake for a few hours and was still buzzing from the stimulants. I was physically, mentally, and emotionally exhausted. When I told Tequila I'd had a tough few days, it had been the understatement of the century.

I sat back and closed my eyes, thinking about Fleming, about the horrors she was no doubt enduring. Then I thought about my other sister. Hammett.

Hammett, Fleming, and I had once been a part of a secret government experiment to create a team of assassins indistinguishable from one another. Along with our four other sisters, now deceased, we'd each gone through training to be the best of the best, not knowing the others existed. Unfortunately, Hammett went rogue, which led to Fleming and me being disowned by our government. Now, like Hammett, we were enemies of the state.

I needed to tell Tequila about Hammett, because she was a wild card. Though she certainly wasn't working for the NIC, she still had an agenda that could interfere with mine. Worse, she potentially had a way of tracking me and Fleming. We each had GPS transmitter chips sewn into our bellies. Anyone with the right software and the right code could locate any of us to within a square meter.

"You trust me enough to sleep?" Tequila said.

"I'm not asleep." I looked at him. "And I don't trust anyone."

"Even your sister?"

"Her I trust."

"Then you trust one more person than I do."

"What about Jack? Do you trust her?"

Tequila shrugged. "I like her. She keeps her word. But she's impossible to trust."

"Because she has morals," I said, recalling my earlier conversation with her in the stairwell.

He gave a slight nod. "She is hampered by her ideas of right and wrong."

"Maybe she's onto something. Maybe if more people had morals, there wouldn't be a need for people like us."

Tequila gave me another sideways glance, but this one wasn't condescending. "The reason people like us exist is because there are morals. Those in power wish to enforce their idea of morality on others."

A cynical way to look at life, but I couldn't disagree with him. I had limits. Lines I wouldn't cross. Naturally I felt that if all people had the same limitations, we'd all get along better. But that wasn't the answer. Wealth, property, religion, politics—they were all ways to gain and display power, and power at its essence was the desire to control people, to coerce them or force them into agreeing with you.

"So that's your philosophy?" I asked.

"I don't have a philosophy. I'm just a thug who hurts and kills people for money."

"Are there jobs you won't take?"

"No."

"You'd hurt women? Children?"

"If I don't do it, someone else will."

"So you really have no morality."

Tequila shrugged. "Moral absolutism is bullshit. There are always shades of gray. If you say you're moral, you either have to live your entire life without ever hurting anyone or anything, or you're a hypocrite. At least my way is honest."

Hammett also had zero morality. But I couldn't make the argument that her way was the better way to live. Did that mean I was being dishonest with myself? I'd turned down assignments before, but there was always someone else to send instead, and the person I refused to kill wound up just as dead as if I'd done it.

Imposed morality.

Was that the fate of humanity? Either allow people to control others, or pure anarchy?

"We're not the good guys," I said.

The barest of smiles crossed Tequila's lips. "Of course we are. We're all the heroes in the movies of our lives. We can all justify everything we do. But that doesn't mean it's easy to get to sleep at night."

I slumped down in my seat, closing my eyes. I wanted to prove him wrong. To go to sleep, with a clear conscience.

But sleep wouldn't come.

***

I opened my eyes about an hour later, when I felt the truck start to slow down. We were coasting into a rest area.

"Pit stop?" I asked.

"Meeting our supplier. Do you have some money in that gym bag?"

"Yes."

"Good. Easier to pay him than to kill him."

I had no idea if Tequila was kidding or not, and I didn't want to know.

He pulled into the semi lane rather than the car lane, and drove toward the tree line. Parked by itself was a black Corvette. And standing next to it…

"That's our supplier?"

"Jack recommended him. Said he has everything."

I frowned. "Don't kill him, no matter how rude he is," I said.

"That's what Jack texted me."

I picked up my gym bag and followed Tequila out of the truck.

"Hiya, hottie," said Harry McGlade. "And which one of the dwarves is this?"

Tequila's eyes bored into him.

"Ahh," Harry said. "You must be Grumpy. I managed to find everything you needed, along with a few extras that you should find helpful."

I sniffed the air, smelling cocoa. It seemed to be coming from McGlade, and something about it was off.

"Did you just eat chocolate?" I asked.

"Nope. That's my Axe body spray. Dark Temptation. Does it make you want to lick me all over?"

"No. It's making me nauseous."

"There's also a deodorant," he said, lifting his arm. "Smell."

I made a face. "That's supposed to attract women?"

"It should. It's almost five bucks a can." He swatted several flies that were buzzing around him.

"You're attracting something, all right. Where's the stuff?"

"It's in the backseat."

"How much?" I asked.

McGlade held up a pudgy hand. "First of all, 'Thanks, Harry, for driving to Wisconsin and helping me out.'"

I managed to say, "Thanks, Harry," without chewing off the insides of my cheeks. "How much?"

"Free," he said. "As long as you bring it back. You break it, you bought it."

I raised an eyebrow. "Why so generous?"

"Remember those box seats to the Bulls game? When you spring your sister, you two owe me a date."

I folded my arms across my chest. "That's what you want? Really?"

"I won't make sex mandatory, but I won't discourage it. In fact, once I rev up the seduction machine, you and your sis will probably start wrestling over who gets first crack at me."

Ugh. "I'd rather pay you."

"There's also that other option we discussed," Tequila offered.

"That's the deal, babe. Take it or leave it."

I sighed. "I'll take it."

"Seal it with a bump and grind?" McGlade gyrated his hips in a manner that made me unhappy.

"How about a handshake?"

We shook, and I realized for the first time that his hand wasn't real. It was a very detailed prosthesis. And, incredibly, it began to vibrate when I held it.

"Just had that installed," he said, winking.

Ugh.

Tequila removed a large duffel bag from Harry's backseat and set it on the trunk of the Corvette hard enough to bounce the shocks.

"Ouch! Watch the paint job, Brainy Smurf! I just got this car!"

Tequila stared at him again, in a way I wouldn't want to be stared at. "You talk a lot."

McGlade scanned the parking lot, looking over Tequila's head. "Who said that?"

I put my hand on Tequila's shoulder, figuring he was going to snap the private eye in two. But instead he surprised me by smiling.

"You are completely without morals, aren't you?" Tequila asked.

"You say that like it's a bad thing," McGlade said, smiling back.

Tequila glanced at me, not smug or cocky, just certain. Then he unzipped the duffel bag, and McGlade spent a minute describing all the goodies. And there were a lot of goodies.

Which put me on the spot. I did NOT want to sleep with this guy. Maybe after we saved Fleming, she could take one for the team. She seemed to be much more liberated than I was when it came to men. Though I was beginning to understand the hypocrisy and inherent evil in imposed morality, a large part of me did want to impose some of my morals on Harry McGlade. Either that or let Tequila kill him.

When we finished, Tequila shouldered the bag, and McGlade stuck out his hand. His real one.

"I'm Harry McGlade, by the way."

"Tequila."

They shook, and it seemed friendly enough.

"Bring her back for me, Tequila. She owes me a date."

He winked at me again, slapped Tequila on the shoulder like they were best buds, and then climbed back into his Corvette.

When we got back in the truck, Tequila said, "So are you gonna—"

"I don't want to discuss it."

"With that guy?"

"This topic is closed."

"Apparently you don't refuse any jobs either."

That was the last we spoke to each other until we reached Baraboo.

Hammett

"The enemy of your enemy can be your friend," the Instructor said. "Or they can be one more enemy."

Hammett's boss had booked the conference room at Crazy Clown's Motel and Waterpark in the tacky midwestern tourist trap known as the Wisconsin Dells.

Coulrophobia. Fear of clowns. And why not? Clowns were just plain creepy.

On the positive side, it was as inconspicuous a location as imaginable. And it being the off-season, it was incredibly cheap. Hammett hadn't stayed in a fifty-nine-dollar-a-night room since, well, *ever*.

On the minus side, the hotel was crawling with children and water-based attractions, both of which she hated. Training at Hydra involved being repeatedly drowned, and like Chandler, Hammett hadn't ever fully recovered from it. Being in a cheap motel, surrounded by indoor waterslides and pools and the ever-present stench of chlorine, made her foul mood even fouler.

As for children, seeing them reminded Hammett of herself as a child, and she didn't like to go there.

The conference room, like the entire facility, was tacky, cheap, and falling apart. Plastic drapes with a palm-tree pattern. Threadbare carpet. A Formica conference table with some chips in it, revealing the particleboard beneath. Colored linoleum chairs with splits in the cushions and flimsy aluminum legs. Hammett had requested some pitchers of water, and they'd brought clear plastic carafes and matching plastic cups, opaque from years of dishwasher abuse, lukewarm and without ice.

If she hadn't been working, Hammett would have hunted down and sanctioned the motel's managers and owners, on her own dime, just to show her displeasure. But she was there to interview possible members of an assault squad, and had no time to pursue her baser needs.

Her boss had set up the potential candidates. The talent pool was limited to who was available and in the immediate area, and Hammett hoped to make it quick so she could leave this terrible excuse for lodging. She'd find someplace else to sleep tonight after the op, even if it meant breaking into a nice home and killing the homeowners. There was no way in hell she'd stay at the Crazy Clown, which had balloons painted on the dresser and a mattress the width of a pizza box, no doubt resplendent with dubious stains and bedbugs.

While she waited for the candidates to arrive, Hammett logged in to her tablet PC and checked up on her sisters. As expected, the GPS blip on the screen indicating Fleming was in Baraboo, at the black site hidden beneath the defunct Badger Ammo factory. Chandler's blip was heading north from Chicago, no doubt going after Fleming.

Hammett had a score—a big score—to settle with Chandler. But Fleming was the mission, so that bit of vengeance would have to wait. As her mind conjured up deliciously awful scenarios where Chandler begged for mercy and Hammett refused, she reviewed the encrypted CVs of the men who were attending the meeting. Standard freelance grunts, none of them really standing out except for a South American who did some stuff that Hammett had to reread three times to make sure she truly grasped its depraved depths.

Hammett heard the approach of footsteps from the outside hall. The first to arrive was a white guy, early thirties, who opened the conference room door a crack and poked his unshaven face through. He had wide eyes and an expression somewhere between amused and alarmed.

"I'm Jersey," he said.

There was no one named Jersey on Hammett's list. She crossed her legs, her ankle sheath within reach.

"Who are you looking for?"

"Oh. Uh, looking for Carl. Carl Phillip Thompson."

Hammett exercised her incredible self-control by not sighing in mental anguish. "Phillip?"

"Phillip? Oh, shit. The *F* sound messed me up. Fred. Carl Fred Thompson."

Charlie Tango Foxtrot. So this moron was here to audition. That was the problem with short-notice calls.

"You said your name was Jersey?"

"Name's Ned. Ned Fracktel. People call me Jersey."

Fracktel was on the list. Explosives expert. Supposedly one of the best. Hammett cast a casual glance at his fingers, and he was only missing one. A good sign.

"Come in. Have a seat."

"Is there coffee?"

"Just water."

The man walked in, obviously shaky. He needed coffee like a dude with dysentery needed an enema.

"You're from Jersey?" she asked.

"No. Omaha."

"Ever lived in Jersey?"

"Naw."

"Own a lot of sports jerseys, Ned?" Hammett was determined to find out how he got his nickname.

"No. When I was twelve I blew up a cow with some dynamite. Jersey cow. Lucky break. I almost did a Nigerian dwarf goat. Hate to be called that as a nickname. Doesn't really roll off the tongue, you know? Doesn't really fit me, either."

"Did you bring your equipment with you?"

"Brought some. Can access more, depending on the job. What's the job?"

"I'll explain it when the others arrive. You've done break-in work?"

"Lots. Metal. Rock. Even reinforced shit. Not as much fun as wetwork. I like the squishy stuff. Blood is pink when it vaporizes, like a party balloon. You think we could call for some coffee?"

"No."

Hammett spent three minutes listening to Jersey drum his fingers on the Formica, growing more and more annoyed. By the fourth minute, she was imagining creative ways to kill him, beginning with cutting off his remaining nine fingers and making him swallow each one, without coffee.

The door to the conference room opened abruptly, and Hammett hadn't heard the approach. Two men stood there, neither centered in the doorway. The one on the left was tall, dark black, almost movie-star handsome, sporting canvas khakis, matching tan Colorado boots, and a loose-fitting black sweater, bulky enough to be concealing all sorts of weaponry beneath it. He looked every inch a military badass, including the intense stare lacking any spark of empathy. On his right, in a tailored sharkskin suit, was a brown-skinned Latino. Also attractive, trim, his jacket cut for a shoulder carry, same empty eyes, his ice blue.

"I came for tea," he said, the slightest Mexican accent. He gave a slight head point to his partner. "That's Casper from Texas."

Hammett took a quick glance at her list, then brought her focus back to the men. She had a good guess as to who these two were.

The black man, a former Force Recon Marine named Isaiah Brown, frowned slightly. "Casper? Should I call you a beaner?"

The Mexican was Javier Estrada, a freelancer who worked with the Alphas, a badass paramilitary team who protected the major drug cartels. He shrugged. "Sticks and stones, brother."

"I get it," Jersey said, pointing and nodding. "A spook and a spic."

The guns that appeared in the duo's hands were drawn and aimed at Jersey so fast that Hammett felt immediately aroused.

"I'm Jersey," the explosives guy said, raising his hands. "No offense meant, guys. Poor white trash, grew up ignorant, never learned about diversity. Shooting me would be a waste of lead."

Neither man's gun hand wavered. These were serious bad boys. And Hammett liked bad boys.

"Tuck in and zip up, gentlemen," she said, "there are kids and clowns all over this shitty hotel. Sit."

Isaiah shrugged, tucking his Colt 1911 back into his pants. Javier cracked his neck to the side like Pacino in *Scarface*, then holstered his Glock 36 slimline under his left armpit, the jacket fabric draping smoothly over it. They sat on opposite ends of the table, both away from Jersey.

"You've worked together before?" Hammett asked. Their curriculum vitae showed they each had ample experience, but didn't mention them as known associates.

"Met a few years back at a gun show," Isaiah said, "then again in the lobby a few minutes ago."

Hammett glanced at her digital tablet again. "Mr. Brown, I see you've been working consistently. Mr. Estrada, I notice you've been off the radar for a while."

Javier shrugged. "Had this thing going in Alaska. Didn't end well. Just getting back into the game."

All of them except for Jersey, who was playing with the stump where his right index finger used to be, turned to look at the door before it opened. An overweight guy in a black Guns N' Roses T-shirt—which had faded to light gray—took a step inside and quickly said, "Charlie foxtrot tango. Christ, you all look so goddamn serious."

This was Merle Hosendorff, vehicle expert.

"Have a seat, Mr. Hosendorff."

"Speed," he said. "Call me Speed."

What is it about mercs and stupid nicknames? Hammett thought. Then she remembered that Hammett wasn't her real name either. Nor was it one she'd picked for herself. But then it was a helluva lot better than the one her foster parents had given her. Betsy.

Does Betsy sound like the name for someone who'd killed over fifty people, bare-handed?

Speed sat next to Jersey. According to his record, he could drive, fly, or sail any kind of vehicle, and repair them if needed. Hammett didn't figure they'd need anything more complicated than insertion and extraction, but it never hurt to be overqualified for a position.

She checked the time on her tablet. The last recruit was late, and she decided to begin the briefing without him.

"Gentlemen, you're all familiar with black sites. There's one—"

"Twenty-five kilometers south of here, in the old Badger Ammunition factory."

None of them had noticed the man slip into the room. He was thin, South American, and spoke with a slight lisp in a thick accent that might have been Bolivian. He had a clipped black mustache and oily, swarthy skin. Like Javier and Isaiah, this man was a bad boy. But not a bad boy you wanted to take to bed. This one was a bad boy you didn't want to be left alone with.

His CV listed him only as Santiago. His specialty was interrogation—a specialty that would be required once they had Fleming. Hammett was no neophyte at making people talk, but her sister had proven pretty tough. Santiago could supposedly make people confess in languages they didn't even know.

"You're aware of this because…?" Hammett asked.

"Because"—Santiago smiled, and it was an ugly smile, filled with crooked yellow teeth—"I've been there before. I did some work for them, in an unofficial capacity."

"So you know the layout?" Hammett only had satellite photos of the area and a sketchy blueprint that might or might not have been accurate. Truth told, breaking into a black site was a risky, potentially fatal endeavor, and she wasn't keen on it. Insider intel could mean the difference between success and failure.

"I do."

Hammett smiled, and though her teeth were white and even, she knew her grin was every bit as ugly as Santiago's.

This mission had just become much more possible.

Chandler

"I've taught you to trust no one," the Instructor said. "But sometimes you'll be forced to rely on other people. Tread carefully. The only thing worse than betrayal is incompetence."

I wasn't sure what to expect from Baraboo, Wisconsin. Red gambrel-roofed barns with silos and quaint split-log lodges, perhaps. Things that I'd seen in travel brochures for the area. And while those items were scattered around the countryside, along with billboards touting Circus World Museum and Tommy Bartlett and water parks in the Wisconsin Dells, the things that held my attention most were the imposing tree-covered bluffs and the sheer size of the US Army's Badger Ammunition plant.

We'd just emerged from the river town of Sauk City and passed a tiny grass-field airport and a handful of farms when the fence began. Twelve feet down the highway, I had to wonder if it was electrified.

Beyond the fence, row after row of old warehouses, barracks, and factories stood, some in disrepair, some with sagging roofs and half-torn-down walls, some nothing but concrete foundations surrounded with scrub grass. Once a busy plant serving the war effort, the place was now overcome with age and vegetation, nature taking back what was hers.

Contaminated land, dilapidated ruins, and an ongoing effort of environmental cleanup made a good cover for a black site. People could go in and out. A heavy guard could keep an eye on the place. And yet no one would ask any serious questions about what was really happening behind that fence.

We drove along the roads surrounding the site, looking for the best approach. Yellow stalks stubbled several surrounding fields, some of the corn already cut down in preparation for winter. Highway 78 flanked the plant to the east, following the Wisconsin River, and Highway 12 bordered the western side. As Tequila had previously said, the forested bluffs of Devil's Lake State Park looming to the north seemed like our best bet. But there was so much terrain to cover, we decided to split it into sections.

"I'll go in here. The elevation should make it easier to take in the whole area."

Tequila nodded and said nothing, as usual.

"What approach are you taking?"

"Through the park. I'll text you."

"Great."

"Before I drop you off, you need to pay me."

One of the longest sentences he'd uttered in the past hour. Figures that it would be about money. "You're quite a mercenary." I mentally calculated the cash I had left. His advance would take most of it. "You haven't done anything to earn it yet."

"But you know I will."

Tequila took 78 to 133 heading north, turned left at a campground, and followed a small road called Helweg, bordering the park on the southeast corner. It continued to follow the edge of the park going west and came to a dead end at a cornfield that was still standing. He stopped, staring through the windshield, his hands on the steering wheel. "The money?"

On the way up, I'd sorted the supplies Harry had not-so-generously provided, stuffing the items I needed into my gym bag and leaving the rest for Tequila. I counted out ten grand, trying not to let Tequila see I didn't have much more than that, slipped it into the bag with the other supplies I was leaving him, and hopped out. I didn't like trusting him, but at this point, I had little choice. "You don't do the job, I'll find you."

"I'll text."

I slammed the door and hiked northwest into Devil's Lake State Park.

The park itself was beautiful, though I couldn't see the lake from my location. The air smelled of leaves starting to turn, wood fire, and pine. Only natural sounds reached me, wind through boughs, the chatter of birds, the soft pad of evergreen needles under my feet.

The terrain was rocky and inclined sharply, outcroppings of Baraboo quartzite everywhere, and even though I was moving at a ground-covering jog, my progress was slower than I liked. Most of my work entailed moving around city landscapes, and I had to admit I was more comfortable with traffic and crime than wild raspberry bushes and a seemingly inexhaustible variety of burrs. They stuck to my jeans and socks and pricked my legs, holding on with a vengeance no matter how hard I tried to pick them clean.

I angled my path westerly, heading for the spot of highest elevation, somewhere I could get a good view of the whole layout at once.

Reaching the crest of the bluff, I shimmied up the trunk of a squatty maple and pulled a set of binoculars from my gym bag. I didn't have to climb high to get my view.

If I'd thought the plant was expansive from the ground, the space we were dealing with was even more daunting from up here. Barracks lined the area to the west. Factories, old warehouses, and some suspicious mounds in the earth dotted acre after acre of land. Two large open-water concrete reservoirs dominated the northern end, just below the bluff where I perched. A network of gravel and dirt roads connected each of the clusters of factories and train tracks cut through the plant's center. Several large dump trucks kicked up dust near the barracks area to the west, and a large backhoe bit into a pile of wood refuse and dumped it into the biggest wood chipper I'd ever seen.

I focused on the areas boasting less activity. If Fleming was here, she could be almost anywhere. At least until you read the signs. And heading my way was a neon one bigger than all the billboards we'd passed on the drive up.

The helicopter was designed for stealth, but that didn't mean it was totally silent. While it didn't give me the beating sensation in my chest, I picked up the sound of the blade before I saw the sleek black body.

It circled the area, approaching from the south. Although I was fairly certain it wouldn't be able to spot me, I snugged a little farther into the leaves anyway and watched its descent.

It chose a cluster of old buildings close to the middle of the acreage on the northern end, and once it lowered down into a clump of trees and brush surrounding the structures, I lost sight of it completely, even with the benefit of my vantage point.

To learn more, I'd have to get closer.

A man dressed in black emerged from a door one building over. In his hand, he held a tablet computer, his eyes glued to the screen. He crossed the short space to the area where the chopper had landed and disappeared behind a clump of ratty box elder trees.

My pulse kicked up a notch. If the man I'd just spotted had the software to track me, they knew I was here. That damn GPS tracker. Medical supplies beyond the most basic first-aid kit weren't among the items Harry had provided, and what I had in mind was a bit more involved than simple bandages and cold compresses could handle. I slid down the tree.

Even after what I'd seen, I didn't expect company so quickly.

I heard him long before I saw him. A man, probably tall, moving through the forest with the tromp of a giant.

I crouched low behind an outcropping, making myself as small and unobtrusive as possible. The adrenaline pouring into my system made my vision clear, my other senses sharp. The scents of leaves and pine were joined by the man-made fragrance of shampoo, an inexpensive herbal, and leather. A twig snapped, then a boot tread slipped on rock. Finally the jingle of keys moving in a jeans pocket, and quiet.

I couldn't see him from my hiding place, but judging from the footfalls, there was only one. If they'd pinpointed my location, I would expect them to send more.

I pulled my weapon from my waistband and slipped it into my jacket pocket, finger on the trigger. Moving as quietly as my target was loud, I inched to the side of the rock and peered through the trees.

He was standing near a fallen pine tree, not dressed in black like the man below, but in jeans, boots, and a leather bomber. He had dark hair and a strong build, and from all appearances was a guy who just happened to be enjoying a walk through the woods...if you didn't count the pair of field glasses he was focusing on the spot where the helicopter had just landed.

Interesting.

I rose to my full height and stepped toward him.

He spun around and looked me straight in the eye. Jumpy.

"Doing a little bird-watching?" I asked.

"Uh, yeah." He squared his shoulders, obviously sensing something wrong, even though from all appearances I was just a hiker enjoying the woods, same as him. "Nice day, huh?"

"A little cold for my taste."

"Not as cold as it will be in a month."

"You spend a lot of time out here?"

He narrowed his eyes, sizing me up. "I live nearby. Where are you from?"

"Chicago. Just doing a little hiking."

"Perfect weather for that."

Every detail about him screamed civilian. He even had the weather small talk down. But though there weren't any laws against civilians using a little magnification, the binoculars bothered me. I nodded toward the landscape below. "What is this place?"

"Old ammunition factory. Owned by the US government."

"Interesting."

"You have no idea." He glanced at the spot where the helicopter had landed, then dipped his right hand into the pocket of his jacket.

I was on him in less than a heartbeat.

I dove for his wrist and seized it with both hands, right above left. Without giving him a chance to react, I jerked it downward. If done fast and hard enough, a move like this can produce considerable shock, almost amounting to a knockout blow.

I was slightly off balance in my attack and he was a big man, so I flowed into the next move immediately.

I swung his arm up, shoulder height, twisting it toward me and forcing him off balance. I stepped forward and under his arm, twirling in toward his body as if performing a dance move, and twisted his arm behind his back.

He staggered forward and fell to the ground.

I moved with him, driving my knee into his back and pinning him face down on the forest floor. After the beatings I'd taken in the past day, it was good to know I still had it…well, at least enough not to have my ass handed to me in every fight.

"Who are you?"

It took him several seconds to answer. "What the hell is with you Chicago people? Are you mugging me? We're in a state park, for crying out loud."

"Is that a cheesehead rule? You can be mugged, but never in a state park?"

"What?"

"Who are you?" I repeated. "Your name. What is it?"

"David Lund."

"What are you doing here, David Lund?"

"Bird-watching, like you said. I was keeping an eye on the helicopters."

"Why?"

"They fly in and out all the time. But whenever I've asked what's going on, no one will tell me a damn thing. Are you with the army?"

"I'm asking the questions, David."

"Look, if you're a mugger, my wallet is in my back pocket. If you're some sort of military, you've made your point. I'll stay away from now on."

I hoped David Lund was who he said he was, because I kind of liked his coolness under pressure and smart mouth. It would be a shame to have to kill him.

"Why do you care so much about these helicopters?" I asked.

"Why do I care?"

"That was the question."

"Maybe because as a citizen in a democratic republic, I'm supposed to keep my government in check. Will you let go of my arm before you dislocate my shoulder?"

I didn't move. "You think they're hiding something."

"Where there's smoke there's usually fire."

"And why have you decided to cast yourself as fireman?"

He blew a derisive laugh through his nose.

"Let me guess. You really are a fireman."

"Firefighter."

What were the odds? "Can you prove it?"

"If you'd get off me."

"Are you armed?"

"Why would I be armed?"

I checked his jacket pocket and found a computer printout of a map featuring the ammunition plant.

"I was going to show you that when you suddenly decided to kick my ass."

Running my hand down one side, then the other, I came up with similarly innocuous items. Car keys, change, a pen. Except for an impressive set of muscles, appealingly solid under my fingers, he had no weapon.

I pulled out his wallet and flipped to a Wisconsin driver's license for David Lund, local boy, and another ID that showed him to be a certified fire inspector. If he was CIA or a similar agency, they'd done a flawless job with the details—something they aren't exactly known for.

I released his arm and thrust myself off his back. "Turn around slowly, stay seated, and let me see your hands."

He did as I said, brushing leaves and mud off his jacket and out of his hair.

He was a good-looking guy, dark hair curling a little at his collar, brown eyes, and bone structure that jibed with the Nordic last name. His shoulders were broad, thighs strong. It was probably due to the adrenaline, but I had to admit, I could imagine him dressed in a firefighter helmet…and nothing else.

"So you really are a firefighter?"

"What else would I be?"

Unfortunately a firefighter's skills didn't do me much good going up against the people I was facing, and now I'd complicated the situation by assaulting a civilian.

"So…going to tell me who you are?" he asked.

"No."

"Just my luck. I run into a mysterious woman in a forest, and she beats me up and refuses to give me her name. That's not the way the *Penthouse Forum* stories usually go."

I couldn't hold back a smile and had to admit once again that his sense of humor and composure under stress impressed me. It made sense that a firefighter would be good at controlling and compartmentalizing emotion.

For a second, I flashed back to Victor Cormack, who I guess I could call my ex, although our breakup had been a little rough. His cover had been working for the fire department, but as an EMT. He'd also been cool in tough situations, good-looking, funny. I'd been impressed with him, too.

God, I hated being so predictable.

"Listen, I'm really sorry for being so paranoid. It must be my city upbringing. I see threats at every turn."

"Don't worry about it." He finished brushing forest debris from the front of his jacket and jeans. "I'm not as fragile as I look."

"If there's a word that doesn't fit you, it's fragile."

"You'd be surprised. For instance, if you refused to go to lunch with me, I might be crushed."

"You're asking me out?"

"Trying to."

And if I wasn't about to save my sister, I might take him up on it. "I'm a little busy."

"Hiking?"

"And other things."

He glanced over his shoulder. "Those things don't have something to do with the ammunitions plant, do they?"

"What makes you think that?"

He arched his brows and shot me a who's-kidding-whom expression.

"Trust me, you don't want to get tangled up in this."

"So it does."

Speaking of the plant, I stood and brought my field glasses to my eyes. I spotted movement. Three men this time, all dressed in dark clothes. From this distance I couldn't discern the reason behind the stir of activity, but I had a guess.

"I really am sorry I overreacted, but I have to go."

I turned and headed east. I wasn't sure how I was going to accomplish what I had to do next. I checked my TracFone. No text from Tequila. Next I scanned for clinics in the area.

I heard him behind me, his strides still loud as a thundering horde, keeping pace with mine. He seemed to be exactly what he was, but I'd been fooled before. Still, he might offer an opportunity to take care of my problem.

I called Information, had them connect me to the Sauk County Fire Department. A woman picked up.

"Is Lund in?"

"He's not," she said with the voice of a heavy smoker. "Is this Val?"

I went with it. "Yeah. Can you give me his cell phone again?"

"Sure. He'll be thrilled to hear from you.

She rattled off the digits, which I memorized and punched in.

Behind me, a phone rang.

"This is Lund."

I turned, watching him catch up, his phone to his ear.

"You just asked me out a minute ago," I said.

He glanced up at me, saw me on the phone, and smiled. It was a nice smile.

"You're calling to accept?"

"I don't know. Would Val be upset?"

"You must have talked to Nancy, the district dispatcher."

"And Val? Tell me about her."

"Val…she's great, but she's clearly stated she isn't ready for a relationship."

He didn't seem entirely happy about that fact, so as a matter of personal self-interest and limited time, I decided not to dig deeper.

Flirting was a useful tool, especially for a female operative, and I'd actually had to study its subtleties in training. But if Lund couldn't help me complete my mission, I couldn't waste time with seduction, whether he was cute or not.

Best to find out straight away whether playing with him was worthwhile. "Your EMS, is it part of the fire department?"

He frowned, as if trying to figure out why I was asking. "Not technically, no. You know, you look like you're dubbed in an old kung fu movie, because I'm watching your lips move but the sound in my phone is delayed."

I knew what he meant, because he looked the same. I almost considered striking a tiger stance and threatening his master with my drunken monkey style, but I managed instead to stay on task. I tucked away my phone and asked, "Does it operate out of the same building?"

"It's next door. We serve the same district but operate as two separate departments. Why? Are you injured?" He narrowed his eyes as if finally seeing shadows of the bruises I'd masked with makeup. "Don't tell me you pinned me to the ground that easily while you're injured. They're going to take away my man card."

It had been a rough week, and my physical condition was debatable, but I didn't see a point to rubbing it in. "I'm fine. I have something else in mind."

"Something you're not going to explain?"

"You're catching on. Is there a clinic close by? Maybe an office for an ob-gyn?"

He gave me a once-over. "You're pregnant?"

Obviously I was going to have to be more specific, not that my next statement would clear things up. "I'm looking for ultra-sound equipment."

"In this area? You're probably going to have to try a hospital."

I shook my head. "I've had my fill of hospitals."

"If you just need the machine, I have one that was designed for dairy cattle. Although I can't guarantee it works."

"Where is it?"

"My in-laws' farm. Not far."

In-laws? I glanced at his hand. "You're not wearing a ring."

"Excuse me?"

"Never mind. Would they sell it to me?"

"Since they're dead, and cows haven't lived in the place for years, you can have it. On one condition."

"What's that?"

"You tell me who you are and what you're doing here."

I sized up David Lund. I was hesitant to trust anyone, but I did need his ultrasound. "OK, I'll tell you. But first we have to get out of here."

"I'm not going anywhere."

"So now you've decided to be stubborn?"

He shrugged and made a show of leaning against the peeling trunk of a birch. "Now I have something to bargain with."

I knew a lot of ways to make him hand over the machine without giving anything in return. Unfortunately for me, I also believed civilians shouldn't have to face the same brutal realities as those of us who'd chosen this life. I thought of Tequila. No doubt, he'd just take what he wanted, no matter who got hurt.

"Do you have first-aid supplies? Something more involved than butterfly bandages and ibuprofen?"

"I believe in being prepared. I have whatever you need."

"All right then, David. I'll tell you what I can."

"Call me Lund."

"Lund." I needed to get this show on the road. I scanned the forest around us, ears tuned for any movement. "I want the same as you, to find out what's going on in the Badger Ammunition plant. Only my reason is more complicated than curiosity or being a good citizen."

"I'm listening."

"I believe this place is a cover for a black site."

He didn't look as surprised as I expected. "Like Abu Ghraib? In Wisconsin?"

"I need to get in there undetected."

"And how will an ultrasound and first-aid supplies help you do that?"

I didn't answer.

"OK, how about a name?" he asked. "Who are you?"

"You don't need to know."

"Let me guess, if you told me, you'd have to kill me?" He chuckled.

I didn't crack a smile.

"You're not serious."

"I won't kill you…probably. But other people might. Just give me the ultrasound and walk away, Lund."

He gave me a smirk and shook his head. "You're not telling me you're some kind of spy."

"I'm not telling you anything."

"I don't believe it."

Now I was insulted. "I *did* just kick your ass."

He rubbed his jaw. "Yeah, well, I'm a lover, not a fighter."

I just bet he was, but that was not a distraction I needed at the moment. "Now where is the ultrasound?"

"Why should I tell you anything? You haven't answered my questions."

"Hello? Ass kicking?"

"You're going to have to do better than that."

Just in the brief time I'd been around David Lund, I had a pretty good feel for who he was. Firefighter. Went into the profession because of a desire to rescue others. Liked to think of himself as a hero.

I took a deep breath, hoping what I was about to do was smart. "My sister is being held there against her will. I'm going to get her out."

He canted his head to the side and watched me, as if deciding whether to buy the story or not. "Sounds like you should call the police."

I shook my head. "The police can't solve this for me. In fact, it would be very bad if they got involved. I know that sounds overly dramatic, but I'm serious. This issue is beyond police. I call them, and people will die who don't have to."

He thought for a few seconds, then shoved himself up from the tree trunk. "The ultrasound is old, and I don't think it's ever been used."

"I can deal with that. I'll also need a sharp knife and bandages and some method of sterilization."

"You don't ask for much, do you?"

"You have those things?"

"Sure. And your name?"

"Call me Chandler."

"Like the mystery writer? What's your sister's name? Dashiell Hammett?"

I didn't answer. He sighed.

"All right, Chandler, follow me."

The White House

"Our contact has briefed you?"

"Yes, Mr. President. I'm...shocked by this."

The president stared at his VP. The veep was older, his hair slicked back and no doubt dyed, giving him the Ronald Reagan look. As a running mate he'd been capable, carrying the states the party delegates had predicted he would, but as second in command he'd disagreed with the president in public, many times. Especially this last term. The president could understand why—he was distancing himself from some of the president's unpopular decisions so he could run on a more conservative platform, which was the direction the country seemed to be moving in. The president acknowledged the reason for this, but he privately bridled at every contradiction. They were supposed to be a team, not every man for himself. The VP should stand by his commander in chief.

"I'm as shocked as you are, Jim. Apparently the Hydra project was a need-to-know basis. Plausible deniability."

"So who took it over when your predecessor left office?"

"I don't believe he was aware of it, either. This goes back a few decades. I don't even know who's running the damn thing now. An assassination arm of the military…do you have any idea how many laws and treaties this violates? Not to mention the goddamn Constitution."

The VP winced. The president knew he was deeply religious, and hated taking the Lord's name in vain. It was pure hypocrisy, as the man was an adulterer, and fiercely coveted the White House. Perhaps some of the Ten Commandments were more breakable than others.

"What's the next step?" the VP asked.

"The Hydra agent is being debriefed. But I've also got my own team on it. People I can count on."

"Who?"

The president hesitated, and in that moment he realized he no longer trusted this man. But then, that was the reason he'd called him into the Oval Office. "I understand you're calling for a press conference. I've seen your speech."

The vice president remained silent, his expression blank. He had tiny dark eyes. Mole eyes.

"I'll be blunt," the president said. "If you're willing to blame me publicly for this fiasco, I'll leak your indiscretions to the press."

"The party wants me to be your successor."

"The party doesn't know about your penchant for young prostitutes. I assume your wife doesn't, either. You want to hang me out to dry, publicly? You'll hang alongside me. Do we understand each other?"

After a brief stare-down, he answered, "Yes, Mr. President. I'll have them rewrite the speech."

"You might think I'm a lame duck, Jim. But this duck still has some fight left in him. You want to see how much fight, cross me."

"The party won't be pleased."

"The party is the least of my worries. You can go now."

The vice president nodded, took a quick look at the eagle-emblazoned Resolute desk, then scurried away, closing the door behind him.

Tequila

The man named Tequila passed the south shore of Devil's Lake State Park and took Burma Road to its end, a mile north of the ammunition plant. He pulled behind a copse of trees, where his SUV wouldn't be seen from the trail, and spent five minutes gathering up dead branches and dead leaves from the previous autumn, arranging them on his vehicle to disguise its shape. Satisfied it was adequately camouflaged, he shouldered a backpack filled with supplies and began to hike south.

His pace slow and deliberate, Tequila kept close tabs on his surroundings. He spotted a camera strapped to a tree at shoulder length, but deemed it to be for park rangers rather than government spooks—one of those placed on game trails and set off by motion detectors to count deer or bear or bigfoot or whatever else the rangers needed to keep track of. He broke open the steel casing with a palm strike, then took the SD card inside. When given the option, Tequila preferred not to be photographed.

For someone born and raised urban, Tequila was strangely comfortable in the woods. Though he had no real experience camping, hunting, or fishing, he often visited forest preserves in northwestern Illinois and took walks. Sometimes he didn't walk anywhere, preferring to stand in one place. He enjoyed the stillness of it, the sense of being immersed in nature while also observing it in a detached way. Once he'd stood in the same spot for more than three hours, becoming so much a part of the scenery that a cardinal had landed on his shoulder.

He continued south, pausing often to listen, not needing the map or the compass to assess his location. Half a mile in, he spotted a white-tailed doe nibbling on an elderberry bush. Going into stalking mode, slow and silent, Tequila crept up behind her. The animal was oblivious to his presence until he reached out and gave her a small pat on her flank. She bounded off into the surrounding trees.

For some reason, the deer made him think of Chandler. She was competent, no doubt. Well trained, motivated, and probably very good at her job. Attractive, too. But she was still young, and he sensed a naïveté about her that she would no doubt rather die than admit. He knew other gymnasts on the Olympic team that were like that. Stubborn, overconfident, and caught completely unaware when life came up and smacked them upside the head.

Discipline, hard work, and talent weren't enough. The better you were at something, the more the tiniest mistakes became amplified.

Chandler seemed primed to make a mistake.

So why was he helping her? He didn't need the money. And while he liked Jack Daniels, he could have refused. Unlike many in his line of work, Tequila took no pleasure from the things he did. He prided himself on doing the job well, but there was no personal satisfaction in it. He had no ego to satisfy. He wasn't a hothead, an adrenaline junkie, or a sadist. He hadn't taken any jobs in a while, even though he still kept up his exercise and training regimen. He might as well have been retired.

But Chandler's situation provoked something in Tequila. She had been betrayed, and a family member needed her. Once upon a time, Tequila had been in a similar situation. Many people had died, including some who shouldn't have.

Tequila didn't believe in regret, so he didn't believe in redemption. Karma, like morality, was BS.

But helping Chandler save her sister appealed to some inner part of him. A part he was pretty sure had died years ago.

There was only one problem. If Chandler was right, and this was truly a government-run black site, there was no possible way two people would be able to infiltrate it and escape with a prisoner. It was one thing for the government to grab some foreigner named Khalid and torture him in a third-world country as long as someone cried terrorist. The American people were happy to suspend the Bill of Rights if it meant they slept better at night. But a secret prison, on US soil, detaining and torturing US citizens? If the president thought the missile debacle in the UK had hurt his reelection campaign, he hadn't seen anything yet. And as a result, he'd be sure not to let *this* secret become known. He'd have it protected with lethal force.

They wouldn't be able to save Chandler's sister. They wouldn't even get close. And chances were high they'd die trying or wind up in cells alongside Fleming.

But that didn't stop Tequila from continuing his hike south to Badger Ammo's perimeter fence. It was chain link, still new and shiny, three meters high and topped with razor wire. No electric fence warning signs, which would have been necessary since it was adjacent to a public park. No cameras in this area, either, and Tequila had an idea why as he stared out over the plant.

The area was huge. A giant, rolling, overgrown prairie filled with several dozen buildings, reservoirs, a spiderweb of roads. And he could only see part of it from here.

It would take a gigantic budget to post cameras every few dozen meters on a property that stretched over twelve square miles, not to mention a control room the size of NASA.

Which meant locating the prison entrance wouldn't be as difficult as Tequila had expected. He'd been anticipating seeking out activity to pinpoint the site, but there was already a lot of activity on the grounds. Construction workers, trucks, helicopters coming in. Covering this much area, on foot, looking for a secret entrance to a secret prison without being discovered—it could take a very long time.

But looking for areas where cameras were present would be a lot easier.

Tequila made sure his jeans were tucked into his boots. Then he snugged the straps of his backpack and scurried up the fence with the speed and agility of a monkey. When he reached the concertina wire on top, he unzipped the rear pocket on his pack, removing some pliers. The cutters weren't large, and the wire was thick, but the muscles in Tequila's hand made up for the loss of leverage and he snipped through with only moderate effort. He vaulted the fence, landing like a cat, and jogged along the tree line until he reached a road. Tequila followed it, his eyes constantly in motion. When a dump truck rumbled by, he ducked into a tangle of wild blackberries. He nestled among their thorny stems and picked a few ripe specimens, chewing them as the truck passed.

Glancing up at the sun, he headed west, winding up at a paved clearing, weeds breaking up through the asphalt. Having studied the map earlier, he knew this was the cannon area, where munitions were tested. He jogged past a dilapidated building, its blast-resistant walls still standing firm against the ravages of time and nature, and came to a rusted fence. Another building was attached, and Tequila noted the antique gun mounts, probably once used for howitzers. He sighted down the line of fire to a hillside, a giant concrete bunker carved into it. Within the enclave, a giant mound of sand. To test their propellant, they'd fire into the mound, checking depth of penetration. That was to be expected.

What was unexpected was the kennel. New fences, six feet high, filled with six doghouses. One of the hounds, a pit bull and mastiff mix who must have weighed as much as Tequila, slept in the corner of the pen, its massive head on its paws.

It hadn't seen or smelled Tequila yet, so he stayed perfectly still. He normally didn't mind dogs, but those bred to kill held a special dark place in Tequila's heart. He'd dealt with bad dogs before, and he didn't want to tangle with them again.

Attached to the kennel was a camera, aiming at the sandpile.

Was that the entrance to the prison? Did that explain the guard dogs?

Tequila looked around for other cameras but didn't spot any. He studied the kennel, and noted that the gate on the side had a gearbox attached. No doubt it opened automatically.

Tequila didn't want it to open while he was there. But he needed to check that enclave. Which meant that the dogs had to be dealt with.

Blowing out a sharp breath, Tequila reached into his shoulder holster.

Chandler

"Pain is temporary," the Instructor said. "It either fades, or you die."

The hike to Lund's house didn't take long, and we ran into no undesirables on the way. It was a good sign that they didn't have the software to track me. But Hammett did, and I couldn't imagine my psychotic sister giving up. That left me with no choice. The GPS chip in my belly had to be removed.

My hunky, calendar-worthy firefighter lived in a comfortable two-bedroom cabin in the woods, which seemed like the best situation for sex I'd come across in a while. Unfortunately, with Fleming suffering who-knew-what at her captors' hands, Tequila set to contact me at any time, and the unpleasant task at hand, I had neither the time nor the focus to bring to Lund's bedroom.

And where there were in-laws there was usually a wife, and even as horny as my death-defying past few days had made me, I did not do married men, even though I had no qualms about killing them.

Lund grabbed a first-aid kit the size of Harry's entire duffel and ushered me to a red pickup.

"How far away is the farm?" I asked.

"Ten minutes."

I checked my phone. No texts from Tequila. "Then we'd better get going."

The drive took seven. I kept an eye out for tails all the way, but there were no vehicles on the roads, let alone following us. Lund turned into a circular driveway and stopped in front of a white two-story farmhouse and an honest-to-goodness red gambrel-roofed barn. "This place is yours?"

Lund shrugged one shoulder, as if not happy about the idea. "It belonged to my father-in-law."

It wasn't my business, but I wanted to know. Hell, I had to know. "Does a wife come with that father-in-law?"

"My wife died."

One shouldn't be happy about a thing like that, so I changed the subject. "Does anyone live here?"

"Nope. It's been on the market for almost a year. Want to make an offer?"

I sized the place up. Remote. A good view of the road. Not far from my ultimate destination. "Maybe for the day."

He gave me a questioning look, but before the words could reach his lips, I grabbed the first-aid case and my gym bag and climbed out of the truck.

The air smelled of old hay and cow manure spread on the nearby field, mixed with a touch of fuel oil exhaust from an old furnace. Our boots ground against the driveway's gravel. Overhead, a flock of Canadian geese honked on an early flight south.

He tromped up the steps to the porch, fished a key from his pocket, and opened the door. The inside floor plan was typical farmhouse; small spaces, narrow hallways, one bathroom. The decor was typical, too. A flowered sofa with a plastic slipcover, shag carpet in the living room. Harvest gold in the kitchen. A wheelchair waiting at the base of the steps, as if its owner had just been carried up to bed.

Lund opened a small closet next to the door and pulled out what looked like a small suitcase. We brought it and the first-aid duffel to the living room, where a wide bay window peered out at the road in front.

"So your in-laws weren't into redecorating, huh? Not since the seventies?"

Lund didn't answer, looking out the window as if he didn't want to focus on what was inside these walls.

"Sorry. I didn't mean to be insensitive."

He shook his head. "It doesn't matter to me. I've always hated this place. Bad memories."

Fairly certain I didn't want to go there, I nodded to the case he was holding. "So how do we set this up?"

He placed it on the coffee table and opened it. "I don't know. I don't think it's ever been used."

The device itself looked like a hard-shelled shoulder bag, complete with strap. Lund plugged a cord attached to a cylindrical probe into one outlet in the device, and a pair of goggles into another. I opened the first-aid kit and sorted through the supplies, pulling out isopropyl alcohol, local anesthetic, gauze, and bandages. I also located a folding lockback knife, utility scissors, a set of forceps, and tweezers.

I still had several syringes of Demerol in my gym bag, but I'd have to watch how much of it I used. Too much, and I wouldn't be able to function; not enough, and the pain would overwhelm me. As a general rule, I preferred erring slightly to the side of not enough.

I'd rejected the idea of venturing up to the bedrooms on the second floor. Although the ones to the front of the house would provide a good view of the road, escape would entail jumping out a window. I was better off on the first level. I collected some old towels to soak up the blood and, with Lund's permission, piled them on top of the couch's plastic slipcover.

"I'll clean and lock up when I'm done. You won't even know I was here."

He eyed my collection of supplies. "What are you going to do?"

"None of your concern."

"You're using my house, my ultrasound machine, and my supplies. And I'm not the type to stand around and watch while someone does something crazy."

"That's the point. I don't want you standing around. You can go. It'll be fine."

"I'm *really* not the type to leave someone who looks like she needs help." He planted his feet, underlying the message that he didn't intend to move.

I didn't like the prospect of having him around while I was vulnerable. I was fairly certain he was who he said—even the few photographs scattered around the farmhouse showed him with a young woman, probably his dead wife—but in my line of work, the only people who lived to see tomorrow were the ones who didn't resort to trust.

"I'd really rather be alone."

"Then tell me what you're going to do. Reassure me that it's not something insane, and I'll leave."

"Somehow I doubt you're going to think this is sane."

"Try me."

I took a deep breath, then shucked my jacket and pulled my sweater over my head, realizing a second too late that I was still not wearing a bra.

"My God, what happened to you?"

"What?" I asked, suddenly self-conscious. That wasn't the reaction I normally got from men when I disrobed.

He knelt down beside me. "You're covered in bruises."

Of course he was right. Bruises ranging from fresh red to purple to fading yellow covered my torso. Abrasions marred the skin on my elbows, hands, and knees. Over the past days, I'd gotten so used to being a human punching bag it hadn't occurred to me that seeing the evidence might freak out a regular person.

And I had to admit, I was a little disappointed that he'd focused more on the bruises than on my bare breasts. "I told you, it's been a tough week."

"You need to go to the hospital."

"It's OK. I just got out." I held up my hand before he could say anything. "It's the truth. They couldn't wait to get rid of me."

I shoved my jeans down, relieved to at least be wearing panties, and felt him looking at the injuries covering my legs. Slipping the goggle-looking device on my head, I positioned the ultrasound next to me on the couch.

The goggles sat right above my eyebrows, so I had only to glance up to see the image. The wand was about ten inches long and built to be inserted in a cow's rectum. Lucky for me, Lund was right about it never being used, and the rubber casing was clean and white. It took some effort to get the thing to work, but finally the sound waves registered on the screen above my eyebrows in the form of blurry gray shadows.

I laid the wand against my belly, cold against my skin. The shadows contorted and changed as I moved the wand, trying to figure out which internal organs were which.

Intestines, too low. A rib, too high. My stomach, just right.

A dark spot registered on my duodenum.

Lund inched toward me, his face close enough to kiss, and stared up at the monitor. "What in the hell is that?"

"A tracking chip."

"You're being tracked? Why?"

"By my employers. Or my former employers." Fleming and I seemed to be on our own now. "I have to take it out."

For a few seconds he stared at me, as if trying to make sense of what I was telling him. "You're going to do surgery on yourself?"

"More or less. If they made it easy to remove, I wouldn't have left it in this long."

"How long have you had it?"

"Years. But I didn't find out about it until recently. Been kind of busy since."

"This seems a little…uh…extreme."

Of course it seemed extreme to him. He was a regular guy who lived a regular life and followed a much more clear-cut moral code. The only thing he knew about people like me was what he read in books or watched in the movie theater.

"The black site, my sister, I wasn't kidding about any of that. They're going to kill her, probably after torturing her for a good long time. I can't get her out if they can see me coming."

The look on Lund's face was somewhere between disbelief, disgust, and awe.

I sterilized the skin around my belly button and readied one of the syringes of Lund's local anesthetic. Taking a deep breath, I plunged the needle into the muscle.

It hurt like hell.

Lund grimaced right along with me. "I have something stronger. Or better, you could go to a hospital."

I shook my head. "I need to keep my head clear for this. Maybe later on the something stronger."

I gave myself two more shots and waited for the drug to numb me. Once my belly felt like someone else's flesh, I picked up a wrapped scalpel.

Lund grabbed my wrist.

"Let go," I said.

"You can't cut yourself open." His grip tightened, as if he was contemplating prying the instrument from my fingers. He glanced at me, then the image on the screen.

"Lund, back off. Don't make me hurt you."

He released my hand and held out his palm. "Let me help."

"I can't. I'm sorry." I wasn't sure why I felt it necessary to apologize. This was my life, my body, and I'd only met this guy an hour ago. But the crease between his eyebrows and tension in his jaw told me how tough it was for him to stand by.

"Then what do you want me to do? Watch?"

"I want you to go home."

"If something goes wrong…"

"Go home, Lund. Thanks for your help so far, but I have a lot to deal with here. I don't need to add holding your hand to the list."

"You aren't even wearing gloves, Chandler. Haven't you ever heard of the germ theory of disease? Even if you survive this, the infection will kill you."

He was right, of course, and the fact I wasn't processing it was testament to how exhausted I was. I got off the couch and went to the kitchen sink, turning up the water as hot as it would get, then started scrubbing my hands with soap. Lund joined me, putting his hands under the stream like we were an old married couple doing dishes.

"I'm doing this myself, Lund."

"If I need to assist, you want my hands to be clean or dirty?"

I sighed, annoyed at his persistence. My irritation relaxed a notch when I cast a glance his way and saw he was—finally—staring at my breasts.

"It's OK," he said, catching the amusement in my eyes. "I'm a professional firefighter. We've seen everything."

"Really?"

"It's true."

"Rescue a lot of topless women, do you?"

"Several times a week. It's a regular thing."

I allowed myself a tiny smile. "Maybe it hurts me that I'm just one of the crowd."

"Trust me," Lund said, his eyes crinkling. "You are *not* one of the crowd."

"You're still not getting inside me."

"Excuse me?"

"Cutting me open, Lund. Get your mind out of the gutter."

He cleared his throat, hunching over just enough that I could sense he was getting turned on. I let it go. This wasn't the right time for flirting, and I knew I was just doing it to delay the inevitable self-surgery.

At least, I told myself that was the reason.

Lund produced two pairs of latex gloves from his pack, and we snapped them on and washed our hands again. Then he gave them each a liberal squirt of iodine.

We went back into the living room, and I assumed the position on the couch. I eyed the monitor and unwrapped the scalpel. Tequila would be texting me any minute. I needed to get on with this.

"This is a really bad idea," Lund said.

I pressed the blade to my skin.

"I should help. I've done some triage work."

"You touch me without permission, and I'll use this scalpel on you."

I looked up at the image and positioned my knife right below my navel. Gritting my teeth, I made the first cut, a very small slice through the skin and subcutaneous fat layer.

Cold chased the blade, the pain starting a beat later. Not too bad, thanks to the numbing, but still a sound resembling a growl surged from my throat.

If I could avoid severing muscle, I wouldn't be nearly as disabled, and healing would come faster.

My hand shook. Pulling in a breath, I pressed my fingertips into the first incision I'd made.

Sweat bloomed on my skin. Tears streamed down my face, and I was helpless to stop them. I blinked, trying to make sense of the watery image on the screen.

David Lund suddenly closed his fingers around mine, slipping the knife from my hand. He positioned the ultrasound at my belly button, and the image of the chip reappeared on the screen.

"If you can hold the skin open, I think I can reach it."

I didn't protest. There was no point. He was right; I did need help. As determined as I was, I couldn't keep my head clear and fingers steady in the face of this much pain.

He took the viewing visor from my head and put it on his own. "Ready."

I dug my fingertips into the wound. A whimper stuck in my throat, a pitiful sound like a suffering animal. One more breath, and I stretched the sides apart.

I'd been shot before. Stabbed. Punctured, burned, abraded, and bruised. But I hadn't done any of that to myself. My own fingers, in my own wound, was a sensation so intensely violating that I had to concentrate with all of my power not to pull them out.

The ultrasound in one hand, Lund probed inside me with the tweezers.

I wanted to see, needed to know what was going on, but with tears streaming down my cheeks and stars narrowing my field of vision, all I could focus on was his face, both intense and concerned.

"Please," I said through clenched teeth. "Please hurry."

I could feel him moving inside me, first the tweezers, then his fingers. Something shifted, and a scream broke through my lips.

"I got it," he said. "I got it."

Darkness edged my vision. I closed my eyes, no longer able to see. "Now I need some of that something stronger," I whimpered, then blackness swallowed me whole, and I no longer needed a thing.

Fleming

"Captivity can take away identity and destroy hope," the Instructor said. "Recognize the techniques they are using to crush you for what they are. Find something to hold on to. Once your hope is dead, your body will soon follow."

"Stop it! Please...please stop! I told you what you want! That's all I know!"

Fleming couldn't escape the sound of the woman's—Chandler's?—screams. They wound through her mind, pulsed behind her closed lids. She could taste their desperation, feel them cling to her skin like the stench of blood.

She wanted to run. She wanted to fight. She could do neither. She closed her eyes, but the light followed her, drilling into her mind. No darkness. No place to hide. No relief.

She clamped her teeth down on her bottom lip. She couldn't let herself break. She couldn't give them what they wanted. She had to find a way.

"No...no...please...no..."

Fleming held her hands over her ears the best she could with the splints on her fingers. Hours must have passed since she'd been thrown in the cell. She had no way to measure time, no outside light to distinguish night from day. It felt like she'd always been trapped here, and always would be, the woman's pleas endlessly thrashing against her resolve.

Malcolm hadn't come, and part of her wondered if he ever would. Maybe this was her punishment for the damage to his hand. She had to listen to the shrieks forever—cold, naked—and fear the voice was Chandler's.

"Stop...please, stop...I'll tell you whatever you want to know... just no more."

As brutal as her training had been as times, it wasn't real life. She'd never felt this vulnerable. Never felt she was a second away from death, or worse, a second away from losing everything that mattered.

It wasn't just her legs, the gunshot injuries, the ever-present pain that weakened her. That pain alone couldn't break her, quash what hope she had left, leave her with nothing. But listening to this shattered woman who might be her sister, feeling so help-less...it wasn't long before it all mixed together in her mind, until she couldn't sort one thing from the other.

"Oh God...no. I've told you all of it. I swear...just...please... don't..."

Wait.

Maybe she *was* losing her mind, but she could swear she'd heard those exact words before. And not just the same words, but the same cadence, the same scream following.

"Please! I'm begging you...no!"

This wasn't a woman being tortured.

At least not here, not now.

It was a recording. Set on an endless loop. A tactic.

As part of her training with the Instructor, she'd been locked away for days, nothing but the sound of electronic humming in her head. That time, instead of the nonceasing overhead lights, she'd been left in complete darkness. Food had been delivered through a slot in the door. She'd had no contact with another human being for a week.

Fleming knew all the ways to break a person down. Suffering through them had once been part of her training. Implementing them had once been part of her job.

That didn't make her immune to their effects.

But now that she knew the woman was a recording, she could focus on that. She could take note of the repeating words, concentrate on something besides the feelings they engendered.

And just maybe she could manage to hold on.

Hammett

"The difference between a highly trained operative such as yourself and a garden-variety killer is intent," the Instructor said. "Only psychopaths kill for fun."

Hammett knew she sometimes killed for fun, and that made her a psychopath. At least, that's what her training taught her. Hammett's own opinion of herself was somewhat different. She recognized in herself an alpha predator. One who did what she wanted to, answering to no one. If she used, hurt, or killed for her own satisfaction, it was not psychopathic, because it wasn't a disorder. If anything, it was an advantage.

Santiago, however, had a serious disorder. That guy was insane.

Shortly after solidifying plans at that awful clown motel, Santiago and Speed had gone off in search of a vehicle while Hammett used her tablet to transfer funds into her team's bank accounts, pausing occasionally to flirt with Javier and Isaiah, even throwing a few pity smiles Jersey's way. Seduction had also been taught at Hydra, and men were particularly easy to manipulate. Hammett flirted so frequently that she was often unaware of it. But in this case it was to foster good morale and allegiance. The only tricky part was to make sure no jealousy took hold. The goal was team-building, not team-destroying.

When Speed texted FOUND WHEELS, Hammett led her team into the lot and found him in an eighteen-wheeler parked alongside the hotel, alongside the outdoor portion of the water park. It was a Mack, the cab bright red, hauling a trailer adorned with a hyperrealistic graphic of people on a beach enjoying soft drinks.

Jersey climbed into the cab with Speed, and Hammett led Isaiah and Javier around the back, opening the trailer door. They found Santiago with the unfortunate driver, who had been tied and gagged, sitting on a stack of cola cartons.

The man had been partially flayed. He wriggled, screaming, the exposed muscles in his chest glistening like strawberry jelly. Santiago stood over him clutching pliers and a utility knife, the look on his face not dissimilar to a pregnant woman, glowing.

"My man, that's just nasty," Isaiah said.

Javier unbuttoned his suit jacket, leaving his hand on his belt.

Hammett checked to make sure the lot behind them was empty, then closed the door.

"This one's a fighter." Santiago's voice was almost a purr. "I may keep him around for a while to play with."

"Just kill him," Hammett ordered, annoyed. "Play on your time, not mine."

Santiago emitted an extended, drama-queen sigh, then slit the driver's throat.

Hammett frowned. She'd done worse to people, but there was a time and a place. And, for the most part, a reason. Murder, especially bloody murder, left evidence. Random murder in public places was asking for attention.

As the truck driver bled out, Hammett drew her Wilson Tactical Supergrade .45 ACP from her hip carry with a speed rivaling that of any famous dead cowboy, pointing it at Santiago's face.

"I want to be clear that I won't tolerate screwing around while on this op. You're being paid professional rates. Act like a professional."

Santiago's eyes narrowed, but he tilted his chin up to the gun and pressed his lips against the barrel.

"Promise," he said after the kiss.

Hammett was aware that Isaiah and Javier had shifted their weight, angling away from her. She sensed the tension in their bodies, could almost taste their eagerness to pull their weapons. Dropping to one knee, she spun and pressed her gun to Javier's belly while simultaneously pulling the M-Tech tactical fighting knife from the tearaway sheath on her right calf and holding it inside Isaiah's thigh.

"Do you gentlemen promise as well?" she asked, smiling brightly.

Both had their hands on their guns but hadn't drawn them.

"I like fast women," Javier said, but his eyes were cold.

"Is that a yes?" Hammett checked her peripheral. Santiago's body was relaxed, his expression amused.

"I am a consummate professional," Javier said, letting his arm fall to his side. "But I admit, when this mission is over, I'd be interested in doing some decidedly unprofessional things with you."

"Mr. Brown?" Hammett glanced his way.

Isaiah put his hands down. "I, too, am a professional."

"No come-on, Mr. Brown?" She was almost insulted.

"I'm married."

Hammett tucked away her weapons almost as quickly as she'd drawn them, then smoothed out the Velcro split in the calf of her boot-cut jeans. Funny. The man would kill for money, but somehow considered cheating improper.

His loss. And no matter, in the long run. While flirting was useful in commanding men, it didn't have quite the impact of proving you could murder him before he blinked.

"Impress me," she said, looking pointedly at Isaiah, then letting her gaze linger on Javier.

The truck revved, slipping into first gear. Hammett turned away, walked deeper into the cab, avoiding the growing pool of blood on the trailer bed, and took her tablet computer from her purse. She spotted three blips on her GPS map. Hers, Fleming's, and Chandler's.

Chandler was close.

Hammett considered her sisters. Chandler was good. Almost as good as Hammett was. And Fleming, despite her handicap, had proven incredibly resilient. She wondered, briefly, if it would be possible to recruit them. After all, she'd previously done so with their other siblings. Hydra was excellent at leaching humanity from its trainees. Causes were foolish. Even revenge, satisfying as it might be, was a waste of their particular talents. Money and power were much worthier pursuits.

But recalling all the trouble those particular two sisters had caused her, Hammett dismissed the notion.

It would be more satisfying to watch them die. Horribly, if possible. And though vengeance wasn't professional, missions sometimes result in collateral damage. If Chandler got in the way, she'd be eliminated.

With extreme prejudice.

Tequila

Tequila finished up with the dogs and then kept his position, waiting and watching. No guards came out to investigate. He couldn't find any other cameras other than the one over the kennel, aiming at the sandpit in the enclave.

He decided to get a higher look, and searched his pack for the case Harry McGlade had loaned them. Inside the stainless-steel box, encased in foam, was a toy helicopter no bigger than a robin.

But this was one seriously pimped-out toy copter. Front- and rear-mounted pinhole cameras. Global positioning tracking device. A thirty-minute battery. And several things no consumer protection agency would ever approve of: a gun barrel that fired a single .380 round, and a M6 detonator/blasting cap with a shaped shrapnel charge.

"You blow it, you bought it," McGlade had said. "And this sucker is worth more than most new cars."

Tequila took a few minutes to assemble the rotors and familiarize himself with the controls, X-axis/Y-axis sticks with a dial for rotation and buttons marked SHOOT and BOOM. There were also two LED displays that were surprisingly clear, and an LCD that reported longitude and latitude.

He directed it to lift off, and the thing hovered in the air with only a slight buzz and hummingbird-like flutter of the rotor. After playing with it for a few minutes, he had to admit he wanted one, but not for the firepower.

Not far from Chicago was the Stillman Nature Center, and on Tequila's last visit he'd seen a great horned owl that had appropriated a squirrel nest in an enormous oak tree. He'd wanted to climb up and get a closer look in the nest, but didn't want to risk being thrown out of the preserve. The helicopter would be an ideal way to satisfy his curiosity.

He landed the chopper on the roof of the cannon building, affording him a good view of the area via the tiny chopper's camera, and then he tugged one of his custom .45s from his shoulder rig. After whistling twice, he took careful aim and shot the kennel camera fifty meters away, blowing it to bits.

One eye on his Rolex Submariner and the other on the LCD screen's view of the enclave, he slipped inside the building and leaned his back against the rusting, blast-resistant door. The building's interior was dark and hot and musty-smelling, punctuated by the occasional beam of sunlight streaming in through various broken windows.

Exactly thirty-six seconds had ticked by after he shot the camera when a hatch opened up in the sandpile. Two men in generic black jumpsuits, their sidearms holstered, emerged from the hole. Performing a standard military sweep of the area, they converged on the kennel.

Tequila pushed the stick on the helicopter, and the tiny machine rose off the roof. He took a wide arc around the kennel, then aimed for the enclave, intent on flying the copter into the entrance to take a peek.

One of the guards picked up a piece of the camera and said something into his walkie-talkie that Tequila couldn't make out, and they began to head back to the enclave. Damn. Too soon. The helicopter hadn't gotten to the hatch yet. In seconds it would fly directly into their line of sight.

Tequila mule-kicked the steel door, hard. The *clang* reverberated through the building.

The guards' heads turned in his direction. They drew their weapons and immediately began to jog his way.

Tequila lurched up from the door and went into motion, dividing his attention between escape and steering the helicopter toward the entrance. Eyes glued to the LCD as he tried to fly sideways and keep the camera on the guards, he stumbled on some refuse on the floor.

He recovered his balance before going down and made it into the corridor. The building was large, the size of a modest home, with several rooms branching off the narrow concrete hallway. In moments the guards would enter, and he would be caught in what cops called a vertical coffin, a long hallway with nowhere to go but dead. He needed to find a place to hide.

He yanked open the nearest door, revealing a completely empty room. The next was the same, barren of all furniture, not even a closet to hole up in. Racing down the corridor, he peered in door after door, looking for cover. But each room had been stripped, no tables, no cabinets, no equipment.

He checked the LED, saw he was flying erratically, missing the hatch by several meters. Tequila reversed direction on the helicopter and hovered. The camera swung around to reveal the guards right outside the building entrance, one of them reaching for the door he'd just kicked.

In seconds they'd be inside, and the best he could do was sit in an empty room and wait to be discovered.

Unless he killed the guards.

He considered that for a moment. It would solve his immediate problem, but their absence would put the compound on alert, making it impossible to save Chandler's sister.

Self-preservation, or help the woman?

The door opened.

Tequila looked up, hoping for rafters or even a lighting fixture, but there was nothing but bare walls and a poured concrete ceiling.

Tucking the remote control in his waistband, light doused against his body, he jumped anyway. He kicked one leg on the near wall, launching himself over to the far wall. Tequila kicked himself off that as well, using momentum and his leg muscles to propel himself higher, like an Olympic floor exercise, only vertical.

One final kick, and then he straightened out his body, stretching hard and fast, wedging himself against the shadowy ceiling with his toes on one wall and his fingertips on the other, his body bridging the hallway, nine feet up.

He held his breath as the guards entered the corridor.

A cramp seized Tequila's fingers, the muscles unused to bearing his weight in this awkward position.

The guards began to walk his way, weapons at the ready, their boots scuffing concrete.

Using the sound of their footsteps to mask his movement, Tequila spun like a pig on a spit, rotating his back to the floor. Stretching his body taller than he thought possible, he braced with one hand, using the other to place the remote on his chest. He craned his neck to see the screen, his forehead touching the ceiling, and used his free hand to control the helicopter, flying it toward the hatch entrance.

The guards walked beneath him—

—and stopped.

"Could be another damn deer," one of them said.

"Deer destroyed the camera, then ran in here?" asked the other. "Why would it do that?"

"Nature fighting back. Could be it got sick of being hunted, wanted to lash out."

They shared a chuckle.

The cramp in Tequila's fingers bloomed into full-on agony. His arm began to shake. It was a familiar feeling, going back to his long-ago training days, his coach screaming at him that muscle fatigue was all in the mind, even though he'd been hanging from the rings for over an hour.

He concentrated on flying the toy chopper, but controlling it with only one hand was difficult, and once again he overshot the hatch door.

"Maybe it was someone from the damn cleanup crew. Getting nosy. Saw us coming and ran in here."

"That would be a mistake."

Tequila heard the sound of a gun slide being racked, the cartridge loading. The arches of his feet began to spasm.

"Wait, what time is it? I think those union pricks left for the day."

"So maybe this piece-of-shit building is falling apart, and the camera blew up because it's typical military-issue crap."

Another chuckle.

Tequila's shoulders began to seize.

He figured he could hold on for maybe another four seconds.

The guards didn't move.

Three seconds.

Two…

One…

Tequila's muscles gave out. But he didn't. He remained in place, even as the cramps became so bad he completely forgot about the helicopter.

So bad he forgot about everything.

But he still held on.

Tequila thought he heard the guards begin to leave, but couldn't confirm it. He was locked into a private hell of his own making, forcing his body beyond the limits of endurance, holding out until even the screaming voice of his coach was drowned out by the pain signals being beamed into his brain.

Don't fall!

DON'T FALL!

DON'T FUCKING FALL!

He fell.

He turned in the air.

He landed on one leg and one knee, cradling the remote to his belly.

The Ukrainian judge gave him a 2.3.

But the guards were gone.

Reality returned, and he bit his lower lip not to cry out from the agonizing, knotted cramp in his left hand and feet and back and...everything. The helicopter had fallen sideways into a jumble of weeds, and he worked the controls frantically with his right hand, trying to get it to lift off.

Seconds ticked by.

The pain wouldn't abate, but he got the chopper up, the cameras now level.

He winced.

The guards had nearly reached the sandpile.

The helicopter was between them and the entrance.

Tequila said, "Ah, hell."

Then he stood up and kicked the metal door again, convinced the *clang* echoing down the hall was tinged with regret.

As before, the guards' heads swiveled around, and this time they sprinted to the cannon building.

Tequila looked up at the ceiling. There was no way he could do that again. He had to find another way.

He made his way up the hall. A window glowed at the end, its filthy, shattered glass held in place with rusty chicken wire.

Tucking the remote into the crook of his arm like a halfback, he sprinted, hunching his shoulders and then throwing himself into the air at the window—

—bouncing back off because it was reinforced with iron bars.

Tequila landed on all threes, refusing to drop the remote control, even as his head rang. He shook himself like a dog and stood up, just as the guards reached the door.

Chandler

"A mission is only as good as its team," said the Instructor. "If your backup fails, you fail. And failure can mean death."

When I came to, my first concern was the sensation of a sharp stick drilling into my stomach. Memories flashed through my mind—the chip, the pain, Lund with his fingers in my belly...

I startled, eyes wide, immediately jackknifing to a sitting position, unable to hold it because the pain took away my breath.

I still reclined on the sofa, but the plastic and towels were no longer beneath me. Instead a blanket covered my bare shoulders and a bandage wrapped my aching middle. My cropped hair was damp with sweat. It was nearly dark outside, a yard light filtering through the farmhouse window's wavy glass.

A rustle came from somewhere in the room, and Lund's face appeared in my field of vision. "How are you doing?"

"You're...still here."

"Where else would I be?"

"How long have I been out?"

"About twenty minutes."

"Oh, shit." Once more I tried to sit up. Agony seized my stomach, sharp and precise, like an icepick into my belly button.

Lund brought his hands to my shoulders. "You're not going anywhere."

Apparently he was right. At least until I could get another shot of painkiller.

"The chip. Did I get it?"

"No."

I couldn't prevent a surge of tears at the thought that I'd have to go in again.

"But I did." He held up something pinched between thumb and forefinger. "Tiny little bastard."

"Let me see."

He handed it to me. It was nearly the size of a dime, just like chips I'd taken from my sisters, and like those other trackers, it held a tritium battery. A nice little radioactive gift from my Uncle Sam. "We need to get rid of it."

"I'm sure there's a hammer around here somewhere."

"No, not destroy it."

"Then what?"

"Send it somewhere."

A slow smile spread over his lips. "So they think it's you."

"Exactly. Maybe Europe."

"I always wanted to visit Italy."

I gave him a smile. "Then Italy it is. FedEx?"

"I'll drop it off."

I made another attempt to sit up, this time succeeding after much pain, groaning, and concerned looks from Lund.

"I need another shot," I said.

"I already gave you one. Give it a second. You need to rest. Or better yet, go to the hospital."

"Don't nag."

"Sorry, dear."

I couldn't stop my laugh, and pain racked my midsection. "Where's my phone, honeybuns?"

He picked up my jacket, pulled it from my pocket, and handed it to me.

I checked the screen. Only one text from Tequila, stating that he might have found the entrance. This had taken longer than I wanted, too long. "I need to get back."

"You're working with someone?"

"A guy is helping me."

Lund raised an eyebrow. "So I'm just one of many?"

"If it makes you feel any better, I haven't let him put his fingers inside me."

"I guess I can't be too jealous, then." He handed me my sweater and jeans. "We can mail the chip, then you'll have to let me swing by my house for my deer rifle."

It took me a second to realize that, like Jack, he thought he was going with me. "You don't want to get mixed up with these people."

"They've probably already seen me checking the place out."

"You weren't connected to me then. I'm serious, Lund. They'll find out who you are and target everyone you love. Family—"

"No family."

"Girlfriend."

A shadow of regret passed over his face. "No girlfriend, remember?"

"Then ex-girlfriend."

Lund scratched the blond stubble on his chin. "She's a cop. She can take care of herself pretty well."

"Not in this case. Look, I'm grateful for your help, but you're not going anywhere near the plant. I'll hike through the park and jump the fence there."

"Then how do you get out?"

That was a good question, one Tequila and I hadn't exactly covered. Fleming couldn't exactly run, and I currently wasn't in any shape to carry her. I might need a little more help from Lund after all, if he'd agree to stay far away from the action. But there was still the problem of his truck being easily traceable.

"Can you steal a car? Meet us somewhere in the park?"

He stared at me as if I had lost my mind. "I don't steal cars. At least, not on the first date."

"You can't use your truck."

Lund's kind eyes crinkled. "I have a better idea."

Tequila

Still unable to use his cramped left hand, Tequila drew just one of his .45s as the guards entered. He pulled the trigger four times, drilling each guard in the face. They were dead before their bodies hit the floor.

Tequila checked his watch. It would be a few minutes, tops, before the base radioed in and the guards didn't answer. After that he'd only have thirty-six more seconds for reinforcements to arrive.

He texted Chandler, explaining the situation. Then he picked up the remote, once again guiding the helicopter out of weeds, and succeeded in aiming it into the open hatch without overshooting. The doorway led to a circular staircase, descending half a dozen meters before opening into a corridor. It was dim, lit by low-wattage bare bulbs positioned at regular intervals from wires hanging from the ceiling. The walls were damp, crumbling concrete. Using the helicopter, Tequila followed the hall to its end, an iron door.

He memorized the coordinates on the remote, then checked them against his map of the compound. The tunnel let off at the water filtration plant, a large structure composed of four rectangular concrete retention pools.

That had to be where the prison was.

Tequila landed the copter behind the door, slipped the remote into his backpack, and whistled twice, once short and once long. Then he jogged to the kennel and set a small charge of Semtex-10, a yellowish plastic explosive, with a remote detonator.

Figuring he didn't have much time left, he jogged back to the cannon house, his cell phone in his pocket set to vibrate, ready for Chandler's reply.

Hammett

"One day you'll be forced to kill someone you know," the Instructor said. "An ally. A friend. Maybe a family member. Don't let your feelings for them get in the way, or else they might kill you first."

The truck came to a stop at the designated spot on Highway 12, a kilometer before Badger Ammo's entrance. Hammett checked the time, knew the construction workers had gone home for the day.

All that was left were the guards. Since this was a black site, Hammett had no doubt they'd been trained by the government. But if they were really good, they would have been in the field, not babysitting a secret prison. According to Santiago, there were three shifts of eight men, plus a spook named Malcolm who functioned as a warden of sorts. Erring on the cautious side, Hammett instructed her team to assume there were at least twenty guards at the prison.

A challenge, but not an insurmountable one.

She waited for Jersey to come around and open the trailer door, happy to be away from the stench of warming blood and Santiago's body odor. The air outside smelled of forest, diesel exhaust, and a faint hint of manure spread on nearby fields. Birdsong and the occasional whoosh of traffic speeding by were the only sounds. The cool breeze on her face felt good as she strolled around to the cab to confer with Speed.

"Thirty minutes you're out in front. If it's sooner or later, I'll text you."

Speed nodded, but he wasn't looking at Hammett. Instead he was looking skyward. She followed his gaze and noticed three—make that four—hot-air balloons. One red. One blue. One white. And the fourth so close she could see the star pattern on it. Flying high above the road, the trees, the world. There was a serenity to the scene that disturbed Hammett for some odd reason. Maybe it was the incongruity of it. They were here to kill a bunch of men, and bright-colored balloons floating gracefully through a tranquil sky before dusk didn't fit.

"Perfect northern wind," Speed said. "Slow and easy. Probably started south at Sauk Prairie Airport, hoping to land at Thiessen Field, near the orchard."

"Hoping?" Hammett asked. She wasn't sure why she cared, but the four fat dots in the sky had caught her off guard.

"Ever been ballooning? You can't steer those things, so you can never be sure where you'll land. And it's getting close to dusk. I'd rather fly a chopper in a hurricane than a hot-air balloon at night. Especially with all the power lines around."

"Thirty minutes," Hammett said, tearing her eyes away from the balloons as a burner on one fired to life with a low roar. She led Jersey, Isaiah, Santiago, and Javier off road and into the grass. They double-timed it north to Badger, stopping fifty meters from the perimeter and hunkering down in a ditch behind a five-foot chain-link fence. Isaiah broke out some field glasses while Hammett studied the map.

"One guard at the entrance booth, one at the gate," Isaiah said. "The main entrance has three security cameras. The booth, the driveway, the parking lot. Also spot a rover on a four-wheeler at two o'clock heading east, looks like he's circling the perimeter. Gun mounts on the handlebars."

"The prison is here." Santiago pointed to the water filtration plant.

It would be a good hike back to the entrance, especially carrying a cripple.

"Where are the ATVs?" she asked.

"Never saw where they kept them, but there's a locked garage here, off the parking lot."

"I've got keys to every lock ever made," Jersey said.

She shot him a look out of the corner of her eye. He'd better not be bullshitting. "OK, we go with the plan we discussed. After penetration, we secure the vehicles and do a northern buffalo-horn formation on the target. Isaiah, right horn. Javier, left. Jersey and me as the chest. Santiago the loins."

Hammett reached into her pack, passing out headsets and walkie-talkies. They set the frequency and did a sound check.

"Radio silence unless needed. We want the subject alive. Let's move out."

They moved.

Chandler

"Facing your fears is crazy," the Instructor said. "When you have a choice, it's better to run the hell away."

Lund's better idea turned out to be horses, and I had to agree with his assessment—even though riding would be painful, it was tough to trace a horse. We took his red pickup, driving in companionable silence. He only spoke when we neared our destination.

"It's a private stable. I bought one of the horses when Val had to sell off a couple, and we have an arrangement that I can borrow the other two whenever I like."

"Sweet deal."

I was tempted to ask about the particulars of this relationship, but knowing them might end up making me feel guilty, either for taking the horses or—if the opportunity arose—taking Lund. So I said nothing.

The farm was secluded and surrounded by trees. Climbing out of the truck, I smelled the usual outdoor smells, the sharp tang of horse manure and sweetness of alfalfa hay adding a new note to the mix. The afternoon was late, dangerously close to starting its slide into evening. Another V of geese honked from the sky.

I saddled two mares, Banshee and Bo, and a gelding named Max, while Lund drove a few miles to town and mailed the GPS chip to Italy. Banshee, a striking bay with the standard dark brown coat and black mane and tail, was eager to get out of her stall and opened her mouth for the bit like she couldn't wait to be ridden.

Bo was a liver chestnut, and she lifted her right front leg and arched her neck strangely when I approached. I'd checked her hoof to make sure there was nothing lodged in the sole and found nothing before I finally figured out it was her way of begging for treats. I hunted around until I found some horse snacks—in this case dried apple chips from a pouch that I discovered in the feed room.

The palomino, Max, was rather plump, and he snorted at me, pawing the ground and dancing around his stall. I spent a minute soothing him and stroking his coat before leading him out, then fed him a few apple chips until he chilled out and I could brush him down and throw on a western saddle.

When Lund returned, we set off, me on Bo, Lund on Max, Banshee trailing on a lead rope behind us.

It had been a long time since I'd ridden a horse, though I got into the rhythm soon enough. Normally it was a fun experience; being outdoors, sharing a single mind with the animal, the tactile sensations of the swaying gait under me and my hands on the reins. But this wasn't a joy ride, and I was so focused on what lay ahead, I might as well have been on the El.

By the time Lund and I had reached the park, my inner thighs were already sore, and I wished I'd taken time to buy a bra. For probably the first time in my life, I was glad I wasn't a D cup. The incision in my belly hurt, but between the pressure of the bandage and the drugs, I was doing much better than I could have guessed. At least when I finally showed up, they wouldn't be waiting for me. With any luck, Hammett and anyone else trying to track me would soon be busy searching Naples.

The sun hung low in the west now, the orange hues already casting a soft glow on everything. I figured two hours before sunset, and then only a little bit of dusk light left. I had buckled on the holster Harry had included in his supply duffel. Around my waist, I'd fastened an additional Paracord S3 Cobra survival belt. I also wore a Stratofighter folder strapped to my ankle, and a Ghost Hawk neck knife on a ball-chain necklace. The extra clips for the Beretta were in my front pockets, the cell phone on my hip. The gym bag full of McGlade's equipment was tied to the skirt of my saddle. I heaved it onto my back, fitting on the shoulder straps, then tightened a chest strap under my breasts.

Lund had packed other equipment on his horse—first-aid supplies, water, and the ultrasound machine.

I took in my surroundings, scanning the trees, looking for movement, and trying to hear any signs of human activity over the creak of my western saddle and hoofbeats of my mare. The flap of bird wings and hum of crickets singing their last songs before cold weather set in were the only sounds that reached me.

Until the gunshots. Four in rapid succession.

The sound was distant, but loud, echoing up over the trees and carrying to the lake and probably beyond.

My horse spooked, steel shoes scraping stone, and I had to take hold of her mouth and bend her in a tight circle to bring her back under control.

"What the hell was that?" Lund held the reins of his dancing mount in one hand, the rope tethering the third horse in the other. "Was that gunfire?"

It was a moot question, so I didn't respond. Shooting wasn't part of the plan, which meant something had gone wrong.

"Don't you think it's a little reckless to use firearms in a place that's contaminated with explosive material?"

He had a point, but I decided not to draw attention to the fact that everything about this plan was reckless.

My hip vibrated, and I checked the text on my phone: TWO DOWN. ENTRANCE BY CANNON BUILDING. PRISON UNDER WATER FILTRATION PLANT. I'LL HOLD THEM UNTIL YOU GET HERE.

Good to know it wasn't Tequila who'd been shot.

"Come on," I said.

We set off at a ground-covering trot. A western saddle is designed for the rider to sit the bouncy gait, which worked if the horse was moving at a slower jog. I'd done basic horseback training with the Instructor, and I'd enjoyed it so much, I'd followed up in my free time at a stable north of Chicago. That's where I'd become hooked on jumping, and as I rose forward in my western saddle, I couldn't help wishing for the Hermes Steinkraus I'd used while training over fences.

When we reached the clearing where I'd first met Lund, we brought our animals to a stop.

"I'm going on alone. We'll meet here?"

"I'll be here all night if need be."

"Don't let anyone see you, Lund. I'm serious. They might have cameras."

"I know."

"One good shot of your face, and they'll track you down."

He swung off his horse. Holding the reins and rope in one hand, he took hold of Bo's bridle with the other. "Don't waste time worrying about me. I can handle myself."

"I kicked your ass a few hours ago."

"That's only because—"

"You let me?"

He actually blushed a little. "Hell, no. I didn't know what hit me until it was all over. I was going to say it was because you're one of a kind."

This guy was far too nice. That was a problem, because I found nice unspeakably sexy.

"Sorry for messing up your come-on line," I said, lowering my voice.

He gave me a grin. "There are more where that one came from."

"I hope so." I swung off and stood beside him. My pulse was elevated, my heart pumping fast. I wanted to blame the spike on the sounds of shooting in the plant below, but I suspected it was the man. And I was relieved he seemed to be noticing more than my bruises.

This was the wrong time, wrong place, and wrong guy.

Which naturally meant I did the wrong thing.

"Be safe, Lund." I grabbed one of his solid biceps, tugged him down to me, and brought my lips hard against his. He responded with equal intensity, opening his mouth, delving deep, the timing of his lips, his tongue, synced with mine, and heat washed over my skin. The kiss lasted only a few seconds, but when I released him and pushed away, my legs were trembling.

I didn't look at him again, just marched straight down the hill and had covered a hundred feet before I remembered I needed to be invisible.

Getting my shit together, I shifted my weight to the balls of my feet and moved with the trees, blending my silhouette with theirs. I regulated my breathing, slowed my heartbeat, focused my thoughts. I liked Lund a lot, but stumbling around with lust on my mind would get me killed. And if that happened, I'd never know if he fucked as well as he kissed.

I checked my phone, but there was nothing new from Tequila. I keyed in BREACHING FENCE, then I shimmied up one of the trees hanging over the razor wire.

I climbed the tree until I was on the other side of the fence, bounced on the limb, then let myself drop. The fall was about ten feet, and when I hit, I absorbed the impact with my legs, then flowed into a roll and came up on my feet.

A road stretched in front of me, the asphalt half crumbled, weeds poking through the cracks. I crossed it in a full run, then plunged into the trees on the other side. The terrain on this side of the fence looked much the same as the park, and I moved westward quickly and silently through the trees, keeping my eyes out for landmarks.

I'd traveled through the forest for a few minutes when I came to the corner of a concrete wall. A chain-link fence topped it, about four feet high. On one side, the forest snugged up tight to the barrier. On the other, goldenrod and Queen Anne's lace lined the base, their withered flowers reaching my waist.

I chose the path of least resistance, wading through the prairie flowers. When I reached the end of the span, the grade of the surrounding area rose, and I could see that the structure wasn't a wall at all, but the side of a reservoir.

The walls formed two squares, their inside surfaces sharply sloped into vats of water one hundred feet square. Algae floated in globs on the water's surface, and a green, rotting smell hung in the air. A walkway with a yellow pipe railing flanked one side, three ancient orange ring buoys piled at the edge.

To my right, a circular driveway looped out of the trees, and parked close to the reservoir's walkway were two four-wheeled ATVs. Pulling out my Beretta, I inched forward.

I smelled the wisp of cigarette smoke before I spotted the sentry.

He stood on a lookout platform near the entrance to the walkway. Glowing cancer stick in his mouth, he clutched a set of binoculars in his right hand and was peering at the vista below.

Two ATVs meant two guards. I scanned the area for his buddy, but came up empty. He had to be fairly close, otherwise he wouldn't have left his ride, but there was no sign of him anywhere.

My back flattened against the cold concrete, I eyed the four-wheelers. With one of those, not only could I reach Tequila before he missed me, but also we would have a way to get Fleming out in a hurry.

I was betting Mr. Smokebreak had the keys.

All I had to do was take them.

Giving the area another once-over for the second man, I shoved my weapon back in its holster and approached the sentry from behind, choosing to attempt the quiet kill so I wouldn't alert his buddy. Walking on the balls of my feet, I moved silently as a cat, knees soft but ready to spring. I raised my arms, extended the fingers and thumb of my left hand, and made a fist with my right. About three feet away, I jumped.

I struck him across the throat with the inner edge of my left forearm, at the same moment punching hard into the small of his back. He staggered and gasped in a breath, pulling in smoke. Sputtering and coughing, he let the cigarette drop to the platform.

Not skipping a beat, I clamped his throat tight in the vee of my elbow and grasped my left biceps, then pushed his head downward with my right hand, cutting off his carotid artery.

Without blood flow to his brain, he passed out in a few seconds. But passed out wasn't good enough.

For a second, I hesitated, even though I knew what had to be done. Despite the fact that I'd killed plenty of men before, and this guy was a guard at a black site and no innocent, I couldn't help but see Jack's wide eyes and hear her whisper in the back of my mind when I'd asked her if she could slit a man's throat or cut off digits to get information.

You do those things?

The guard tensed, starting to come to. I increased pressure, depriving his brain once again. Once he lost consciousness, I changed my grip and gave his head a wrench until the neck snapped, then I lowered him to the platform.

Yes, Jack. I guess I do.

But that didn't mean I felt good about it. Hands vibrating from the adrenaline dump that usually accompanied taking a life, I went through his pockets and recovered a cell phone, a pack of cigarettes, and the ATV keys. I headed to the circle drive to claim my reward.

Then I caught peripheral movement at the tree line.

I jerked sideways, diving for the ground just as two bullets punched into my back.

Fleming

"The only thing to fear more than your enemy," the Instructor said, "is your enemy when he's pissed off."

The screaming in the adjacent cell stopped.

Fleming was already cold, shivering, and naked on the concrete floor, but she knew what turning off the recording meant.

Sure enough, her cell door opened a moment later.

A guard came in first, older than the previous one, a long stick in his hand. Fleming recognized it as a cattle prod by the electrodes on the end.

She tried to drag herself backward, but the prod touched her chest with a sharp *crack!* Though she'd never been stabbed with a hot poker, Fleming could guess it felt just as terrible. She cried out, shrinking away from the pain, the stench of ozone and burned skin clogging her nostrils.

Malcolm stepped into the room next, his hand swaddled in white bandages. The look in his eyes was somewhere between doped-up and furious. He hadn't bothered to reapply his concealer makeup, and his port-wine stain was as dark as a raspberry.

"Three fingers," he said, his voice slurring from pain, painkillers, or both. "That's how much your little stunt cost me."

He nodded at the guard, who juiced her again.

Fleming was able to knock the prod away, but she felt the urge to scream and keep screaming. Instead she ground her teeth together and met Malcolm's eyes. "It'll be OK. You only need two fingers to jerk that tiny thing between your legs."

Malcolm's eyes practically popped out of his head. He shoved the guard with his good hand, and Fleming was zapped two more times.

"You disfigured me, you crippled little bitch."

Fleming found her voice. "Haven't you checked a mirror lately? God beat me to it."

She tried to brace herself, knowing it was impossible, but the attack didn't come. Instead, Malcolm squatted down on his haunches, looking so angry his face twitched.

"Here's what's going to happen to you. I'm going to hurt you until you tell me everything I want to know. And then"—he smiled—"I'm going to keep hurting you anyway."

Fleming tried desperately to come up with some comeback, some retort, but fear closed up her throat.

"Get the cart," he ordered the guard. "We're going to strap her down and have ourselves a grand old time."

The White House

It had taken a lot of digging, threats, and bribes, before the president was properly debriefed on Project Hydra.

His findings were illuminating. In some instances, Hydra had altered the course of history. It had averted wars, taken out key enemies, and helped the United States remain the world's biggest power. A rogue Hydra agent was responsible for the missile launch on the UK, but two other agents had thwarted the attempt. One of them was the woman in custody.

The president called his contact. "Where is Fleming?" he demanded, using her codename, the only name he knew.

"She's being interrogated." His contact's voice was flat, impossible to read, as always.

"Interrogated? She's a goddamn hero. This country, and the world, owes her a huge debt."

"May I ask where you've gotten your information, Mr. President?"

"Where are we keeping her?"

"She's…at a black site."

The president closed his eyes. He knew what went on at black sites. "Jesus. Which one? Egypt? South Korea?"

"Baraboo."

"Where is that? Poland?"

"Wisconsin."

"We've got a secret prison on US soil?" He didn't normally have heart palpitations, but he was having them now. "Do you have any idea of the PR nightmare I'm living right now because of the London incident?"

"Very few people know about the Baraboo site."

"And apparently I wasn't among them. Who set this up?"

"I did. And we'll keep it quiet."

"I want her flown to me immediately."

"That might be…tricky."

"I don't care how goddamn tricky it is—make it happen, or Baraboo's next prisoner will be you."

Tequila

Tequila whistled twice, long and short, then went behind the cannon house and detonated the charge on the kennel, blowing off the door.

They came three minutes and eight seconds later. Four men, armed with handguns, coming through the hatch and spreading out, their long shadows trailing behind them.

Tequila didn't want to waste ammo, so he'd appropriated one of the dead guard's guns, a 9mm Sig, and fired four times into one of the blast walls. Then he squatted with his back against the building and watched.

The men converged on the gunshots.

Tequila raised the dog whistle to his lips once more, and blew three times in quick succession.

He didn't hear anything.

Neither did the men.

But the dogs did.

Ever since his bad experience with dogs trained to kill, Tequila had studied up on commands. Most attack dogs were trained with a dog whistle, the advantage being that it was so high frequency that the enemy didn't know an order had been given. When Tequila discovered the kennel, he'd worked for fifteen minutes with the dogs, learning their commands with the whistle he always carried in his holster.

Three rapid blows meant "Attack."

The four dogs each targeted a guard, bolting silently from the open kennel.

Shots were fired.

No dogs were hurt.

But the guards were.

When the last one had had his throat torn out, Tequila blew the Stay command.

Then he waited for more guards to come.

Hammett

"War is hell," the Instructor said. "If you want to win, be worse than hell."

Hammett had to assume that guards patrolling with long arms would attract unwanted attention, especially so close to a small community like Baraboo. Which is why they stuck with handguns.

Big mistake.

When they got within striking distance of Badger Ammo's entrance, she motioned to Isaiah, who carried a 30-06 Winchester 70 bolt-action rifle with a Redfield scope, which she'd purchased at a department store in the Dells using her fake ID.

He didn't say a word, just waited for her to tell him what she wanted.

Hammett liked that in a man. "See the sentry at the gate?"

He nodded.

"How about the guard at the entrance booth?" The man had emerged from the little hut and was now pacing in casual little circles, taking a smoke break.

Another nod from Isaiah.

"Show me what you can do."

Isaiah blew the forehead off the sentry at the gate, the single crack echoing back from the Baraboo bluffs to the north. Two seconds later he fired again, and the entrance booth guard gave a twitch and fell to the gravel.

Served the moron right. Every pack of cigarettes had a warning on it stating that smoking was hazardous to your health.

Isaiah glanced at Hammett over his shoulder, raising an eyebrow as if silently asking, *Impressed?* Hammett shrugged. They were head shots from forty meters away, but she could have done that with a handgun after half a bottle of Bombay Sapphire. "How about the cameras?"

Isaiah took aim at the nearest, mounted on a post. He fired. The camera stayed where it was.

"You missed," Javier said.

"Did I?"

Hammett checked with the binocs, and saw Isaiah had severed the power line to the camera. Now *that* was a tough shot, even for her.

"Get the other two and meet us at the garage."

They each drew a sidearm and jogged up to the gate, out of Isaiah's line of fire as he made easy work of the other two cameras. No doubt the guards had already been alerted to their presence, but Hammett preferred to keep her face from being recorded. Jersey led the way, Javier covering the left, Hammett right, Santiago bringing up the rear.

When they reached the steel garage door, Hammett chanced a look and noted a heavy-duty disc padlock on a serious-looking hasp.

"No problem," Jersey said. "I've got a universal key."

Hammett shot him a look. "So you said."

He removed his rucksack and knelt down as he went through it, coming out with a Serbu Super Shorty shotgun, an adorable twelve-gauge no more than seventeen inches long. He unfolded the foregrip on the pump, took aim, and fired. The slug instantly devoured the top half of the lock. The rest clinked to the asphalt.

Not bad.

Javier lifted the door to interior darkness, and Hammett flipped on the 190-lumen flashlight mounted to the trigger guard of her Supergrade. The garage smelled like gas and exhaust fumes and an underlying bouquet of dirt. She swept the interior and immediately noticed three ATVs parked along the west wall. Hammett approached one.

No keys.

She pressed the talk button on her radio.

"Speed, can you hotwire an ATV?"

"Lady, I could hotwire a racehorse."

"Bring the truck in, park behind the garage, and get in here." Hammett nodded at Javier, who went off to greet him.

Gunshots punctuated the air, not from her team but from somewhere within the plant. Hammett dug out her tablet and checked the GPS tracker. One blip for her, one for Fleming, but Chandler seemed to be in Baraboo, a few miles away.

So who was shooting?

"Check that out," she ordered Isaiah.

He nodded and jogged off.

"You seem concerned," Santiago said, standing uncomfortably close to her.

"Watch the door."

He did as she said, but the creepy psychopathic sadist was right. She *was* concerned.

Hammett didn't like it when guests showed up uninvited. If it wasn't Chandler, there was someone else it could be. Someone who knew she was here.

Her boss.

The only person in the world Hammett really feared.

Chandler

"The only safe place in a gunfight," the Instructor said, "is somewhere else."

I rolled with the bullets' impact, somersaulting and coming up on my feet, first in a stagger, then in a sprint, heading away from the shooter, surprised I wasn't dead. It felt like I'd been walloped with a baseball bat in the upper back, but there was none of the searing pain that always accompanied being shot. Instead I felt a dull throb, as though I'd been wearing Kevlar.

My gym bag was crammed with supplies. It had stopped the slugs and saved my life.

I hoped that didn't mean I had to sleep with Harry McGlade.

I pushed away the revulsion and focused my attention on the here and now. I had more pressing matters on my mind than unpleasant sex, like avoiding an even more unpleasant death.

Three more bullets tore into the ground in front of me. I veered right, circling the reservoir, making for the closest tree line as I tugged out my Beretta. More gunfire, right on my heels, and I ducked into the woods and put my back against the trunk of a large white pine. My best guess, taking into account the trajectory of the shots, was that the other sentry also hid in the same tree line, roughly fifty meters to the east.

The guard I'd killed had a radio. No doubt this one was calling for reinforcements. I could probably escape into the forest, take a roundabout way to Tequila, but that would take time, and soon he'd have guards all over him, same as me.

Our best chance, and Fleming's, was for me to reach those ATVs.

So I ran. Not away from the sentry, but toward him.

Sunset was quickly approaching, and the thick canopy gave me enough shadows to hide in that I wasn't an obvious target. After twenty meters, I still didn't see the guard, so I stopped to listen.

The scream of hawks overhead. Some mosquitoes buzzing. Gunfire in the distance.

But nothing to give away the guard's position.

Where was he?

I crept forward, gun at the ready, scanning a wide arc in front of me, stopping every few steps to listen.

Then I smelled it, faint but unmistakable, completely inappropriate for the environment.

Chocolate.

But where was it coming from?

I turned a slow circle, squinting into the woods.

Nothing.

Continuing east, the smell grew stronger. And it took on a musky note. A familiar, unpleasant musky note.

Was the sentry wearing that silly chocolate body spray that Harry had slathered himself in?

That's when I heard a twig snap, directly above me.

I'd made a rookie mistake, forgetting that ambushes could come from any direction, not just in front or behind. I managed to get my gun up just as he fell on top of me.

He hit me hard, an elbow to the top of my head, a gravity-fueled chop to my gun hand.

My Beretta spun away, into the bushes. I fell to my knees. Splashes of light burst behind my eyes. Dizziness swirled around me. But I managed to fight through the pain, surprise, and confusion, and had just enough awareness left to pull the sidearm from the holster on his belt, point it into his belly, thumb off the safety, and squeeze the trigger.

Click.

Empty. Which explained why he tried to jump me rather than shoot.

I saw the fist coming down, and I managed to lower my head so he hit the top of my skull. It hurt, but it probably hurt him just as much. I rolled backward with the punch, coming up on unsteady legs, and faced my attacker for the first time.

He was big. Pro wrestler big.

And boy, was he ugly. He had one of those pushed-in fat faces with the little piggy eyes that were too close together, the kind you'd associate with the progeny of cousins who marry.

No wonder he needed body spray. Maybe he was hoping to attract a blind woman...one who had a hankering for rancid chocolate.

I reached for the Ghost Hawk blade hanging around my neck, but only felt the chain; it had swung around to my back. Before I could grab it, Axe slammed into me with a football tackle—actually lifting me up off my feet.

Next thing I knew the wind was knocked out of me, and I was riding the world's fugliest runaway train, smashing through bushes and brush, through the tree line, and plowing me into the fence surrounding the reservoir.

It would have crushed my ribs like pretzel sticks if the chain link hadn't bowed inward, acting somewhat like a stiff safety net.

He continued to shove me, shoulder in my gut like he was pushing his football coach on a training sled. I couldn't reach my ankle, but I did manage to pull the Ghost Hawk around and yank it free. It was a small weapon, no more than two ounces, a finger loop on the bare tang. The blade was shaped like bent trapezoid, with four edges to it and a hole in the center, sharp as hell. I dug it into his back until I scraped his shoulder blade.

Axe howled, pulling me off and plucking the knife from my finger as easily as picking a daisy. I smelled blood under the cloud of chocolate. Then his enormous hands encircled my neck and half my face.

I didn't have the leverage to pull free. I shot a hand between his legs, trying to get a grip on his balls. He increased pressure.

I kicked, missing, my world becoming blurry. Once more I reached for my ankle sheath, but he pushed me backward, the vise tightening around my neck. Feeling concrete under my boots, I surged forward, hoping to throw him off balance, make him slip.

He dragged me back a step, countering.

My ears were ringing now, the blood to my brain being cut off just as I'd done to the other sentry. I tripped over something—the ring buoys—pulled hard as I could, and steered my opponent into them, hoping he'd get tangled. Axe bobbled a little, but his grip on my head didn't let up.

I grasped for his testicles again, at the same time throwing all my weight away from him.

He countered, smashing my body into the fence. Chain link clanged. He slammed me against the fence again, as if trying to break through the rickety thing and throw me into the water.

I clawed at his crotch and bucked my body, my strength fortified with adrenaline, but it was no use. He forced me into the fence a third time, and this time, it broke. I grabbed Axe's arm, digging my fingers into his jacket like claws, holding on. He bobbled for a moment, almost catching his balance, then tipped forward with me, and we both slid down the steep concrete wall and plunged into the water below.

Cold closed over my head. I pulled at the arm still holding me, and then all at once I was free.

Free, but underwater and unsure which way was up.

Though I feared water as much as I feared anything, and though I still lacked air from the stranglehold, I forced myself to relax and reorient.

Buoyancy took over, and my body began to float. I went with it, using my arms and a strong scissors kick, breaking the surface, sputtering, the foul water in my mouth, algae dripping from my hair.

Hands closed around my throat from behind.

Now that I was free of him, I'd be damned if I was going to let him take control again. I went back under, forcing Axe to go with me. Grabbing his hand, I used my fingernails to dig in. My nails are pitiful, short and not particularly strong, but my grip is one of my best qualities. I can crack walnuts with my bare hands, and once upon a time managed to hold on to the landing gear of a helicopter while it was taking off.

My nails wormed their way into his grip, and then I was holding his index fingers, big as sausages. I bent them back, straining until I saw red. He thrashed, trying to get into position to kick me, finally releasing my neck in his effort to get away.

Not so fast.

I tightened my hold on both fingers and then snapped them back, breaking all six knuckles. We both breached the surface, and I gasped in a breath and a dose of fetid water, then twisted under one arm and attempted to pin it behind his back. To counter, Axe rolled over, forcing me under to maintain my hold. My head hit the wall behind me. I turned to the side, trying to slip out, but he wrenched his arm free and used his mass to drive into me, pinning me to the wall and trying to force my head below surface.

I took a gasping breath, then dove feet first, sweeping upward with my arms, heading for the bottom.

Axe spun and grabbed my left wrist, then gripped me to him in a bear hug, his head out of the water, mine under.

I tried to flip him, but he was too big. If we were wearing swimsuits, I could have taken a bite out of his chest, but instead all I got was a mouthful of his jacket and nasty water. I punched at his gut and crotch, I flailed at the sides of his head, but none of it made him loosen his grip.

I'd drowned too many times in my life…hell, too many times this week. And I was *not* in the mood to do it again.

I bent my knee and moved my hand to my ankle, finally able to reach it, pulling the Stratofighter tactical folder from its sheath. With a surge, I drove the four-and-a-half-inch blade into his kidney, then ripped it back toward his spine.

Axe's body seized, and his arms released me. Squeezing out from between his mass and the wall, I kicked to the surface and gasped in breath after breath.

Blood was already spreading in the water, turning it from greenish to brownish. Judging from the Axe's movements, the wound hadn't finished him off, but the water soon would.

I kicked over to him and tried to pull the knife free, tugging hard. It was caught on something, and wouldn't budge. I changed my grip, pulling again, and the Stratofighter came free and abruptly slipped from my fingers, sinking into the murk. Abandoning it, I swam to the corner, a distance away from the dying man. I'd had enough of this particular swimming hole. I wanted out. And now. Reaching my hands upward, I gave a powerful kick, boosting myself a few feet up the inclined concrete.

I slid back down.

Backing up a few yards, I took another shot, swimming as hard as I could, then giving a hard surge up the wall. I hit a few inches higher, clawing with my fingers, pushing with my knees. I stuck on the wall for a few seconds, then descended once again.

The odor of algae mixed with blood clogging my throat and making me gag, I trod water, searching the reservoir for some way out. I might have sent my opponent to a fairly quick death, but if I didn't find a way out of this putrid vat, I was going to join him.

Fleming

"There is no greater pain," said the Instructor, "than being at the mercy of someone who wishes to inflict pain."

Fleming could hear the metallic rattle of a gurney moving up the hallway outside in the direction of her cell. When the guard ducked out to retrieve it, Malcolm had moved back to the door to await his return, as if he believed that despite her burned, injured, crippled shell of a body, as soon as the opportunity presented itself, she'd rise up on her nonfunctioning legs and strangle the life out of him with her bare hands.

Which, more than anything, Fleming wished she was able to do.

"Chicken shit," she called. "You're really that scared of me? What do you think I'm going to do? Trip you?"

"You're not going to be able to do anything when I'm done with you."

Fleming knew he was right. She was going to be tortured. The thought was so frightening to her that it was almost unbelievable. Surreal. An honest-to-God, pinch-me-I'm-dreaming scenario.

She was going to hurt. Hurt terribly.

So she might as well get in a few shots first.

"One hundred and seventeen times," Fleming said, her voice strong as she proudly announced that number.

Malcolm was sucked into it, and made the mistake of asking, "What are you talking about?"

"That's how many times I got laid this year."

It was true, too. Devoted as she'd been to her job, Fleming had a very active social life, and she enjoyed men to the fullest. She had three steady guys who visited her regularly, loyal as puppies and hearty as stallions, and two spare dudes that she could call up if she was feeling especially kinky. Her legs aside, she still had her looks, still had her appetite, and she found that the thing men liked most in women was enthusiasm.

Fleming was very enthusiastic.

"How many times have you gotten some this year, Malcolm? Not counting yourself in the shower, or paying for it."

Malcolm's whole face turned almost as red as his port-wine stain.

"And now that you've got a disfigured hand, no woman in the world would want you. You can't hide that with makeup, you ugly fuck. I bet the whores will charge you double now."

For a moment, it looked like Malcolm was about to burst into tears. Fleming was pleased with herself. Scared as she was, at least she went down swinging.

"I hope that wasn't your jerk-off hand," she said, pushing further. "Although there's nothing wrong with learning to be ambidextrous."

The door opened, and the guard pushed a steel gurney inside, stopping it next to Fleming and locking the brake. On the gurney was a tray filled with horrible things. Things that would be used to hurt her. Her momentary victory deflated, and the fear took over once again.

"That's right, bitch," Malcolm said. "That's all for you. You're going to set a Guinness World Record for suffering." He stepped behind her and ordered, "Pick this cripple up"

Fleming tried to ready herself for something she couldn't possibly ready herself for. Unable to stop, she thought back to all the pain of rehab, all the postsurgery misery, and how she'd rather die than go through that again. This would be worse. And there would be no painkillers. No relief. No end to it.

How could anyone possibly prepare for that?

The guard lowered the gurney, then, holding his arms out to the side in a modified Hulk stance, he prepared for the grab and lift.

But before the big man moved, Malcolm brought the prod to her again, this time connecting with her hip, shocking her good and long, until she thought her skeleton would rip out of her skin. When he finally pulled the device away, her muscles were clenched so tight she couldn't move. The smell of burned flesh coated her tongue, and her diaphragm spasmed, making it impossible to catch her breath. The guard scooped her up and dropped her on the table, her desperate flailing pathetically inept. A few stunned seconds later thick leather straps were buckled on, pinning down her wrists, torso, and ankles. It was old, stiff leather, and Fleming could imagine all the pain of those who'd been strapped to this gurney before her.

She pulled her good hand. There was a little bit of play in the cuff—these were made to restrain men, not women—but she couldn't get her wrist out.

Malcolm hovered over her, his face close. He rested his hand on her naked thigh.

She wanted to spit, but couldn't summon a drop of saliva.

He nodded to the cattle prod. "You're thinking about all the places I could stick this, aren't you?"

She hadn't been, but now she was. Nausea lodged up under her ribs, and Fleming realized she was going to be sick.

"A hundred and seventeen? Is that what you said? I think we'll go for one eighteen. How does that sound to you?" The tray near her head rattled, and he held up an instrument that looked like small branch nippers, the type used for pruning roses. "But first I have a few other things in mind."

Fleming tore her eyes away from the nippers, glancing at the other implements on the tray.

The nausea built like a bomb ready to blow.

Malcolm set the cattle prod on the tray, gripping the garden tool in his functioning hand. "Spread her fingers," he ordered.

Fleming balled her hand into a fist, rolling her fingertips into her palms and hard as she could, but the guard was too strong. He pried her pinky free and jammed her hand tight to the table.

A sickening smile lit Malcolm's pointy, port-wine-stained face. "You took my fingers, now I'm going to take yours."

The fingers on her other hand had just been reset after a different bastard had gotten his jollies breaking them, and the pain was fresh and hot in her memory. She flinched, and she could see in Malcolm's eyes that he recognized her fear.

"Your fingers. Every one of them." He spoke slowly, as if savoring the texture of each word, rolling the sounds over his tongue the way aficionados taste wine. "And then when your hands are nothing but stumps, we'll finish what we started yesterday with your legs."

Her stomach roiled. "Tell me what else you're going to do to me," she said.

"You see that butane torch? I'm going to use that on your—"

That was enough for Fleming. She vomited, hard as she could, her stomach clenching with a mighty contraction. She threw up on Malcolm, on the guard—

—and on her wrist strap.

They stepped away in disgust, but disgusting as it was, it was also very slippery.

Twisting her wrist, she lubricated her leather strap with mucus and bile, and then tugged with all she had, popping her arm free. She stretched out and yanked the cattle prod from the tray, feeling its heft, and cracked the guard across the temple with enough force to shatter bone.

He went down, and Malcolm was too busy gagging from the puke to recognize what was happening.

Big mistake.

Fleming twirled the prod like a baton—thanks Fremd High School for the majorette lessons—and gave him half a million volts right in the eye.

Malcolm folded like an ironing board, screaming and clutching his face, flopping onto the floor. Fleming dropped the prod, quickly undid the straps on her chest and hand, and sat up on the gurney, reaching for the other instruments of torture on the tray.

The first was a bottle of isopropyl alcohol. She bit off the plastic cap and sprinkled it all over Malcolm as he howled.

Then she picked up the butane torch. A model with convenient electric ignition for the interrogator on the go.

"I'm doing every call girl in the world a huge favor," Fleming said, switching on the pointy blue flame.

Fleming wasn't a sadist. Far from it. If anything, she was far too empathetic for this line of work.

But that *whump* sound when she dropped the torch on Malcolm felt pretty damn good. He scrambled to his feet and ran, arms pinwheeling, out of the room and straight into a cinder block wall, knocking himself out.

Unbuckling her feet was difficult, but Fleming was properly motivated. More guards would be coming.

She reached down to check the guard she'd brained, but he didn't have any weapons on him. Her eyes flitted back to the cart, and she palmed the scalpel—

—and brought it to her own throat.

Escape was impossible. She had no guns. She couldn't walk. Even if she had a wheelchair, she doubted a secret NIC black site adhered to the laws requiring handicapped access. Soon reinforcements would arrive, and Fleming would be tortured to death.

The smart thing to do was to end her life. Spare herself the agony. Prevent the lives lost and destruction that would ensue once she was forced to reveal her secrets.

It had to be this way.

It had to end like this.

Right now.

Fleming closed her eyes. She reflected back on her life. All in all, a good one. She'd seen things. Done things. Even after the accident—the only other time before this that she'd considered suicide—she'd still found things worth living for.

There had been adventure, of course. Globe-trotting espionage. Fighting the good fight for the good guys. Making the world a slightly better place. Narrowly escaping death, only to face it another day.

Family. Her loving adoptive parents. Dad taking her to ball games. Baking cookies with Mom. So wholesome and loving it was a glorious, beautiful parody of itself. She missed them terribly.

Men. Her trio of steady lovers would mourn her. So would her two kinky backup dudes. Fleming wished she had a chance to see them once more, to say good-bye. To thank them for all the good times. To taste a final kiss.

She pictured their faces, one by one, and waved to each.

There were regrets, too. She supposed there were in every life. Things she'd still hoped to do. Experiences she still wanted to have. Love she wanted to share.

She'd always hoped someday to be a mother, to feel a baby kick in her belly, to nurse at her breast. To hear the laughter of a child who shared her eyes.

There were places she hadn't seen. For all her travels, she'd never been to Las Vegas. How ridiculous was that? A spy who hadn't ever played baccarat at the Bellagio. A shame, because she had a damn good system for counting cards.

And Chandler...

The sister she'd always wanted and had only just begun to know.

Chandler might even be here now, in this prison. Fleming ached to search for her.

But the safety of the many had to outweigh the safety of the few.

Fleming wasn't the woman she once was. She was beaten down, her body broken, only a shadow of what she'd been. She'd been lucky to be able to take out Malcolm and the guard. But that luck couldn't hold. She couldn't get away. She couldn't fight. She couldn't win.

She knew too much, and the best thing she could hope for was to take that knowledge with her.

She had to do the right thing.

Sometimes doing the right thing was all a girl had left.

Fleming let out a slow, peaceful breath, said good-bye to her sister, and pierced her neck with the blade.

Tequila

Tequila heard gunshots coming from the reservoir. Two different handguns. But that had been over five minutes ago. Chandler should have arrived by now.

Equally disconcerting were the gunshots coming from the Badger Ammo entrance. Rifle fire. And a shotgun.

The guards Tequila and the dogs had dispatched hadn't been carrying anything larger than a 9mm. Which meant a third party had entered the game.

Tequila had sensed Chandler was holding something back. He didn't get the feeling she'd lied to him—he was good at spotting deception—but she'd obviously omitted something important.

He considered calling it quits, getting out of there. For all he knew, Chandler could be dead, and the enemy could be closing in on him.

But he recalled what he'd told Chandler when they first met. He did whatever it took to get the job done.

Running away wouldn't get the job done. So Tequila stayed.

He reached for his phone to text Chandler again.

Simultaneous thoughts and sensations bombarded him.

—the right side of his head became hot and pressurized, as if under a hair dryer—the energy from the bullet's wake generated by air compressed around it, the shock wave.

—his ear became immediately clogged, like it was filled with water.

—he felt the shot hit—in the ear—a millisecond before he heard it.

—that meant it had come from a long distance away, the slug traveling faster than the speed of sound.

—that meant a sniper rifle.

—it sounded like the rifle he'd heard earlier.

—he threw himself to the ground, rolling, pressing his hand to the side of his head.

—his ear went numb—but his probing fingers reported that the top of it was missing, could feel the warm, slick blood.

—he'd dropped his cell phone.

—the bullet had been fired from the south, probably the inert gas production buildings five hundred and fifty meters away.

—the sniper was a damn good shot to have come so close to a kill from that distance.

Tequila rolled onto all fours and scrambled behind the cannon's blast wall, pressing his shoulder against it while removing his pack. Wiping the blood from his fingers, he dug out what looked like a black rifle stock and grip, with the rest of the gun missing. In fact, the gun was complete. The barrel, receiver, and magazines were housed inside the hollow butt stock.

This was a Henry US Survival AR-7. Harry McGlade's version came with two mags, each holding eight rounds of hollowpoint .22 LR ammunition. Tequila assembled it within forty-five seconds. Hands shaking with the flood of adrenaline, he fit the receiver onto the butt and tightened it with a screw at the bottom, then screwed on the barrel. He fed in a magazine, pulled back the bolt, and put the spare mag in his pocket.

His opponent was using a larger rifle, probably a 30-06 or a .308, and he probably had a scope. Scopes had some disadvantages in a firefight; namely, they limited the field of vision. Hoping the sniper was focused on either side of the building, waiting for him to stick out his head, Tequila hopped onto an oil barrel and pulled himself up on the flat roof of the cannon house. Flattening his belly to the concrete roof, he cradled the rifle in the crook of his arms and crawled on his elbows until he was half a meter from the edge.

Tequila brought the weapon to bear, then sighted south. He had a slight elevation edge—his only advantage—and Tequila had to use it before the sniper spotted him.

He had to wait for almost a minute before he caught movement, alongside the east wall of the second gas production building. A tall black guy in a black sweater and tan pants, his rifle barrel resting against the structure's corner.

Moving slowly, Tequila lined up the Henry's peep sight with the plastic sight on the end of the barrel. He felt the wind on his face and adjusted slightly for its direction, and for bullet drop at this distance. Then he squeezed off two quick rounds.

The black man dropped onto his ass, then immediately began to scramble backward as Tequila adjusted to the rifle's sights, firing four more times as quickly as he could pull the trigger. He apparently missed, because the sniper managed to get behind the building.

Time to move. Now that the man knew Tequila was on the roof, he'd probably find another vantage point and pick him off.

Tequila chanced going forward, rolling off the roof, hanging on with one hand, then dropping to the ground and rolling into the brush.

He immediately flattened his body, spreading his legs wide, pressing his chest to the dirt. His only protection was some buckthorn twigs. If he'd been spotted, he'd be dead. He waited for the man to appear again.

A moment later, he detected movement, from the same corner the sniper had been in before.

The bullet dug into the ground only half a meter ahead of Tequila, throwing dirt into his face.

He'd gambled he hadn't been watched, and he'd lost. His hiding spot had been discovered. He had no cover.

The next sniper bullet would surely kill him.

And it would be coming any second.

Chandler

"When you die," the Instructor said. "That's the only time you're allowed to stop fighting."

I trod water for several minutes, wondering what to do, gunshots echoing throughout the compound.

I studied the fence rimming the reservoir. The steep concrete was impossible to climb, too steep to even cling to for a chance to rest. The reservoir was cold, and now that I was no longer fighting for my life against a human opponent, shivers took hold of my muscles. If I didn't find a way out, my limbs would grow sluggish and eventually it would be impossible to keep my head above water. Fatigue sucked at my energy reserves. My clothes, my shoes, my pack, they were all were weighing me down.

It seemed as if the entire universe was conspiring to drown me.

Staying afloat with a scissors kick, I unclipped the belt I wore above my holster. As nice as the woven belt looked, I hadn't donned it to make a fashion statement. It was actually made of fifty feet of paracord, braided until it was compact enough to fit around my waist.

My fingers were numb and clumsy, and it seemed to take forever to unravel the cord, which was no wider than a shoelace. When I had enough to work with, I muscled off my gym bag, looking for something suitable to use as an anchor. Pawing past the stacks of waterlogged cash, my fingers seized the first-aid kit. Too heavy. Inside it were some bandages, syringes, pill bottles. All too light. My Beretta would have been perfect, if I hadn't lost it in the woods. My Stratofighter would have worked, too, if I hadn't dropped it. I touched the Ghost Hawk around my neck, but that weighed less than two ounces. Too light for fifteen meters of water-soaked paracord.

A boot?

It was impossible to untie the laces while treading water, so I had to let my head go under while I fought to claw them free. My fingers refused to work right, shaking and stiff with cold. After several tries, I had to admit I'd done nothing except tighten the knots.

A small, completely hysterical laugh escaped my mouth. I was going to die in a reservoir because I couldn't find something between six ounces and a pound to tie to my paracord.

That's when I noticed a pair of eyes staring at me.

They were at water level. Small and black, set in a flat green head covered in black spots.

I reached out, grabbing it.

A salamander. Cool, slimy, wiggling—

—weighing about eight ounces.

It was the most beautiful thing I'd ever felt.

I looped the paracord around its tail and cinched it tight.

Giving a few good strong kicks to raise me out of the water, I gripped the cord loosely in my first and second fingers and started spinning the salamander over my head. The water gave the cord weight and I let out more line with each revolution, until it grew to three times the size I'd started with. Judging the correct timing by feel, I released the cord.

The amphibian sailed through the air, narrowly missing a fence post. I jerked back, and the animal spun around the post several times in a blur, winding the cord tight. I gave it a tug, and it went taut.

So far, so good.

I swam close to the wall, pulled the cord around the backs of my knees, then up under my armpits. The cord was too thin to get a good grip on, so I pulled my sleeves up over my hands and struggled to ascend by wrapping the cord around my palms.

No good. The cord held, but I was too weak, my wet clothes too heavy.

I had no choice.

Letting a low whimper escape my lips, I dropped the water-logged bag. About forty pounds of cash and Harry's equipment sank immediately, but I was able to get up out of the water.

My movement was slow, my boots wet and slippery. I wound paracord around my fingers, and soon they were screaming from lack of circulation. But inch by excruciating inch I got up that gradual incline, and when I reached the top and hooked my elbow around the fencepost, I couldn't help emitting another hysterical giggle.

My salamander buddy watched me unwrap the paracord, and I could have sworn his expression was bemused. He didn't look any the worse for wear from his ordeal, except for a broken tail, bleeding where the cord had dug into it.

"Thanks for the assist," I said, yanking the Ghost Hawk from my neck sheath.

I cut off the salamander's tail just above the knot, quick and surgical. The cute little critter scurried past, beelining for the water, no doubt anxious to share this tale with his friends as a new tail grew back.

I cast a backward glance at the reservoir and the lost cash, lost first-aid kit, lost phone, then pulled up to my feet and went to find Tequila.

More gunshots, from various places in the compound, and I had a sinking feeling that Hammett had finally joined the party.

Just when I thought things couldn't get bleaker.

I made my way back to the first guard I'd killed and patted down his pockets until I located his keys. I took them and his gun, a Sig Sauer P229 that fit loosely into my hip holster, then I saddled up, checked the magazine on the 5.56 mm rifle mounted to the ATV's handlebars, and familiarized myself with the controls. It had an automatic transmission, so I put in the keys, hit the start button, released the brake, and was off and running.

I headed southeast along the weed-choked road, then the road veered south, and I found myself facing another ATV several hundred meters ahead. I steered right, hoping to avoid an encounter.

No use.

The shots peppered the asphalt in front of me. I laid on the throttle and spun in a 180, heading off road behind a clump of bushes, east toward the oleum plant. Automatic weapon fire continued to kick up behind me, and I questioned the intelligence of front-mounting a machine gun on a four-wheeler. I supposed the only reason for guards to have guns was to chase people, and it made some sense to have a weapon pointed at the person you were chasing. But when you were being followed, as I was now, it was a big bowl of fail.

I zigzagged, trying to use the terrain to protect myself, ducking behind hills and slaloming between trees, but eventually I ran up to a creek that was too wide to traverse. I followed alongside, head down, until I came to a small railroad bridge. I'd crossed and was racing for the building in the distance when gunfire blew out one of my right rear tires.

The vehicle shuddered and slipped beneath me, and I turned into the skid, hitting the brakes. But nothing I could do worked. It flipped and sent me rolling across the prairie like craps dice thrown by a spastic hand.

When the world stopped cartwheeling around me, I took quick inventory of my injuries. I'd scraped my right knee, banged my left elbow, and gotten a good-sized knot on the back of my skull.

I slapped at my holster.

Empty. The gun had fallen out.

That's when I saw the Latino man in a sharkskin suit staring down at me, pointing a Glock in my face, and realized with absolute certainty that I was going to be shot in the head.

Hammett

"The secret to winning a war," the Instructor said, "is to not be on the side that loses."

Hammett fought annoyance.

The buffalo-horn attack formation, as developed by the legendary Zulu warrior king, Shaka, was still practiced in modern combat. Its effectiveness was the reason Hammett chose to use it.

She, along with Jersey and Speed, would be the chest of the buffalo, leading a direct assault on the prison, which was located under the water filtration plant. Santiago would bring up the rear, watching for any attack from behind. Isaiah and Javier would be the horns, and come in on either side of the prison, trapping any guards on the perimeter.

But moments ago Isaiah had called, claiming he'd been shot in the leg by a sniper. Not a serious wound—a graze from what he suspected was a .22 long rifle—but enough to keep him rooted until he finished up.

Javier, the other horn, also radioed to say he was chasing a guard on an ATV, and thus out of position.

So Hammett's buffalo currently had no horns. And the longer she waited, the more frustrated she became.

She had one arm around Speed's waist, holding on as he steered the ATV. This annoyed her as well. Hammett disliked riding bitch, even though it freed up her hand to shoot if the need arose. Years ago, Hammett had actually visited a psychiatrist because she thought she might have control issues. But she disliked the doctor constantly telling her what to do, so she killed him.

Speed brought the four-wheeler to a gradual stop, then pointed northwest, toward a blocky white two-story structure at the end of the road. The water filtration plant. Hammett raised her binoculars and watched four men run out of the building, sidearms in hands.

"Rush them," she ordered. "Shoot to kill."

Speed hit the throttle. Hammett let the binocs hang around her neck and drew her Supergrade. When they closed within two hundred meters, Speed cut loose with the handlebar-mounted machine gun. Two men dropped in a mélange of bullets and blood. One ran west, and Hammett clamped onto Speed's butt with her knees, brought up her other hand to steady her firearm, and double-tapped the guy into early retirement. The other wisely fled back into the building, slamming a door behind him.

Hammett ordered Speed to stop twenty meters away.

"Guard the entrance. Kill anyone who isn't friendly."

She climbed off the seat and slowly ran her eyes over the building, scanning for cameras. There were two, one on the roof and one above the door. Hammett shot them both. Jersey and Santiago pulled up alongside her and parked.

"Get the door open," Hammett ordered the explosives expert.

While he huffed it over to the entrance, Hammett pointed at Santiago, pointed east, and then made a circle with her finger, signaling him to search the perimeter. She took the west, modifying her buffalo horn in the absence of Javier and Isaiah.

To her left, more rifle shots, a reminder to stay low. She moved in a quick crouch, navigating the outside of the building, avoiding the thick brush that had grown around its foundation. Hammett found another roof camera, dispatched it with a squeeze of the trigger. The building was attached to a concrete retaining wall that extended back a hundred meters, enclosing the four coagulation pools.

There was another gunshot—Santiago, on the opposite side of the plant—and then more shooting from the east, Javier. Hammett followed the length of the wall until she reached the end, and met Santiago at the midpoint.

"One camera," he said, smiling at her. His lips were wet, and he was slightly out of breath. There was something about the guy that Hammett found absolutely repulsive. Certain people had chemistry together. This was the polar opposite of chemistry. Santiago evoked the same reaction as seeing a spider or a poisonous snake.

"You've got some mud on your face," he said.

Santiago slowly reached his free hand up and rubbed his thumb across Hammett's cheek. He had soft, almost feminine, hands, and she fought not to recoil in disgust. In that moment, Hammett almost felt sorry for Fleming; she wouldn't want to be on the receiving end of this nutjob's full attention.

"Thanks," she managed. "You can take your thumb away now."

He did, then ran his tongue across his lower lip. Yuck.

The explosion echoed out over the compound, and Hammett felt it in the soles of her feet. It was followed by gunfire. She led

Santiago back to the front, jogging, and when they arrived there was a charred, black space in the frame where the front door used to be.

"Better too much than too little," Jersey said, grinning.

Hammett cleared the doorway, Santiago backing her up. The guard who'd run inside earlier was there. Or rather, parts of him were. She showed Speed her palm, indicating he stay there, and then led her men into the black site, careful not to step in any blood.

At first glance, the building seemed to be abandoned and neglected, the decor a hodgepodge of dust, broken furniture, and stripped lighting fixtures. But Hammett noticed fresh mud on the floor, boot marks, and didn't need Santiago to tell her where the secret entrance to the prison was. She followed the trail down a hallway and into a room where, as if in some 1940s black-and-white comedy, the footprints disappeared into a solid wall. Hammett saw the overhead camera, mounted in the ceiling corner. Rather than waste a bullet, she jumped up and smashed the lens with the butt of her Supergrade.

Santiago strolled over to a phone on a table. It was one of those old Princess models, olive green, the receiver gone. He pressed a sequence of five numbers on the phone's keypad. When nothing happened, he tried it again.

"They changed the code."

"Open it," she told Jersey, who already had his hands in his pack.

Hammett checked her tablet PC. Fleming was beyond this wall, only a few dozen meters away. The guards hadn't been problematic, which was lucky but also a bit puzzling; she'd expected more resistance.

But it didn't matter. Soon they'd have what they came for. Perhaps with enough time left over to settle things with Chandler, whose blip showed her to be still in Baraboo.

Hammett allowed herself a small grin. For the first time today, things were going her way. Hopefully the trend would continue.

Tequila fired twice, feinted rolling left, then rolled right.

The bullet kicked up dirt to his left, where he would have been.

In the two seconds it took the sniper to work the bolt and aim again, Tequila was on his feet and running.

He knew about leading a target. So he became a target that couldn't be led. Muscle memory kicked in, a routine from decades ago. Tequila clutched the AR-7 to his chest and, sprinting, jumped into the air, doing a one-handed spring off the ground, following it with a forward flip and a tack roll. He somersaulted alongside his backpack and phone, both of which he grabbed as another shot missed him, and then he bellied down into the tall weeds, hidden from view.

Moving slowly, he elbow-crawled past the kennel, casting a watchful eye toward the dogs. They sat by the open gate, tongues lolling, waiting for his next command. He was tempted to send them out after the sniper, but knew several would get shot or killed during the attack, so he let them be.

He punched in a quick text to Chandler, asking where she was, then focused on the open hatch, ten meters away. The problem was that the area right near the entrance was devoid of cover. If Tequila sprinted for it, he'd be out in the open—and easy to lead—for several seconds.

That's when two more guards walked out of the hatch.

Tequila dug out the dog whistle, commanding the hounds to stay. Then he brought up the AR-7, sighting the first guard.

His head burst open like a Gallagher watermelon before Tequila fired a shot. The second ran for the building, hoping to make it to cover in time.

He didn't. The sniper's bullet blew out his heart.

But that gave Tequila the chance he needed to dash for the hatch. He launched into a run, the three seconds it took lasting an eternity, and he envisioned the bull's-eye on his back, involuntarily hunching his shoulders in expectation of the bullet.

The shot never came. Tequila made it to the opening and ducked down behind the stairs.

He waited, listening.

Silence, except for some gunshots elsewhere on the grounds.

He checked his phone, finding nothing, and realized he couldn't wait for Chandler any longer. Especially since she could already be dead. So he descended the stairs and went to search for Fleming on his own.

The hallway was just as he'd seen it on the helicopter monitor. Dark. Rocky. Dirty. An expected setting for a dungeon. He followed the corridor southeast, moving at a light jog, reaching the iron door after four hundred meters or so. He found the toy copter he'd landed there and quickly returned it to its metal case.

The door was heavy, solid, locked. Splitting the remaining hunk of Semtex in two equal pieces, he shaped a charge around the lock and jamb. Then he stuck a detonator in the center and retreated twenty meters, hugging the wall.

The explosion shook the tunnel, dirt falling from the ceiling, dust and smoke obscuring Tequila's view.

The AR-7 at the ready, he waited for the bad guys to come out.

Chandler

"Use every advantage you have," the Instructor said. "There is no such thing as a fair fight. There are only the survivors, and the dead."

The Latino man didn't shoot me in the face. He hesitated, something crossing over his eyes.

Confusion?

No.

Recognition.

"What the fuck are you doing, you idiot?" I said, brusquely pushing his gun aside. "You couldn't tell it was me?"

"I'm…I thought you were back at the water filtration plant."

"Do I look like I'm at the plant?"

I held out my hand, and he helped me up. But the doubt on his face remained. He might have mistaken me for Hammett, but it wouldn't be long before he realized I wasn't my identical sister. My hair was wet, darker looking than my blond dye job, and slicked back with algae water, making it hard to discern color and length right away. But even so, the guy would notice something eventually, maybe my hair, or clothing, or the rough shape I was in, and then once again I'd be looking down the barrel of his Glock.

I had to kill him before it came to that.

"Why didn't you radio?" he asked.

"Do you see a radio? I fell in the damn water." I changed my expression to alarm, pointing suddenly over his shoulder. "Behind you!"

The man turned, but only partway—a pro. I lashed out with a wet boot, slower than I would have liked, catching his wrist but not hard enough to jar loose the gun. As he spun back, I freed the Ghost Hawk from my neck sheath and chopped at his forearm.

Blood sprayed. His Glock went soaring into the weeds. He ignored the slash on his arm, the loss of his gun, and continued his momentum, turning a 180 and swinging the back of his left hand against my cheek before I could duck under it.

I dropped to my left knee, trying to stop the world from spinning, mastering it just in time to see him draw something from his belt.

A balisong.

Also known as the butterfly knife, the balisong is an ancient Filipino weapon that opens in a fan pattern by flicking the wrist and twirling the fingers. Besides offering the simplicity of one-handed operation, balisongs are high on the intimidation meter. Those who know how to use them really enjoy the process, and few things are scarier than getting into a knife fight with someone who likes it.

This man seemed to like it. Though his arm was bleeding, it wasn't slowing down his balisong acrobatics. The knife flipped open and closed, twirling in a silver blur, the *ching-ching-ching* of the blade against the dual metal handles almost as frightening as the sound of a shotgun racking.

His eyes gleamed, and a sick smile spread across his face. "*Le rebanaré abierto, puta*."

I will slice you open, bitch.

I raised the Ghost Hawk, which seemed ridiculously ineffective against my attacker's six-inch blade. He feinted a thrust, then slashed at my eyes. I parried, the clang of metal on metal causing a spark, barely an inch away from having three of my fingers amputated at the knuckles. I leaned away, kicking out my right leg, connecting with the man's knee.

He staggered back.

I attacked, the energy coming from some deep reserve I didn't know I had, throwing myself at him, seeking to hook the Ghost Hawk into an artery.

Every time I went at him, he wasn't there, or he blocked. Small, efficient moves. And he wasn't even striking back. Just taking pleasure in the footwork.

Slash at the neck.

Blocked.

Slash at the inner thigh.

Jumped back.

Slash at the inner arm.

Parried.

Then I was on the defensive, backpedaling as he advanced with the balisong like a fencer, alternating thrusts and lunges with parries and swings. The rule when knife fighting is to watch the eyes—the eyes betray the attack. But the blows were coming so fast I had to rely on pure muscle memory, barely dodging and blocking in time. And besides, his eyes gave nothing away. Even in the fury of the attack, they stayed focused on mine with an unnerving calm.

More gunshots in the distance. Another slash, and I felt a sting across the back of my hand. A cut opened like I'd been unzipped, speckling my face with blood. This man had skills, along with strength, stamina, and a superior weapon.

I was going to lose.

I got under the next swing, kicked at his crotch, and right after I connected, turned tail and sprinted. Besides his tailored suit, my opponent sported soft-soled Italian shoes. Fashionable, but not the ideal footwear for running through prairieland.

I sheathed my Ghost Hawk and zigzagged my way around scrub brush and construction debris to the building in the distance, the old oleum plant. It could offer me places to hide, and opportunities to get away. The numbness of the anesthetic was wearing off, the tearing pain of Lund poking around in my belly beginning to return. I didn't know how bad it would get, but this wasn't a situation in which I could let pain incapacitate me. I shoved that mental signal in a file cabinet with all the others I chose to ignore, and slammed it closed.

My eyes stayed on my target, the building, but I could hear my pursuer behind me. His footfalls. His breathing. He was catching up.

I wasn't going to lose him. He was too fast. That meant I needed to find the proper area to fight.

I reached the crest of a short incline, the building coming into full view—dilapidated, part of it torn down and bumping up against a mound that was three meters in height and flattened on top. It looked like a multicolored dirt hill, which didn't make sense until I noticed the grinder.

The construction grinder was a monster, taking up the entire flatbed trailer of a semi truck. A long conveyor belt stretched from the grinder to the top of the debris mound, where it deposited the pulverized rubble. But I wasn't focused on that. I was focused on the truck's cab. Often construction workers leave keys in vehicles, especially on private sites. After all, who is going to break into a fenced and guarded army-owned compound and steal a thirty-ton industrial grinder?

I headed for the thirty-ton industrial grinder, intending to steal it. If I could make it inside the cab and lock the doors, that would buy me enough time to figure out how to start it up and drive away.

Not the best plan ever, but it beat going toe to toe with a knife-wielding killer.

Focusing on my target, I shifted all of my reserve energy into my legs, running hard as I could, blocking out everything except that truck.

Twenty meters away…

Fifteen…

I could sense my pursuer right on my heels, and part of me anticipated, expected, the tackle that would end with his knife in my throat.

Ten meters away, I locked my eyes on the driver's-side door handle.

I reached out a hand, imagining pulling it open and diving inside.

Assuming it wasn't locked.

Assuming he wouldn't pin me to the truck like an hors d'oeuvre on a toothpick.

Five meters, and I made a judgment call. Instead of going for the door, I leaped onto the hood of the truck, *Dukes of Hazzard* style, sliding on my belly and turning onto my hip, landing on the passenger side and snagging the door handle.

Open. I got in, slapping down the lock button just as my attacker went for the handle. I slid into the driver's seat, locked that side, then did a quick scan of the dashboard.

This wasn't a normal truck. This was Super Truck. There were so many controls, switches, and knobs that it would have confused a NASA engineer. I managed to locate the ignition, a grin breaking out across my face when I saw the key inside it, and then I hit the brake and clutch and started that bad boy up.

I popped it into first gear, released the clutch, and gave it gas.

Nothing happened.

More gas, and though I heard the engine gunning, the truck wasn't moving at all.

I checked the side mirror and spotted the problem. The truck had pneumatic lifters on either side, raising it up off the ground. That prevented anyone from driving it off while the grinder was on and the conveyor belt still attached.

OK. I needed to raise the braces. I eyed the control panel again, squinting at labels covered with a healthy layer of grime.

A knock on the glass ripped my attention away from the controls.

The Latino was standing by the door, smiling. His cool demeanor remained, and his hair still appeared combed. The only indication we'd been fighting was the blood on his arm.

"I think perhaps we got off on the wrong foot," he said.

I began pressing random buttons on the dashboard.

"I am Javier. At first, I mistook you for my present employer. But I'm sure you knew that. You must be sisters."

The truck began to shake, the whole cab vibrating. I'd turned on the conveyor belt leading to the debris pile.

Javier tried the lock, said, "I just want to talk."

"Kind of busy here."

"What is your name, señorita?"

I hit a few more switches, and the conveyor belt reversed direction, as if trying to take debris from the mound and pull it into the truck bed.

"It is so rare to find an equally matched opponent. Surely you know this. I cannot think of the last time someone's blade even touched me." He held up his bloody arm. "Aren't you even a little bit curious?"

I wasn't happy with his nonchalance. A moment ago we'd been in mortal combat, and now he was chatting me up like we were poolside at a singles resort. "About what?"

"Which of us would be standing at the end."

"You've got the better weapon."

He reached into his jacket and removed a second balisong. A millisecond later it was open, the point tapping on the window. He was just as good lefty as righty.

"I could loan you this. But you would have to promise me not to get blood on it."

Even worse than someone who knew how to use a knife was someone who wanted to show you how much he knew.

"I'll pass."

His face darkened, the sly smile becoming a tight line.

"If you do not want to play my game, we shall play another one."

I went back to fiddling with the buttons and knobs. The next time I looked over, he was gone.

I pressed a green button that started blinking. Then the trunk began to shake, and a godawful noise cranked up behind me.

Great. I'd just started the industrial grinder. The red button beside the green one was probably the kill switch. I reached for it—

Something hit the windshield. I flinched and looked up in time to see a piece of cinder block bounce off the glass—thankfully it was shatterproof. Javier was standing on the hood. He gave a little wave, then hoisted the chunk of concrete over his head and brought it down again, making a long white scratch.

I punched the red button as Javier continued to batter the windshield, but it only had the effect of ramping up the grind speed.

Fuck this.

I need a new—

The windshield popped out of the frame in a complete sheet, slid up the dash, and came to rest in my lap. Javier climbed through, riding on top of it, pressing me back into the seat. His face less than an inch from mine, our lips separated only by glass.

He winked, then gave the window a quick kiss.

I reached over and popped the lock, pulled the handle, and hauled myself out the passenger door. Hit the ground, rolled onto my feet, saw Javier scrambling out of the cab behind me.

I made a quick survey of my surroundings as I tugged the Ghost Hawk out of my neck sheath.

Heard the *ching-ching-ching* of Javier's butterfly.

Straight ahead, only two meters away, loomed the debris pile.

I accelerated toward it and leaped onto a broken piece of plywood, felt it shift, then settle underneath me.

I glanced back.

Javier had stopped at the foot of the debris pile and was looking up at me with his head tilted.

"This is uncivilized," he said over the growl of the grinder. "Climbing around on this dirty mound like animals."

"Then feel free to stay down there."

"These are eight-hundred-dollar shoes. Let me tell you something." He pointed the balisong's knifepoint at me. "If I ruin these coming after you, I will make your death infinitely more unpleasant."

"Even more unpleasant than your constant yapping?"

His face got darker.

I scrambled up the gentle slope. Unsurprisingly, it was made up of all the things that made a building, only ground up into small pieces. Wood, metal, glass, plastic. Wires and pipes. Old furniture and fixtures. Solid enough to hold my weight, but occasionally a foot sank in up to the ankle.

I glanced back and saw Javier climbing toward me on all fours, both of his knives clenched between his teeth, points out, like a furious, charging tusked animal. I made it to the top of the pile, looking around for a stick or pipe or something more substantial than the Ghost Hawk. All that stood out was a small chunk of wood, no wider than it was long.

I snatched it up, then turned to face my tormentor.

Javier stopped when he was several feet below.

He looked at my two-by-four, said, "Seriously? You just aren't any fun at all."

Then one of his butterflies stuck in the wood.

I hadn't seen him throw it. Hadn't even seen his arm move.

Pure dumb luck it hadn't gone through my rib cage. Or had he hit what he was really aiming for?

"Now pull out the goddamn knife and let's have us a proper fight, no?"

I yanked it from the board and switched hands. My training played through my head like old, flickering movies. I knew how to fight with knives. I was good at it.

But obviously so was Javier.

He leaped nimbly, and then we were both standing on the summit of the debris pile. The sun was almost kissing the horizon, casting a soft orange glow and making our shadows gigantic. The air felt almost still, and a hawk screamed overhead. I assumed a fighting stance, legs spread, knees bent, arms wide.

He lunged.

I parried and countered, metal clinging and sparking.

He blocked and thrust.

I leaned away, chopping with the Ghost Hawk.

He parried.

This all repeated five times until we each stepped away, neither at an advantage.

It had all happened in less than three seconds.

"That would have been a sweet YouTube video," Javier said.

Suddenly my left leg was bleeding. Not a serious cut, but deep enough to hurt.

He smiled, the edges of his mouth curling up like a pit viper's.

"That is the thing with knives," he said. "When the blade is sharp and the slice is fast, you don't even know you have been—"

Suddenly his nose was bleeding. He staggered back, eyes wide.

"That's the thing with kicks," I said, bringing my foot back for a follow-up.

He jabbed his balisong at my neck. It was the first time I'd seen the attack coming—a minor narrowing of his eyes. He was angry and couldn't hide it.

I got low and, using his own momentum, scissor-kicked his legs and clamped down. It brought him to his knees, but he grabbed hold of my arm as he went, and we both tumbled down the gradual incline of the debris pile, coming to an abrupt stop faster than we should have.

And then, instant acceleration.

For a crazy moment I felt like I'd been thrown from a moving car and was bouncing along the asphalt. But the rumbling sound, and the sensation of the road moving in the same direction I was, made the realization sink in pretty quickly.

We were on the conveyor belt, moving at a very quick clip.

I tried to kick Javier off my ankle, which his bulk pinned to the ribbed slats of the belt. He was too heavy to budge. I jack-knifed into a sitting position, raising my knife, and then we were both airborne, falling into the bed of the truck, into the jaws of the industrial grinder.

Fleming

"The secrets you possess may risk lives," said the Instructor. "Many lives. You alone have to make the call. Are those secrets worth more than your life?"

Fleming's hand trembled. She felt the bite of the blade at her throat, the blood trickling down her collarbone.

"Do it," she ordered herself.

For all the people she'd killed, both directly and indirectly, Fleming still considered herself a humanitarian. On the surface, that seemed to indicate a lack of self-awareness at best, psychotic delusion at worst. But the assignments Fleming had taken as a field agent, and those where she'd been Chandler's handler, ultimately benefited mankind. Certain people were harmful to society, as cancer harmed a body. Corrupt politicos, fanatical jihadists, murderous traitors, human traffickers, genocidal scientists, mad dictators, sexual predators—these were bad people. Fleming cut them out of the world as a surgeon excised a malignant tumor.

There had been missions in which Fleming had weighed her personal safety against the safety of the innocent, and she always protected the innocent over her own skin.

Now, locked in her head, was information that could kill millions of innocent people. Strong as Fleming was, that information would eventually be forced from her. And those who had the information would use it.

Suicide was the right thing to do. Fleming's death would protect many.

She closed her eyes.

She put more pressure on the blade.

She let her final breath hiss through her clenched teeth.

There was a genuine fear of death—only psychos didn't fear death. But Fleming's resolve was stronger than her fear. It wasn't even a real choice. One woman's life for millions.

Except…

It wasn't one woman's life.

It was *two* women's lives.

There was a possibility Malcolm hadn't been lying. That Chandler was on-site.

Chandler didn't know what Fleming knew. Chandler would be tortured, and killed. But she had nothing to reveal, no secrets to share. The world would be safe.

So it would be OK if Chandler died.

It would be OK.

Right?

Fleming opened her eyes. Tears streamed down her cheeks, mingling with the blood on her neck. She thought about her sister.

A sister who would never give up on her.

A sister who would never desert her.

A sister who would never choose the easy way out.

A sister she loved.

If there was a chance to save Chandler, Fleming had to take it. No matter how many lives it risked.

Because that's what love is.

Fleming opened her fingers and let the scalpel clatter to the floor. She turned to the tray and picked out weapons small enough to carry: a fillet knife with a good-sized blade, a rectangular pack of double-edged razor blades, and an ice pick. She tossed them all to the floor, then swung her legs over the gurney's edge.

"Hold on, Sis," she whispered. "I'll be right there."

Taking a deep breath, Fleming pushed off. She hit the floor with a hard smack, fire shooting up her legs and through her hips, a cry breaking her lips. For a few seconds she lay there, trying to gather her strength, hoping nothing was broken, willing the ache to be merely bruises layered on bruises. Refusing to give in to the pain, Fleming rolled to her stomach, her arms straight, holding her torso erect in a pose a yoga instructor would call upward-facing dog. Then, using her arms and hands, she started walking forward, her useless legs trailing behind.

The concrete was cold and rasped her wounds like sixty-grit sandpaper on raw skin. Her muscles seized with shivers, probably the combination of hypothermia and the aftereffects of adrenaline. She picked up the knife and pick with her good hand and wedged the package of razor blades under the palm end of one of her finger splints. The ice pick handle went into her mouth.

Focusing on the door, she concentrated on moving inch by inch, foot by foot, until she'd cleared the heavy steel portal. The room where she'd been held was at the end of a narrow dead-end hall, half a dozen doors on either side, the far end elbowing to the right. She couldn't hear anything but the distant hum of an electric fan and her own breathing. The space smelled strongly of Malcolm's burned flesh, with an undernote of the same dank mildew of the room where Fleming had been imprisoned.

She eyed the bastard's body. Fleming wasn't sure if he was dead or not and realized with disgust that she hoped he wasn't. Let him live with the pain of burned flesh, the probable blindness from the cattle prod to his eyes. The only thing she regretted was that his clothing was so scorched, she couldn't strip it off him. It would be nice to not have to drag herself around this hellhole naked.

She briefly considered going back into the room and taking the guard's clothing, but she couldn't make herself cross back over that threshold. Fleming had gotten out of that cell, the place she was sure she'd die, and she couldn't face going back. Not for any reason. So instead, she concentrated on the rooms branching off the hall.

She doubted she'd find a map lying around, with a key showing which cell might hold Chandler, but she might be able to score some keys.

Fleming inched up to Malcolm, the knife ready in her fist in case he made a move, not willing to risk even the remote possibility that something would go wrong and she'd fall under his control again.

He was breathing, labored and ragged. But an unpleasant glance at the burns on his chest proved he didn't have much longer to live. His injuries were too severe.

Fleming found the keys on his belt. Taking them in hand along with her weapons, she dragged herself past him, along the dirt floor, and to the first heavy, steel door. Reaching up, she unlocked it, and pulled.

The sucker didn't move.

She tried again, but it was no use. The thing was too heavy, and not only did she have no leverage but, after all she'd been through, her strength was lacking, even in her upper body.

When she'd been in her cell, Fleming had been able to hear sounds—the recorded screams, the movement outside the door. The doors were heavy as hell, but they weren't soundproof.

The guards would be coming. If she was sitting here silently in the hall, she would be captured again.

But if she could find her sister…

Fleming had to risk it. She spit the ice pick onto the floor and yelled, "Chandler!"

Silence answered.

She put all her strength into the yell. "Chandler, I have keys! Where are you?"

Nothing.

Fleming propped herself up on her hip, shivering in the bright light and dank chill, her mind racing. There was a chance her sister wasn't here, that Malcolm had been lying about capturing her. There was also a chance that Chandler was already dead.

"Chandler!" she screamed again, as loud as she could manage.

"Fleming!"

But it wasn't Chandler. This voice belonged to someone else.

Someone Fleming knew intimately.

And it originated just a few doors away.

Lund

Lund checked his watch for what had to be the eightieth time in the past twenty minutes. Still not time to meet Chandler, but the crack of gunfire—and worse, several explosions—made his pulse accelerate and sweat coat his back. Max and Bo jigged a little, picking up his nervousness, ready to bolt.

He patted his gelding and crooned to Bo, but it did no good. How could it? His voice sounded tight even to his own ears. To the sensitive horses, he must have seemed in a full-bore panic.

Lund forced his breath to slow and rolled his shoulders, trying to loosen up. He'd only known Chandler for a short time, but it was obvious she knew what she was doing and was used to handling this type of danger. He recognized the confident calm in her, the same vibe given off by veteran firefighters and cops. Hell, usually given off by him, too.

Lund had to trust she knew what she was doing. But he kept seeing the stubborn woman willing to stick a scalpel into her own belly. Recklessness didn't inspire confidence.

"Good evening, sir."

The voice came from behind him, several yards away. He turned to see the tan button-down and dark jacket and pants of a state park ranger.

Shit.

Normally when gunfire and explosions were blasting around him, he'd be grateful to see the authorities. But Chandler had warned him about calling the police, and after all he'd seen, he believed her. This park ranger's curiosity and the inevitable cops he'd call in would only complicate things and cost lives. If this really was a black site on US soil, the powers that be couldn't afford to let anyone know about its existence. That included park rangers. That included cops. That included him and everyone he knew.

Lund faced the ranger. "Nice night, isn't it? Although I hear it's supposed to rain tomorrow."

"Sir, horses aren't allowed in this park."

Lund knew that, but feigned surprise. "Oh. I guess I didn't realize..."

"You'll have to take them out immediately. And if you parked a white—"

A spurt of gunfire erupted below. The ranger reached for the radio on his belt.

"It's a training drill," Lund said.

The man's eyebrows arched, as if he didn't believe a word.

"That's why I'm here. With the horses. I'm an observer. I should have stayed near the fence line, I know, but the view is better up here. And the blanks they're shooting were making the horses nervous."

The ranger squinted into the sun, low in the western sky. Hair silver and face lined, he looked like he'd been on the job for a while, maybe nearing retirement. Lund would like to think those extra years would make him willing to let a training drill pass. But judging from the skepticism etched into the man's expression, it seemed those years had simply made him harder to fool.

"Was this reported to local authorities?"

"I'm not sure. You know the army. They report to their superiors, and the rest of us might as well not exist."

"Do you have some identification?"

Lund reached for his wallet and offered the man his driver's license and card identifying him as a fire inspector for the county.

"You're not with the army."

"I'm here on behalf of the county, making sure things don't get out of hand."

The ranger paused, glanced out at the ammo plant, and then back to Lund. "Why wasn't my office notified of this?"

Lund forced a shrug he hoped looked casual. "Like I said, you know the army. They're in their own little world sometimes."

"Does the county sheriff know?"

"I'm not sure."

"Why don't I give them a call, find out?"

Not the response Lund was hoping for. "I did talk to the police chief of Lake Loyal, Valerie Ryker. She knew about the drill. Since it's Sunday, you might be able to reach her more easily than the sheriff."

He was taking a leap on that one. Val didn't know anything about what was going on. He just hoped she would back him up.

The ranger seemed to consider the idea. Then he pulled out a cell phone out of a case on his belt.

"I doubt she'll be in the office this late," Lund said. "But I, uh, have her home number, if it's really necessary."

"It's necessary."

Double shit.

Lund pulled out his phone. He called up his directory and selected Val's number, trying not to focus on the fact that his finger was shaking.

He and Val had been through a lot, and more than anything, he wanted to believe she'd trust him and wait until later for his explanation. But there were a lot of things he wanted to believe about Val. A lot of things he wanted, period. And if he'd learned anything over recent months, it was that he couldn't control the choices another person made.

All he could do was make his own decisions accordingly and hope things worked out.

Two rings, and Val's voice came on the line. "Lund? Do you have the horses?"

Of course her first question would be about the horses.

"Yeah. I'm at Badger Ammo, observing the training exercises. A park ranger here wants to know that local law enforcement is aware of what's going on."

"What *is* going on?"

"I made the mistake of riding too far into the park instead of staying at the fence line."

"I have no idea what you're talking about."

"I know. They should have told the park rangers. Someone could think there's a dangerous situation and call the authorities for no reason, waste time and taxpayer money. Someone could even get hurt, as a result."

"Have you been drinking?"

Dammit, Val. Figure out what I need. "He just wants to confirm with you that everything is all right."

"Everything better be all right. What are you doing with the horses?"

"Here's the ranger." Lund handed the man his cell and held his breath.

The ranger brought the phone to his ear, his eyes still narrowed, still focused on Lund. "Chief Ryker?"

Lund tried to read his expressions, but the guy had a face like a mannequin. He made a mental note that if he ever ran into this guy at the Doghouse Tavern, he should never play him in a game of poker.

The moment stretched. Lund patted his mount, for his own nerves as well as the horse's.

"All right. Yes. Absolutely." The ranger clapped the phone shut and handed it back to Lund.

Lund swallowed, throat dry. Either Val had backed him up, or the shit was about to hit an industrial-strength fan. Either way, he needed to know. "So now you see, they did notify someone, at least."

The man offered the same narrow stare. "Yeah, I see. I see plenty."

Chandler

"Fear is a gift," the Instructor said. "Use it."

Hours ago—though it seemed much longer—I'd been gripped and shaken by raw animal panic when my arm was stuck between railroad ties as a train approached and a nut named Rochester tried to kill me.

I might have said that ranked as the worst fear I'd ever experienced, until the moment I fell into an industrial construction grinder as a nut named Javier tried to kill me.

The drop onto the flatbed of the truck was a tiny bunny hop, and we'd both been dropped onto the spinning screws that stretched out twelve meters in length and five meters side to side. Four metal walls kept us, and the debris, from spilling off the edges, trapping us in a giant hopper.

The screws themselves were long spinners, segmented with dozens of thick steel flywheels— high-torque, low-speed shredders that spun in opposite directions. Bladed, intersecting rollers. They caught debris, pinching it together, then forced it through the floor of the chipper. Once they grabbed something—steel, fabric, leather, wood, flesh—they shredded it to hamburger.

I landed feet first onto a small, churning pile of concrete, and the blades spun under the soles of my feet.

Luckily, they were wide enough to stand on.

Unluckily, they were turning in opposite directions.

During training at Hydra, I'd once had to play lumberjack and balance on a floating log. This was like balancing on two logs at once, one going clockwise and one going counter.

I pulled up my left foot, bringing it to my right, trying to find my balance. A piece of rebar sacked me in my leg, then got pulled down into the churning morass. I almost tipped over, dropping the butterfly knife, watching it bounce once, twice, on the blades and then get crunched into pieces and disappear.

Movement, to my side.

Javier had also adopted my log-rolling technique, hips swaying and feet moving in rhythm, looking oddly like a meringue dancer. He was facing me, less than a two meters away.

And he hadn't dropped his knife.

Some plywood floated across the bed between us, then the blades caught it and chewed it up, spitting splinters and sawdust.

I chanced a quick look behind me, saw that the wall of the hopper was two steps—two rows—back. It was as high as my shoulders. On a flat surface, I could vault right over it. That would be trickier while balancing on spinning, bladed wheels. If I tripped, or fell, or missed, then anything at all—a bit of clothing, an edge of rubber sole, a finger, a lock of hair—could get caught in the blades and pull me through a moment later.

My breath coming out in sprinter puffs, I eyed my jump to the next roller, trying to work out the landing in my head, since it was going in the opposite direction and would mess up my momentum.

Javier, on the other hand, didn't seem to be focused on escaping this swirling death pit. Proving himself every bit of the psychopath I guessed he was, Javier chose to go after me rather than save himself. He jumped in my direction, feet hitting off-center, arms pinwheeling wildly before he found his footing.

He was now close enough to stab me.

Javier's eyes locked on mine, and he knew I knew, and that brought out his snakelike grin.

He slashed with his balisong.

I blocked with the Ghost Hawk, then caught his wrist with my free hand and tugged, hoping to yank him off his feet.

Instead I pulled him onto the same roller I was balancing on.

I backed up, my feet in constant motion, hoping I didn't step on anything that would trip me up but unwilling to look because I was concentrating on Javier. I had a fleeting racist thought: if Javier were white, he'd be dead by now. White guys are clumsy. But Latinos seem to have some kind of inner rhythm and balance, and his footwork was fancy enough to get him on *Dancing with the Stars*, assuming the show accepted sadistic mercs.

Face sweating, he edged closer to me, looking more like a bullfighter than a hoofer. Unsteady as we both were, we each kept our knife hands extended and more or less unwavering.

"You are something special, señorita. You move very well. In different circumstances, I would have enjoyed a sensual *bachata* with you."

"I could see doing that with you," I said, "if I'd swallowed poison and needed to vomit."

He took three quick steps toward me, and I went backward, losing my balance and falling to the side. I managed to place my other foot on a swirling mound of hard clay, and was able to spring off it just enough to land on a flywheel a meter away from Javier, and right next to the hopper edge.

"You look tired, *chica*. Why don't you let me—"

I'd had enough of Javier's obnoxious jabbering, so I tugged the Ghost Hawk off my pinkie and threw it at his head. It wasn't big or sharp enough to kill, but it did what I'd intended it to do; knocked the *bailador* off balance and onto his ass.

He swore in rapid-fire, near-hysterical Spanish, all four limbs a blur as he tried to stay on top of the blades, and I leaped to the wall and chinned myself to the top. I turned back at Javier.

"So now we know," I said, "which one of us is left standing."

He screamed, "*Puta!*" as the grinder grabbed his right foot.

I climbed out of the hopper and headed toward the rendezvous point, hoping Tequila was still alive, hoping Lund hadn't been discovered, hoping it wasn't too late to save Fleming.

Javier had thought I was Hammett. That meant Hammett was close.

And that bitch scared the crap out of me.

Hammett

"Sun Tzu was only partially right," the Instructor said. "All war is based on deception. But so is everything else."

After Jersey blew open the door, Hammett checked with her men.

Isaiah was still in position, guarding the rear entrance of the prison.

"A little guy got inside. Moves like the Road Runner, shoots like Wild Bill Hickok."

She told him to stay dug in, then tried Javier and got no reply.

Hammett didn't like to assume things. She preferred her intel to be black and white. But if Javier was as good as he thought he was, guards wouldn't have taken him out.

So who did it? Her boss?

Hammett didn't trust her employer, because she didn't trust anyone. Human beings were liars, cheaters, double-crossers, and operated primarily out of self-interest. If Hammett could have cloned herself, she wouldn't trust the clone.

But taking out Javier didn't make any sense. As far as Hammett knew, her boss had the same agenda that she did: get Fleming. He wouldn't have any tactical reason to take out her men before that goal was reached.

Which meant he already had Fleming, or…

There was another player in the game.

Once again, Hammett looked at her tablet computer, searching for the blips to find her sisters. Fleming was still nearby, in the prison. Chandler was still in Baraboo. Neither appeared to have moved.

Hammett drummed her fingers along her belly, where her own GPS tracking chip was located. She zoomed in on herself as tight as the satellite allowed. Then she began to walk around the room.

Her blinking dot moved. It was such a slight distance that it was tough to notice. But Hammett noticed.

Next she magnified Fleming. Her dot was also moving, barely a snail's pace, but movement nonetheless.

Something to do with the geosynchronous orbit of the satellite? Some software malfunction? Some sort of delay?

Hammett stayed perfectly still.

Her dot didn't move. But Fleming's still did.

Next she focused on Chandler.

She watched for movement. She watched closely.

Chandler's dot stayed in the exact same place. So she was either sleeping, or dead, or…

Or she'd managed to cut out her tracking chip.

Hammett felt a pleasurable warmth radiate out of her body. Though it didn't happen often, she recognized the emotion as happiness. She got on the radio.

"One of the enemy looks like me," she told her men. "She's in the area, attempting to grab the target before we do. She is armed and extremely dangerous. If she's taken alive, you will all get a bonus equal to double the agreed-upon pay."

Tequila

No guards had come to greet him. Tequila stayed put, waiting for something to happen. Eventually, something did.

The explosion came from the south, large enough to kick up the dust in the hallway and get in Tequila's eyes. He wiped it off.

Chandler had some explosives in her pack. Was that her? Or was it the party who had been shooting at him? Either way, it no longer made much sense to crouch in the corner, waiting for action. The action, whatever it might be, was ahead of him. So Tequila moved forward.

The iron door had been blown off one hinge, the other twisted and fused by Tequila's Semtex. He used both hands and all of his strength, and it still took almost a full minute to pry it open wide enough to slip through. It lead to another dimly lit hallway, this one lined with cell doors, complete with waist-high slats for meal delivery.

He went to the nearest one, found it unlocked. AR-7 at the ready, he sidled up next to it and pushed it open, peeking around the jamb. Too dark to see far inside, he dug a mini Maglite from his pocket and swept the interior. The cell was empty except for a dirty cot and a flimsy, plastic bucket.

Tequila eyed the hallway again. One down. Eleven to go, then a bend in the hallway.

He moved on to the second cell.

Fleming

"There are no heroes on the battlefield," the Instructor said. "Only those who survive, and those who die."

"It's me," Fleming said, dragging herself across the floor to the familiar voice. "Are you injured?"

"Been better. You?"

"That makes two of us." She got to the correct door and stabbed the key into the lock. As with the previous door, the key turned. And as with the previous door, it was too heavy and she was too weak to open it.

"Can you help me? I've got the key, but it won't budge."

"It's a magnetic lock. Needs a card."

For the first time, Fleming noticed the protruding gizmo alongside the doorjamb. It looked like a swiper for credit cards. How could she have missed that?

"You either need to find the card, or kill the power."

"Is Chandler here?" Fleming asked.

"I don't know. I haven't been here long. Are you alone?"

Fleming hesitated a moment before giving in to trust. "Yes."

"You need to get out of here."

"I won't leave Chandler. Or you."

"Think, Fleming. You're smart. Be smart about this."

"You didn't leave me."

"No offense, but I don't see that there's much you can do. Are you in a chair?"

Fleming bit her lower lip. "No."

"I heard engines when they brought me here. ATVs. Could you ride one?"

"Maybe."

"Find one. Get out. Are you armed?"

Fleming had a fillet knife, a scalpel, and a pack of razor blades. Was that armed? Maybe those weapons were formidable in Chandler's deadly hands. But in hers?

"I may know where the card is."

"Fuck the card. Save yourself."

But Fleming was already pulling herself back to Malcolm, her body flapping behind her like a broken sea lion, so near the point of total exhaustion that halfway there she passed out, only to revive when her head bounced off the floor.

Finally at Malcolm's side once again, the smell of burned meat choking her throat, she forced a hand into his scorched pants pocket, causing him to moan in unconscious pain. Her fingers locked on to something warm and flat, and she tugged out the magnetic key card—

—warped and partially melted from the fire.

She knew it wouldn't work. It was so bent, it wouldn't even swipe through the card reader. To prove it, she went back to her own cell and gave it a try.

The card got stuck halfway in the slot. When she put more pressure on it, the plastic snapped in half.

Peering back into that terrible cell, Fleming's eyes zeroed in on the guard. Unlike Malcolm's, the guard's injuries had proved fatal; the prodigious pool of blood around his cracked skull was testimony to that. Much as she didn't want to go back in there, one hand followed the other, and soon she was patting down the dead man's uniform, searching for another key card.

He didn't have one.

Fleming bit her lower lip, fighting the urge to scream. Even if Chandler were here, Fleming wouldn't be able to save her. It was doubtful she could even save herself.

"I was hoping to find you here."

A shot of pure terror took the express route up Fleming's spine, making her yelp, and she turned to face the menacing figure blocking the doorway.

Chandler

"Everyone has a limit," the Instructor said. "Eventually, we all shut down. Part of my job is to extend your limit beyond that of anyone else."

I ran as best I could. I was exhausted, light-headed and heavy-footed, aching in so many places that they all blended together. I pressed on, fighting all the signals my brain and body were sending me, demanding I rest.

Marathon runners call it "hitting the wall." Spies call it survival.

My first instinct was to go for the ATV I'd flipped. But Javier could have radioed in those coordinates, which would make it a likely ambush spot. So instead I headed for the rendezvous point with Tequila. If he was still alive and still had weapons, we could always fight our way to the four-wheeler.

I went west, toward the setting sun, keeping my knees high so my toes didn't catch on underbrush. If I tripped and went down, I might not be able to get back up.

Breathing through my mouth, filling my lungs with each intake of air, my concentration wandered to my lousy childhood and lousy young adulthood. From the middle of elementary school on, I was what school shrinks called "antisocial." I didn't play well with others, so they said. They confused my inability to form long-lasting relationships with some sort of internal defect. In reality, it was a survival mechanism. After my parents died, I couldn't find anyone worth having a relationship with. I'd gotten burned a lot, to the point where I equated kindness with deception. So instead of meaningful friendships with generous people, I hung out with losers because it made things easier when they inevitably betrayed me.

I wasn't a sociopath. I was just extremely unlucky.

My pace slowed, eyelids drooping, and I bit the inside of my cheek to stay on task. Battling fatigue, I tried to get my muscles to work using sheer will, since the glycogen reserves were gone.

But will only took me another twenty meters, and then my foot caught a root and I face-planted onto the ground.

I lay there for a moment, breath rasping.

The moment stretched.

I tried to get up, but my arms and legs wouldn't work right. I'd never been so tired. Crazy as it sounds, my brain tried to convince me that it would be OK to take a little nap.

I closed my eyes, my will depleted. In my mind's eye, I saw Kaufmann.

Kaufmann was my parole officer. He was the only person I'd ever been able to trust, to love. Too recently, too soon, he died. And on the heels of losing him, I'd discovered that my long-time handler, Jacob, was really my sister, Fleming. We'd worked together for years, and even before we met face-to-face, before we knew we were sisters, we'd shared a bond.

But for me it was more than that.

I'm sure the shrink I'd been court-ordered to see as a teen would say I was projecting the guilt and anger and pain of my recent loss onto Fleming, but that wasn't all of it.

When I looked into Fleming's eyes, I didn't just see my sister. I saw myself. The self who could love and trust others. The self who was loved and trusted in return. The self I had once buried along with my parents, who had died again with Kaufmann.

The self I wanted so desperately to be.

I wasn't just here to save my sister. I was here to save me, too.

I opened my eyes.

I pushed up against the ground.

I got my feet underneath me.

I started running again. And I wasn't going to stop until I'd saved us both.

Tequila

The woman on the cell floor was naked, dirty, bleeding. Her ruined legs told horror stories Tequila couldn't even imagine. When she turned around, he realized it was Fleming—her face was a carbon copy of Chandler's.

Fleming's expression of surprise quickly morphed into fierce determination, and a blurred moment later Tequila felt a sharp sting in his belly.

He looked down to see an ice pick sticking in his abs, and felt an overwhelming respect for this woman. Respect on a deep, core level. Fleming was a fighter, and he immediately identified with that. Even more, he was impressed by it. The measure of a human being is what finally makes them give up.

Tequila saw the burned man in the hallway, and the dead man in the cell. It appeared this woman didn't know how to give up.

He quickly spread out his hands, letting the AR-7 swing to his side on a strap. "I'm with Chandler. We're here to rescue you."

Fleming's hard expression remained. Tequila noticed she had a fillet knife in her hand, and he didn't want that sticking in him too.

"Who are you?"

"My name is Tequila. I met your sister through a mutual friend. You're at the Badger Ammo plant in Baraboo, Wisconsin, at a black site. Chandler and I had different entry points. I lost communication with her a while ago. Please don't stab me again."

Her expression didn't change. "How do I know you're telling the truth?"

"Chandler said you were her handler. She knew you as Jacob."

"I need more."

Tequila considered it, then said, "She's a stubborn pain in the ass, and almost didn't take my help because she thought I was too old and too short."

"Why did she change her mind?"

"My hand-to-hand is better than hers."

Fleming nodded, apparently coming to a conclusion. "Your ear is bleeding."

"Sniper. Apparently we're not the only party here for you. I'm going to take out this ice pick, OK?"

Tequila slowly pulled the weapon from his belly, where it hadn't penetrated his hard abdominal muscles more than an inch. He gave it a slow, underhanded toss back to Fleming, who managed to snatch it out of the air with her bandaged hand.

"We have to get out of here, Fleming."

"I can't walk." She said it as a statement, not as a complaint.

"You can ride on my back. If I do anything you don't like, you can stab me again."

"It didn't do much good before."

"If it makes you feel better, I'll probably have a scar."

Fleming's face softened slightly.

"I'm taking off my coat," Tequila said, carefully slipping it off his shoulders. "Please put it on. Your nudity is…distracting me."

It must have been the right thing to say, because Fleming reached her hand out for it. Tequila watched her struggle into it, not bothering with snapping up the front.

"There's a man, a few cells over—we need to take him with us," she said. "But there's no key card."

"I have explosives in my pack." He shrugged it off and gave it to her. "Put it on. I can't wear both of you."

This time Tequila saw a small smile pass over Fleming's face, and for the first time he realized why he was there. It wasn't for the money, or because he owed Jack Daniels a favor, or because he saw a kindred spirit in Chandler.

He was there to rescue Fleming, because this woman was worth rescuing.

Fleming

"Trust your gut," the Instructor said. "It usually knows better than you do."

Fleming dug into the pack and removed a chunk of plastic explosive, expertly inserting a blasting cap. She placed it and the remote detonator to the side as Tequila knelt next to her, resting his butt on his heels.

"Your name is really Tequila?"

He nodded, handing her the AR-7. She slung it, and the backpack, over her shoulders.

"Sorry I stabbed you, Tequila."

Tequila glanced around the cell. "I'd say I got off easy. Why didn't you aim for my throat?"

Fleming wondered that as well. When he appeared in the doorway, she'd had every reason to believe he was a threat, and had reacted accordingly. But some bit of instinct had deterred her from a killing blow.

She was grateful for that foresight.

As he helped her onto his back, she was also grateful her stubborn pain-in-the-ass sister had agreed to allow Tequila to help. Hopelessness had become possibility.

Fleming wrapped her arms around his throat—jeez, the guy had a neck like a tree trunk—and he gently folded Fleming's legs around his waist and held her ankles locked together in a single, callused hand. Then he stood up as if she weighed nothing. Tequila smelled like sweat and gunpowder and blood and a tiny trace of sandalwood soap, and he looked like a GI Joe doll come to life. Fleming thought back to an elementary school Halloween party where she'd dressed up as a princess because it used to be a fantasy of hers to someday be rescued by a knight in shining armor. That fantasy ended during Hydra training, when she was taught to rescue herself. But now, riding on Tequila's muscular back, a very tiny, minuscule, infinitesimal, teensy-weensy, girlish part of her felt like swooning.

"Am I hurting you?" he asked.

"Just my pride."

"We've just met, but I'm pretty sure nothing hurts your pride."

"If you're trying to smooth-talk me out of my pants, you're too late."

Tequila bent over, scooping up the Semtex and detonator. "Which cell is he in?"

"Three doors to the right."

She pulled up the AR-7, checked the magazine, and brought it to bear over Tequila's shoulder. He walked to the cell doorway, then stopped.

Fleming was going to ask what the problem was, but then she felt it, too. Someone was in the hallway.

He silently handed Fleming the plastic and detonator, then drew one of his pistols from his shoulder rig. Feeling him tense, Fleming hooked her elbow around his throat, holding on to him and the explosives she carried with one hand, her other extending the AR-7.

Tequila bolted into the hallway and immediately began to backpedal. At the end of the hallway were three men and a woman. All were armed.

The woman was Hammett.

"Another sister?" Tequila said.

Fleming couldn't find the words to answer. The sight of her sister hit like a slap, shuddering through every muscle, zinging along each nerve, and centering in her chest. Fleming stared at the face that was the same as Chandler's, the same as her own, and involuntarily recalled the horrible things Hammett had done to them both.

Hammett was worse than Malcolm. She wasn't power hungry, or a puppet of the government, or sadistic for its own sake. Hammett simply did whatever she wanted to do, without guilt or remorse. At least Malcolm's evil was rooted in emotion. Hammett was a shark. A shark following a blood trail. And Fleming was the chum.

As they raised their weapons and flattened themselves against the walls, Tequila and Fleming emptied their magazines, lead pinging and ricocheting off concrete and stone. Just as the enemy began to return fire, Tequila did a quick pirouette and rounded the corner, bursting into a full sprint. This hall was like the previous one, lined with cells, and they were through it in a flash, coming to a twisted metal door. The air smelled heavy with spent explosive.

"The way out?" Fleming guessed.

Tequila nodded and slipped through.

"Wait—" Fleming said, thinking of the man she'd promised to help.

Tequila holstered his gun and pried the Semtex out of Fleming's hand. He stuck it to the doorjamb. "I'm low on ammo, and they'll be on us in a second."

"We can't just leave—"

"We'll come back for him. I promise. But we need to stop them here."

Fleming swallowed the lump in her throat, then nodded. Tequila sprinted down the hall and yelled, "Do it!" in midstride.

She pressed the detonator, and the corridor shook behind them, roaring in an explosive thunderclap.

Chandler

"Family is a luxury," the Instructor said. "And all luxuries are liabilities."

I was still running, nearing the cannon area, when I heard the explosion. It sounded dampened, muffled, and I felt the ground shake beneath the soles of my feet.

Something underground had blown up.

Fleming was underground.

Panic gave me a surge of extra energy, and I managed to put on a bit of speed. But my legs—heavy with lactic acid—couldn't keep up with the forward momentum, and for the second time I face-planted into the ground—

—right as a sniper round whizzed over my head.

Being shot at is a very distinct, unforgettable sensation. At Hydra I had to stand against a wall while various caliber bullets were shot above and around me. This was definitely a rifle round, probably a 30-06. I peeked through the field weeds, trying to follow the report, instinct telling me it had come from the southwest.

Another *crack*, and dirt erupted a few centimeters in front of my hip. I didn't have sufficient cover, and there wasn't any for a hundred meters around me.

I got up and ran.

Fleming

"The only safe enemy," the Instructor said, "is a dead enemy."

The shock wave from the exploding doorway washed against Fleming's back, dust peppering her in tiny pinpricks. She twisted around and squinted through the smoke, watching the ceiling collapse around the doorway.

Then they were running up stairs, and Fleming was surprised by how familiar it felt. Since the accident, she'd been on stairs either in her chair or on her butt. For the briefest of moments, Tequila's ascent—and the memories it stirred in her—blocked out all other feeling, thought, and emotion. There was only the step-step-step of his feet on the stairs, the unforgettable bouncing of the body as it climbed.

In her dreams, Fleming often walked. But this sensation was so real, so powerful, she hugged Tequila's chest not just to hold on, but with genuine emotion.

All too soon they were at the top, her savior dropping to his knees. Fresh air washed over her, the scents of forest and prairie, the sounds of trees and geese flying south. Through a doorway ahead was the mouth of a concrete cave, and behind that, a field. The elation Fleming felt from jogging upstairs was multiplied by the realization that freedom was only a few steps away.

"Tequila?"

"Yeah?"

The words were sticky in her throat. "Thanks."

"Too soon," he said. "Remember the sniper? South, a few hundred yards, behind the building out there."

Fleming swallowed the lump and brought up the AR-7.

"You want to wait him out?" she asked. "Or run for it?"

"If we wait, they can surround us."

"You can leave me here, get around him. I can cover you. Can you get closer?"

"He might have infrared."

"Risk it."

Tequila released her ankles and tucked her feet into the side pockets of his jeans. Then he dropped to a push-up position, keeping his whole body straight as a board, and pulled himself up the last few steps and over to the doorway with Fleming on his back. They hung back half a meter, giving Fleming a wider view of the landscape. The concrete cave was actually a giant testing pit for cannon fire, dug into the side of a hill. Across the weeds Fleming saw two buildings, and the one at six o'clock Tequila had mentioned. Fleming watched for movement, saw none, and then swept her gaze to the east where she spotted—

"Chandler," she whispered.

Her sister was running toward them, her pace erratic, more than four hundred meters away. Fleming's eyes teared up, and she almost began to sob, her chest shuddering. Fleming knew she was in an emotionally frail state. That was one of the effects of captivity and interrogation. She was thrilled to be free, and it was amazing riding on Tequila's back, but seeing her sister again was overwhelming.

Fleming couldn't remember the last time she'd been overwhelmed by happiness. She was getting ready to call out when the *crack* of a sniper round cut across the compound. Fleming's breath caught as she waited to hear where the bullet hit. But it didn't come near the doorway, or the cave.

Which meant the sniper wasn't firing at them. He was firing at Chandler.

"Tequila—"

"Hold on."

Fleming gripped his neck tight as Tequila hopped to his feet and began to sprint into the open field. It was notoriously hard, even for professionals, to sight between two moving targets on a long scope. So the sniper would have to pick one and stick with it if he—

Crack!

Chandler went down.

Fleming tried to process it, but couldn't. Had she been hit? Had she just gone to ground? Had she even seen Chandler at all?

Crack!

Fleming felt the bullet hit home, tugging at her backpack and making a clanging sound. Tequila immediately changed course, cutting left, and Fleming brought up the AR-7 and fired twice in the direction of the building, the bouncing and jostling making it impossible for her to aim.

Crack!

And then Tequila was skidding, face-first, onto the ground, and Fleming went rolling into the weeds, amazed at how quickly overwhelming happiness could disappear.

Hammett

"There are always obstacles," the Instructor said. "And there are always solutions."

Hammett frowned at the rubble before her. Grit filled her mouth, and all she could smell was concrete dust and smoke. "Can you get through it?"

Jersey shrugged. "Sure. But I might bring the ceiling down on us. Blasting underground is bad news. There was this time, when I was a kid, I brought a puppy into a mine shaft near my house—"

Hammett elbowed Jersey in the nose, not hard enough to break, but hard enough to shut him up.

"I like dogs," she said, her voice steady and eyes hard. "Now clear a damn path."

Any complaint Jersey might have had died in his throat. Instead he dug into his pack and began to set up a charge. Hammett moved away, around the corner with Santiago, back to Fleming's cell.

Hammett pressed her radio. "I need eyes topside."

"Found your look-alike," Isaiah said into her earpiece. "Going for a leg shot, but she moves like a rabbit."

"Stay on her. Javier? You got ears on?"

"*Putita* knocked me into a grinder. Trashed an eight-hundred-dollar pair of Ferragamos, and I almost lost my little toe."

"What have you got for me, other than complaints?"

"Heading to my ATV. We lost them in the chase."

"Stay there, in case she returns. Our main target is with a man, riding on his back." Hammett turned to Santiago, who was toeing the burned man on the ground, making him moan. "Where will they exit?"

Santiago pressed his talk button. "They'll come out near the cannon area."

"Here we go," Jersey called out.

The explosion shook the corridor, bathing them with another flood of smoke and dust. Waving a hand in front of her face, Hammett hurried back to where she'd left Jersey. In her haste, she stepped on him.

Well, parts of him.

The idiot had blown himself up. Even worse, the path was still blocked.

Behind her, Santiago began to whistle something off tune. It took her a few seconds to recognize Patsy Cline's "I Fall to Pieces."

"See if there's anything salvageable," she ordered.

Hammett stormed back down the corridor and rounded the corner. So far, they hadn't encountered much resistance from the site's caretakers. It had been a skeleton crew. Hammett hadn't noticed any prisoners other than Fleming, and her sister had managed to charbroil the lead spook. This had been easier than expected, other than the obvious fact that they still hadn't acquired their target, and that she'd lost a man due to gross incompetence.

Santiago returned, empty handed. He shrugged.

"Who's out there?"

Hammett's head jerked at the sound of the voice, coming from one of the cells.

A male voice. One she knew intimately.

"Grab and secure the crispy critter," she told Santiago. "I'll be just a moment."

Chandler

"If you're forced to be a target," the Instructor said, "be a moving target."

Another crack of the rifle, and I dove for the ground, rolling with my shoulder dropped and my legs tucked to my chest, feeling every one of my injuries as I came to a stop on my side beside some goldenrod and twisted branches of sumac just starting to turn orange.

The sniper seemed to be aiming low, at my legs. They wanted me alive.

That didn't make me feel any better.

I heard the rifle's report once more, but this time the round didn't come anywhere near me. I peeked through the weeds and noticed movement to the west, only a hundred meters away.

Fleming!

She rode Tequila piggyback, wearing his Blackhawks starter jacket and nothing else, the bottom band barely covering her ass. Her bleeding, bruised, dirty legs circled his waist, held in place by the gymnast's jean pockets. She clung to his shoulders with one hand, a rifle clutched in the other. My sister fired twice, surprising steady considering her mount, and then the sniper returned fire, and I watched her and Tequila go down.

No! No no no no—

I got to my feet again and ran with all I had, closing the distance by half, and then Tequila was on his feet and lifting Fleming onto his back again, and my sister stared at me.

Fleming gave me a smile with her eyes, and even though her lips were pinched from pain, they curved into a grin so brilliant and brave, she looked like the picture of a conquering hero.

My lower lip started to tremble. Tears blurred my vision, and at that moment I realized I'd never expected to see her again, let alone so strong, so defiantly alive. I'd wanted it more than anything, planned for it, worked for it, but I'd never truly believed I'd see her sweet face.

My knees felt weak, and I stumbled, catching myself before I fell.

A few more steps and I reached them. No time for hugs, for tears, for spilling the feelings welling inside. No time for the feelings at all. We had to reach the fence, the horses. We had to get Fleming somewhere safe.

I touched my sister's hand, and what passed between us was deeper than words. "We need to go," I said.

"Hell yeah."

Then I shoved the emotion into a compartment somewhere in my psyche as I'd been trained to do, and we went. Another rifle shot, but we were on the road now, behind the cover of trees and scrub, heading back in the direction of the reservoir.

"Hammett is here," Fleming said over the sounds of our feet slapping asphalt.

"I know."

The last time I'd seen my only other living sister, we'd been trying to kill each other on the deck of a yacht. That was a sisterly reunion I was *not* looking forward to.

Tequila moved at a steady run, seemingly not even out of breath. I hadn't even looked at him, noticing only Fleming, but now I could see his ear was wounded, the top of it missing. Blood stained his blond stubble and ran in a stream down his neck.

"Your ear…are you OK?"

"What?"

"Is your ear OK?"

"What?"

"Is your—" And then I caught the glint in Tequila's eye. So the man could do funny, too. Who the hell knew?

"What happened to Hammett?"

"Delayed."

"Permanently?"

"No."

"A girl can dream."

Fleming grimaced and said, "She can find us. The chips."

Of course. I was now clean, but we'd have to deal with Fleming's. But before we could do that, we had to reach Lund.

"That can wait. If we're still here when they get out, she won't have to track us, she'll run right into us."

Her or one of her little helpers.

I thought about my ATV and the long trek back to the spot where Lund was waiting. The upward incline alone would be difficult to manage, even if Tequila and I took turns carrying Fleming. But I knew Hammett. She'd be staking out my quad, figuring I'd return with Fleming.

I held my hand out to Tequila. "I need your phone."

"What happened to yours?"

"A long and soggy story."

He handed it over.

I punched in the number I'd memorized after my call to the fire department. The phone rang, seemingly endlessly, then went to voice mail.

Where in the hell was he?

Scenarios flashed through my mind, all of them ending in Lund being discovered, suffering, and dying. I never should have let him help. He was a civilian, not cut out for this.

"You done?" Tequila asked.

I cut off the call and texted instead, FOLLOW THE FENCE LINE WEST—not the easiest thing to do while jogging. Then I handed the phone back to Tequila and willed Lund to be all right.

"Where did you come in?"

"Follow me." Tequila's steady gait quickened.

I glanced at Fleming. "We can't climb the—"

"Follow me," he repeated.

We cut left, off the road, and pushed through the waist-high weeds, my head light from the effort. I could feel burrs snagging in my socks and pricking my legs, but kept moving.

"The fence isn't charged," Tequila said.

I looked up at the curls of razor wire at the top. "I hope you have wire cutters on you."

The bullet snagged the cuff of my pants before I heard the sound of the shot.

I dropped to the ground, Tequila and Fleming with me, as the crack echoed off the bluffs. Our sniper had found higher ground, and the greater distance didn't seem to bother him.

I could see Fleming through the long grass, staring at me, eyes wide. "Chandler?"

I checked where I'd felt the tug. When functioning on adrenaline, it is possible to be injured and not feel it at first, the body's way to keep one's focus on survival, not relatively smaller things like getting a bullet hole in the leg. But despite the tear, I'd escaped having a round pierce my flesh yet again.

Chalk it up to living right. "I'm OK."

"Where did he fire from? I can't see him. Not even a hint."

I scanned the area but came up empty as well. "Some kind of distance, that's for sure."

"I think I know that guy." Tequila rummaged in his bag and brought out wire nippers. "We can't go over. He'll be waiting. We're going to have to go through. Stay low."

I wasn't about to argue with that.

Cutting through the fence, on the other hand, was not as agreeable. Even with the good-quality cutter, it took forever to sever each wire of the chain-link fabric. Tequila took the first turn, snipping several. When he stopped to stretch out his hand, I took over.

And the whole time, there was no sign of Lund.

Now I wasn't sure if I wanted him to meet us or not. If he rode up with the horses right now, there was no telling what the sniper would do. If it were me, I'd take him out, then each of the animals, cutting off our means of escape.

I handed the cutters back to Tequila, trading for his phone. Lund hadn't returned the text or the call.

"Chandler, go." Tequila clipped the last wire and bent the remaining side open like a flap.

I returned the phone and crawled through the small space. Once on the other side, I helped Fleming, even though she was better at crawling through the space on her belly and dragging her legs behind than I was. Then it was Tequila's turn, and the little man slipped through without a hitch.

The three of us crawled into the edge of the tree line. So far, so good. "I need to find Lund."

"Lund?" Fleming and Tequila said in unison.

It seemed like I'd known Lund for a few days, rather than a few hours. Certainly after this afternoon, I knew him better than I'd known most of the men I picked up for an anonymous good time whenever my work schedule allowed it. But I'd forgotten neither my sister nor Tequila knew he existed. "I recruited some help."

"Help?" Fleming prodded.

"He's a firefighter. He has horses. He also has a shot of Demerol with your name on it."

"Oh, I could use a little of that kind of help." She raised an eyebrow. "Is he cute?"

"Like George Clooney if you took a little steel wool and roughed him up around the edges."

"Ooo."

"I need to warn him about the sniper."

Tequila pointed with his chin into the woods. "I think they're both aware of each other."

Then I heard it. Galloping hooves and breaking twigs. Lund was close enough to have heard the shots. If the thrashing coming through the trees were any louder, it would be echoing off the quartzite bluffs like the explosions and gunshots had.

I sprang to my feet to stop him before he broke the tree line and became a target.

Big mistake.

The first sharp report jangled my nerves, kicking up dead leaves a meter to my right. The second was closer, the sound cracking through my ear and jaw, the bullet whizzing so close I could almost feel it.

I hit the ground, flattening to my belly.

"We need to get deeper in the trees."

I nodded, not sure my voice would work. Fleming was already moving, dragging herself faster than some people walked. To my relief, the thrashing in the trees had stopped, and seeing how close the round had come to me, I was guessing the gunshot hadn't killed Lund, but frozen him in his tracks.

One of the horses snorted.

"Lund, stay there. We'll come to you," I exchanged looks with Tequila but couldn't read his eyes. "Ready?"

"Horses?" he said.

I nodded, thinking about how I thought he looked like the Marlboro Man. "It's time to ride."

Tequila

Tequila eyed the animals. The only horse he'd ever ridden was the pommel variety, and although he could perform some mean kehrswings, wendeswings, flops, and scissors, he doubted the experience translated.

Chandler crossed to the lighter of the two brown horses and started digging into a pack secured to the back of the saddle. Her new recruit, the man she called Lund, sat astride a palomino. That left the dark brown beauty.

"Ever ride before?" Lund asked.

"Not this type."

The man frowned. "Quarter horses are pretty easygoing, and this one gets ridden every day. Banshee is bombproof."

Tequila wasn't sure what that meant in horse jargon, but he figured it would probably come in handy in light of the circumstances.

"I'm David Lund."

"Tequila."

"Unusual name."

Tequila nodded and turned away. In a glance, he could tell Lund was one of those people set on saving the world, like his altruistic friend Jack Daniels. And although he wasn't about to trust the man, he figured he wasn't likely to pull a gun on him either, at least not at the moment. But that didn't mean Tequila was interested in trading small talk.

He stepped to his mount's side and ran his fingers over her silky neck. Her skin shuddered beneath his touch.

"Lift me up on the saddle," Fleming said, having pulled herself to sit on a purple rock. "I'll ride behind you."

"Take the front. I've never ridden before."

I can't manage it. You're going to have to learn fast. I'll ride on the skirt, behind the cantle. You're going to have to take the reins.

He was struck again by what a good-looking woman Fleming was, identical to her sister in most ways, except for a certain aura of stillness that Chandler didn't possess. As if, while her sister was still hungry to prove something, Fleming had already been through the fire and had emerged on the other side. But despite her strength, he could see she was in pain.

"Wait. Chandler? Got that Demerol?" Tequila asked, keeping his eyes on Fleming.

"I got it," Chandler said, approaching with a syringe. She administered the dose, and the lines smoothed from Fleming's forehead.

"Better?" Tequila asked.

Fleming nodded. "How about your ear? Chandler, do you have something for Tequila's ear? He's still bleeding."

"It's fine."

"It doesn't look fine."

He smiled slightly. It felt odd, because he didn't do it too often. "Really, I'm fine."

"OK." But Fleming kept staring, the look of concern on her face making his ear hot in response. Both ears, actually.

"Really, I've been hurt worse."

She nodded as if finally satisfied. "You and me both."

For a second they just looked at each other, Tequila in no particular hurry to break the moment, then Chandler swung onto her horse. "We'd better get a move on."

Tequila looked at Fleming, wearing nothing but his jacket, and then eyed the saddle.

Oh, hell.

Tequila pulled off his boots and stripped his jeans down his legs. "You're not sitting on the back of that saddle bare-assed."

Pulling the boots back on, he handed the pants to her and stood there in his black boxer briefs.

She gave him a slightly loopy smile, and he wasn't sure if she was amused or just enjoying the Demerol. After she'd pulled on the jeans, he lifted her into the saddle, then, placing his hands as if it really was a pommel horse, sprang on board.

His feet didn't reach the stirrups.

This just kept getting better and better.

"Should these be…adjusted somehow?"

"The stirrups? Sure." Fleming leaned to the side, and for a second he thought she was going to topple off.

He twisted in the saddle to steady her. "Never mind. Not important."

"It's not all that hard to—"

The sound of an engine buzzed in the distance.

"ATVs," Chandler called from her horse. "Go, go, go."

"My car." Tequila raised a hand to point. "That way."

Chandler nodded and laid a heel into her horse's side. Chandler and Lund took off. Tequila's horse followed without any encouragement from him.

It was a miracle Tequila stayed on. He grabbed the saddle horn, the hard leather seat smacking his ass and sending him bouncing three inches in the air with each stride.

"Pick up the reins," Fleming said, the warmth of her breath fanning his ear.

Reins…reins…

Tequila found them crossed over the horse's shoulders, right in front of the saddle. He took one in each hand, still gripping the saddle. Most of his life he'd prided himself on the fact that he could balance on anything, but now his sense of equilibrium seemed to have totally deserted him.

"OK, sit up on your seat bones and drive your weight through your heels. You don't have to hold on with your legs. Head up, heels down, that's the key to balance."

Balance...balance...

He did as she said, not that it was at all comfortable while wearing boxers. It seemed as if the animal fought against him, refusing to keep a steady rhythm. Just as he started wondering if he'd ever get the motion right, the horse broke into a much smoother, rolling gait.

"Good." Fleming crooned. "You got it."

He released his hold on the saddle, moving with the horse, finding the groove, letting his posture and balance take over.

"OK, the reins. Hold them in your left hand."

He gathered them. Reaching around his body, Fleming folded her hand over his, positioning the strips of leather so they ran into his hand through his fingertips and out through his palm. She moved his index finger between the two reins and adjusted them so they dropped in a loose loop before reaching the horse's bit, then she kept her hand on his. Tequila had been carrying this woman for the better part of ten minutes, but this touch was more intimate by tenfold.

The horse didn't speed up or slow down, just kept up her steady pace, following the others. Fleming moved her hands to either side of his waist, holding on. Her body was close enough to feel her softness against his back, and warmth spread over his skin.

"Now, just move your hand in the direction you want to turn. Think of it as the rein pushing against the horse's neck, and she'll turn away from the pressure."

He tried it, and Banshee responded so fast, he nearly fell off. "She handles like a sports car."

"To stop, raise your rein hand and shift your weight back toward the cantle."

"What if I push you off?"

"I'm not going anywhere," Fleming said, tightening her grip on him.

They reached the wheel rut path he'd followed part of the way into the ammo plant. Chandler glanced back over her shoulder, and he gave her a nod.

Behind them, the ATV engines grew louder, gaining ground.

"Squeeze her with both legs." Fleming started to make a kissing sound in his ear, a phenomenon that both confused and aroused him until he realized she was doing it to encourage the horse.

He pushed his heels into Banshee's sides and she bolted forward.

The ATVs still sounded like they were gaining.

Tequila liked nature, and he liked Fleming holding him, and he was even warming up to this riding thing, but he still couldn't wait to get off the horse and into his car, the way people were meant to travel.

They reached the spot where he'd parked, just off the paved road, and Tequila raised his rein hand, as Fleming had instructed. He leaned back into her, lightly.

"Harder," she said. "I won't fall."

Tequila sat back into the cantle. The horse took a few strides to slow, but she eventually came to a halt.

The SUV. Where the hell was it?

It was the right spot. He was sure of that. But the vehicle he'd so carefully hidden with leaves and branches was gone.

Lund turned back and stopped his horse beside them. "Was it a white SUV?"

"Yeah."

"I ran into a park ranger. That's why I was detained. He said he had it towed."

Hammett

"If at first you don't succeed," said the Instructor, "do it again, and this time you damn well better get it right."

"I thought your nickname was Speed," Hammett yelled over the racket of the ATV. She swore that if he didn't move this machine faster, she'd throw the fat bastard under the tires and take over the driving herself.

The Supergrade was in her right hand, her left arm snaked around Speed's generous middle. Javier drove behind her. They had taken too long to get out of the tunnel, too long to cut through the fence, and they needed to push it to catch up with Fleming and her munchkin bodyguard before they got away.

Isaiah had been too far away on his sniper's perch to join the chase, so he stayed with Santiago at the site. He was searching for the videos of Fleming's interrogation, on the off chance she'd spilled something, while Santiago interrogated the prisoner, with strict orders not to kill him.

Damn Isaiah for not stopping them at the fence. Damn Javier for failing to capture Chandler. Damn Santiago for being a psycho. Damn Speed for his shitty driving. And most of all, damn that loser Jersey for getting himself killed.

It was impossible to get good help these days.

Hammett punched Speed in the side with her knee. "Faster."

He accelerated. The jumbled path over rock and brush smoothed out into an unpaved road, tire ruts in long grass. As the road straightened and they drew closer, Hammett spotted Chandler ahead and understood why she and her little group had made such good time while Hammett had been struggling to get her shit together. Where she'd managed to scrounge up horses, Hammett didn't know. But there were three of them. Chandler and a man Hammett didn't recognize each had their own mounts. Fleming rode behind the blond shrimp.

None of them would be riding long. Not if Hammett had something to say about it.

And Hammett always had plenty to say.

They closed the distance. As fast as the horses could move, the ATVs were faster, especially over even ground. But even though they were bearing down on Fleming's horse, who was bringing up the rear, shooting while driving over uneven terrain was never a sure thing, even for Hammett, and she couldn't take out the short prick without risking hitting her crippled sis. Dead Fleming would be no good to them.

Chandler was an easier target, though Hammett preferred her alive. And shooting at her legs carried the risk of hitting the horse, which was senseless. Hammett had no compunctions about killing a human being, and she enjoyed a good steak or pork loin, but she did feel compassion for dogs and horses. And cats. And those domesticated Siberian foxes.

A target of hers in Chernogolovka had a silver fox named Fyodor, and she played fetch with the cute little guy for over half an hour after she slit his owner's throat. He had the most adorable bark, a cross between a Chihuahua yipping and a cat purring.

If she didn't have to leave her home all the time to travel around the world, killing people, Hammett could easily imagine having a few foxes. And a doggie and a horsie.

"Speed!" Hammett pointed at the fallen tree branch on the path ahead of them.

Apparently Speed didn't notice it. Or he noticed, and didn't care. The front wheels hit hard, the vehicle shuddering, then taking flight, giving a buck that almost sent Hammett cartwheeling across the forest floor. She managed to hold on, her teeth clapping together hard enough to make her whole head ache.

If Speed made another move like that, she really was going to have to kill him.

Ahead, the horses had reached the paved road leading out of the park and were racing alongside in the ditch. She and Speed bounced onto the asphalt, and he cranked the engine, gaining fast. Beside her, Javier fired a burst from his mounted machine gun, making the horses swerve into the woods.

"I want them alive," she snarled into the radio. "Watch your fire."

"I'm aiming for the horse," Javier said.

"Don't."

Hammett directed Speed to follow, and they cut through the front yard of a small farm and raced across a field stubbled with shorn corn stalks.

The farmland was heavily rutted from a muddy harvest, and the rough terrain slowed them down. Able to move more nimbly, the horses gained, and by the time they broke into an alfalfa field, Hammett was considering abandoning the mission and her principles and just gunning down everyone and everything.

A roar erupted overhead, louder than the ATV's engine. Hammett looked up, surprised to see one of the balloons they'd noticed earlier, now closer to the ground. The sound had been a blast of flame from the propane burner. Two more balloons were up ahead on a distant hill, hovering over an airstrip half surrounded by rows of stunted apple trees.

Hammett knew where Chandler was headed.

Good thing she hadn't killed Speed, the man who could drive anything.

She scanned the area, looking for a way to circle, to cut off Chandler, but the underbrush streaking past on one side and the pitted field on the other left no options, not until they reached the hay.

But she had a better idea.

Hammett focused on the shrimpy bastard riding with Fleming. Take him out, and her crippled sister would be easy pickings. Then Chandler would be the one scrambling to catch up.

And to do it, she would have to get up close and personal. Just the way Hammett liked to make her kills.

Tequila

Tequila hadn't had time to mourn his truck or lament the fact that he would have to buy a new one for cash because he didn't believe in insurance. He squeezed Banshee's sides, urging her to run faster, her hooves thundering over the cornfield's uneven dirt. The ATV was hard on his mare's heels, and although he kept waiting for the bullet to hit, the shot never came.

They must want Fleming alive.

Ahead, Lund had taken the lead. He charged into a field of alfalfa, Chandler on his gelding's right flank. Beyond him, Tequila could see a red hot-air balloon hovering low, and a blue one looming in the sky to the west.

The ATV roared closer, the sound grating at the back of his neck and throbbing through his injured ear. He glanced over his shoulder and spotted Hammett rising up behind a heavy guy in an old black T-shirt, a pistol in her hand, the barrel leveled on him.

Tequila had to do something.

When he'd told Lund the only horse he'd ridden was the pommel horse, he hadn't been kidding. The event was considered one of the most difficult in men's gymnastics, and while he'd never medaled with his routine, he'd been pretty good.

Tequila glanced back at Fleming. "Duck."

She folded forward against the back of the cantle, clenching the stirrup flaps.

Trying not to think too hard about what he was doing, he gripped the fork of the saddle, one palm on either side of the horn, and shifted his weight onto his hands, raising himself out of the seat. He started with a circle. The horse's rhythm made the movement more difficult, but she was as bombproof as Lund had promised, and it only took moments for Tequila to adapt to her stride. Splitting his legs in a flair, he spun over Fleming's head and drilled his right heel into Hammett's forearms.

The gun fired, her shot flying harmlessly into the air. The ATV swerved, and so did the horse, but somehow Tequila kept his balance, his movement unhindered.

Hammett stayed on too, kept her grip on her weapon, and brought it back up.

Tequila completed another circle and nailed the driver this time, connecting with the fat man's shoulder, the force shuddering up Tequila's legs but only slightly slowing his circle. The ATV veered off course, up the other side of the ditch.

"Tequila, the fence!" Fleming yelled.

He piked into a handstand, then lowered his chest and split his legs on either side of the horse, his ass smacking back in the saddle.

A three-board fence stretched in front of them, barring them from the airstrip where the balloons were touching down.

"I don't have stirrups."

"You're really worried about that after what you just did?"

"I don't know how to jump."

"Just stay with the horse's motion."

Ahead of them, Chandler sailed over the meter-high fence and landed with the grace and poise of a professional show jumper.

Tequila knew it wouldn't be as easy for him.

"Weight in your heels. Give the mare her head. She'll follow the others over."

Lund cleared the barrier a couple of strides behind her, his jump an ill-timed hop that left him clutching the horse's neck, bumping his shoulder into her mane. Incredibly, he made it to the other side and stayed on the horse, sloppy as he looked.

A burst of gunfire exploded behind them from one of the front-mounted guns, bullets shredding sumac and hitting the painted boards. The fence rushed up fast.

"Keep your head up," Fleming urged. "Focus past the jump. Whatever you do, don't look down."

"There are two of us. The extra weight—"

"You can do this. And don't ever comment on a girl's weight."

Tequila could feel the horse's muscles coil beneath him, her hindquarters gathering, taking the fence in stride. He figured there was no way in hell they'd make it.

Then they were flying.

He glanced down at the horse, instinctively grasping for the saddle horn, and felt his butt rising out of the saddle as Fleming clenched him tight.

Look forward. Always forward.

He forced his chin up and focused on Lund's back, the balloons beyond.

The horse landed, front hooves first, throwing Tequila forward. He tensed his stomach muscles just as the horn punched him in the gut. Fleming held on, moving with him.

The horse kept going, her rocking gait allowing Tequila to regain his balance.

Between the saddle horn and Fleming's ice pick, Tequila's gut was killing him. He knew he looked even sloppier than Lund, and he was sure the USSR judge gave him a 1.5. But fuck that guy, they'd made it.

Another burst of fire came from behind, but Banshee kept moving, leaving the ATVs hauling Hammett and her men trapped behind the fence.

"Good job," Fleming said.

Tequila nodded, ignoring the compliment and already focused on the spot where Chandler was heading.

The closest hot-air balloon.

Chandler

"When you find yourself in a tight situation," said the Instructor, "the best thing you can do is remain flexible. Plans fall apart, but opportunities you never envisioned can save you, as long as you are ready to improvise, adapt, and overcome at a moment's notice."

The fence did the trick. The buzz of the four-wheelers faded, the gunfire ceasing as we pulled out of range. I hadn't been sure either Lund or Tequila could make the jump, but it had been a necessary gamble. If I'd let the chase continue, one or more of us would have been shot. We were low on guns and ammunition, and in most circumstances horses couldn't outrun ATVs.

But horses *could* jump.

I raced for the airstrip, Bo's strides steady and long beneath me. The smell of hot horse hung in my nostrils. I'd glanced over my shoulder to make sure Lund, Tequila, and Fleming were in good shape, then I turned my attention to the next part of the plan I was desperately cobbling together in my head. It wouldn't take Hammett and her men long to go around the fence. We had to be out of here by the time they did.

A few people milled about the airstrip, curious onlookers and the balloons' crews, who spread large tarps on the ground next to the two balloons that had landed in preparation for deflating them and packing them up.

More civilians gathered in the adjacent orchard and farm market, where some kind of festival seemed to be closing out the weekend. The rumble of voices and pulse of a tuba playing polka music wafted in the air like the smoke rising from a booth selling food, the smell of charcoal and bratwurst competing with the fragrance of horse. The sun was already hunkering low behind the western bluffs, twilight closing in.

Unfortunately the first choice on my hijack list, a small airplane, was nowhere to be found. And while there were cars in the orchard parking lot, they were a good distance away, and we'd risk Hammett catching up to us in the time it took to reach them. Worse, I doubted my sister would be careful to avoid the old ladies and small children who often attended festivals like this while she was shooting at us.

I eyed the balloons, a more immediate plan taking shape.

I pressed my calves into Bo's sides, a searing pain reminding me of one of my many injuries, and she surged forward. We bore down on the closest balloon, its envelope still fully inflated. The crew had just tied it down and was climbing from the basket. They stared at us, galloping toward them, oblivious to what was about to happen.

I glanced back at Lund, then back to the balloon, hoping he would catch what I was thinking.

Then I pulled Bo to a sliding stop and jumped off in one movement. Lund stopped beside me, but instead of dismounting, he grabbed Bo's reins. I stared up at the massive red balloon, at least eighty meters tall, and strode for the basket. Then I began untying tethers.

The crew just stood and watched, as if not quite believing I was stealing their balloon. Eventually a woman who I pegged to be in her fifties stepped toward me.

"Hey, what are you doing?"

I drilled her with a serious stare. "We need to borrow this."

"You can't do that."

I kept untying.

"Hey, stop! I'll call the police."

"You do that." I didn't want to hurt the woman, but I might have to if she didn't back off.

Tequila and Fleming reached us, stopping Banshee next to me.

"This is our balloon," The woman plopped her hands on her hips and jutted out her chin. "You can't just take it."

Tequila said, "What's your name?"

"Midge."

"We're going to take your balloon, Midge. That's not your choice. But you do have choice of whether or not I break your nose first."

The woman stared wide-eyed at Tequila for a moment, her obvious horror shifting between his eyes and his bloody ear, then took a step backward. "I'll keep my nose intact."

So maybe she wasn't so dumb.

After unleashing the last tether, I climbed into the basket and helped Fleming slide off the saddle and into the gondola beside me. While piloting a balloon was one thing *not* taught at Hydra, I'd gone up in one a few years ago after meeting a cute guy in a bar who was an avid balloonist.

The main principle behind ballooning is simple. Because hot air is less dense and thus lighter than cold air, it rises. Each of the colorful craft was constructed from panels of nylon reinforced with webbing that extended from the bottom of the balloon's envelope to the top. At the bottom, or skirt, two propane burners heated the air. As the heat's energy made the air molecules move faster, the air grew less dense than the air outside the envelope, and caused the balloon to rise.

It takes skill to pilot a balloon with precision, but the controls are as simple as turning on a gas stove or firing up the gas-powered grill cooking that bratwurst. Just the turn of a valve, and propane from the tanks in the basket fuels the flame in the burners. The larger the flame, the faster the air heats inside the nylon envelope, and the more quickly the balloon ascends. To lower the balloon, the pilot only has to pull a cord opening the parachute valve at the balloon's top and let out the heated air.

From there it is a matter of moving up or down to catch the specific air currents that will take you where you wanted to go. At that moment, the only particular direction I was interested in was *away*, so I opened the propane valve and cranked the burners.

The flame roared, and a moment later the basket started to lift.

On the ground, Lund grasped Banshee's bridle and Tequila leaped off his mount, raced to the balloon, and jumped, catching the basket as it lifted. Then he gracefully pulled himself over the edge and safely inside.

Gathering reins from all three horses in one hand, Lund looked up at me and raised the other in a wave. I waved back, realizing too late that we hadn't gotten a chance to say good-bye. Leading the other two horses, he rode his gelding in the direction of the orchard crowd.

I didn't have time to watch him go. Only twenty feet up, I spotted Hammett and a heavy guy in a faded Guns N' Roses tee racing across the field in the ATV, followed by three others.

"Ammo?" I yelled at Tequila over the roar of the flame.

He pulled out his right .45 and handed it to me. "Four rounds in this one, plus the AR-7."

"Empty," Fleming said, checking the magazine on the rifle.

I aimed Tequila's gun at the lead ATV and fired once. I missed, but it got Hammett's attention. She'd go after us rather than chase Lund. At least, that's what I thought. While Hammett and her driver did race for the second balloon, the man on the other ATV—ah hell, it was that asshole Javier—made a beeline for Lund and the horses.

I aimed carefully, leading the target, and fired my three remaining rounds at Javier, missing all three times.

I turned to Tequila. "Get Fleming to safety. I'll meet you at noon at the Baraboo antique mall."

Then I gripped the side of the gondola and prepared to vault over. A firm hand grabbed my shoulder.

"We're forty feet up," Tequila said. "At best you'll break something major."

"I have to save Lund."

"I think your friend can take care of himself."

I watched, helpless, as Lund and the horses headed for the apple trees, Javier in pursuit.

"We've got other concerns right now," Tequila said, pointing.

My sister was at the other balloon, waving a pistol at the crew trying to pack up.

I tried to crank the propane, but it was already firing at its maximum. Hammett had weapons. We had none. If we didn't want to be blown out of the air, we had to widen the gap between us.

High enough to clear trees, we caught a current moving northward. I slowed the flow of propane to the burners. The wind was strong up here, and we cleared the orchard and floated over trees, then a patchwork of farm fields. Lights from Baraboo twinkled farther north, the black ribbon of a river flowing through its center.

Unlike flying an airplane, where the direction and velocity can be precisely controlled, piloting a balloon is about planning, guesswork, and improvisation, adjusting to wind currents moment to moment. And at the moment, I was wishing the wind wasn't as strong and the sun wasn't setting.

"How much fuel do we have?" I asked Fleming.

Sitting on the bottom of the basket, she checked the gauges on each of the canisters. "Not much."

Just what I was afraid of. The balloons had already completed their flight for the day and used their fuel. I glanced at Tequila. "Look for a place to land."

Tequila signaled that he'd heard over the roar of the flame. "Parking lot."

Along the highway, I could see several big-box stores—wide-open spaces, and plenty of cars to steal. But it was still a good distance away, and I wasn't sure we'd make it that far.

The farm fields below would be a safer bet, but once we had landed, we would have only our feet to get us to safety.

The roar of the burners diminished, and I realized we were down to one canister of propane. On the other side of the fields but closer than the city of Baraboo, giant metal poles jutted out of the rural landscape, high-tension wires glistening between them in the fading twilight.

"We're going for the fields." I shut down our last burner to conserve fuel. As we cleared a last few trees and centered over the fields, I pulled the Kevlar cord attached to the parachute valve, releasing some of the hot air. Slowly we started to descend.

Big mistake.

Wind currents move in different directions at different altitudes. As we dropped, instead of heading down or west toward the big-box stores, we changed direction, floating northeast, straight toward those latticework metal towers holding four high-voltage wires, two on each arm.

I adjusted the valve, trying to bring us back up a little. The only burner left fired for a few seconds, then it too went quiet.

We were out of fuel.

"Three o'clock," Tequila called.

I turned to see Hammett's balloon. She was still at least a hundred and fifty meters behind us, but I could see her raise her weapon.

"Get down! Get down!" I yelled to Tequila, not that it would help much. If she could hit us with a handgun at this distance, a wicker basket wasn't going to provide much protection.

The crack of gunfire reached us. Then another.

Tequila fumbled with his pack.

"You have more ammo?" I asked, my spirits trying to rise.

"Nope. But I have something," he said. "Something that might work."

The wind had us now, driving us east. I yanked the parachute valve cord hard, taking a chance that a crash landing would be better than getting tangled in wires buzzing with enough energy to fry us all instantly, but the direction didn't change, and the balloon didn't drop fast enough.

The power lines came up fast on my right and I fought to keep from screaming in terror. Instead I managed to yell, "Heads down!" just as the balloon's skirt hit the high-tension wire, just above the balloon's burners.

Lund

When Lund took the horse's reins, watched Chandler vault into the hot-air balloon basket, and spotted those chasing them heading for the other balloon on the ground, he'd been concerned about her safety. It had never occurred to him to worry about himself.

Until one of the ATVs had started after him.

The driver was dressed in a suit, of all things, one foot bloodied and shoeless like some kind of wounded warrior businessman. The machine gun mounted on the front swung around, the barrel seeking out Lund and the horses.

Flanked by a throng of innocent families on one side and an orchard across the road, Lund had opted to make a dash for the apples, and now he and the horses were running for their lives.

Three sets of steel shoes clacked over asphalt, then they plunged into the lane between trees. With their top branches removed to make harvesting the apples easier, the trees looked stunted; their limbs twisted downward like gnarled, grasping hands. Long, irregular shadows stretched from the trunks, practically camouflaging the dents of tire ruts between the rows.

But it wasn't enough to conceal three horses.

The ATV's engine grew louder, closer, buzzing over the drum of Lund's pulse, urging him on like a set of sharp spurs. Max bunched with tension beneath him, and Lund gave him his head. Bo reached out for a branch as they passed, snagging an apple with her teeth and trying to chew it around the bit. Banshee brought up the rear, balking, the bridle dangerously close to pulling over her ears and turning her into a free agent.

The horses were fast approaching exhaustion, all three dark with pungent sweat. Lather foamed at the edges of their saddle pads and across their necks and chests. The smell of hot horse blanketed the air, and Lund felt the heat come off Max in humid waves. He doubted they could keep up this pace much longer without a breather.

He took a backward glance, spotting the vehicle jump onto the road, dip into the ditch, and plunge into the tree row directly behind them.

Lund had watched Val's niece practice for pole-bending competitions on Max, weaving in and out of a line of broomsticks stuck upright in buckets of sand. He laid the reins against Max's wet neck and a leg against his side, and the gelding swerved to the right between two trees.

Low branches whipped Lund's cheek and tore at his jacket. The other horses were slower to follow. Leather slipped through Lund's hand, and for a second he thought he was going to lose them.

A spray of gunfire rattled trees and shredded leaves. Apples rained to the ground.

The mares surged alongside, seemingly unhurt but spooked by the gunfire. Ahead, three people froze in the middle of the lane, staring at the horses charging them down.

"Out of the way," Lund yelled over the thrum of galloping hooves. "Run!"

They bolted, their bag of self-picked apples scattering across the grass.

Seconds later, the ATV crashed through the tree line behind them, spraying another round of bullets just as Lund swung through to the other side, Max and the other two horses slaloming like champion pole benders.

His pursuer echoed the move once again, engine roaring like approaching doom, but this time no bullets peppered the orchard.

Out of ammunition? Lund could only hope.

He directed Max through the far row of trees, but this time Mr. Suit kept to his side of the row, moving faster, gaining ground. Lund guided the horses over another row, tearing his focus from the ATV just in time to spot the orange light of sunset shining on the wire fence at the end of the row—five feet if it was an inch.

Shit, shit, double shit.

Max spotted it, too.

Lund had seen reining horses performing sliding stops at one of Val's niece's horse shows the previous summer. Unfortunately he'd never actually ridden one.

Max stopped dead, tucking his hindquarters under him, skidding to a stop. Lund kept going.

His chest grazed Max's neck as he sailed over, and before he'd totally registered what was happening, the ground rose to meet him.

He reached out his hands to break the fall and hit chest first as if diving into second base. Air exploded from his lungs. And even though Lund heaved gasp after gasp, he couldn't seem to replace it.

A jumble of hooves rumbled past him. In the distance he could hear the ATV's engine slow and circle back around.

Chandler

"Today we're going to learn about electricity," the Instructor said. "The main thing to learn is: stay the hell away from it."

I hadn't thought we'd been moving fast, but the impact on the high-tension wire made the basket swing almost parallel to the ground like a crazy carnival ride. As the gondola reversed direction, the balloon collapsed rapidly, spreading itself across the length of the line almost to the nearest tower, and coming to rest on the insulator. Judging from the towers' height and the distance between them, these were high-voltage lines, at least 130,000 volts and as thick as my wrists.

As anyone who's ever played around with an electric fence knows, electricity always wants to ground itself. Jump in the air while touching the hot wire of a fence and you are as safe as a bird sitting on a power line. Stand on the ground and try that, and the electricity will seek the path of least resistance in its quest for a ground, in this case through your body. With an electric fence, you get zapped. With a high-tension power line, you're fried.

That's why there were insulators between the wires and the towers—without them, electricity would jump to the towers, seeking the ground. Anything that connected wire to ground—a rope, a pole, a tower, a vehicle that wasn't properly insulated—would work. If there is some direct path through you to the ground, electricity will take it.

We were hanging at least thirty meters in the air, so that wasn't my immediate concern. What had me scared out of my mind was arcing.

Because there was so much voltage going through the wires, an energy field formed around them. This energy liked to jump to nearby objects. An arc is basically a lightning bolt, which shoots off the wire and fries anything with sufficient mass that comes close.

In this case, us.

And like lightning, an electric arc could blind, burn, or blow holes. To prevent that, we needed to energize our bodies to the same voltage as the line, as those birds did, due to their limited size. The nylon envelope we hung from was a poor electrical conductor, so we weren't energized, hadn't bonded on. By touching the wire with something metal and holding on to the other end, I could prevent the spark from jumping. The electricity would run safely through us without the unpleasant and deadly burn, and since we weren't touching the ground, it wouldn't explode out of our bodies.

At least that was the theory.

But there was nothing in the basket that would allow us to bond on to the wire. Tequila's AR-7 was no good—it had a plastic stock. No metal pole or antenna or wire. The only thing metal were the cables holding the gondola to the burner.

The burner.

"Shield your eyes!" I yelled, and as the basket continued to sway I hopped onto the edge in a crouch, holding onto the pipes. Perched precariously there for the swing back to the line, I kicked the nearest burner. Its bolts held it firm.

The line threw a spark, zapping the wicker basket like a scene from Frankenstein's lab, causing it to ignite. Fleming was quick to grab the fire extinguisher and snuff out the flames.

"What are you doing?" Tequila yelled.

"Bending the burner to touch the line!"

Either Tequila understood how electricity worked, or he was the most trusting man I'd ever met, because he joined me on the basket's edge and lent his foot to the cause. As we rocked, Tequila and I kicked that bastard until it bent off the pole at a right angle.

"Now swing," I told him.

As if we were competing on a playground, we rocked the gondola back and forth, the burner getting closer and closer to the wire, sparking each time. Finally, when we were again parallel to the ground, the burner caught on the wire with a brilliant flash of light, then stuck there. Tequila and I hung off the edge of the basket, and Fleming rolled onto its side, like an ice cube in a spilled drink glass. The metal tube that attached the burners to the basket also ran along the lip, and electricity thrummed and tickled our palms.

"Touch the rim of the basket," I told Fleming. Then I turned to Tequila and told him not to let go.

"Wasn't planning on it."

We chinned up into the basket, then Tequila helped Fleming onto the top, continuing to hold her hand as he followed her up. I reached for Tequila's hand before letting go of the lip, so we all stayed connected. The wire crackled right next to us, hooked onto the burner, its induction making all the hair on my arms stand up.

"If we lose contact, it will arc at us. We have to make sure we're linked to the line at all times."

We all instinctively ducked when we heard the gunshot. I looked to the east and saw Hammett's balloon, a hundred meters away and seventy meters above us. She was leaning out of the gondola, holding her .45 in a two-handed grip.

"I got an idea. Backpack," Tequila said, holding out his hand to Fleming. He placed his leg atop hers, then dug out an aluminum case with a bullet ding in the side. Tequila removed the remote control helicopter Harry McGlade had loaned us.

"I don't think we can all fit inside," Fleming said.

He winked at her. "Trust me. Good things come in small packages."

I could swear I heard my sister sigh like a lovesick teen. Tequila fished out the remote control and then the diminutive whirlybird was up in the air, heading toward Hammett's balloon.

Hammett

"In the field, you'll sometimes be confronted with things that don't make sense," the Instructor said. "If you waste time puzzling over them, your enemy will have the advantage."

As she took aim at the tiny musclehead with the gymnastics chops, Hammett saw a bird fly up out of his hands.

By the time she processed what she was seeing—a toy helicopter—it had closed to within ten meters.

"It's a remote control chopper," Speed said.

"Get down!" Hammett ordered, diving for the floor of the gondola.

"Why? It's just a toy. It can't—"

The toy fired a single bullet, entering Speed's head through his nose, exiting out the back behind his right ear. He folded himself into a pile next to Hammett, an expression of surprise frozen on his stupid face.

Hammett looked up, raising her weapon and seeking the helicopter. It wasn't in her vision. She killed the propane, listening for the buzz of its tiny propellers, and heard it somewhere above. Chancing a look, she saw it alongside the outside of her balloon, halfway up.

Could those little spinning blades rip the nylon? Hammett doubted it. And even if it had a few more bullets, they wouldn't do much to a thirty-meter-tall balloon.

That's when the helicopter exploded.

For a moment, there was just ear-numbing sound and a spray of smoke and toy parts. Then Hammett saw the rip in the envelope. A rip the size of a twin-size bedsheet.

The balloon began a rapid descent, and Hammett realized, with hyperawareness bordering on awe, that she would probably die when she hit the ground. Working fast, she kicked on both propane burners and opened them up fully. It slowed the balloon down, but not by much, and from this height impact would surely be—

BANG!

The thought was knocked right out of her head, and Hammett found herself face-to-face with a latticework of aluminum supports. She hadn't hit the ground. Hammett had hit the tower.

Taking advantage of the luck in the case it was short-lived, she immediately tucked her gun into her holster and scrambled out of the gondola and onto the electrical tower. Crossing a span hand-over-hand, Hammett got away from her balloon—in case it caught fire—and made her way to the maintenance ladder on the corner. She was still thirty meters from the ground, and about five from the high-tension wires above her. As her envelope deflated, she searched for Chandler's balloon, seeing the basket fifty meters away, its envelope almost directly above her.

Hammett began to ascend.

Lund

Lund forced his lungs to function, his ears to stop ringing, his head to clear. Using his hands, he lifted himself up in a push-up, then scrambled to his feet. He had no horses, no weapon, and nowhere to hide.

The ATV's engine buzzed from the end of the row. The slight sheen of the man's sharkskin suit blinked between twisted branches. He'd be around the row and on top of Lund in a matter of seconds. And though the man had missed while moving at full speed, a stationary shot at point-blank range would be much easier.

Lund glanced around for a branch, but the orchard was well kept, and there was no dead wood to be found. He stepped back into the tree line just as the vehicle cleared the row and the man's narrowed eyes focused on him.

Lund wasn't sure if it was possible to brace yourself before being shot, but he tensed anyway. He wondered, in a nonsensically detached way, what his last thought would be, and how long he'd be able to hold on to it before he died.

But the ATV didn't fire. Perhaps it indeed was out of ammo, and Lund had caught a break.

The man got off the bike. He was a little shorter, a little broader. Lund had been in his share of scraps throughout the years, and could hold his own in a fair fight.

But the suited man was a professional. And pros weren't concerned about fighting fair.

He smiled, and carefully removed a black object from his pocket. Lund immediately thought it was a gun. But a moment later there was a metallic clicking sound—the black object was the handle of a thick-bladed folding knife, four inches if it was one and looking substantial enough to hack down a sapling.

"I like knives," the man said. "They are so personal. So intimate. There is nothing quite like looking closely into a man's eyes, seeing the disbelief as his blood drains from his body."

Lund backed up, feeling a prickly branch poke the back of his head.

"Nice shoe," he said. "What happened to the other one?"

The suited man's smile soured.

"I am going to cut a hole in you big enough to stick my foot in. Then you can be my lost shoe."

Lund was sure he wouldn't like that. He reached up, to the tree branch. "You like cutting people up. But how's your fielding?"

"What?"

Recalling his college days pitching for the Minnesota Golden Gophers, Lund plucked an apple from the branch. Heavy and hard, it was green as the grass and not yet ripe. Perfect. He threw a wicked slider, aiming at the man's face.

The suited man plucked the apple out of the air with his left hand, a harsh slapping sound as fruit met palm.

Undaunted, Lund grabbed another, this time slinging a curve.

Wicked knife dropping to the ground, the suit snatched the second apple, equally adept catching lefty.

"That is the best you can do?" the man asked, flashing a wide grin. "Throwing apples at me?"

Lund plucked a third and let loose with his best pitch, a fastball, and drilled it dead center into the suited man's nose, smacking the cocky grin right off his face and knocking him onto his butt.

"You only got two hands, asshole," Lund said, taking off before the guy had a chance to recover. He headed in the direction the horses had gone, yanking his phone from his pocket as he ran. Punching up his directory, he stabbed it with a finger. Then he held it to his ear and prayed for an answer.

One ring. Two.

"Chief Ryker."

"Val, I need your help."

"Where the hell are you, Lund?"

So she wasn't happy with him. He couldn't blame her. But regardless of how she felt, she'd come through with the park ranger, echoing every bit of his training drill story and fibbing that she'd been in personal contact with a representative of the US Army.

Lund knew he was pushing her trust coming back for more, but at this point, she was his only option. "The orchard to the west of Devil's Lake."

"So the nine-one-one calls are about you. There's gunfire reported."

"Anyone hurt?"

"Not that I've heard."

A miracle. Unless you counted the guy he'd just taken out with an apple.

Up ahead he saw the dark shadow of either Banshee or Bo through the trees. The horses had stopped to eat apples or grass, no doubt. He could only hope they didn't founder after all the running they'd done. Val's niece would string him up. From the sound of it, Val already wanted to. "Listen, I need—"

"What's going on, Lund? And what are you doing in the middle of it?"

"Long story. Can you hitch up my truck and—"

"Already did. I'm at the park looking for you. And the sheriff's department is on the way."

"Good. The faster you can get here, the better. And Val?"

"What?"

"I hope you have your gun." He cut off the call, not wanting to explain any further. With the sheriff's department on the way, there was no time to lose. He had to get out of here if he was to have any chance of helping Chandler, wherever she might be.

By the time Lund had gathered the horses and made it back to the road, his red truck was pulling the four-horse stock trailer up the hill toward him. Val was out of the driver's seat almost before she stopped.

Val was a beautiful woman, and one of the strongest Lund had ever known. One of those blond-haired, blue-eyed, stoic Norwegians, she also had a knack of making him feel as though she didn't need him, as if she didn't need anybody, a fact that probably shouldn't grate on him as much as it did.

At least, not anymore.

A crease dug between her eyebrows, her mouth pinched in a frown, and she glared at him as if pondering how she'd like to drag him back to Lake Loyal and throw him into the PD's single holding cell. "All right, Lund. Time to come clean."

A county sheriff's cruiser crested the hill from the other direction, light bar flashing. To Lund's relief, the county car turned into the orchard's farm market parking lot on the opposite side of the road.

The last thing he wanted was to answer questions. Val's or the deputy's. He needed to make this quick. "There's a man straight through the trees, near the fence. He was the one shooting."

"At you?"

He nodded.

"At the horses?"

Lund chose not to answer that one. "I hit him with an apple."

"What?"

"Never mind. We have to get out of here, Val. Fast."

She shook her head. "Get out of here? Are you nuts?"

"You don't understand. This is not a law enforcement matter."

"Gunshots aren't a law enforcement matter?"

"It's beyond you or the deputy over there. This is…it's…"

"It's what?"

"Complicated. You have to trust me. We need to load the horses and get the hell out of here." He turned away from her and led the animals to the rear of the trailer.

Val followed, tossing him a halter and lead rope for Banshee and taking Bo and Max's reins. "We'll load them, then you can explain. How's that?"

He didn't answer, figuring silence was the most expedient option. Val was cooperating for the moment, and anything he said would likely mess that up. He'd deal with the explanation when they got to that point. He swapped Banshee's bridle for her halter and led her into the trailer, tying her in front. Then he helped Val load the other two and climbed behind the wheel.

The moment Val got into the truck, she narrowed her eyes, giving him that cop stare that made him want to squirm even in cases when he had nothing to hide. "Talk."

Val's cell rang, and she glanced at the readout. "Oneida. I have to take this." She answered, questioning the dispatcher of the village of Lake Loyal's police department in a low voice.

Taking advantage of the distraction, Lund pulled out onto the road, driving away from the deputy to the intersection with Highway 12.

When Val ended the call, he could feel her eyes return to his face. "You wouldn't know anything about two hot-air balloons that were stolen and flown into power lines north of here?"

Lund turned north.

Out of the corner of his eye, he could see her shaking her head. "How on earth did you get involved in…whatever is going on?"

He gave her the CliffsNotes version of what had happened in the past few hours, skipping the part where Señor Suit shot at the horses.

"You didn't answer my question."

"A woman named Chandler needed my help."

"A woman?"

He'd like to think he heard a note of jealousy in her voice, but even if the feeling was there, he doubted Val would ever admit to it. "She works for the government, or at least she did. Her sister is with her, and she's injured. We need to help them."

She brushed her hair back from her face and gave a heavy sigh. "I'll go along with that, provided this trip ends at the station, so I can find out exactly what's happening."

"Chandler won't agree to that."

"She doesn't have to agree. I have handcuffs."

Lund didn't think Chandler would agree to being cuffed either, but decided there was no point in trying to explain. "These are the good guys, Val."

"Then they shouldn't be afraid to talk to the police."

"Val, you don't understand. Badger Ammo, it's a black site."

"A black site?"

"As in a make-people-disappear black site."

"I know what a black site is, Lund. But here? In Wisconsin?"

"I know it's hard to believe. But everything I've seen suggests it's true. And that the people running it aren't afraid to kill to keep it quiet."

"Kill? You haven't told me everything, have you?"

"And what are you going to do, Val? Rush in? Arrest people? Take on government agencies we've never even heard of because officially they don't exist?" He shook his head. "Please, Val. I need your help."

She froze, staring at him, as if watching their past play through the back of her mind. Finally, she nodded. "You have feelings for her?"

Lund didn't want to answer. It would only hurt Val, even though she was the one who'd pushed him away. Even when he'd worked through all that had happened between them and was ready to look past it, she'd said she wasn't ready for a relationship, that she might never be.

He cleared his throat. "We just met. But I like her a lot, yes."

"I'd say it's more than that."

"Maybe I can't wait any longer, Val. Maybe I need to move on."

"I know these last few months..." Val looked away. "You deserve to be happy, Lund."

"So do you, Val."

Raising her chin, Val squinted out the window. "Is that your girlfriend up there?"

Lund looked in the distance to the power lines, and saw two brightly colored hot-air balloons draped across them. One was tangled in the tower; the other's basket seemed to be hung up on the line itself. Atop the basket were three figures, one of them standing up.

"That's Chandler," Lund whispered.

He floored the gas pedal.

Chandler

"Gravity wants to fuck you," the Instructor said. "Play hard to get."

As Hammett climbed the tower near the top of our almost-deflated balloon, I crawled to the end of the basket and reached for the skirt. Gathering nylon in both fists, I tugged.

The envelope was heavy, and it didn't budge. I pulled again, Tequila adding his strength to the effort, but we still couldn't move it. Sighting down to the end of it, I saw why. The parachute valve at the top of the balloon was snagged on the ceramic insulator attached to Hammett's tower.

I knew what I had to do, much as I didn't want to do it. Imagining my veins filled with ice water, I stood up and prepared to face my sister.

"I'm going to free the balloon envelope," I said. "It'll fall, and should drop low enough so you can climb down it, to the ground. Don't touch the balloon and the ground at the same time."

Tequila stood up. "I can do it."

"This isn't your fight."

"I'm a gymnast."

"You practiced the balance beam? I didn't know that was a male event."

He touched my shoulder. "Chandler..."

"I got this. I need you to get Fleming to safety."

His hard look softened, and he nodded. I felt a hand tug at my calf and stared down at my sister. She reached up to me, extending a fillet knife.

"Kill the bitch," Fleming said. Her face displayed complete confidence in me.

I wished I shared her conviction.

I took the knife and tucked it into my back pocket. Then I tentatively touched the wire, feeling a strong and somewhat painful spark, knowing it was only induction and it wouldn't kill me.

But it wasn't pleasant. Not in the least. I've never stuck my hand into a beehive, but the buzzing, and stinging, was probably close to what it felt resting a bare palm on a high-tension wire. I placed one foot onto it, then the other, and slowly stood up, feeling the heat through the soles of my shoes. The hair on my neck, and over my temples, began to stick out. A slight, cool breeze blew in from the south, and I sucked some in through my clenched teeth.

My sense of balance was pretty good, as long as I didn't let heights mess with my head. But no matter how many times I found myself high up, I still couldn't get used to it. Looking at the basket beneath my feet was fine. But then I took a few steps and the basket was gone, leaving me on a wire with nothing but ninety feet of air between me and the ground.

The trick with being high up is desensitization. When you spend a lot of time at great heights, you can become acclimated to the point it no longer bothers you.

I've never gotten to that level. I respect heights like I respect electricity, water, guns, explosives, fire, vehicles, and the many other ways a human being can get killed. But I've never reached the point, either in training or in the field, where I fully got used to it.

So when I looked down—the unfortunate side effect of watching my footing on the wire—I saw how high I was, and my stomach wanted to jump up my throat and slap me for my bad judgment. But I kept my balance, and walked two steps in open air until I reached the skirt of the balloon. I crouched slowly—in the heyday of the Playboy Club they called it a bunny dip—and with great care I gathered up a handful of nylon fabric and let it fall off the side of the wire. Then I moved, step by step, tugging the nylon off the wire and letting it drop. It was excruciating work. My muscles cramped up. I was constantly adjusting my balance. If the wind kicked up any harder, it would blow me right off the wire. But slowly, surely, the balloon fell free, and then its weight took over and the bulk of the envelope slid off the wire until it hung in a big U, one end attached to the basket, the top still attached to the insulator.

Chancing a look ahead, I saw that Hammett had reached the top of the tower, and she had a hand on the insulator coils, right where my balloon was snagged. We were about ten meters from each other.

"Be a dear and free that for me," I yelled.

She didn't follow my request. Instead, she drew her gun.

I considered my options. To my left was another wire, attached to the one I was on by large aluminum separators, about a meter away. But jumping to that wire meant I'd lose my connection with it while in the air, and arcing would zap the shit out of me. I needed to keep at least one limb on the wire at all times.

I considered turning back, but we'd still be stuck on the wire, and Hammett would come for us. So would whichever secret branch of the military ran the black site. Even if I dealt with Hammett, we still needed to get off this wire before we were all conveniently disappeared by my loveable duplicitous government.

I stayed in a crouch, keeping myself a small target, waiting for Hammett's move, and I realized she wasn't aiming at me. She was using her gun to draw a spark from the wire ahead of the insulator, bonding on like I'd done with the propane burner.

But her gun wasn't very long, and when the spark zapped her, it was a doozy. Hammett cried out, her gun falling to the ground, but the bitch managed to get her hand onto the wire without falling off.

"I bet that hurt," I yelled.

Hammett began to laugh. Instead of it being a sisterly bonding moment, her insane cackle seriously creeped me out. In between guffaws she said, "I'm going to show you *hurt*."

I stood up, the breeze whipping through my short hair, and clenched my hands into fists.

"Bring it," I said.

Hammett and I had both been trained by the Instructor, so her balancing skills were on par with mine. We closed the distance between us quickly, but before we were near enough to engage, she stood on one foot and pulled something from her ankle sheath.

A straight razor. I hadn't known Hammett for long, but this weapon seemed particularly appropriate for her. Razors were a psycho's best friend.

I reached into my pocket, pulling out the fillet knife Fleming had given me.

"OK," I said. "Let's do this."

And we began the most dangerous high-wire routine in the history of mankind.

Hammett

"When facing an equally skilled opponent," the Instructor said, "cheat."

Feeling the surge of the high voltage flowing from the wire through her shoes and making her arm hair stick out, the hyper-awareness from the thrill of balancing on a thin line at such a great height, the solid excitement of the pearl razor handle in her fingers and the jointed steel tang under her thumb, and the sight of Chandler approaching with a fillet knife, Hammett couldn't help but smile.

She felt wonderfully alive. A curious reaction, considered death was all around her.

Years ago, Hammett had latched on to Hydra training like a starving calf latched on to a teat. It had been a lifeline. An outsider would have viewed Hammett's upbringing as normal, bordering on quaint. Suburban nuclear family, middle-class down to the white picket fence, with smiling adoptive parents who were always hugging little Betsy in pictures.

But the smiling was just a front. A mask of normalcy hiding the monster. And she still didn't like to think about the monster.

By the time of her stepparents' deaths, Betsy had fully embraced what psychiatrists call "thrill-seeking behavior." But it was always without purpose. Betsy wanted an outlet for her aggression, but lack of direction meant her energies were wasted satisfying base urges.

Hydra allowed her to do things she never even dreamed of. She got paid for her self-destructive indulgences. And now, balancing on a high-tension wire thirty meters above the ground, about to engage in a knife fight with her identical sister, Hammett couldn't think of anywhere she'd rather be.

Chandler had adopted a fencing stance, front foot with the toe pointed forward, back foot perpendicular. When she advanced, it was front foot, back foot, front foot, back foot, never crossing one over the other. It was woefully predictable; fencing duelists maintained the same axis line, suitable for wire walking.

Hammett, however, had other ideas.

She ran forward, taking fast, tiny steps on her toes, rushing at Chandler as if they were on solid ground. Chandler hunched down, leaning back on her rear foot, raising her knife in one hand, throwing up an arm block with the other.

Hammett came to a quick stop just out of slashing distance, and then twisted her hips, kicking at Chandler's knife with a football punt. Chandler pulled back, her blade slashing harmlessly across the bottom of Hammett's shoe. Hammett retained her balance on one leg, pivoted, and brought the same foot across Chandler's face, connecting solidly with the side of her sister's head.

Chandler extended her arms at her sides, an obvious effort to keep from falling. That left her wide open to attack.

Hammett's foot found the wire, and she leaned forward, slashing with the razor. Chandler managed to block with the fillet knife, and there was a clink of metal on metal. Though Hammett liked the theatricality of a straight razor—it scared the piss out of many a target when she opened it up—it was best suited for close-up work on an unarmed opponent. Against a knife, a razor came up lacking. Which Hammett learned all too well when Chandler followed up the parry with a poke at Hammett's chest, the knife tip penetrating her left breast.

Hammett recoiled, and Chandler seized the advantage, using her fencing moves to force Hammett backward, fast enough to make Hammett focus on staying on the wire and abandon attacking.

After backpedaling eight or nine steps, Hammett was confronted with the startling realization that she might actually lose, and in this case losing was fatal. She had wanted to beat Chandler in a fair fight, but there really was no such thing as unfair in a fight to the death, so she dug a hand into her back pocket and removed the carefully folded piece of paper that she always carried with her; an origami envelope, filled with a mixture of regular table salt and pepper.

Bending the envelope in half behind her back in a much-practiced move, most of the contents spilled into Hammett's palm, and with the wind behind her she threw the salt and pepper into Chandler's eyes during her next lunge.

The effect was immediate, and devastating.

Chandler staggered, immediately raising her free hand to her eyes to clear them of irritants. Then her rear foot slipped, and she toppled off the wire.

Chandler

"When an opponent cheats," the Instructor said, "cheat back."

I had no idea what Hammett had thrown into my face, but it stung my eyes and temporarily blinded me. And then I was falling.

As my back foot stepped into open air and my body followed, I crooked my left elbow and snagged the wire on my way down. For a crazy moment I swung, and I clamped my teeth around the knife handle and barehanded the wire, pins and needles jumping through my palms. I shook my head like a dog, blinking away tears, and blurrily saw the parallel companion wire a meter ahead of me.

Above me, I sensed Hammett moving in, no doubt anxious to slash my fingers off. Without waiting for that to happen, I jackknifed my lower body like a trapeze artist, and swung toward the other power line.

My heels caught the edge, and I used momentum, muscle, and good old-fashioned fear to get my knees onto the wire. Then I let go with my hands, and I was hanging upside down.

That's when the fear really kicked in.

I gave in to it for a moment, letting my body respond to the raw, animal panic in all the usual ways. Dry mouth, sweaty palms, hammering heart, hyperventilation, adrenaline surge, inability to focus. It seemed like minutes, but couldn't have lasted longer than a few seconds before I regained control and let my training take over.

I plucked the knife from my mouth, coughed, and spat into my free palm, using the saliva to wipe my stinging eyes. From smell and taste I guessed Hammett had used salt and pepper, rather than something potentially more lethal, such as lye or powdered glass. This was good. It meant my blurriness was temporary, so I could scratch "permanent blindness" off my list of immediate fears.

"What are you doing over there, Sis?"

Hammett's voice activated my startle reflex, but I forced myself to betray nothing but calm.

"Just hanging out," I said through clenched teeth. "You should come over."

And that's what the bitch did. In a single graceful move, Hammett tucked down, flipped, and then was dangling by her hands on the wire, directly across from me. I blinked away tears and watched Hammett smile, her teeth locked around the straight razor handle.

I put my knife back into my mouth, reached up, and unhooked my knees. Then I changed my grip on the power line and faced her just as her feet were rushing at my chest.

I twisted, bringing up a leg, catching her bent knee with mine. She kicked out with her free leg, and I locked that one up as well, trying us into a knot as we hung there.

I continued to rapidly blink, tears and spit getting blown off my cheeks by the wind. Hammett tried to tug me toward her, lifting herself up so I had to bear her weight, but sore as my hands were, I wasn't about to be pulled off that wire.

Then my sister did something I didn't expect. She took one hand off the line and removed the razor from her mouth. I immediately did the same with my knife.

"If you cut me with my legs still wrapped around yours," I said in forced tones, "we'll both fall."

"I was thinking I just cut an artery, you bleed out."

"I can do the same to you."

Hammett's eyes flashed. "Prisoner's dilemma."

Though we weren't together at Hydra, I assumed Hammett and I had the same training. The prisoner's dilemma was a classic example of game theory. Two people are arrested. If neither rats out the other, they each get short prison sentences—the best possible scenario. But if one rats out the other, the other goes to jail for a long time, and the rat goes free. If both rat, they both get long sentences. While it is in the collective interest to keep silent, self-preservation kicks in, always resulting in a double betrayal. I played the game with the Instructor many times, his way of proving that you can never trust anybody.

"You know how this ends," I said, adjusting my grip. "We both die."

Hammett's eyes narrowed. "Human nature sucks." She raised the razor.

"Don't do this, Hammett. You can't win."

My sister smiled. "But I can try."

She slashed down with the razor, and I thrust the fillet knife forward, blocking her blow. Our steel locked together, I turned my wrist downward, poking at the back of her hand. Hammett pulled away, and my fillet knife sunk into her thigh.

Our eyes locked, and I could guess my panicked expression mirrored hers.

Then Hammett let go of the power line.

Her legs remained tangled in mine.

For the longest second of my life, I hung there, one-handed, holding both of us.

Then my hand slipped, and we fell.

Fleming

"Life is tragedy," the Instructor said. "Get used to it."

Clenching Tequila's hand in hers, so tight she was no doubt hurting him, Fleming watched her sisters fight on the power line.

She gasped when Chandler fell and hung by her knees.

She yelled when Hammett joined her beneath the wires, locking legs.

And when they fell, something inside Fleming broke, and she screamed like she'd never screamed in her life.

Lund

It was damn near impossible to drive while also watching Chandler do her high-wire act, but Lund managed to get to the field under the electrical towers without wrecking his truck or harming the horses in the trailer.

When driving over the grassland became too bumpy, he threw it into park. Then he fumbled for his cell phone to dial the fire chief in Lake Delton. Baraboo's fire truck only had a three-story ladder. He needed one of the big boys, one with a hundred-foot hydraulic telescoping platform, to cherry-pick Chandler off the line. He tried to search his list of contacts for the number, pressed the wrong button, and wound up in the programming menu.

Cursing himself, he slowed down and went name by name, carefully selecting the correct number, setting his jaw as it rang once, twice, three times—

"Lund."

Val had her hand on his arm, gripping it tight. Lund looked up and saw Chandler and the woman she was fighting, hanging by their hands, the big bow of the deflated balloon in a wide arc ten meters below them, flapping in the wind.

Lund squeezed the phone. He had the urge to do something, anything, but could only sit in his truck, every muscle tensed, eyes glued and powerless. He'd only known Chandler a short time, but he felt something between them, something more than the physical attraction they shared. Lund had fought some terrible blazes alongside some very good people. The bonds formed in combat were strong ones, and he shared lifelong friendships with men he'd met in the midst of a firefight, friendships forged in an instant when lives depended on another's actions.

He knew Chandler. Recognized her bravery, her self-sacrifice. Understood her on a base, core level.

She was one of the good guys.

"This is Chief Potash of the Delton Fire Department. I'm away from my phone right now. If this is an emergency, dial nine one one."

Lund swore, disconnected, and dialed Delton direct. He only knew a few of the men who worked there, so it could take a bit of convincing to get them to travel outside their district, but maybe he'd get lucky.

"They're still fighting," Val said, her voice distant, incredulous. "How can they still be—"

And then Lund watched Chandler and her opponent drop off the line, into empty sky, and his mind filled with disbelief, because that wasn't supposed to happen to the good guys.

Chandler

"You ain't dead," the Instructor said, "till you're dead."

When you hit the ground during sparring, there are moves and tricks to absorb the impact. Some of these can help counteract the effects of a fall from as high as four or five meters.

There is no training that can help you survive a thirty-meter drop. Brace yourself? Go limp? Land legs first? Back first?

None of it matters. From that height, you are lasagna when you hit.

There is no way to mentally prepare yourself to become lasagna, especially when the raw panic of falling overwhelms your ability to think. I'd always hoped for some insightful, poignant last thought, something that succinctly summed up my life and what I'd learned from it, but when Hammett and I fell off the wire, all that went through my head was: *Shit.*

I looked up, hands outstretched, and watched an arc of electricity reach out and zap my fillet knife, then stretch and wink out. Before I had the chance to brace myself or go limp or do anything that required more than my reptile brain, we hit, much sooner than I expected.

Even more surprising, we didn't turn into pasta.

Hitting ground didn't stop our downward trek, and as we slid in on an angle, the reality of my luck went off in my head like a school bell. We'd landed on the balloon envelope I'd removed from the power line, hanging in a bow beneath us. Because nylon didn't conduct electricity well, it only had a small charge, similar to static. My hair stood up on my neck, but there was no discomfort, no heat like that of standing on the wire.

Still entwined with Hammett, I turned onto my side, trying to grip the slippery nylon, dropping the fillet knife in my efforts, unable to grab hold but eventually coming to a gradual stop as we reached the center of the bow.

For a moment, Hammett and I lay there in the world's largest and highest hammock, silent and shocked.

"That was lucky," she said.

Then the end ripped free from the insulator, and we were falling again.

I kicked my sister away and gathered up the fabric in my arms and legs, like a koala bear clinging to a tree, getting friction burns on my bare skin but determined to slow myself down before slamming into the earth. The nylon continued to tear, and I dug an arm inside the hole, my armpit busting through seam after seam after seam. But I wasn't slowing down fast enough, and soon I'd slide off the end of the balloon and drop to the ground at too high a velocity to survive.

Then I felt Hammett's hands on mine, seeking my shoulders, and my hands found her waist, and we clung to each other, the torn balloon nylon between us, pressing our bodies together in a wrestling clinch and coming to a painful, friction-filled stop with a few feet of envelope still left to spare.

I gasped, chanced a look down, saw we were still about fifteen feet up. High enough to break ankles, but we'd live.

"Prisoner's dilemma again," I said between panting. "If we work together here, we can—"

Through the envelope, Hammett elbowed me in the face.

Goddamn, she was an asshole.

I released her, sliding down again, managing to snag onto the line that opened the parachute valve. I slid down those two feet and then dropped off, leaving my hands above my head, electricity arcing from the envelope and giving me a painful zap in my right index finger; and then I hit the ground with my ankles tight together, immediately dropping and rolling to absorb the shock of impact.

Hammett dropped next to me, and from a prone position, I kicked her in the face. She rolled away, my toe connecting with her cheek, and I got up on wobbly legs in time to see Javier speeding toward us on his ATV.

"Chandler!"

The voice came from behind me, and I turned and saw Lund running up. Next to him, drawing a weapon, was a blond woman. She was trim, attractive, and moved like a cop. I guessed it was the infamous Val. My joy at seeing Lund again was tempered by my instant dislike for his ex girlfriend.

"Shoot the four-wheeler," I told her.

"I'm a police officer. Both of you raise your hands above your heads and get on the—"

I was on Val before she finished her sentence, coming up in under the gun, twisting, levering it away from her, and then tripping her backward so she fell onto her ass. I could do the same move without the tripping part, but it felt right for some reason.

Her gun was a Glock, no safety. I aimed at Javier, a head shot, and fired just as he swerved.

The hammer fell on an empty chamber. Damn townie cop played it cautious.

I fired again, but Javier was now racing away, Hammett running alongside. He slowed enough for her to hop onto the back of his bike, and I emptied the clip at their retreating forms, trying to aim through the dirt the tires kicked up. They didn't slow down, but I saw sparks as I pinged the back of their ride. Unfortunately, none of my shots was a kill shot, and they zoomed away leaving me pissed as all hell. We'd never catch them in Lund's truck.

"Val..." Lund said.

I turned, ready to chew out Blondie for being a wuss and not carrying a live round in the pipe, but to my surprise she was right there, already swinging a haymaker at my head.

I took it on the chin, as hard a shot as I've ever received, and even though it hurt like crazy I stood upright and stared her down like it was no big deal. Her eyes got wide with obvious fear, and I thought about all the things I could do to amplify that emotion in her.

"Chandler," Lund said, "she's here to help."

"Learn to load your weapon, cop," I said. Clint Eastwood couldn't have been scarier.

To her credit, Val didn't melt into a blubbery pool of cowardice. "There are more accidental firearm deaths due to—"

"Shh," I interrupted. Then, before she could go on, I'd shoved her gun back into her holster and was walking away.

Above, I saw Fleming, clinging to Tequila's back as he climbed down the balloon envelope, hand over hand.

I looked back at Lund, saw the poor guy paralyzed with indecision as two women stared him down. He looked from me, to Val, and back again, as if watching a tennis match. When he took a step to Val, my heart died a little bit.

"I swear, you'll get an explanation. But right now I need you to drive the truck while I talk to Chandler."

Val stared hard at him in a way that made me think she was probably a pretty good cop, then gave him a clipped nod and headed for his truck. Lund walked over to me, and my heart promptly forgot about its minor setback a moment ago, and beat with new possibilities.

"Are you OK?"

I nodded. He took a step closer.

"Val is…she's a good person. I trust her."

I nodded again.

"When I saw you up there, I—"

"Lund?"

"Yeah?"

"Just kiss me already."

His lips curled into a quick, boyish grin, and then I was in his arms, feeling safe for the first time in I don't know how long. The kiss was soft, gentle, nice, but as much as I liked nice, it wasn't enough for the moment. I circled his neck with my arms and crushed my lips to his, hard and needy, taking him, claiming him. My tongue touched his, and I felt a spark that was just as strong as any I'd felt on the power line. And in the back of my mind, I hoped Val saw it all.

Fleming

"Combat is like politics," the Instructor said. "It makes for strange bedfellows."

"I don't want to interrupt them," Fleming said. "They're so cute."

She was clinging to Tequila's back while he hung off the end of the balloon roughly three meters up, watching Chandler passionately kiss Lund.

"No problem," Tequila said. "I can hang on for as long as you need."

Fleming gave him a little extra hug, then called down to her sister, "A little help here."

Chandler and Lund looked up, then immediately broke the embrace and positioned themselves beneath the duo.

"Ready?" Tequila asked.

"Yes."

Ever since the coast guard had fished them out of Lake Michigan, Fleming had been out of her element, at the mercy of those around her. That Chandler had watched out for her didn't come as a surprise. She knew what her sister was capable of, and it was far more encompassing than her amazing physical skills. Chandler had a big heart. She'd proven it to Fleming before they'd ever met face-to-face, and she'd proved it every moment since.

But Tequila had been a welcome surprise.

Fleming didn't know anything about him, but she didn't have to. He was obviously reserved, even cut off emotionally, and yet the way he'd taken care of her in the prison, when he gave her his jeans so she didn't have to ride half naked, how she was piggybacking him again like it was the most natural thing in the world for him, suggested there was more to the guy than met the eye, even though he seemed to resist accessing it.

Gently but firmly grasping her hand, he removed her off his shoulders and held her at arm's length.

"You'll get shocked when I let you go," he said.

"So will you."

"I can handle it."

"So can I."

She took a deep breath. For a few seconds, Fleming swung back and forth, hanging by Tequila's hand as if they were a couple of acrobats at Baraboo's nearby Circus World Museum. Then he released her, and the electric spark stretched between them like a tether—painful, but perhaps not as painful as letting him go.

Fleming fell into Chandler and Lund's arms.

"Hiya, Sis," Chandler said.

They hugged hard, both teary-eyed.

Chandler allowed Lund to take her, and Fleming looked up just as Tequila dropped off the envelope, doing a double flip in the air before landing on his feet.

Fuck shining armor. Fleming's knight wore black boxer briefs and was built like a Roman god. She allowed herself a quick, unabashed ogle as he walked over, and then she let out a girlish sigh.

"No kidding," Chandler said, also eyeing Tequila.

And they looked at each other and squeezed hands and giggled like schoolgirls. Like regular civilians. Like sisters.

"Did I miss something?" Tequila asked.

Fleming and Chandler giggled again. Tequila rolled his eyes, held out his arms, and took Fleming from Lund, whisking her over to the trailer.

Lund opened the back, and they all squeezed inside with Banshee, Bo, and Max, who were still wearing their saddles.

The trailer was an open stock-type, built to haul four horses, and Lund pushed to the front and lowered Fleming to the floor in the open space next to Banshee. The trailer started to move just as the scream of sirens filtered in from outside.

Chandler eyed Lund. "We can't get pulled over."

"We won't be. At least not for long."

"They're going to want to check out what we're doing here."

"Don't worry about it."

"We can't—"

"Val is driving the rig, Chandler. She's police chief of a town near here. She understands that you can't be found. She'll get us out, and no one will be the wiser."

Fleming didn't know who Val was or what was going on, but even though she didn't totally trust cops, she was relieved to have one on their side.

The trailer rumbled over gravel, then reached a smooth paved road. Tequila stood between Fleming and Banshee, seemingly guarding to ensure the mare didn't make a wrong step. Chandler and Lund stood near Bo and Max's heads, speaking in low voices. Chandler administered another shot of Demerol to Fleming, and two for herself.

They made it down the road without being stopped by police at all, and as the truck wound down country roads, Fleming's eyes closed and she fell asleep to the gentle rocking of the trailer and the scent of horses.

* * *

The truck came to a stop, and Fleming woke. Pulling herself up as tall as she could, she peered through the slats in the upper portion of the trailer, but the sun had finally set and all she could see were trees and the black sky, speckled with stars. She had no idea where they were. She sought out Tequila, saw him standing in the same position he'd been in before she fell asleep. Fleming knew how terrible she must look after all she'd been through, but she also knew lust in a man's eyes when she saw it, and through all the pain and exhaustion it made her feel warm all over.

She must have shown something in her face as well, because even in the dim light she could see Tequila blush.

Lund jumped out the back, and Chandler knelt down beside Fleming. "You're going to think I'm crazy, but we need to remove your tracking chip."

Of course they did, and Fleming probably would have thought of it herself if she wasn't so out of it. "Where do you want to do it?"

"Here in the trailer. Lund has the supplies."

As if on cue, Lund slipped back in the trailer and shuffled between the horses, carrying a duffel bag, a small, hard-cased device slung over his shoulder. The truck remained still, the trailer only shifting slightly as the horses adjusted their feet.

"Don't worry," Chandler said. "He's experienced. And very gentle."

Fleming felt a momentary sense of panic. Not at the thought of an impromptu operation in a horse trailer, but because she hadn't yet told Chandler.

"At the site, while I was escaping, there was another prisoner there. We have to go back for him."

Chandler's face screwed up, almost comically. "Are you kidding? There is no way in hell I'm ever going back to that place."

"I have to. I owe him. Years ago, when I fell in Milan…he risked everything for me."

She shook her head, still not understanding.

"Chandler…it was the Instructor."

The White House

"She escaped, Mr. President."

"How on earth did that happen? It's my understanding she has no use of her legs."

"As I said, these women are formidable."

The president closed his eyes and shook his head. He resisted the impulse to throw his encrypted cell phone onto the floor. Not that it would do anything. The phone was supposed to be shockproof.

"Do you know where she is?"

"She's with Chandler, and we have a way of tracking them, but we don't know how long that is going to be viable."

"What are the chances of her coming in on her own?" he asked.

"Zero. She feels her country has betrayed her."

"No shit." But at least they remained loyal to each other, which was more than the president could say about his party. This situation had brought out the worst in them.

"But we have a plan in place to recapture her, and her sister Chandler. We'll know more soon."

"What about the rogue agent? Hammett?"

"She'll be taken care of."

"See that she is."

The president hung up. He no longer believed he could trust his contact. In fact, he no longer knew whom he could trust. So far, the only ones who seemed to be on his side were the Hydra agents, Chandler and Fleming. And their country had betrayed them. Which meant, what? They needed to be silenced? Would he be forced to kill patriots—heroes by any definition—just to keep a dirty little government secret?

Unfortunately, he knew the answer to that.

Chandler

"I can't state this often enough. You must learn to live in the moment," the Instructor said. "Not just while carrying out an assignment, but in every aspect of your life. There's no point in putting things off when the future may never come."

Fleming's chip came out more easily than mine had, but that was probably a combination of Lund and me now having experience and it not being my own duodenum this time. Once the procedure was done and Fleming's incision was dressed and bandaged, Lund took the chip and tossed it into the back of a dump truck on its way to who knew where. Then he rode the rest of the way back to his in-law's dairy farm in the truck with Val.

I stood in the back, watched Tequila fawn over Fleming—or at least his nonfawning version of fawning—and tried not to think about the Instructor.

The last time I'd seen him, I'd been unsure about whether I could trust him, and that feeling hadn't changed. But although I didn't know the details of what he'd done for Fleming after her devastating fall in Milan, I recognized the look in my sister's eyes when she said she had to go back. And no matter how ambivalent I felt about our mentor, I wasn't about to let Fleming down. I had a hunch Tequila would agree, although I doubted he would lower his rates.

Of course none of us was in any kind of shape to do anything about it now. We needed time to regroup, arm ourselves, and come up with a plan.

Once we reached the farm, Tequila carried Fleming to the house. I paused for a moment, standing in the gravel drive, loaded down with the first-aid duffel and ultrasound. By the time I realized Lund was not getting out of the truck, I felt exposed and awkward and realized Val was sizing me up from the driver's seat, her piercing blue eyes seeing more than I wanted.

"I just...thank you," I managed to say.

She nodded, then she shifted into gear, and I watched her drive away with the horses...and the man.

My teenage years hadn't been normal, no dating or going to prom. But if I had experienced such things, I imagined this is what it would feel like to watch the boy I was crushing on go to the dance with the head cheerleader.

Giving myself a mental shake for being so pitiful, I followed the others into the house. I should feel lucky to be alive, and not just me but Fleming and Tequila, too. We'd escaped from the prison, we'd shaken Hammett, and now we could recover and reload and figure out what the hell we were going to do next.

In the harvest gold living room, Tequila set Fleming down on the ugly couch, and she winced.

"You're in pain," he said.

"I'm used to it."

Tequila reached into his jeans pocket and removed a lighter and something else.

Sinking onto an armchair next to the fireplace, I raised an eyebrow. Talk about teenage flashbacks. "Is that...?"

"Purple kush. Medical-grade marijuana." He glanced at Fleming. "Have you ever?"

Fleming rolled her eyes. "Duh. I went to college."

"It'll take the edge off the pain, without making you loopy like morphine." Tequila lit the joint, taking just enough of a hit to get it started. Then he passed it to Fleming.

The sweet smell wafted through the old farmhouse. After the first puff, the tightness in Fleming's face began to fade. Two puffs after that, and my sister was grinning.

"Damn. It's gotten a lot stronger since I was in school," she said.

I frowned. Much as I felt for Fleming, this didn't seem like an ideal time to get high. We were safe for the time being, but we were out of ammunition, only had Tequila's .45s and his survival rifle, and we hadn't even discussed our next move.

"I didn't picture you as a stoner," I said to Tequila. "I figured you for one of those health types. My body is my temple, that sort of thing."

Tequila shrugged. "Tough to sleep sometimes. It helps."

He held it out for me. I tried to think about the last good night's sleep I had, but it seemed too long ago to recall.

We seemed to be safe, for the moment, but I wasn't ready to let my guard down. Hammett wouldn't give up so easily. We weren't the only ones who would regroup. She'd come at us again. And the fact that the Instructor was a prisoner at the black site offered up a whole new problem. Did Hammett know he was there? If so, what would she do to him?

I might not be sure whether or not I trusted the Instructor, but I knew I certainly owed him a debt. If we were to spring him, it had to be fast. Whichever clandestine part of our government controlled the black site, they no doubt already knew it had been breached. That meant sending in a cleanup team.

Every minute that passed, our odds at a rescue attempt got worse. And even though I hadn't discussed it at length with Fleming, I was sure we would be attempting it soon, and I didn't want to add pot to the mix.

"No thanks," I told Tequila.

He took a hit himself, letting out a long stream of smoke as Fleming cozied up against his side. He passed the joint back to her, and she hit it again.

"Oh my God, you've got a body like a stripper," she said. Even in the low light I could see that the whites of her eyes had become pink. "And thighs like tree trunks."

She was right. Still in his underwear after donating his jeans and jacket to Fleming, Tequila was all muscle. His legs from boxers to boots looked more sturdy and solid than any man's I'd ever seen.

"Let me feel your muscles." Fleming reached for Tequila's chest, placing her palm on it. "C'mon. Flex for me."

He shrugged, and his pecs popped under the white T-shirt.

"Oh my God, I want to fuck you so bad right now."

"I think she's had enough," I said. I hated being such a buzz kill, but someone had to be the responsible one, at least until Fleming got back to herself.

Tequila gently took the joint from Fleming and pinched out the burning end between his thumb and index finger.

"Maybe she's right. Maybe I've had enough pot." Fleming slipped a hand under the hem of Tequila's shirt and lifted it up to expose an impressive eight-pack. "But not enough of this. Can I see you naked?"

"Ah, Sis?"

Fleming shot me an exasperated, and very high, frown. "Chandler, I thought I was going to die just a few hours ago. I'd like to live a little now, if you don't mind."

Of course, I couldn't mind. She was right. And from the look of Tequila's boxers, he wasn't minding much either. "Fine. But take it upstairs, won't you?"

"Oh, you're no fun." Fleming laughed, a sound that soothed even my prickly mood. She looked at Tequila and started easing down the zipper of the Blackhawks jacket to show a little cleavage. "Want your jeans and jacket back?"

Tequila's eyes glinted. He stood, then scooped her up and headed upstairs.

I thought about Lund, pictured the last kiss we'd shared, and the moment was ruined when I remembered he'd gone off with Blondie Cheerleader Cop.

What was wrong with me?

I wasn't an emotional person. On top of that, I'd been trained to compartmentalize, kill without a thought and sleep like a baby at night. I'd had plenty of one-night stands, enjoyed myself, and walked away without a twinge of longing. And now I was breaking down in the middle of an op over seeing my sister and awash in jealousy over a guy I'd just met?

I had to laugh at how just a day ago, Jack Daniels had labeled me a sociopath. I hadn't liked the label, but I certainly preferred it to "emotional basket case."

I heard a loud clunk, and at first thought Tequila might have dropped Fleming. Then their moaning, with a few pleasure-filled yips from my sister, echoed down the stairs.

The yips became squeals. And, ultimately, screaming. Screaming, accompanied by swearing, "God" and "yes" repeated over and over.

I wondered if I sounded like that. I didn't think so, and pondered if that had to do with some inhibition on my part, or perhaps it was due to my poor judgment in picking partners.

I curled in the armchair, thinking about lighting a fire. After contemplating the effort it would take and the threat of smoke from the chimney conjuring up unwanted curiosity, I abandoned the idea. Staring at the night through the bay window, I willed myself to fall asleep, but even a simple doze seemed beyond reach. It occurred to me that I should at least clean up and dress my wounds, but instead I just sat there.

The past days had turned my life upside down, and all I could think was that my emotions were struggling to catch up, to make sense, to process. It was a choice of that or believing I was losing my mind, and I preferred the first option.

Rest. That's what I needed. Maybe then I could get my act together.

I wasn't sure how much time had passed when a stream of headlights split the darkness outside. Armed with only a paring knife from the kitchen drawer, I took position beside the door.

The porch creaked, heavy footfalls thumping up the old wood. The doorknob rattled, and Lund pushed inside.

I had to admit, I was more than relieved.

He carried an assortment of plastic shopping bags and wore a satisfied grin. "Did I miss anything?"

As if in answer, a second full round of thumps and screams started from upstairs.

Lund raised his eyebrows at the sounds. "I knew I should have done something about those termites."

I laughed, but my attention was torn between the man and something in Lund's packages that smelled deliciously like rotisserie chicken. I stepped closer, trying to get a peek. "Worried they'll break through the ceiling?"

"Worried? At least someone is having fun in this house." He headed for the kitchen, and I followed. "I will admit to being a little surprised. I mean your sister...she was in a pretty bad state, and then the chip..."

I shrugged a shoulder. "The opportunity presented itself."

"The opportunity?" He set the bags on a countertop and turned to look at me.

"When you might die tomorrow, you take whatever you can get whenever you can get it. Don't put off until tomorrow what you can do today, that kind of thing."

He held my gaze, only a few inches between us. "Seems like a good way to live, even if you aren't planning to die tomorrow."

"Is that one of those come-on lines you promised?"

"Would you like it to be?"

It didn't take too much thought to come up with my answer. I grabbed for the hem of my sweater.

But before I could pull it over my head, he took hold of my wrists. "In a hurry?"

I peered up at him through my lashes. "Yes."

"Why not take our time?"

Because I felt like I'd been waiting to fuck him since we'd met. Because I'd just spent the past hour listening to my sister and Tequila ripping down the house. Because until a minute ago, I'd thought I'd lost him to his ex.

Because I was more comfortable with sex than with wallowing in emotion.

"Just eager, I guess," I said.

A slow grin spread over his lips. "Nothing wrong with that. But first, will you let me show you something?"

Always a sucker for letting a guy show me something, I released the sweater and let my gaze wander down to his crotch. "Whatcha got?"

He smiled. Turning to the plastic bags, he pulled out four takeout containers holding one full chicken each. "I thought you might want to eat first."

If there was anything better than a ready, willing, and handsome lover, it was one who brought me food. "Why, was I eyeing that chicken like a starving fox?"

"Let's just say, that's how I want you to look at me. If feeding you first gets me that, I'm willing to wait. Now sit. I'm going to serve you."

I smiled at him.

"Go," he ordered.

I crossed the tiny kitchen in two steps and lowered myself into a chair at the Formica table. My stomach approved the decision. My sex drive wasn't so happy…until Lund brought a chicken and a bag of apples to the table and pulled up his own chair. He rested his hands on my thighs, opened them, and slipped a knee between mine. Then he tore off a chicken leg and brought it to my lips.

I sank my teeth in and flavor filled my mouth, Lund watching me as if absorbed by my every movement and expression. At first I couldn't stop giggling, then slowly I started to *feel* fascinating, sexy, erotic, as if I really was the captivating creature he saw.

Eating was a necessity to me, a way to fuel my body for the job I had to do. But as I took bite after bite, it became something else, something ridiculously sensual and overtly sexual. I found myself wanting to strip off my clothes, run chicken over my body, preferably followed by Lund's tongue.

I finished the leg, and he followed by prying the breast meat free and feeding it to me. I devoured it and licked his fingers clean. He brought me an apple, and I crunched deep. It was so fresh, juice dripped down my chin, and he wiped it off with a rough finger. He offered me another taste, and another. I moved to the edge of my chair and pressed myself against his knee.

He brought more chicken, and we took turns eating, each feeding the other, our eyes devouring one another, me rubbing against him. Finally he crooked a brow. "Ready for dessert?"

"Yes." It was more a breath than a word.

But even though I'd given the answer, he didn't move. Instead, he ran his eyes slowly down my body, and I swore that even through my sweater, I could feel his gaze circle my nipples as if it were his tongue.

I let him pull me up from the chair, and he grabbed one of the plastic bags on the counter, then took my hand and led me upstairs. I liked to be in charge, in control at all times, moving at my own pace. But with Lund, it was different. It wasn't as if he was preventing me from taking over, more like I didn't want to. I was perfectly happy following, waiting to see what he'd do next.

I assumed we'd take one of the bedrooms, but instead, he turned into the sole bathroom in the house and closed the door behind us. He ducked into the old tub and turned on the spigot, then he pulled my sweater over my head. My jeans came off next, his fingers raising goose bumps over my skin as he skimmed them down my legs. My panties followed. Then he unwound the filthy bandage around my waist. Leaving it all in a pile on the bathroom floor.

He dipped a hand into the bag and brought out a bottle of shampoo. Setting it on the tub, he repeated the procedure, this time emerging with conditioner, then body wash, then one of those shower scrubs in bright purple.

"For me?"

"I hope you like roses. It seemed a bit generic, but it's all they had." He caressed my cheek, then slid his fingers up my cheek-bone and into my hair.

"I love roses," I said, not that I'd cared one bit about the flower before this moment.

He switched the spigot to spray, then pulled off his own shirt. His chest was precisely the way I pictured it, muscular, just the right light sprinkle of hair, washboard gut, just like a goddamn romance hero.

"Get into the shower. Wet yourself down."

The way he said the words made me almost ready to come right there. Instead, I reached for my inner dignity, stepped into the tub, and let the warm, clean water sluice over me while I watching him take off his jeans.

He wore tighty whities, which was so cute, I had to control myself yet again, especially when I saw the bulge stretching that elastic to its limit. He pushed the jeans to his ankles, exposing thighs every bit as muscular as they'd appeared through the denim. By the time he'd stepped one foot free and then the next, I was thoroughly wet and wanted to scream with impatience.

He smiled at me and hooked a thumb in the waistband of his briefs.

"For God's sake, get naked or I'm going to kill you."

That conjured a laugh, not exactly what I was hoping for, but then sure enough, he pushed the white cotton down, and for the second time in twenty-four hours, the man made my knees tremble. "Please," I said.

Another laugh, but he climbed into the tub. I reached for his cock, but just as when I tried to strip down in the living room, he took hold of my wrist. "What's the hurry?"

"I need it."

"I have more planned." He held up the bottle of rose-scented shampoo.

"Maybe you need a reminder, but I can kick your ass."

He smiled. "That might be fun, but first the roses."

I shook my head, but he proceeded anyway. Taking the bottle of shampoo, he squeezed out a generous amount and started massaging it into my hair.

His fingers felt amazing on my skull, both soothing and rough. He swirled lather around my temples and caressed the nape of my neck. I could feel tension falling away, the pain of my injuries falling away, reality falling away, leaving only him and me, warm water and the scent of roses.

He guided me under the water and rinsed the shampoo clear, followed it with conditioner, then reached for the shower wash and purple scrub.

Teasing the cleanser into a thick foam, he then moved it over my skin. My back first, then over my buttocks and down the back of my thighs to my heels. Then he came back up, on the insides of my thighs this time. I spread my legs, giving him space. But instead of going for the money, he scrubbed my butt again, then turned me around and washed my arms.

The rough texture raised shivers over my skin. He was gentle in the scraped places, firm in the unmarked ones. Skimming over bruises and massaging what screamed to be massaged. He brought the scrub to my shoulders, my clavicle, then swirled it around my breasts.

I brought my hand again to his cock, reveling in the weight of his testicles, but again he pushed me away.

"Enjoy," he said. "And then I promise I'll fuck your brains out. OK?"

I made a sound in my throat, something akin to a purr, as he skimmed the rough scrub down my belly and nestled it between my legs, moving in gentle circles.

Tremors seized me, shook me, and I gripped the soap dish built into the tiled wall to keep my footing. He concentrated on that spot for a while, until my cries subsided, then finished the trek down my legs.

Before he came back up, I grabbed the bottle of shower gel and filled my palm. Once he straightened, running the scrub back up my belly and over my breasts, I cupped his balls in my gel-filled hand and started washing.

He brought his lips to mine, and his mouth claimed me, demanding, delving deep. His whole body moved with his kiss, his chest crushing to my breasts, his cock surging in my hand. I never knew a kiss to be so erotic, and even though he wasn't touching me at that moment, I could feel the wave building in me again and crashing to shore.

I cried out into his mouth, and he swallowed it, kissing me harder, accepting everything I was.

The spray washed us both clean, and I reached for more of the rose gel, wanting to feel him reach the spot I had, wanting to hear him call out in passion. Again the hand encircled my wrist, but before I could protest, he was kissing his way down my neck, stopping at my breasts, licking and lightly tugging on my nipples with his teeth while his fingers worked lower.

I came, my whole body shuddering, and Lund dropped to his knees and kissed me there like he kissed my mouth, his tongue exploring, probing, moving slowly and then picking up speed. He seemed to know my body better than I did, drawing out every slow lick, every swirl, pulling away as I leaned against him, teasing me beyond endurance.

"Please. Oh please."

Then he clenched my bottom, pressing his face hard against me, giving me what I'd asked for—more than I'd asked for—until I was reduced to pure sensation and could only clutch his hair and scream and swear and repeat "God" and "yes" over and over until my legs buckled.

Then Lund was picking me up off my feet, leaning my back against the tile, and entering.

I screamed again, louder this time, not from aggression or anger, but from sheer mindlessness.

He thrust into me, filling me up, making me whole, giving me everything I'd searched for, and some things I'd never known I wanted. And when another wave of ecstasy crashed over me and carried him along, I understood I had been swept too far off course, and that now nothing could ever be the same.

Hammett

"Anyone can be your enemy," the Instructor said. "Some day, I might be."

Hammett sat in the empty security office, in the black site underneath Badger Ammo, staring at a bank of television screens.

She was horny as hell.

Almost dying did that to a person. Psychologists babbled bullshit about it somehow reaffirming life. Physicians preached science about the effects of adrenaline and dopamine and serotonin. Hammett didn't care about the reason for it. When a mission ended, she wanted to grab the nearest human being, man or woman, friend or foe, and fuck their brains out.

But this mission hadn't ended. Their target had gotten away. Hammett was sure Fleming's tracking chip had been removed, and was now on its way to Boise, or Lima, or Moscow, and the only way to find her was through other means.

Hammett crossed her legs, ignoring the persistent throb in her crotch, and twirled the knob that fast-forwarded the digital surveillance video of Fleming's captivity. Mostly there was nothing happening. But the interrogation scenes were revealing.

Hammett knew, firsthand, how tough Fleming was, and it had initially pissed her off. But watching her sister trash-talk her captors was…

Well, truth be told, it made Hammett feel kind of proud of her. In her career, Hammett had endured more than her share of what could generously be called *duress*. She knew how hard it was to resist torture. Her broken, crippled twin sister had done an admirable job keeping it together, and when she killed that guard and set that creep Malcolm on fire, Hammett confessed to giggling.

But the most interesting thing Fleming had done during her black-site stay was get Malcolm to punch in a code on the transceiver, which made it explode.

That was very, very interesting.

Fleming skipped ahead to the parts where that steroid midget showed up, and let it play out. She learned his name was Tequila, but she doubted that was real. He didn't look like a merc, exactly, but he was paid talent for sure. Maybe he'd be traceable. Maybe not.

Santiago knocked on the open door, and Hammett inwardly cringed. If it had been Javier or Isaiah, she might have jumped him. But she'd rather dry-hump a tarantula than that South American nutjob.

"The warden has unfortunately expired."

"What did he give up?"

"Everything. Swiss bank account numbers. The names and addresses of every member of his family. He wet the bed until he was twelve, lost his virginity at nineteen to a fat trailer-park whore, and offered to suck me off if I stopped."

Hammett sniffed the air, smelling BBQ.

"Did you order food?" she asked.

Santiago picked something out of his teeth and smiled.

"Christ, you were *eating* him?"

"He said he wouldn't expect reinforcements until tomorrow," Santiago said, ignoring the question but pausing to slowly lick grease off his lips. "And then, just a small insertion team. Only very few people know about this site. Even the president is out of the loop."

"Go into town. Pick up some pizzas, or burgers. Something the rest of us can eat." She mentally added, *You creepy goddamn psycho.*

"I'll add it to my expenses."

"Do that."

Santiago crept away, and Hammett went back to the video. Earlier, she had skipped past the pathetic scenes of Fleming dragging herself up and down the hallway like a trained seal, but this time Hammett stopped when it looked like Fleming was talking to someone. Someone in another cell. Hammett cranked up the audio.

The Instructor.

Hammett got on her radio. "Santiago, scratch that last order. You and Isaiah, meet me in the security office. Javier, maintain a watch on the front door."

The Instructor was there, and Fleming knew he was there. That changed everything.

Hammett stood up, cracking her knuckles. It was time to have a much longer, harder talk with the man who had trained her.

Chandler

"When you start to consider forming personal attachments," the Instructor said, "it's time to get out of the game."

When I awoke the next morning, snuggling next to Lund in one of the upstairs beds, I smelled like a garden and was sore in all the right places. The only thing I hadn't counted on was the uneasy jitter under my ribs.

I'd been ready for sex. I hadn't been ready for whatever it was that had happened along with it, and I wasn't sure how to deal with it.

The mission hadn't changed. The Instructor still needed to be rescued. But I was no longer convinced we had to be the ones to do it.

"You OK?" Lund asked, sitting up, the blanket falling away and exposing his chest.

"Fine."

"Worrying about your other sister?"

"Yeah." It wasn't entirely a lie. I was thinking about Hammett, where she was now, what she was doing, how we could be ready for whatever she had planned next. Admitting to that seemed much easier than explaining something I couldn't understand myself.

Lund gave me one last steal-my-breath kiss, pulled on his clothes, and ventured downstairs.

I wrapped clean bandages around my belly, dressed my various cuts and scrapes, and gave myself just enough Demerol to take the edge off, then dug through yet another plastic bag of things Lund had purchased for me. Cargo pants, a long-sleeved tee, and he'd included underwear and a couple of sports bras. I put on the clothes, covering up the bruises over my ribs and the whisker burn on my thighs, girding myself for whatever was ahead.

I returned to the kitchen to find Lund dishing up more food. Tequila and Fleming sat at the table with two empty chicken containers, a few apple cores, and an empty container that appeared to have once held coleslaw. Fleming gave me a knowing smile, then gestured to the old wheelchair she had commandeered. "Lund said I can do with it what I want, but I'll need some supplies."

I'd seen what my sister could do. The custom rides she'd designed for herself back in Chicago had more in common with tanks than the chair she was sitting in now.

"Just give me a list," Lund said. Hair tousled, he looked as if he'd popped straight out of some beefcake calendar, *A Year of Hot Firefighters*. Looking at him, I expected to have the overwhelming urge to relieve him of some of those clothes. But instead I felt something else entirely.

I felt fear.

Not of him. For him.

I kept my voice even, betraying nothing. "We also need rounds, rifles, whatever we can get. I have a feeling it isn't going to take long for Hammett to make her next move. We need to be ready."

"Rounds shouldn't be a problem," Lund said. "Weapons might be tougher to get on such short notice. But I have an idea."

Fleming raised her eyebrows. "Idea?"

"Someone local. No waiting period. No registration. But we'll need cash."

I looked at Tequila.

He stared back, not saying a word, even though I was pretty sure he'd picked up what I meant to imply. Seconds ticked by.

I finally gave in and said the words. "I need to ask you for a loan."

"It's day two."

"A loan, Tequila. Not a gift."

"Tomorrow you owe me another payment."

"I lost the money in the reservoir. I'll pay you back and for additional days as soon as I have a chance to get to one of my stashes."

"That wasn't our deal."

"With interest."

"I'm not a bank."

Fleming ran a finger along Tequila's arm. "It would be nice to have something more than a pack of razor blades to defend myself."

His eyes shifted in her direction, then returned to me. "Going rate."

"OK," I said before he changed his mind. I held out my hand.

He dug into his pockets and slapped the ten grand I'd given him into my palm, then he glanced at Lund. "Some interesting things in that old barn out there. Iron railings, old motorcycle parts."

"Yours for the taking," Lund said. "There should be some welding equipment around here, too."

While they discussed ideas for tricking out Fleming's chair, I stuffed the money Tequila gave me into the pockets of my new cargo pants and focused on my sister. "Can we talk?"

"Sure."

I gestured for her to follow me into the living room. Once there, I perched on the edge of the sofa and searched for the right words. "The Instructor. I know you feel you owe him."

"And you're wondering why?"

I nodded. The man had trained all of us, me, Fleming, Hammett, and our other four sisters, now dead. But even though I felt some connection to him because of that, I wasn't itching to charge back into that prison. I needed to know why Fleming was. "You said he helped you in Milan?"

"I was in the hospital after my fall, no passport, no identification, in a haze of morphine, and with Italian police doing their best to tie me to the assassination."

I nodded. In such circumstances, we were on our own, and in the eyes of the United States government, we didn't exist. "And he pulled strings?"

"He came to the hospital himself, dressed as a doctor, and wheeled me out of there."

I let that sink in, not sure what to say.

"He risked everything for me, Chandler, but it's not just that. After the accident, there were times..." She looked away for a moment, and I waited for her to continue. "There were times I was pretty low, and he saw me through, encouraged me, forced me to go on. He gave me a life when I thought I no longer had one. I just...after all that, I can't just leave him."

I felt myself nodding. I wouldn't go back into that prison for the Instructor's sake, but I couldn't refuse my sister. "OK. We'll get him out."

"Thanks," she said.

I was about to return to the kitchens when she stopped me.

"I have to show you something." She brandished a laptop. "I'm rigging it to track Hammett."

"Where did you get that?"

"Lund. Didn't he tell you?"

"No."

"Too busy showing you his other goodies?"

I thought about the food, the clothes, the bath products, but I knew Fleming was referring to the man himself. Any direct answer wouldn't do those particular treats justice, so I simply nodded. "You and Tequila seemed busy last night."

Fleming grinned. "The guy is like a piece of gym equipment. I swear, it was the most satisfying workout I've had in my life. You should try him."

I gave an uncommitted tilt of the head.

Her grin widened. "You really like him."

"Tequila?"

"Lund."

I opened my mouth to give a flip answer, something funny, preferably steeped in saucy innuendo, but no words came.

"You like him so much, you're speechless."

I couldn't deny it, and I had to admit that bothered me. A lot. "I must be tired. I think the past few days have caught up with me."

"Chandler. This isn't good."

Sometimes I forgot how much Fleming knew about me, even though we'd first met face-to-face only a few days ago. But after all the missions she'd worked as my handler, she knew most of my secrets. In fact, there were times I was convinced she knew everything about everything.

"I'm fine," I said, crossing my arms.

"No, you're not. He's a hunk. He's smart, funny. I'll bet he's hung like that horse of his."

"His horse is a gelding. And I can testify to the fact that Lund is not."

"Don't obfuscate the point, Chandler. You're falling for him."

"I don't know. He makes me feel..."

"Makes you feel what?"

"Different. Not like myself."

"And I'll bet that's one of the things you like about him."

Was it? Maybe it was. I wasn't convinced. Feeling this emotional, about Fleming, about what had happened with Lund, it was exhausting and exhilarating, but most of all it made me uneasy. "He's a regular guy, Fleming. How can I be with a regular guy?"

"I wouldn't exactly call him regular."

"OK, he's amazing. But he doesn't live in our world."

"Chandler, after all this is done, *we* might not live in our world...or any world. Seriously, even if we get out of this alive—and it's a big if—our covers have been blown, Hydra is gone, we are not only out of a job, we don't exist. Seems like it might be the perfect opportunity to reinvent ourselves. Be whatever we want. Have what we've never been able to have."

Maybe I'd been disappointed too many times to trust my feelings for a man, but I just couldn't embrace this as wildly as Fleming seemed to think I should. "I'm exhausted. I'm beaten up. I feel as emotionally raw as a teenager. And he's a calm port in a storm."

"Maybe. But *maybe* there could be more."

I shook my head, not able to think about this one more second. "Can we talk about something else? A shopping list? Something?"

Fleming gave me a sympathetic press of the lips. "Something easier, you mean?"

"Yeah."

"There is something else we have to discuss. But it's not easy."

"What?"

"The transceiver. There's something you need to know."

I gave her a frown. "You mean my old cell phone? That transceiver? The one at the bottom of Lake Michigan?" Our dip in the lake seemed like it had taken place forever ago, when in reality only days had passed.

She nodded. "That's the one. Except it's not in the lake."

"Where is it?"

"Now? Destroyed." She filled me in on Malcolm's questions, how he'd produced the phone, how he'd demanded she give him the code to unlock the device, and how she'd provided the self-destruct code instead.

"So it's no longer a factor." I said, more than a little relieved to be rid of the thing. When I'd carried it, I'd had no clue about its many capabilities. But since Fleming had designed the device, she knew all of them.

She just stared at me.

"It's no longer a factor," I repeated. "Right?"

"It's not the only one out there."

I groaned. "And?"

"And it's part of my job to keep tabs on the other. To make sure it doesn't fall into the wrong hands, and take care of things if it does."

I thought for a moment. "And why are you telling me this?"

"Because I think that's part of what Hammett is after."

"Hammett is psycho. How are you sure she doesn't just want to kill us just for the hell of it?"

"Because she could have had her men mow down all of us when we were escaping on the horses, but she didn't. She risked moving in close when she didn't have to. She tried to shoot Tequila and later tried to kill you."

"But she avoided targeting you."

Fleming nodded. "I think she knows I have the codes for the other transceiver. I think that's what she wants."

"So what do we do?"

"Stop her." She eyed me as if there was more, but she was working her way up to telling me.

"And?"

"And I share the codes with you, so no matter what happens to me, one of us will be able to control that other transceiver."

I wanted to reassure Fleming that sharing the codes wasn't necessary, that nothing bad would happen, that she could carry out that duty herself, but in light of all that had happened in the past days, such reassurances would be empty…not to mention utterly stupid.

I reached for Fleming's hand and gave it a squeeze. "OK, I'm ready. Lay the codes on me."

***

With all Fleming and I had talked about hanging in the back of my mind, I collected Lund, and we drove out in his truck, leaving my sister and Tequila working on programming the computer and customizing the chair.

"What did you and your sister talk about?"

The tires hummed on the highway for several seconds before I could formulate an answer. "The computer. It was very nice of you to let her use it."

"Just the computer?"

"We discussed how much we appreciate all you've done for us. The place, the horses, all the food and supplies."

"That's all?"

"We touched on what weapons are on our wish lists."

"No girl talk?"

"Weapons *are* our girl talk."

Lund pulled over onto the side of the road, gravel under crunching under his tires. When he looked at me, his face was creased with disappointment. Uh-oh.

I frowned. "Jesus, Lund, you want to talk about it, don't you?"

"Apparently you don't."

"I thought I was the chick."

His face pinched even further. Part of me wanted to hold him. Another part of me wanted to slap him, to get some much-needed distance.

"Look, Chandler, maybe what we had last night was just a typical weekend for you—"

"Let's not go there."

"—but it wasn't that for me. I was with a wonderful woman last night, and this morning she's gone."

I folded my arms. "Maybe I just used you for sex, Lund. Isn't that every man's fantasy? Now you can write that letter to *Penthouse Forum* like you wanted to."

"I know you, Chandler."

That got a derisive laugh from me. "You don't even know my real name, Lund."

Lund put his hands on my shoulders, turning me to face him. "I know what it's like to be alone. To work hard at a job, giving it your all. I know about the sacrifices. How hard it is to get close to someone when you think you have nothing left to give. I know what it's like to risk your life, to not know if you'll still be breathing by the end of the day."

I'd made a big mistake. The biggest of them all. I'd slept with a good man. The best thing I could do, for both of us, was push him away. So I went with the surefire relationship killer.

"I'm a government assassin, Lund. Not a spy. Not a patriot. I kill people because I'm told to. Where do you think this is going to all end up? In a wedding chapel? Me barefoot and pregnant in your in-laws' house, waiting for you to come home with some flowery fucking soap to wash my back?"

My words hung there. I kept my face hard, but I felt myself breaking down inside. Because right when I asked that question, I'd realized how I wanted him to answer.

I wanted him to say yes. Yes, that's how he wanted it to end up. Yes, he accepted me for who I was, and was willing to be with me anyway. Yes, he could be enough for me, and the scenario I'd thrown at him wasn't meant to be sarcastic, but instead it was my deepest, truest hope.

But Lund gave me nothing, other than sad eyes. And I said nothing, just sat there, arms crossed over my chest, determined that would be enough to hold me together.

He pulled back onto the highway, and asphalt hummed under the tires. Soon he turned into a dirt rut driveway and steered around a half-collapsed, split-rail fence. Another gambrel-roofed barn poked through overgrown brush and trees, this one so old and neglected there was barely any paint left on the weathered boards. The roof sagged in the middle, a portion of it gone entirely. A trailer stood where the farmhouse had likely once been.

"This is your source?" I asked, emotion shoved firmly into some compartment I wasn't sure I still had. Business as usual.

"Not *my* source exactly."

"Have you ever bought weapons here before?"

"Never had the need."

"Of course you haven't."

He parked near the double-wide and twisted in the driver's seat, his eyes digging into me. "When we're done here, if you want to go your own way, I understand. I'm here for as long as you and your sister need my help. But, what we did last night…that can't happen again."

His words stung. I thought about apologizing. Taking it all back. Or turning on my inner vamp, seducing him right there in the truck. But before I had a chance to do either, Lund was climbing out his door.

I exited the vehicle and glanced around at the dilapidated farm. Lund's in-laws' place was the Ritz compared to this. "Are you sure there's anything of value in this place?"

"It's the only place to get some of the things on your wish list around here, at least that I know of."

"All right. Lead the way."

The air smelled like early fall, wood fire, and a touch of rot from the barn. Gravel and quackgrass crunched under our boots, birds twittered around us, and to the east I could hear the beat of a helicopter blade. I checked the sky to make sure the aircraft wasn't heading in our direction. The sky was vibrant blue, spotted with nimbus clouds, and except for a V of Canadian geese, it seemed to be clear.

"Now this could get touchy. I need you to follow my lead. The guy we're dealing with, he isn't the most predictable—"

A click registered in the back of my mind, a sound I'd recognize anywhere, the hammer of a revolver cocking, the cylinder turning, putting a round into position to fire.

The gunman was behind an old cellar door, just a few feet from me. With a swinging blow from my right hand and a twist of my left on the gun, I could shift out of his way and disarm him. But I couldn't shift Lund to safety at the same time.

There was only one thing I could do. I tackled Lund, pushing him to the ground, covering him with my body as I turned to face the threat.

Not one of the black-clothed CIA thugs nor one of Hammett's lunatics, the man holding the .45 Bulldog revolver was dressed head to toe in camouflage, but the straggly brown beard and shoulder-length hair threaded with gray was definitely not up to military specs. Regardless of where this guy was from, the hand holding the gun was steady, and I didn't doubt he could be dangerous.

"Let me see your hands." His voice creaked and popped, as if it didn't get much use.

I raised my hands.

"What the hell?" Lund started to rise.

"Stay down. I've got this."

"Don't hurt him, Chandler," Lund said. "He's our guy."

"Did you forget to call ahead?"

"He never answers his phone." Lund sat up, raising his hands as well. "Kasdorf, please put the gun down. I'm Lund. The firefighter. Remember me? This is Chandler. We need your help."

Kasdorf squinted at us for a few seconds as if he couldn't place Lund, then lowered the Bulldog and slipped it into his holster. "What do you want?"

Lund stood and then helped me up. "I want a favor."

"What kind of favor?"

"Weapons. Ammunition. I want you to sell us some."

"You're doing this for the police chief?"

"She doesn't know a thing about it, and I give you my word she never will."

I could only surmise he meant Val. Lund had borrowed her horses for me, asked her to smuggle us out instead of arresting us, and now he was swearing to keep my secrets. I had a feeling that if Blondie ever found me so much as jaywalking in her town, I would be looking at cavity searches and jail time.

Kasdorf bobbed his head in my direction. "How do I know this one ain't a government agent or something?" For a moment, he looked as if he were contemplating going back to the gun.

I wasn't quite sure how to answer that one.

"You know the old Badger Ammo plant?" Lund asked.

"Yeah, what about it? Place is a black site for the CIA."

"Actually, you're right," I said.

"Of course I'm right. I live here, don't I?"

Lund nodded to me, a hint I should continue.

"They took my sister, tortured her. We broke her out last night, but you know how those people are. They aren't going to let us get away. They're going to come after us, and we need to be ready."

"I ain't just giving you my collection."

"I have money," I said. "I'll pay you well."

He glowered at me for a few seconds, and I could swear I heard a harrumph. "We'll see about that."

I expected him to lead us into the trailer home, but instead he turned to the cellar and pulled the steel cover open. Steps led down into the earth, and I caught the scent of recently poured concrete.

He started down and motioned for us to follow. I went and then Lund, lowering the door behind us. The basement held very little, as far as I could see in the dim overhead bulbs. A chest freezer lined one wall, and a shelf full of Ball canning jars filled with pickles and tomato preserves. Something yellow, red, and green took up another wall.

"Is that corn relish?"

"My mother made it."

"I had it once when I was little. It's amazing."

Kasdorf stared at me, then a smile twitched at the corners of his mouth. He picked one of the smallest jars from the shelf. I could tell by the gentle way he lifted the glass that it was precious to him. He handed it to me.

"Can I pay you for it?"

"My mother would want you to have that. You and your sister."

"That's a very generous gift. Thank you."

"But the guns and ammunition? Them you'll pay for." He turned back to the wall and pulled at something behind the jars. The shelves swung toward us, accompanied by a slight sucking sound, like the opening of a freezer door.

He stepped inside and we followed, a thrill shimmering up my spine at the array of wonderful, dangerous toys covering the walls like a munitions Toys "R" Us.

Fleming

"Sherman called war 'hell,'" the Instructor said. "Sun Tzu called war 'art.' Pack for both."

Was there anything sexier than a hunky man with an arc welder? Fleming didn't think so.

She sat in a rocking chair on Lund's back porch, laptop in lap, hacking into Hydra's encrypted database server to find out where Hammett was holing up. This was in between stealing numerous glances at Tequila, who was near the barn, reinforcing her new wheelchair with spires from an old wrought iron fence. He had his shirt off, and the sweat on his chest glinted in the sunlight. Though she'd never admit it to anyone, Fleming had always had the hots for Darth Vader, and seeing Tequila in that black welding mask made her want to crawl across the pinecone-strewn lawn and violate him in delicious ways.

Fleming smiled to herself. She'd slept well, partly because of the drugs, partly because of the sex, but mostly because Tequila had given her a temporary reprieve from her fear and pain. She was sore—it had taken three ibuprofen and half a dozen small shots of Demerol before she'd been able to get out of bed—but she'd managed to avoid nightmares. That was surprising, considering that she often had nightmares on good days, and the ordeal she'd just been through could be classified as one of the worst in her life. But she hadn't dreamt of Malcolm, or the black site, or Hammett. Nor did she have the usual walking dream, only to wake up and be once again devastated by her condition.

Last night, Fleming had dreamed of being a wife and mother.

It hadn't been a particularly vivid dream, nor was it overly happy, but it made her think of Chandler's dilemma with Lund. You can't be in this business and have a family. Period. As safe as Tequila made Fleming feel, he was just the latest in a series of boy toys, and she couldn't see developing anything more than friendship with him. But earlier, Fleming had seen the look of worry on Chandler's face, and she understood the deeper feelings it covered up.

Chandler, like Fleming and probably Hammett, couldn't allow herself to get close to people, because it inevitably ended in tragedy. Either for the beloved, or personally. Caring about someone meant putting someone ahead of you. For an operative in the field, that was death.

Plus, there was a chicken-versus-egg dynamic. Were they incapable of having meaningful relationships because they were assassins? Or had an inability to have meaningful relationships pushed them toward this line of work?

Over the past few days, Fleming's interaction with Chandler had gone from businesslike to intimate. Chandler connecting with Lund was another step in that direction. This was dangerous, especially since they still had a mission to complete.

Fleming considered the Instructor. She owed him a lot for what he'd given her, the skills to be the best of the best. She also despised him for what he'd taken from her, namely, her humanity. After rescuing him, what next? Could Fleming go back to business as usual? Did she even want to?

A pair of fat blue dragonflies landed on Fleming's rocking-chair arm. They were mating, connected to each other in a heart-shaped loop. Yet as unwieldy and uncomfortable as the copulation appeared, they were still able to fly.

For shits and grins, Fleming tried to imagine a domestic life with Tequila, but she couldn't picture what that would be like. Instead of a computer in her lap, what if it were a baby? What if Tequila were planting bushes in the yard, rather than outfitting her wheelchair for war? What if Chandler had gone out to buy ingredients to bake cookies instead of guns?

The dragonflies flew off, erratically. Fleming half expected a blue jay to come swooping down to gobble them up. But they managed to live for at least as long as Fleming watched them.

It didn't matter. Winter weather would kill them soon.

She went back to her laptop. Months ago, Fleming had used a worm, concealed in a rootkit, to install a backdoor on Hydra's server. She didn't know which program was the GPS tracker, and since each program was numbered rather than named, Fleming had to look at each individually. Many were password protected, which required cracks. She had various cracking programs stored in her file locker, which she could access remotely.

It wasn't a difficult task, but it was slow going.

"OK, wheels are reinforced," Tequila said. He wiped a sweaty arm across his sweaty brow, looking like he'd been chiseled out of marble. "It's a lot heavier."

"Are you mistaking me for some fragile waif, Tequila?"

"Just want to make sure you'll be able to get this sucker rolling with me in your lap." He tossed her one of his rare grins. "Of course, with the cycle parts…"

Tequila's focus snapped toward the road, and Fleming heard it a second later; vehicle coming.

"It's Lund's truck," Tequila said. How he could determine that by hearing its engine, Fleming didn't know, but she liked the fact that even though he knew who it was, he still disappeared behind the garage. He might not have been trained by Hydra, but his abilities, and instincts, were top notch.

Lund pulled up and parked on the grass, and he and Chandler got out without looking at each other.

Uh-oh. Trouble in paradise.

Chandler took a duffel bag from the backseat and slung a rifle over her shoulder, while Lund trudged up to the porch, gave Fleming a bland nod, and stood there like a man wanting a smoke but out of cigarettes. Chandler walked up the porch stairs without looking at Lund, and Fleming could feel the tension between them radiating like microwaves.

"Got some oldies but goodies," Chandler said, setting down the duffel with a heavy thump.

She dug into the bag. "Ceska Skorpion, chambered for .32 ACP."

Chandler handed the submachine gun to Fleming, who admired its lethal beauty. Oldie was right—this looked to be 1960s—but the owner had kept it cared for, cleaned, and oiled. She checked the thirty-round curved magazine, unfolded the wire-frame stock, and pulled the bolt back.

"Two extra mags for you." Chandler passed them over. "You also have an AR-15, standard five-five-six NATO, converted to full auto."

Chandler unslung the rifle, and Fleming hefted its weight. A fully automatic AR-15 was basically an M-16, made famous by Rambo and any movie set during the Vietnam War. This had an extra mag taped upside down to the one in the well, and Leupold optics.

"Nine-mil Beretta," Chandler said, handing Fleming a pistol, butt first. "And a KA-BAR." The Marine fighting knife was seven inches long, in a leather sheath.

"Got my ammo?" Tequila had managed to materialize on the porch without Fleming noticing.

Chandler nodded, handing him some boxes.

"How about you, Lund?" Fleming asked. The poor guy had his hands in his pockets, looking like the last kid picked for the kickball team.

"Lund has done enough," Chandler said. She focused on Fleming, on Tequila, on anyone except the man she was discussing. "He's lending us his truck, but he isn't coming along."

Ouch.

Chandler was right, of course. Lund had proven helpful, and resourceful, but he didn't have the training they had. Still, her sister didn't have to kick a guy so obviously down. Fleming wondered what had gone down during Chandler and Lund's shopping trip. It couldn't have been pleasant.

"Thanks for the truck, Lund," Fleming said. "We really appreciate all you've done."

"Not a problem." He nodded agreeably, but tension in the muscles along his jaw gave away how he really felt.

Fleming leaned in closer and lowered her voice. "You're a fighter. Fighters don't give up. On anything."

He nodded again, but his expression didn't change.

"We'll be back. Chandler will be back." Fleming wasn't sure he wanted to hear her message at the moment, but if he was worthy of her sister—and judging from what she'd seen, he was—he'd be ready to fight for her when they returned.

Fleming's computer beeped, the latest password broken, and she checked the program. "I found the GPS tracker." She waved Chandler and Tequila over.

Moving her fingers along the touchpad, she quickly located Hammett's receiver, and zoomed in on the map. Pulling in a sharp breath when she spotted their sister's location, she tilted the computer so Chandler could see.

Chandler's reaction was similar. "She's back at the ammo plant?"

"Looks that way."

"This is your other sister?" Tequila asked. He stepped closer, also eyeing the screen. "The maniac on the wire?"

Fleming nodded. "Hammett."

"She must know the Instructor is there." Chandler's voice rose barely above a whisper.

"Yeah," Fleming answered. The time for mulling over relationships and dragonflies was over.

"We'd better move."

"Yeah."

Chandler

"If you're going to risk your life," the Instructor said, "it had better be for something worth dying for."

It was past lunch when we rolled into Baraboo, and the three of us were famished. We stopped at a busy deli that boasted more than two hundred types of cheese—imagine finding that in Wisconsin—and I ordered some sandwiches while Tequila and Fleming waited in the truck. We ate on the way to a Walmart, where I used Tequila's money to buy two pairs of 50x binoculars, three Motorola thirty-five-mile walkie-talkies, batteries, a climbing stick, a tree seat, two fanny packs, a TracFone, superglue, a first-aid kit, appropriate clothing, a night-vision monocular, bottled water, beef jerky, protein bars, pepper spray, and some braided paracord bracelets. Also in town was a medical supply store, and we outfitted Fleming with two forearm crutches and some aluminum leg braces.

Then it was off to the police station to get Tequila's car out of impound. I could have done that earlier with Lund, but it would have required spending even more uncomfortable time with him. Our morning munitions shopping trip had been hard enough, and even though I'd avoided looking at him when I announced he wasn't going to Badger, I'd sensed his feeling of powerlessness; and I knew not allowing him to help was probably the worst thing I could do to a man like Lund.

Not that I expected my announcement to stop him, which is why I'd taken his truck.

Of course, having a vehicle bearing Wisconsin plates and a state park sticker was handy as well, as long as we kept it in the park and away from Badger. As we wolfed down our cheese sandwiches and shopped for supplies, we hashed over our plan, and by the time we loaded up our purchases, we were good to go.

I was to accompany Tequila to the same spot where he'd dropped me off the day before, near the farm. Fleming was going to enter Badger via Devil's Lake State Park, taking Lund's truck. Apparently my sister could drive by using a cane to operate the gas and brake. I took her at her word. She was going to take Lund's truck to the end of Burma Road, right at the perimeter fence, and set up a watch in a high hide.

"You climb trees?" Tequila asked.

"You forgot last night already?" she asked, winking.

I averted my eyes so I didn't have to witness the rest of the exchange.

When the flirting was finally over, Fleming promised to contact us when she was in position, and we were on our way.

* * *

Tequila drove to the end of Halweg Road, where he'd dropped me off yesterday. Rather than risk another tow, he pulled into the woods, down a shallow ditch, and parked behind a copse of dogwood trees so his truck wouldn't be immediately visible.

"So, you seem to have hit it off with my sister pretty well," I said to Tequila as we trekked into the woods.

He grunted, noncommittal.

"She seems to like you, too."

Another grunt. I grunted back, to see how he'd respond. He didn't reply at all.

Fascinating company, as always.

We stayed inside the tree line, hiking in silence, and after heading west about two kilometers we passed the reservoir where I'd dropped my bag.

"Your money is at the bottom, if you want to dive in," I said.

No reply.

"It's full of cool salamanders," I told him.

Tequila remained silent. I'd had better conversations with walls.

The prison was five hundred meters southwest, but neither of us knew where the front entrance was, or what we'd be facing. While waiting for Fleming to call, I used the binocs to do a slow sweep of the area. The whole compound seemed to be deserted. There weren't even any construction workers. I wasn't sure if that was a good thing or a cause for concern. It was doubtful they knew we were coming back, especially this soon. But the Instructor might have talked, in which case there would be a reception for us.

I checked the time on my TracFone, then glanced at Tequila. He was sitting, crossed-legged, on a patch of wild grass, his expression blank.

I was too tense to sit here with him Zenning out and not saying a word. No one had that much inner peace, especially me. "Jailhouse Rock," I said.

His eyes met mine.

"You told me you'd teach me."

"Now?"

Wow. So my sister hadn't humped all the talk out of him, not that he'd had much to begin with. "We've got some time. I've never heard of JHR before. Where is it from?"

Tequila rolled easily to his feet. "It's also known as Fifty-Two Hand Blocks and Brick City Rock. It's the only indigenous American martial art."

"Who invented it?"

"Black guys in jail. It's a system used for fighting in closed, confined areas. Lots of blocks, lots of feints and dodges. I like it when I'm toe-to-toe with an opponent, because it confuses them."

No shit.

"Where did you learn it?"

Tequila didn't answer. I wondered if he'd gone to prison, realized his past was none of my business, and moved on. "Show me."

He beckoned me closer. "This move is called skull and crossbones. Throw a jab."

I planted my feet in a boxing stance, then threw a quick punch at Tequila's face. He twisted sideways and caught my hand between his right palm and left elbow, deflecting the power and direction of my punch while also positioning himself on my unguarded right side. It was the same move Rochester had done to me at the hospital.

"Again," Tequila said. "Slow."

I threw the same punch, slower, and watched how he moved.

"Again."

We repeated it three more times at reduced speed, and then he said. "For real now."

I threw a right punch, fast as I could, and he blocked, used his palm to hold my wrist, then moved the elbow along my body and gave me a firm tap in the cheek, showing how easily he'd gotten inside my defenses.

We drilled it three more times, then I changed things up and tried a left jab. He countered just as easily, but on the follow-through he dropped to one knee and gave me a short uppercut in the ribs, pulling it so he didn't hurt me.

"Now you."

The first few times, I was having trouble finding the right place for my elbow, but after a dozen attempts I was getting the hang of it.

"For real," I said.

Tequila hit, hard and fast, and I used skull and crossbones to deflect the punch, then lightly caught him in the temple with my elbow.

"You learn quick," he said, rubbing his head.

"Show me more."

"Catch and kiss. Punch me."

Once again I threw the jab and he caught the fist between his forearms, then kissed my knuckles.

I laughed. "That's 52 Blocks? But that's so sweet."

Still holding his lips to my hand, Tequila bent my own arm at the elbow, and keeping it locked within his arms, pushed back, making me smack myself in the nose. I fell onto my ass.

As I blinked away starry motes, Tequila helped me up.

"Jailhouse Rock uses distraction. For every move thrown, there are handfuls of feints and shuffles. When the body is in constant motion, the opponent doesn't know where the attack is coming from, or how to hit back. And if you can confuse your opponent for even a second, that's enough time to land a blow."

Tequila began to do a *kata* of sorts, but it seemed freestyle rather than practiced. He quickly touched his elbows, head, chest, and sides while weaving and bobbing, using both hands, in constant motion. It was a bit different from Rochester's style. Tequila was a little tighter, a little faster, and Rochester's was more rhythmic and flowing. But in each case it was very tough to land a hard blow, and I had no idea where the next attack would come from.

It reminded me a bit of a street performer on Michigan Avenue who played spoons, clicking them together against various parts of his body, keeping it going until his limbs were a blur.

I tried to follow Tequila's pattern, but four or five moves in, I realized he had no pattern. It might as well have been dancing, if there were a dance in which you tried to kill your partner.

And that's how it finally clicked for me. Instead of copying Tequila, or Rochester, I took half a dozen repetitive motions and made them my own. I faced Tequila, bobbing left, touching my head, right, chest, down, crossing arms, left, touching elbows, finding my own speed, my own groove. Then, when I was presenting just as hard a target as Tequila was, I popped the jab.

He blocked, skull and crossbones, and tried to catch and kiss, but I ducked, bobbed, and cut an elbow into his ribs. Tequila stepped away, stuck the jab, and I blocked with my palm and elbow, then continued the motion and tapped my elbow into his cheek.

"Good," he said, which was a strange thing for a man to say after I'd hit him twice.

"What are some other moves?"

He showed me how to knee skip—advancing on your opponent while bouncing from knee to knee, and a variation of the skull and crossbones, where the follow-up was a spinning backhand, which again knocked me onto my butt. I also learned how to pull an uppercut short to drive an elbow into the opponent's sternum, then clip him under the chin.

By now, both Tequila and I were sweating pretty good. I wondered why Fleming hadn't called yet, and then thought, inappropriately, about her calling Tequila a piece of gym equipment and suggesting that I try him.

As we sparred, I had no doubt Tequila was good in bed. He had flexibility, endless endurance, and might have been the strongest man I'd ever met. Also, trading punches with him was a strange, but very real, turn-on. Who needed overlong showers and rose-scented bath gel? Sometimes a girl didn't want to be tenderly caressed, or erotically fed. Sometimes she just wanted to fuck.

Tequila threw a combination, and I ducked under it with a knee skip. When I stood up I was in his arms, face-to-face.

We stared at each other for a moment. I looked at his mouth, his lips, and inappropriately thought about Lund. Lund was dangerous. A serious distraction. He made me think and feel things that messed with my head.

And the best way to get a man out of your head was to move on to another one.

So I put my hand behind Tequila's neck, pressed my heaving chest to his, and kissed him.

Fleming

"If life gives you lemons," the Instructor said, "toss those fuckers back in life's face and demand better."

When Fleming left the Walmart parking lot, she'd felt confident they'd thought of everything. But now that she was sitting in a traffic jam in the south entrance to Devil's Lake State Park, she realized there was one very important thing that they'd forgotten.

Yesterday's events had changed everything, and not just for the three of them.

Fleming knew she was in trouble when she tried to turn near the orchard and found the road to the south side of the park blocked off, a police car and bright yellow sawhorses barring the way. Moving on to the next option, she'd circled the park and approached from the other side, intending to circle the lake from the east on South Shore Road.

That had been ten minutes ago. Because of all the commotion yesterday, Devil's Lake was on high security alert. Which Fleming had no time for.

The school bus in front of her inched forward, spewing a cloud of exhaust in its wake. Fleming followed, controlling the gas and brake with the cane in one hand, manipulating the steering wheel with the other. Stopping and going while park rangers checked each car moving through was a giant pain in the ass, but the time it took was even worse. Chandler and Tequila had to be in place, and now that they knew Hammett was with the Instructor, they needed to proceed before there was nothing left of their mentor to rescue.

The bus pulled past the checkpoint and continued on to the information center and parking lots lined with other buses, near the lake. Fleming pulled forward, glad to be breathing clean air again, and leaned an elbow out her window. She put on an engaging smile, full wattage.

The park ranger who stepped to her window had silver hair, and although he looked like he was ripe to retire, there was a shrewdness about his eyes that told her that even if this wasn't the guy Lund had tangled with, he would be equally tough to snow.

But Lund had help. Unfortunately Fleming didn't happen to have an ex who was police chief to vouch for her. She was on her own.

"Beautiful day, isn't it?" she said.

"Ma'am, what is in the back of your truck?"

Fleming stifled a groan. Apparently he believed in cutting right to the shit of things.

She fitted her lips in a pout, channeling her inner Marilyn Monroe. "I don't really know. That stuff belongs to my husband."

Ranger Rick pressed his lips into a skeptical line and walked back to the truck's bed. When he finally sauntered back to the window, Fleming added a touch of cluelessness to her sexy pout. "Everything OK?"

"Actually no. There's no hunting in the park, ma'am."

"Hunting?"

"The tree stand, the ladder..."

Hell.

"Like I said, that's my husband's stuff. I'm no hunter." She produced a shiver. "Lucky for me, he never hits anything, though. I don't know what I'd do if he wanted to hang a Bambi head on my wall."

Ranger Rick stared at her. He couldn't have seen anything but the tree-stand equipment. The assault rifle was safely behind her feet, tucked under the seat. He'd have to order her out of the truck to discover that.

Please don't order me out of the truck.

"Can you get out of the truck for a moment?"

Shit.

There wasn't a chance Fleming was going to do that. She was going to have to bring out the secret weapon.

Fleming thought about Milan, about the pain afterward, and worse, the loneliness. She summoned her experience at Malcolm's hands, and the anguish of watching Chandler fall from the wire. And then...

She cried.

Big blubbering tears blurred her vision and splashed down her cheeks. "Please, I just want to sit in the park for a little while. It's been a hell of a week. My husband is leaving me because he says it's my fault that he can't get it up, and my sister is calling me a selfish bitch even though you wouldn't believe what she did, or maybe you would. It all started when..."

The ranger couldn't get Fleming through the line fast enough, and once she was driving around the curve of the lake, purple-rocked bluffs and majestic pines rising in all directions, she allowed herself a small smile.

Years had passed since she'd been in the field, but she still had it.

She found Burma Road with little problem. Although she'd been a little loopy with freedom and Demerol when she'd taken it on horseback not even a day ago, she could remember every detail of the land.

Lund's truck took the terrain easily, even plowing over a small downed tree with no problem, and soon she had reached the fence. Time for the challenging part.

After she turned off the ignition, Fleming took a few minutes to listen to the sounds of the forest return to normal after her intrusion. Birds chirped, wind rustled in the trees, and a rodent burrowed somewhere nearby. Normal sounds. Nothing amiss. The scents were normal, too. Forest and moss, a faint note of wood fire, and the last wisps of truck exhaust as they cleared.

Satisfied she was alone, Fleming heaved herself out of the truck's cab and positioned the crutches under her arms, her hands supporting her body's weight.

She'd walked with crutches and leg braces before, and although most people probably thought it was freeing for her to walk at least to some degree like she used to, it had never felt that way to Fleming.

It had been one thing to ride Tequila's back as he ran up the stairs. That experience had felt like walking, like freedom, like the way she remembered it to be. The struggle of shifting each crutch and forcing her legs to follow wasn't walking. It was a visceral reminder of all she'd lost. Shuffling, but not really walking. Moving, but not really getting anywhere. Like rubbing her face in her disability. She'd rather sit in a wheelchair and move around at will any day.

Unfortunately, for this she couldn't use a wheelchair.

Fleming heaved herself over to the truck bed and pulled out the climbing stick they'd picked up at Walmart. A pole made of tubular steel with crossbars jutting out on both sides. When assembled, the fifteen-foot climbing stick was designed to be strapped to a tree, providing an instant ladder. It broke down into three five-foot sections, and the whole thing weighed under twenty pounds.

The weight wasn't a problem for Fleming, the bulk was. Not that she'd ever complain, and it gave her a private thrill that neither Tequila nor Chandler had objected to her climbing a tree when they'd discussed the plan earlier. Fleming had dreamed of returning to the field for years. Her little manipulation of the park ranger had scratched a part of that itch, but getting up in that tree and taking in the view through the scope of the AR-15 would be even more satisfying.

Unless, of course, she fell and killed herself. Or worse, broke her legs in even more places.

Leaving one of her crutches leaning against the truck's rear quarter, Fleming lifted all three sections of the climbing stick out of the bed and tucked them under her arm, using them as her second crutch. She knew just the tree she wanted, a tall sugar maple that had already lost enough of its brilliant orange and golden leaves to give her a great view, yet still held enough to hide her presence from the ground.

The path to the tree, however, was slow going. Shift the crutch forward, follow with that leg. Shift the pole next, and then that leg. Twice she slipped on moss-covered rock. Once she sank into soggy ground, losing her crutch, falling onto her face. But slowly, tortuously, Fleming reached the trunk and began the task of assembling her ladder.

As painful as the walking had been, the ladder was easy. Fleming strapped the bottom section to the tree, then attached the next five-foot section. Leaving her crutch and the other piece on the ground, she used her hands and arms to climb up the rungs. Only when she reached the strap did Fleming force one braced leg over a rung to hold her in place while she strapped the second section in place. The process for the third was more of the same, and soon she was fighting her way back to the truck on a single crutch to fetch her tree stand.

The tree stand came in two pieces, a footrest and a seat, each of which secured around the tree trunk. They snapped together for easy carrying, and the combination weighed less than the climbing stick.

Another thing they'd purchased was a camo jacket; that and the dark cargo pants Lund had bought Fleming earlier would combine to make her invisible among the trees. At the moment, however, it was just making her sweat. Unsure she could manage another trip back to the truck, she threw the straps of the assault rifle and her laptop case over her shoulders, the tree stand under, and grabbed her second crutch.

By the time she'd reached the tree, her hair was soaked where it touched her neck, and she could feel the drips of perspiration running down her back and gathering under her chin. Fleming thrust her arm into a loop of the tree stand and pulled it over her right shoulder. The rifle and computer rested against her back, the straps riding across her chest.

Fleming stared up at the tree. The vantage point she sought was about ten meters up. Thinking about the height made her throat close up.

The wire, yesterday, had been higher than that. But she hadn't been alone. Tequila and Chandler had been with her, and there was so much happening that Fleming never had the chance to be self-indulgent when it came to personal fears. But now, all by herself with only her thoughts to accompany her, Fleming began to relive the biggest tragedy of her life—the fall that ruined her legs.

She recalled the moment, the details in high definition and 5.1 Dolby. Milan, after midnight. Clinging to the side of a five-story building, climbing down after a sanction, relying on a wire to support her weight. Halfway to the ground, the wire snapped, and Fleming fell more than twenty feet to the alley below. Shattered bones had broken through the skin of her legs in half a dozen places. Still conscious, feeling every bit of the pain, she had ditched her mission gear and crawled ten meters into the street, where she'd screamed until she was discovered.

It was a nightmare she used to have daily. Lately, she'd escaped with just having it a few times a week.

But now it was live and in her face, and it scared her so badly she felt light-headed.

Fleming sucked in a deep breath. She noticed that her hands were trembling, and when she clenched them together, Fleming realized how cold they were.

"OK, I'm afraid," she said to herself. "I don't want to fall again."

Acknowledging the fear was the first step. The easy one.

The second step was harder. Getting back on the horse that just bucked you off.

"I don't want to fall again," Fleming repeated. "So I won't."

She remained where she was.

"Action, then motivation. Do it. You won't fall."

Fleming clenched her jaw and began the climb.

Her abused muscles already exhausted, her fear making her bladder seem like it was half her body weight, each rung gained on the climbing stick required an Olympic effort. Fleming tried to distract herself with her thoughts, her observations about dragonflies, the challenge she'd thrown at Lund, her feelings for Tequila, or at least her memories of the sex. It worked for several rungs, then romance and loneliness and conflict no longer pushed back the pain and fatigue and fear, but instead it all blended together until she couldn't tell where physical pain left off and emotional longing began.

"Almost there," she said through clenched teeth. "Don't look down. You got this."

Fleming reached for the next rung, only three from the top. Her sweaty fingers curled around the aluminum tubing—

—and slipped.

For a moment, Fleming hung there in open space, her entire being reduced to mindless, animal panic.

And then her greatest fear was realized, and Fleming fell.

Lund

Lund tried to focus on outfitting Fleming's chair, but struggle as he might to occupy his mind with motorcycle parts and weaponry, his thoughts kept worming their way back to Chandler.

He couldn't figure her out. How could he feel like he knew her one minute, and the next she was a stranger? How could everything feel so right between them last night, and today Chandler acted like she didn't care?

He and Val had gone through their difficulties, but no matter how many times she'd pushed him away, told him she might never be ready, at least she'd never pretended that the feelings between them didn't exist. What kind of a person did that?

And why was he hooked on her nevertheless?

Lund really needed to have his head examined. Or at the very least, go for a long run until the frustration burned out of him and he was too tired to think about her anymore.

The prospect of running in boots wasn't pleasant, but he'd almost decided to try when his cell phone rang. He yanked it from his pocket and checked the readout.

The name of the caller was blocked.

He answered, disgusted with himself that more than anything, he wanted it to be Chandler. "Lund."

"Is this that fireman?" a scratchy male voice asked.

"Who is this?"

"Kasdorf."

Great. The guy had probably decided he wanted more money for the weapons he'd sold them. Lund prepared himself for dickering. "How did you get my number?"

"Asked to talk to the fire inspector. Fire station gave it to me."

He'd have to talk to Nancy about her habit of giving out his cell number to anyone who asked. "What is it?"

"This morning you were here talking about Badger Ammo. Thought you might want to know what I saw."

"What?" Lund was leaning forward now, like a kid trying to make his sled move faster. Unfortunately the technique didn't work when it came to pulling information out of Kasdorf. "What did you see?"

"Helicopters."

"Helicopters fly in and out. We talked about that. I've seen them, too."

"Not like the ones flying earlier today."

"Today?" A dose of adrenaline dumped into his bloodstream. Chandler hadn't said anything about activity at the site. Did she know? When she, Tequila, and Fleming arrived, what would they find? CIA? Soldiers? "How many?"

"Hell if I know. A bunch. And they were bringing in soldiers. And one of them, it wasn't the usual black chopper without tags. It was an Apache, with a thirty-millimeter, front-mounted chain gun. Those things can cut through a brick wall."

Cold rushed through Lund, then a wave of heat. By the time he found his voice, Kasdorf had ended the call.

He didn't pick up when Lund called back.

Damn, damn, damn.

Lund stared at his phone, every cell in his body vibrating. There was nothing he could do. Chandler hadn't given him the number for her new phone, and had taken his truck. Val wasn't accepting his calls, and there wasn't a chance in hell she was going to let him near the horses, not that he wanted to drag her or the horses in deeper than he already had.

He was powerless to help, inadequate, useless. Chandler was walking into a compound filled with soldiers, and he was stuck at this godforsaken farm.

Unless…

Chandler

"Take what you can get," the Instructor said. "Then take even more."

It was like kissing a tree. Tequila didn't so much as flinch. No lip action. No tongue fencing. No arm around my waist, snugging me close.

I pulled back, confused. Never kissed a guy before who didn't kiss back. "Everything OK?"

"What are you doing?" he asked.

"Coming on to you. That's not obvious?"

"Why?"

The passion I'd felt a moment earlier was rapidly becoming annoyance. We'd been sparring, working up a healthy sweat, and we obviously had a connection. So what was his deal? "A girl can't get horny? Only men are allowed?"

Tequila stared at me, his face a stone mask. I pulled away to arm's length.

"What's your problem, Tequila?"

He folded his arms across his chest. "I'm not the one with the problem."

"Who has the problem?" I asked. "Fleming? If it's my sister, she said this was OK. She even encouraged it."

"I like your sister, Chandler. And I like you."

OK. So what was the problem? I cozied up again, running my palm down his washboard stomach, fiddling with the top button of his jeans.

"I like you, too," I said, giving him a naughty smile.

"But I'm not an eraser."

My smile vanished, and I narrowed my eyes. "Excuse me?"

"What Fleming and I did last night, that was healthy. We were celebrating life. Right now, you just want to use me to erase Lund from yours."

I wanted to say he was wrong, but of course, he wasn't. I put my hands on my hips. "So what if I do? That's a bad thing?"

"You don't want me, Chandler. You want him. But you won't get him if you sleep with me. You don't want to get laid. You want to punish Lund so he hates you. And I won't help you screw your life up more than it already is."

Annoyance became anger. "Who the hell are you to tell me my life is screwed up?"

Tequila put his hands on my shoulders and held me in a vise-like grip.

"You're a train wreck, Chandler. You kill complete strangers for the government. You've almost died half a dozen times in the past twenty-four hours and haven't stopped once to think how fucked up that is. I'm not sure if you're constantly putting yourself in danger to punish yourself, or if you truly have a death wish, but when you go down, everyone around you is going to go down as well. I don't want to be one of those people."

I broke his grip and tried to slap him. He caught my wrist.

"Grow up," he said.

Grow up? This munchkin was telling me to grow up? Furious now, I went to knee him in the crotch. He gave me a double-handed push, knocking me onto my ass.

OK, you want to play? We'll play.

I kipped up to my feet, pivoted my hips, and went for a spin kick. He caught my leg, leaned back, and tossed me aside, sending me twirling to the ground.

"What are you trying to prove, Chandler? You want to kick my ass, because you think then I'll sleep with you? Or do you think that will make you right? Give me a break."

I stood up again, fists clenched, and began to bob and weave. I threw a jab, Tequila blocked it, but I did the spinning backhand move and caught him on his chin, hard enough to make him stagger backward.

Quick learner? Damn right I was a quick learner.

I followed up with another kick, and he caught my foot between his knees before I had a chance to punt his balls out through his nose. Then he slapped my cheek, open-handed, released my leg, and hit me in the gut so hard I wound up on all fours, throwing up my cheese sandwich.

"I don't know your background, Chandler, but let me guess. Abusive parents. Flunked out of school. Got arrested young. Learned to use sex to get your way. Never had a stable relationship in your life. You know you're good at your job, but being good at killing isn't how you're supposed to help yourself."

I spat, then screamed at him, "So how the hell am I supposed to help myself!?"

My words echoed out over the compound, making me sound tinier than I already felt.

"Quit," he said.

I opened my mouth to reply, but wasn't sure what I was going to say.

Quit?

Could that be the secret to happiness?

Could it really be that easy? Just leave all this behind me and start fresh?

"I had a sister, once," Tequila said. "She died. In this line of work, you can't let people get close. But living without people in your life…that isn't living."

"But you're still in the game."

He shook his head. "I retired. After she died. Except for an odd job now and then, or a favor to an old friend."

I let the fantasy play out. If I wasn't an assassin anymore, I could be anything. There were endless possibilities. I had enough money socked away to take my time in choosing a new career. One where I didn't get shot at. One where I didn't have to kill people.

One where I could have an honest-to-goodness steady relationship.

Being with Lund, while I was an operative, was impossible.

But if I was no longer in this business…

"Your sister? Is that what made you quit?"

He surprised me by shaking his head.

"So what did it?" I asked.

"I realized something. Every time I hurt someone, or killed someone, the person I was really hurting and killing…was me."

I felt strange, as if his simple statement had drawn my anger out like poison from a snakebite, and something akin to melancholy had taken its place. What he was saying made sense. "Tequila, you're…right."

Tequila's look remained skeptical. "Seriously?"

"I'm a quick learner, remember? Although you probably just saved me half a million dollars in psychotherapy."

"So you're quitting?"

Could it really be that easy? Maybe it could. I wouldn't know unless I did it. "We need to see this mission through to the end."

He folded his arms.

I couldn't leave the Instructor at the mercy of Hammett. It wasn't due to any nobility or even loyalty on my part, not to him. But it was important to Fleming, and I was not going to let her down. "But when it's over, Tequila, I'm done."

"Really?"

"Yeah."

"You're not just saying this because you're still trying to sleep with me?"

I laughed. "Please. You're cute, but that was so five minutes ago."

Tequila walked over, held out his hand, and helped me to my feet.

"Thanks," I said. "If you've got anything else you want to teach me, I'm a willing student."

"About 52 Blocks? Or life?"

"Either."

He rubbed his chin, apparently thinking. "There's a move called Spitting Razors, but it's dangerous."

"What does it involve?"

"Spitting razors."

"Show me."

He removed a pack of double-edged razor blades from his front pocket, and unwrapped one. Holding it between his thumb and index finger, be began to bob and weave, but also somehow juggled the razor blade at the same time, tossing it into the air, snatching it with the other hand, slashing, tossing, switching hands, going around the back with it, and then he threw the razor blade up by his face—

—and sucked it into his mouth.

Before I could say, "*No fucking way*," he'd spit the blade out from his lips into his empty right hand and was holding it to my neck.

"You keep the blade flat on your tongue, and then sort of spit and blow at the same time, shooting it to either hand."

"That's insane."

"It's the ultimate move of Jailhouse Rock. All the best fighters know it."

Tequila tossed the blade to his other hand, then tossed it back inside his mouth, catching it in his teeth and grinning. Plucking the razor out with two fingers and offering it to me, he asked, "Want to try?"

I nodded. What was the worst that could happen?

Fleming

"Often the difference between survival and death," said the Instructor, "is keeping a clear head when the shit hits the fan."

Fleming dangled by one hand for half a second before she fell.

Then gravity took over, a sensation she remembered all too well. She flashed back to Milan, the raw fear as she plummeted, the pain when she hit, the physical and emotional agony of rehabilitation.

Fleming cried out, weightless for a heartbeat, then her legs slammed the rungs below, braces clanging, pain jarring up her spine, panic threatening to push her into madness.

Not this time. Not again.

Not. Ever. Again.

Fleming stifled the cry and stretched out her arms, seeking to snag them on a branch.

Her shoulder gave a painful jolt, and she came to an abrupt, jaw-jarring stop, hanging around a thick tree limb by her armpit.

Fleming looked around, blinking away the tears assaulting her eyes, struggling to get her bearings. She swayed against the trunk, her leg braces clacking against the aluminum climbing pole with each swing.

"There. That wasn't too scary."

Setting her jaw, mastering her fear, Fleming grasped the rungs, unhooked herself, and resumed climbing, hauling her useless and screaming legs behind her. She reached the spot and tried setting up the stand, but the braces were so awkward and clumsy, it was obvious within a minute that she needed to rethink this plan.

She shrugged the tree stand off her shoulder and hooked it on the climbing stick's top rung, then started unbuckling her right leg. Fleming followed with the left and dropped the braces down to the base of the tree, flashing them the finger as they clattered to the ground.

Her legs still hurt like hell, but without the braces it was easier to move. She resumed setting up the stand, balancing it on a branch, positioning the contraption to one side and a little behind the trunk. When she'd finished her adjustments, she climbed into the seat and removed the laptop from its case.

Waiting for it to boot up, Fleming rubbed her sore shoulder and positioned her weapon's barrel on the brace. She could keep this posture for hours, if need be, or at least she had been able to back when she was in the field. It felt good. Familiar. But despite the rush another taste of the life brought her, she couldn't help feeling something was missing, too. That whatever it was that used to sustain her just wasn't quite enough anymore.

She suspected Chandler felt the same way, when she allowed her feelings to squeak through. But what did that mean for either of them? She honestly couldn't say. However, of the many memorable things the Instructor had said, one that stood out was, "If you're thinking it might be time to quit, it's time to quit."

Bringing herself back to the moment, she peered through the scope and did a sweep of the compound. The air was warmer than yesterday and growing more humid, clouds starting to form in the sky. The building across from the cannon testing area was to the right; the water treatment plant, which housed the secret prison, loomed slightly to the left; and by the water reservoir, farther left, she spotted Chandler and Tequila in what looked like an intimate embrace. Fleming searched her feelings for jealousy, and didn't find any. But something still didn't sit right. It took her a moment, but Fleming realized what it was: she didn't like Chandler hurting Lund.

Tequila was fun.

But Lund was something else. Something serious. And Chandler shouldn't piss that away.

Fleming thought about radioing them to interrupt their tête-à-tête, but then saw that they were sparring, not making out. Maybe her sister was wiser than Fleming gave her credit for.

She took two more sweeps, spotted no activity, checked the laptop, and brought her walkie-talkie to her face.

Chandler answered, sounding out of breath. "In position?"

"Yes. And everything looks clear."

"What took you so long?"

"The park has tighter security than the White House." An exaggeration, of course, but still. "And I'm not as good at climbing trees as I used to be. You OK? You're lisping a little."

"I cut my lip. Tequila just superglued it."

That must have been the embrace Fleming saw. "I have a bead on our psycho sister."

"Visual or via computer?"

"Computer." She studied the blip on the screen. "She left Badger and is heading north to the Dells. I hope she didn't take the Instructor with her."

"Guess we'll find out."

"Guess so. You ready to rock and roll?"

She could almost feel Chandler's smile. The line was one Fleming had used all the time when she was Chandler's handler.

"Ready, Sis. Let's blow this thing and go home."

Fleming laughed. Home...it was sounding better and better. "*Star Wars*, huh, Chandler? You're such a nerd."

"You got the reference, so you're a nerd, too. And Han shot first."

"Hell yeah, he did. Make sure you shoot first as well."

"Roger, and out."

The White House

"It's all under control, Mr. President. We've got them where we want them."

"Is the plan to take them alive?"

"That's the plan."

The president gripped his encrypted cell phone so hard his knuckles turned white. "You recognize the security leak they represent."

"I do, Mr. President."

"That leak needs to be plugged."

"I understand, sir. We'll make sure it is."

"These women…they're heroes. This country owes them."

"They understand the risks, Mr. President. All soldiers do."

"My veep, he'd say we're going to hell for making this decision."

His contact didn't reply.

"Make sure their families are provided for," the president said.

"They have no family, sir."

At least that much, he supposed, was good news.

Chandler

"Don't go seeking revenge," the Instructor said. "But if the opportunity for revenge presents itself, take it."

We approached the reclamation plant at its northeast corner. Tequila and I circled the perimeter in different directions, looking for the entrance. I went left, keeping my AR-15 at my side, finger resting on the trigger guard. I didn't sense anyone nearby. In fact, I hadn't sensed anyone since we'd breached the fence. That was odd. Where were the workers? Had everyone, including Hammett, abandoned the place? If so, what were the odds the Instructor would still be here? And if he'd been taken elsewhere, were Fleming and I supposed to track him down no matter how long it took? I didn't want my last mission to drag on for weeks or months. I wanted out of this life, and it couldn't come fast enough.

I reached the front of the building. There was a shallow, elongated pond alongside a dirt path, which led up to a metal door that had been blown off its hinges. I smelled traces of explosives, and something underneath it. BBQ?

"I'm at a doorway," I said into my radio.

"I lost sight of Tequila, but I can still see you," Fleming said. "Tequila, you there?"

"I'll catch up in a minute. Checking out a retention pool."

"I'm going in."

The doorway opened into a dilapidated office. What little furniture remained was twenty years out of date and beyond repair. There were holes in the walls and ceiling where pipes and lighting fixtures had been ripped out. It was dark, ten degrees warmer than outside.

I listened, hearing no unusual sounds, but I got a little spike of adrenaline, like I'd leaned too far back on a chair before catching myself. It was a feeling I was familiar with, and one I'd learned to trust.

Someone was in the room with me.

I knew due to a combination of things. Feeling eyes on me, smelling the pungent odor of someone who'd been sweating for a while, sensing the ambient heat of a fellow human being nearby. I wasn't alone. And whoever was watching me was close.

I pulled the night-vision monocular from my pocket and powered it on. It worked by amplifying ambient light, and in the viewfinder the room lit up bright green. I did a slow 360, finger on the trigger of my rifle, holding my breath so I could hear better. I saw a desk with an old phone on it, a bookcase, another blown door leading to an empty hall, the remains of a couch. But there was no one in the room.

After I'd turned a complete circle, I pocketed the monocular and saw one of the scariest things a spy could see; a red pinpoint of light over my heart.

A laser gun sight. My butt clenched in something I called the pucker effect.

"Move and die," a male voice said.

I chose not to move. I couldn't see where the shooter was standing, couldn't locate him by his voice. There wasn't anyone in the room, but he sounded close. In the floor? The ceiling?

"Drop the rifle. Nice and slow."

The alternative was getting my heart blown out the back of my chest. I unslung the AR-15 and let it drop to the floor.

"Now the machine gun, and the sidearm."

Something about the voice. Something familiar. I eased the Skorpion off my shoulder. As I did, I passed it in front of the laser light, to see if I could determine its point of origin. The shooter responded to my unsubtle attempt by aiming the light into my left eye, temporarily blinding me. I closed the eyelid and let go of the Skorpion. My Beretta was next. And though I still had the KA-BAR knife strapped to my calf, I felt practically naked.

"Knife, too. Hurry now."

I unstrapped the KA-BAR, letting it fall.

"Been waitin' for you, my pretty girl."

Ah, hell. This guy.

"Did you miss Ol' Rochester?"

Noise, to my right, and I squinted into the dark and saw the bookcase move, swinging out on hinges to reveal a hidden closet. My good buddy Rochester stood there, grinning ear to ear. The weapon with the laser sight was a magnum of the Dirty Harry variety.

"A gun?" I said, louder than necessary, hoping Tequila was close. "I thought you were more hands-on than that."

"I am, Miss Chandler. I'm going to put my hands on you like you never felt before, girl."

He holstered his gun under his shoulder as if it embarrassed him, then began to pat his chest and elbows, bobbing and weaving in a steady, unsettling rhythm. It was the same pattern that had freaked me out so much the first time we met, and led to him kicking my ass.

"You remember this, girl? I bet it gave you nightmares."

I let him approach, keeping my hands at my sides, waiting for his attack.

It came in the form of a jab, fast and hard.

I clocked with skull and crossbones, then extended the elbow and clipped him in the chin.

Rochester staggered back, confused. Then he smiled again, his white teeth streaked with blood.

"I see you been practicin'. Rocking the jailhouse, huh, sweet thing?"

He moved in again, the tempo of his palms on his body increasing, and lashed out a roundhouse.

I caught it.

Kissed it.

And sent it back with enough force to break his nose.

Rochester staggered a step back, but as I was crouching to grab one of many weapons, any of my weapons, he caught me in the chest with his boot, sending me sliding across the dirty floor on my ass. I turned, getting on all fours, and then I was on my feet as he closed the space between us.

"I got something nice for you, girl. Nice and sharp."

Nice and sharp? I tensed, guessing what was going to happen next.

I saw his cheeks bulge out, his mouth open up, and just as he spit my hand sprang out and snatched the razor blade from the air, grabbing it before he could. A millisecond later he was clutching his throat, blood pumping through his fingers, because I'd opened up a slit in his neck down to the trachea. His eyes went wide with shock, and probably pain.

I tossed the razor blade to the floor, wiped my fingers on my shirt, then stared at Rochester as he tried to speak.

"You got something to say, sweet thing?" I asked. "I know. You think you're going to die from that big, nasty cut in your throat. But don't fret. Ole Chandler won't let you go out like that."

I snatched up my 9mm, drilled two into Rochester's face, and then got on the radio.

"That shooting was me. I think I found the entrance."

I squatted, patting down Rochester's body. A few hundred in cash. ID in the name of Jules Blech—maybe his name had a lot to do with his sadistic streak. More razor blades, a bag of weed, a brass key, and a key card. I took it all, plus the laser sight on his magnum, which I was trying to fit onto my Skorpion when Tequila arrived.

"Won't fit," Tequila said. "Different rail size."

"I noticed," I said, pocketing it anyway.

"I see your 52 Blocks buddy doesn't scare you anymore."

I wondered how Tequila knew this was the man I'd mentioned, but he either saw Rochester's JHR tattoo or the bloody razor blade, and made a correct assumption.

"I've got a friend," I said, "who taught me how to deal with him."

"A friend?"

"He's a good guy, but he talks too much."

Tequila, predictably, didn't reply.

I picked up my weapons. Then I stood, gave Tequila a clap on the shoulder, and headed for the open door. It led into a hallway, and then down some concrete stairs. At the bottom were a bank of rooms: security center, locker room, toilet, another office, kitchen. It was the kitchen where the BBQ smell originated, but my stomach did cartwheels when I figured out it wasn't food making the odor, but some dead burned guy. I didn't look too closely, but his arms and legs were bound with wire, and the expression on his face revealed he hadn't died peacefully.

We continued our search, coming to yet another steel door blown off its hinges by explosives. Didn't anyone pick locks anymore?

Through that doorway into a hall. Stone walls, concrete floor, dirt ceiling held at bay with wooden supports, single bare bulbs strewn up every few meters. The hall was lined, both sides, with cells. We turned a corner, finding an open door and another dead guy who smelled as if he had been there a little while.

"This was Fleming's room," Tequila said.

I saw the instrument tray, upended on the floor, all the torture implements, and wanted to kill the dead guard a second time.

"Anyone here?" I yelled, my voice echoing down the hall.

"Who's there?" a man called back.

We followed the voice, used the brass key and the keycard, and opened the correct cell door.

There, sitting on the floor, filthy clothes stained with blood, was the Instructor. He stared up at me, his eyes clear and bright.

"Chandler. Jesus Christ, it's good to see you."

Lund

Lund glanced at the motorcycle parts Tequila had found in the barn. Pulse thrumming in his ears, he made a beeline across the yard. The barn's door needed lubrication, but with a hard tug, it squealed over the runners, sliding wide.

There were many things about Lund's father-in-law that he'd actively tried to forget, mostly how he'd beaten his wife and heaped unspeakable abuse on his daughter, Lund's deceased wife. But there was one thing he wished he'd remembered before now.

He slipped into the barn. The place hadn't seen activity for years, and now both he and Tequila had entered in the past few hours. As a result, dust hung thick in the air, and he had to squint to see through the interior gloom.

The smell of cow manure still permeated the place, although the acrid bite had long since faded in intensity. A center aisle stretched the length of the barn and a row of stanchions lined each side a quarter of the way in, providing capacity for four rows of cows. By the time Lund first saw the place, the milking itself had been moved to the more modern barn behind the old barn, and this one had been relegated to housing cows in bad weather. Later, the front of the barn was converted to storage.

He eyed the jumble of stuff that choked either side of the aisle now.

Tractor parts, a pair of aluminum trash cans, and one of those pop-up campers. A dozen calf hutches, and a western saddle so old and dry that one stirrup fender had snapped in half.

It couldn't be here. Not the item he was looking for.

He walked through the junk until he reached a ladder made of two-by-fours and nailed to the wall. Above the ladder, a hole led up into the haymow.

As he climbed, birds fluttered and sailed through the cavernous space overhead. The mow smelled of dusty hay, old but still slightly sweet. Less than fifty bales piled at one end, the rest long since fed to cows or sold to nearby farmers. Bird droppings covered much of the floor not strewn with loose hay, white against the dark wood.

Lund spotted the tarp immediately, crossed the floor with urgent strides, grabbed the edge of the tarp, lifted it off—

—and stared at a Harley-Davidson FL Panhead.

The bike seemed to be in nearly perfect condition. The fenders and gas tank were cherry red, only a few dings in the paint. Even the tires were the classic whitewalls, in solid shape despite needing air. Lund had never been a huge motorcycle fanatic, mainly because the hobby was too costly for his bank account. But with a bike like this, he was more than willing to learn.

The thing he needed from it most now, though, was basic transportation.

He yanked open the haymow's big slider and walked the bike down the earthen ramp. He found a tire pump in the barn, topped off gas and oil, and soon he was ready to roll.

Besides a certain lack of comfort in the old seat, the Harley handled like a dream. A heavy bike, it was pretty stable, and he was grateful Wisconsin had few helmet laws, since he didn't have one.

The road leading to his cabin and the park beyond was closed. Luckily he knew the deputy babysitting the roadblock, and with a flash of his driver's license to prove his address, he was on his way.

After a quick stop at his cabin to get his deer rifle, he retraced the path they'd taken in their escape from Badger the day before. When the pavement ended, he parked the bike, hoping it wouldn't end up on the impound lot like Tequila's, and covered the rest of the distance at a brisk jog.

He stopped when he spotted his truck parked near the fence.

The forest was quiet, unusually so, and an uneasy tension gripped the back of his neck and shoulders. Standing still, he scanned the trees, sniffing the air like a deer checking for danger, realizing that danger had likely already found him.

Fleming

"Field work is equal parts waiting and watching," said the Instructor. "Those who stay awake and alert are the ones who live to see the excitement. Those who snooze, die."

It wasn't right.

Fleming focused on the compound through her scope. Fifteen minutes had passed since she'd taken up her position, and in all that time she hadn't seen one hint of movement down below. The demolition crews Chandler had told her about were nowhere to be found. Idle dump trucks were parked in rows, front-end loaders scattered at various worksites unmoving, not a rumble of engines or a cloud of kicked-up dust in the whole place.

Still as a graveyard.

She didn't see anything at the entrance guard tower, either. No movement in the booth. No cars in the front parking lot. Fleming wasn't even sure if the gate was locked. Security seemed to be tight in the park and the orchard and everywhere in between, but at the ammunition plant itself, it was nonexistent.

Then she heard the shuffle of footsteps tromping through leaves.

Fleming slowed her breathing to counteract her natural spike in adrenaline. Tracking the sound, she pivoted in her chair and brought the rifle around.

One set of steps, one person. A man, she knew from the heaviness of the tread, then a slight smell reached her, riding the wind.

The fragrance of roses.

She slipped her finger to the trigger.

Lund

Lund wasn't sure what made him look up into the trees. Not a sound—there was none. Not a scent—all he smelled were leaves, pine, and a hint of wood fire. The only way he could explain it was a change in the pressure of the air.

But whatever the reason, when he did look up, he peered straight into the barrel of one nasty-looking assault rifle.

"Don't shoot." He dropped his deer rifle and raised his hands like he was in some old western, his heart pumping out of his chest.

"Lund?"

That voice. He knew it. "Chandler?"

"Close. Fleming."

The rifle lowered, and he could finally focus on the face behind it.

"I almost shot you," she said.

"Yeah, I know."

Lund still couldn't quite breathe. Here he'd brought a weapon, only to drop it at the first indication of trouble. But he wasn't going to beat himself up about it. Yesterday he'd seen the people he was up against in action. He was no match for any of them. He was trained to save people, not kill them. He probably shouldn't have even brought the damn gun.

"Why are you here? Wait, how are you here?"

"I got a call. Can you warn Chandler?"

"Warn her? What's wrong?"

"A guy called me. The guy who sold us the guns. He watches this place pretty carefully, and he saw helicopters flying in earlier today. Lots of them."

Even from the ground, Lund could see alarm widen Fleming's eyes.

"How many?" she asked.

"He wasn't sure. But he mentioned seeing soldiers."

"Here?" She brought the rifle to her shoulder and scanned the ammo plant through the scope.

"You don't see them?"

"I don't see anyone. That's what has me worried. Is this guy reliable?"

"Depends on how you define reliable."

Fleming glanced down at the laptop he'd given her. "Unless..."

"Unless what?"

"Unless they don't want to be seen. Meaning it's a trap."

Lund was just about to panic when Fleming whirled to the side, focusing the rifle at something in the forest behind him.

He followed the trajectory of her aim and found himself looking into yet another rifle barrel focused on him. Then, from the other side of Fleming's perch, he heard the unmistakable sound of a shotgun racking.

Chandler

"Trust no one," the Instructor said.

"Where are you hurt?" I asked.

The Instructor's face was a mask of dried blood, his clothing caked with the clotting stuff. He coughed, spat between his legs onto the cell floor.

"All over," he said. "Can you help me up?"

I moved to do so. Though I was unsure if I could trust him, I had relied on him many times in the past. This was the man who had trained me, and in doing so had held my life in his hands countless times. Much of what I was today, both good and bad, could be attributed to the Instructor. I may not have known his real name, but without a doubt he was the most influential, and important, person to have ever been in my life.

I felt a hand on my shoulder—Tequila holding me back. He knelt next to the Instructor before I could, but rather than help the man up, he gave him a thorough pat-down.

"Who are you?" The Instructor asked.

"Who are you?" Tequila replied.

Tequila didn't find any weapons, and I helped the older man to his feet. The Instructor's age was hard to guess. He didn't seem any older than the day I'd met him. Graying hair, grizzled features, gruff voice. He probably came out of the womb looking like a drill sergeant.

"Hammett is here," the Instructor said. "She wants Fleming. Is Fleming safe?"

"Yes."

"Where is she, Chandler?"

"Why are you here?" I asked.

He blinked. "I don't know. Got jumped in Chicago. Woke up here. Not even sure where here is."

"Where are you injured?"

"Hammett and her boys worked me over, but I'll manage. Where are we?"

"A black site."

"Baraboo?"

I nodded.

"This administration has gone to hell," the Instructor said, spitting again. "A secret prison on American soil. Why doesn't the president just wipe his ass with the Constitution?"

Said the man who trained me to kill people for the government. I'm pretty sure state-ordered assassination wasn't part of the Bill of Rights, but given the Instructor's current condition, I could understand his bias.

"We're getting you out of here," I said. "Can you walk?"

He nodded. "I think I know why Hammett wants Fleming. Are you sure she's safe?"

I got on my radio. "We got the package. He wants to know if you're safe."

"I ran into a snag. There's a cemetery a kilometer west of you. Meet me there."

"How are you getting there?"

"Your firefighter friend is giving me a ride."

Lund? Goddamn Boy Scout. "Why aren't we going for the trucks?"

"Compromised. I'll brief you at the cemetery. Out."

Shit. I tried to picture the map of the compound in my head. The cemetery was an old one, here before the military acquired the land and built the Badger Ammo facility. If we double-timed it, we could get there in under ten minutes.

"You have this guy here"—the Instructor stuck his thumb at Tequila—"*and* a firefighter friend? You're Miss Popularity lately, Chandler."

"Don't make me regret saving your ass. Let's move."

Fresh air was a relief after the stuffiness underground, but the clear sky was starting to cloud up, and the temperature had risen, humidity hanging in the air.

As we jogged, I should have kept my mind in the game, but instead I thought about Lund. This mission was almost finished, and I wanted it to be my very last one. So, what next? Tell him I quit? That I wanted to be with him, and see where it led? Even though I'd just met the man, there was something about him that made me feel good about myself, in a way I hadn't felt in a long time. Maybe it wouldn't end with wedding bells, but if there was someone who could lead me back into the world of normalcy, Lund would be a good bet. And the fact that he'd shown up here hopefully meant I hadn't killed whatever feelings he might have had for me.

Maybe I would get a real chance at a happy ending.

The cemetery was small, less than fifty meters wide, surrounded by a short fence. I was surprised to see it carefully maintained, the grass neatly trimmed, no weeds or overgrowth. Our society was a twisted one. We treated our dead better than we treated the living.

The air was strangely quiet, no geese honking or birds of prey overhead, no sounds from birds at all, nothing but the patter of our footsteps on dry grass. Fleming was sitting on the ground, her back to a tombstone, her legs in their metal braces and stretched out before her. I didn't see Lund and felt a twinge of disappointment. Fleming had probably sent him home. When we entered the cemetery and approached her, Fleming smiled at me, and I knew something was very wrong.

A split second later, she was pointing her AR-15 at us.

"Hands in the air," she said. "Or I will shoot you."

"Not Fleming. Hammett."

"We're surrounded," Tequila said.

I checked left, then right, and saw Javier on one side, a black man on the other. Both had guns on us.

"Hello again, *puta*," Javier said. "You owe me a new pair of Ferragamos."

Tequila and I raised our hands. Then we were being disarmed, someone taking our weapons, and I clenched my jaw when I saw who was doing it.

The Instructor.

And in that instant, I realized how stupid I'd been.

My sister lowered her rifle, unbuckled her leg braces, and sprang to her feet with the grace of a dancer.

"You removed the chip," I said.

She nodded, still flashing that shark grin. "Hurt like a bitch."

"And it was you on the radio, telling us to come here."

"We all sound the same. You, me, Fleming."

"So what were you?" I asked the Instructor. "Bait?"

"I was expecting Rochester to take you prisoner."

Of course, if anyone knew my training and fighting style intimately, it was the Instructor. When Rochester first came after me, I'd known he was there to neutralize me. I just hadn't guessed who sent him.

Or maybe I just hadn't wanted to face it.

"He was very good," the Instructor said.

"So am I."

"Obviously." The Instructor studied me through narrowed eyes. "Yet here you are, with your hands in the air. You still need me, Chandler."

"I need you like I need an extra asshole."

"Want to tell me what's happening?" Tequila asked.

I glanced at Tequila. He hadn't trusted the Instructor. I wished I'd taken my cue from him, instead of pushing aside my doubts. Hell, I wished we hadn't tried to save him in the first place. That we were all back at the farm right now, or better yet, heading down the road.

"You two haven't been officially introduced. Tequila, this is my sister, Hammett. Hammett, Tequila."

Hammett grinned at him. "Hello, tough guy." She'd even put on Fleming's shoes, and had done her hair in the same style.

"Sorry about your balloon," Tequila said.

Hammett's expression hardened. She strolled up to Tequila and punched him square in the jaw. He took the punch, and spit out some blood and a tooth.

"Apology accepted," Hammett said.

I glanced around the cemetery, almost afraid to voice the question. "Where are Fleming and Lund?"

Hammett's smile snaked back over her lips. "Let's go check on them."

That prick Javier raised his shotgun, herding us deeper into the graveyard. I saw Lund and Fleming under camouflage netting, their bodies lying next to each other.

It felt like I'd swallowed a block of ice. "Are they…?"

"Just drugged," Hammett said. "Should be wearing off soon. Go wake them up. They should be conscious for this next part."

I went to them, kneeling down, not sure who to check first. Tequila saved me from my indecision by going to Fleming, sitting her up, and lightly slapping her face. I checked Lund's pulse—strong—and gave him some gentle shakes.

"Ch-Chandler?" he said, droopy eyes opening.

"Wake up, Lund. We're in some shit."

"Go figure."

When Fleming awoke, she wrapped her arms around Tequila. Then she met my eyes and mouthed, "I'm sorry."

My throat felt thick, and I mouthed back, "Me too."

"I owe you ladies an explanation," the Instructor said. "After the fiasco in Chicago, I needed a place to take you both so you could be properly debriefed. But the only place available to me was this facility in Baraboo, and I had to get you here without explaining why to the agency that runs it. A power-hungry little grub named Malcolm tried to find out on his own what the fuss was about, and he did as inept a job as I'd expected. I apologize for that, Fleming. You deserve better."

"You had Hammett take him out," I said.

"Fleming did most of the job before Hammett arrived." The Instructor glanced at Fleming, a strange look on his face, something resembling pride. "I was right about you. You're as tough and resourceful in the field as you always were."

I could read where this was going. "And that's why you became a prisoner. In case Fleming managed to escape."

"And once you had my trust, you'd try to get the codes from me," Fleming said.

"That was the plan. But it changed when Hammett discovered your interrogation tapes. I had no idea the transceivers could be detonated."

"Can someone explain what's happening to the viewers just tuning in?" Lund asked. He should his head, a little bleary, but the same cool-under-pressure guy I'd liked from the start.

"Fleming created a method of encryption that's unbreakable," I said. I wasn't sure how Lund would take any of this, but I supposed that no longer mattered. The longer I talked, the longer we'd all stay alive. "She built it into two cell phones, called transceivers. With one of the cell phones and the proper code, you could launch our country's nukes."

"Jesus Christ. So that thing in England the other day? That was you guys?"

I pointed my chin at Hammett. "It was her. Fleming stopped it."

Lund glanced from one of my sisters to the other. “So now they want the codes. Do they have the phone?”

“That phone was destroyed,” Hammett said. “Fleming punched in a code, and it self-destructed. But there’s another phone. And *that’s* the one that interests me.” Hammett stared at Fleming. “You gave Chandler that phone because she could carry out orders. If it was needed, she could either launch or defuse a nuclear missile strike. She was a fail-safe. But you loaded the transceivers with explosives. And that tells me you have another fail-safe in place, don’t you, Sis?”

“It won’t work,” Fleming said. “You need to have the transceiver with you.”

“To launch a strike, yes. But to detonate the transceiver? You needed to be able to do that anywhere, anytime, without any special equipment. Because if Chandler went rogue, you needed to be able to stop her.” Hammett smiled. “Am I right?”

I looked at Fleming. “The transceivers can be remotely detonated?”

She didn’t say anything, but the look on her face said enough.

“Why didn’t you tell me?” I asked. But I knew the answer. If I were compromised, Fleming needed a way to destroy the transceiver. And me with it. I wondered why she hadn’t done that a few days ago in Chicago, but then realized she’d never had the chance.

“Wait a minute,” Lund said. “Who has got the other cell phone?”

“The president,” I told him.

“The president’s cell phone can explode?” Lund asked. “What’s the point of that?”

I exchanged a look with Fleming. Her expression was flat, but I could see the pain beneath.

“Checks and balances,” Hammett answered for her. “If the current leader got out of hand, he could be removed.”

Lund shook his head. “That’s…insane.”

Hammett shot Lund a look of disgust. "No, a populace who thinks patriotism is all about wearing flag lapel pins and watching fireworks on the Fourth of July is insane. This is reality."

"Assassination is faster than an election," I said.

Hammett nodded. "We tried to do it the hard way, by launching a nuclear attack on a friendly nation. Let public opinion hang this president. But *someone* fucked that up."

"You would have killed millions of innocent people," Fleming said.

"Don't be ridiculous. Nobody's innocent. Least of all you, Sis."

Lund shook his head. "I don't believe you people. You planted a bomb on the president of the United States, and you're talking like it is part of the balance of power. He was elected by the people."

Fleming took a deep breath, then spoke. "Technically, he was elected by the electoral college, with a campaign financed by lobbyists, special interest groups, big business, and foreign powers. The president starts wars based on personal agendas, detains American citizens without due process, tortures in blatant defiance of the Geneva Convention, and is responsible for greater abuses of power than anyone currently living. If he got out of control, there was previously no way to stop him. Now there is."

"Who are you to make that decision?"

"The only one with the technological capability," Fleming said. "So it had to be me. I didn't want the power, or the responsibility. But the alternative was leaving absolute power unchecked."

"So, what now?" Lund asked.

He sounded tired, dispirited, and I guess I couldn't blame him. This was a glimpse into the world I inhabited. Fleming, Hammett, the Instructor, and to some degree, Tequila, lived in it as well. Lund lived in a better world. Not an ideal one, but at least his made sense. Lund was all about fairness and justice and doing the right thing. The rest of us were weapons used to gain power. The country, and the world, was corrupt.

I could imagine how Lund felt. It was like being in a beautiful meadow, finding a stone, and turning it over to see all the creepy, crawly, ugly creatures underneath. Those creatures were always there, but we normally didn't have to see them.

Lund stared at me like I was one of those creatures. And I guess I was.

"Now?" the Instructor said. "Now Fleming gives up the code, we use it, and the vice president gets sworn in, a man more favorable to our position than the current POTUS."

"And if he isn't more favorable, what then? You kill him, too?"

The Instructor shrugged.

"You're going to kill the president," Lund said, as if he still couldn't believe what he'd heard.

"Where did you find this guy?" the Instructor said, jerking a thumb at Lund. "Mayberry?" He turned to Lund. "Let me clue you in, son. The president sends our troops to die in wars we shouldn't even be involved in. He kills people in secret prisons every day. He uses me, and these ladies, to kill people abroad and in our own country. He's got more blood on his hands than all of us here put together."

"He's a dick," Hammett said.

"There's one thing you didn't think of," Fleming said. "I won't give up the codes."

"Yeah, you're a tough little cookie," Hammett said. "But what if I start killing all your friends here?"

Fleming and I exchanged a glance, and hers said, *I'm willing to die.*

Mine didn't match hers.

"Fleming," the Instructor said. "I've been in constant touch with the president since yesterday, and his last directive to me was to make sure this security leak gets plugged. You know what that means. All of you are supposed to die."

"Assuming I believe you," Fleming said, "that doesn't make me change my mind."

"Then let's start with the altruistic firefighter," Hammett said. "I'm going to count to three, then put a round in his brain. One…"

Lund's jaw clenched, and he glared at Fleming. "Don't tell this bitch anything."

"Two…"

His eyes flitted to mine, and I wasn't sure what I saw there. Resignation? Regret? Fear?

Love?

I couldn't breathe, my lungs, my throat, all of me squeezed as if by some giant hand.

Lund, like Fleming, was willing to die for the cause. Except it wasn't Lund's cause, wasn't his fight. He was a civilian, and I never should have brought him into this. What did he think he was doing? Rushing to the rescue? Saving the world? I doubted Lund had blood on his hands, but the president did. And of the two, I cared for Lund a lot more. Hell, I didn't even vote for the current guy.

"Three!"

"I know the codes!" I said.

Everyone stared at me.

"I'll do it," I said. "I'll do it."

"Chandler…" Fleming said.

Lund shook his head. "Chandler, don't."

Tequila, predictably, didn't say anything.

"Stand over there," the Instructor ordered, pointing next to a tree.

"Got a sniper on site? These two aren't enough?" I asked, looking at Javier and the other guy.

"Just do it."

I complied.

The Instructor reached out a hand, and Hammett handed him a leather satchel. He slung it across his chest and pulled a piece of paper from inside. "Here's the phone number to the other transceiver," he said, handing me the typed note. "Call it and read the script, or your friend dies."

"Chandler?" Lund stared at me, but I couldn't read his expression. "You can't do this. You can't."

"Your life for the president's? It's not even close."

Hammett winked at Lund. "I think she's sweet on you, buddy."

"Put it on speakerphone," the Instructor ordered.

I did, and dialed the number. It rang twice, and then, "This is the president. Who is this?"

"Read it," the Instructor said.

I swallowed into a parched throat, and began reading the message. "Mr. President. I work for Hydra, a secret assassination arm of the military. You're familiar with it. Hydra is upset with the job you're doing, and because we're patriots, we have no choice but to relieve you of your power."

I punched in the code Fleming had shared with me earlier. There was a loud *POP!*, then static.

For a moment, nobody moved or spoke.

I'd killed many people on my job, and this one had been the easiest. But the weight of what I'd done began to seep in, and I became light-headed.

John Wilkes Booth. Lee Harvey Oswald.

Codename Chandler.

Of course, if the world ever found out what I'd done, I wouldn't be remembered by my codename. My real name would be discovered. The US wasn't going to let a presidential assassin get away with it. I'd be hunted to the ends of the earth, executed by the country I'd sworn to serve, and be the source of debate, conspiracy theories, and hatred for as long as human beings lived.

If the world found out.

"You just killed him?" Lund asked.

"I did what I had to do to save you," I said. "This country will always have a president. But you...you're irreplaceable."

Lund stared at me with an expression I couldn't read, his eyes wide, his mouth slightly open. I hoped it was relief or gratitude and not disgust.

Hammett had her tablet PC out, tapping at the touch screen.

"CNN.com," she said. "President was just pulled out of a press conference. They think he was shot." Hammett tapped the screen a few more times. "I just bought a slew of stock options this morning. Think the Dow will crash? If so, I'm rich, bitches. Cha-ching!"

"What now?" Fleming asked the Instructor. She hadn't looked at me since I'd punched in the code.

"Now, provided the fireman can keep his mouth shut, you're free to go," the Instructor said. He took the phone and note I hadn't realized I was still holding, slipped them into a small bag and stuffed it in a satchel slung around his shoulder. "Everyone take a week off. I'll call you soon with your next assignment."

"You're letting us leave?" I asked.

The Instructor pointed up at a nearby tree. I noticed the video camera, hidden in the branches. "I got your speech on tape. You'll work for me again, or I leak it to the press, and your face will be on every television station and website on the planet."

I blinked. The bastard had me. I glanced at my two identical sisters. He had all of us. I had just started dreaming of a normal life, and now those hopes were gone, held hostage by a man who would never, ever let me go.

Hammett's eyebrows crinkled. "That's my face, too."

"It's all your faces." He tapped the bag. "And your fingerprints."

I stared at his hand, the bag, then back to the camera. I couldn't believe how stupid I'd been. I'd actually handed him half his evidence.

Hammett made a growling noise deep in her throat.

The Instructor gave her a shake of his head. "You already work for me, so I don't need any leverage. This is just an insurance policy for Chandler and Fleming, so they stay in line."

"You can take that video and shove it up your ass," Fleming said.

Hammett raised her rifle, aiming at Fleming. "Then I guess it's game over for you, Sis."

The Instructor took a step toward Hammett. "We need her. She's still got the encryption code in her head."

Hammett shot him a mean glance. "Then give me the recording. Find some other way to control her."

The Instructor spread out his hands. "Hammett..."

Hammett swung the rifle barrel from Fleming to the Instructor. "I'm not kidding. Give me the goddamn video. I'm not spending the rest of my life as Public Enemy Number One."

The Instructor raised his hands over his head as if surrendering, but I saw him touch his index finger to his thumb.

A signal, for whoever was watching the camera.

I had a feeling things were about to go from bad to worse.

Hammett's radio crackled. "It's Santiago...there are troops fucking everywhere! I surrender! I surrender!"

"You son of a bitch," Hammett said, putting her rifle barrel to the Instructor's forehead. "You set me up."

The Instructor shook his head. "Just a precautionary measure. We're partners, Hammett."

"I'm bouncing," the black guy said. "Too much heat."

"Later, *chica*," Javier said, winking at me. The two took off. Jumping on two ATVs hidden behind a swell of earth, they headed south.

I looked to the west, saw half a dozen armed men converging. They were in ghillie suits—camouflaged so we hadn't noticed them earlier. More came from the east.

Tequila, so fast he was a blur, came up behind the Instructor and pulled his sidearm, aiming it at Hammett. Half a second later, Hammett was behind me, gun pressed to my back.

"Let her go, or I kill him," Tequila said. "Then you don't get your video."

"You have until three to let him go, then Chandler dies. One..."

I tried to make a move, and Hammett clubbed me in the side of the head with the rifle stock.

Pain rattled through my skull. I dropped to my knees, the world wobbly, and she crouched behind me.

"Two…"

"Chopper coming in," Fleming said.

I heard it, flying in from the south, fast.

"Three!"

But it wasn't Hammett who'd said it. It was Lund.

Hammett crumpled, slumping against my back and sliding to the ground. I peered over my shoulder to see Lund holding a broken piece of tombstone in his hands.

Above, the chopper swept in. It was a war bird, an Apache, opening fire with its front-mounted barrel gun.

Tequila pushed the Instructor aside and dove onto Fleming. Lund tackled me, covering my body with his, as large-caliber gunfire ripped the cemetery to shreds.

Tequila returned fire, his pistol rounds pinging off the copter's reinforced fuselage. I searched for a fallen machine gun, saw one ten meters away, then crawled out from beneath Lund to go for it. Wind stirred from the Apache pummeled my face. The bird lowered a ladder.

The Instructor.

I raced for the weapon, scrambling on hands and knees. I grabbed it, brought it to my shoulder, and turned just in time to see the chopper sweep away over the prairie, the Instructor clinging to the ladder beneath.

"We're being surrounded," Tequila said. "At least two dozen men."

Fleming had crawled over to Hammett, and I saw her pressing something to Hammett's chest. A gun?

No. A handful of syringes. I noticed Hammett's pack was open and contained a few more.

"It's what she drugged us with," Fleming said. "I upped the dosage. I'm guessing she'll be out at least an hour, unless Lund put her in a coma."

I glanced at Lund, who looked deathly pale.

"We should kill her," I said.

Fleming slung Hammett's pack over one shoulder. "We can discuss that later."

"OK, let's move," I said. "Tequila?"

"Got her," he said, kneeling next to Fleming.

"Lund, can you…?"

He nodded, scooping up Hammett in his long arms.

I grabbed my other weapons and took point, leading the group back to Lund's truck on Burma Road. The troops were closing in on foot, but we had a two-hundred-meter head start.

Hopefully it would be enough.

Lund

Lund had always liked to believe he was good at compartmentalizing emotion and doing what needed to be done, but at this point he felt like a marathon runner hitting the wall.

A limp Hammett swinging over his shoulders in a fireman's carry, Lund concentrated on putting one foot in front of the other. The forest was quiet, at least as much as he could discern. His ears were still ringing from gunfire, his body aching from the long trek to the tree line carrying Chandler's evil look-alike, but he wasn't close to depletion yet.

Chandler jogged ahead, then Tequila, carrying Fleming. The two of them moved like rabbits through the trees and brush, quick and silent. He felt loud and clumsy as an elephant, trying to keep up.

Only a few hundred yards, and they'd reach his truck.

Once they reached his truck, they could drive out of here.

And as soon as they were out of here, they'd be safe.

He still couldn't wrap his mind around what had happened back at the cemetery. On some level, he didn't believe that the president was dead, that Chandler had actually killed him. He couldn't make sense of that. Especially the fact that she'd done it to save *him*.

He forced his feet to keep moving. They were almost to the truck. Just through this thicket and they would—

Chandler held up a hand, signaling him to stop.

Lund froze midstride, then he smelled it.

Cigarette smoke.

Someone was close.

Chandler waved her hands, indicating without words that she planned to circle around and approach from the other side. Tequila and Fleming nodded. Lund wasn't sure he understood exactly, but he nodded too.

She set off to the east, her steps silent.

Hunkering down behind a thicket of brush, Lund spotted his truck and a man wearing camo standing near the front fender, a cigarette stub clenched between his lips. He held an assault rifle, but his casual body language suggested that he hadn't sensed their approach. Taking one last drag on his smoke, he flipped the butt to the ground and stomped it out.

Lund detected movement behind the man. It was only a subtle shift of the bushes, barely discernible, but then he spotted Chandler creeping low, moving up behind the man like a tigress stalking her prey.

She inched closer. Closer. Until she was just inches behind.

Her move was fast, perfunctory. Her left hand clapped over the guy's mouth and yanked back his head. Her arm moved in a flash, her knife blade opening his throat before Lund was sure she'd moved at all.

And as blood flowed and the body slumped to the ground, Lund looked into Chandler's eyes. And in them he saw nothing at all.

Chandler

"When God closes a door," said the Instructor, "blow a hole through the damn wall."

I slipped behind the wheel of Lund's truck and started the engine while the others piled inside. The radio came on with the turn of the key, and a frantic voice launched into speculation about the president's condition. I left it on, letting the clueless commentator's words wash over me like the lash of a whip. But instead of feeling the sting of what I'd done, I felt nothing at all.

It took only minutes to drop Lund at a sweet-looking Harley. We decided to leave Tequila's truck for the time being. Fleming and I stripped Hammett of all clothing while Tequila dug into his duffel and produced a pair of handcuffs to secure her wrists—the one item left of Harry McGlade's we hadn't lost or destroyed.

I was sure Hammett would properly appreciate the faux fur lining when she woke.

The plan was to circle country highways until we were each sure we weren't being followed, then we'd meet back at the old farm to pick up Fleming's chair and a few supplies, and figure out our next move.

A few miles into our drive, I switched off the radio. Fleming didn't say a word. Fine with me. The last thing I wanted to discuss was how I'd betrayed everything we were sworn to uphold and had screwed her, Hammett, and myself in the process. I'd rather listen to the newscaster's ill-informed blather.

I spent the miles mulling over the first time I'd met Hammett, a particularly unpleasant experience back at my ex's apartment in Chicago. I wondered how Lund had come up with the red Harley

Panhead. I even contemplated the possibility of offering Hammett to Harry McGlade, naked and bound with fur-lined handcuffs, to cover my debt.

But despite my best efforts at distraction, sometime before we reached the farm my thoughts wormed their way back to the Instructor and the president, and every muscle in my body started shaking. It was all I could do to steer the truck into the farm's drive and park it near the house.

Tequila raised an eyebrow at me, and Fleming said, "Give us a minute."

He got out of the truck. Then I was alone with my sisters.

I wasn't sure how long I sat there, gripping the wheel, staring through the bug-spotted windshield, before I regained some semblance of control.

"Chandler?" Fleming called from the backseat. "She's not going to be unconscious forever."

I forced myself out of the truck and opened the back door. Avoiding my conscious sister's gaze, I heaved Hammett's limp body over my shoulder and held on to her legs.

"Are you OK?" Fleming asked.

"Are you?"

"Don't turn this on me."

"Why not? After what the Instructor did, I'll bet you're pretty upset."

She shook her head as if disgusted with me. "I think there are more important things happening now."

"Like the president's assassination? Exactly what I don't want to talk about." Not now. And especially not with someone who knew me as well as Fleming did. "I'll come back for you after I have Hammett secured."

Fleming nodded, but I knew it wouldn't end there.

"Listen," I said. "I did what I had to."

"I know. We both did. I just wish you could have made your choice before this."

"My choice? You were there. I had no choice."

Her eyebrows arched. "There's always a choice."

"You think I should have let Hammett kill Lund? Then she would have killed Tequila. Then you. The Instructor would have had her kill everyone until I made that call, until I punched in the code, and you know it."

"Yes." She looked injured by the reminder.

I wished I could take it back. Hell, I wished I could change everything that had happened. "Then why are you busting my chops?" I could feel Hammett shift her weight and groan, the sound more a vibration through my back and shoulder than a sound.

Fleming shook her head. "I'm not."

"Then why am I standing here?"

"I just think you should decide what you want, Chandler. Really decide, instead of putting it off and letting circumstances steer your life for you."

"I'm not doing that."

"Who are you trying to kid? I've been watching you for years."

Since she was my handler, I couldn't exactly argue with that one. "And I've been an exemplary operative."

"The best."

"Then what are you talking about?"

"For starters? Let's discuss what you did with Lund."

"You're judging me? I don't sleep with half the men you do. Not one-tenth of the men."

"I don't shy away from having a good time. And up until this moment, it's been the same for you. But Lund is different, and you know it."

I couldn't argue. "What does that have to do with anything?"

"You care about him. It's obvious. And he cares about you."

"So?"

"So, do you love him?"

My throat felt tight. "Maybe. I don't know. We've only known each other for—"

"Chandler, dammit, answer the question."

"I think I might," I whispered.

Fleming's expression didn't change, not discernibly, but something about her eyes softened. "Then why did you push him away this morning? Why not give him the number of your new cell phone?"

She told me about the warning Lund had received from Kasdorf. How he'd risked his life to reach me. How if I'd only been less obstinate, the events in the cemetery wouldn't have had to turn out the way they did.

How I really could have changed everything that had happened.

"You've been looking for a way out, Chandler. I think I knew this about you before you did. But when it's right in front of you, you're too damn stubborn or suspicious or selfish to take the leap."

I could feel my sinuses burn, and for a moment I thought I'd cry. When I finally found my voice, it sounded rusty, as if it hadn't been used in a long time. "I…I was afraid."

"Of what? Lund would never betray you."

"No. He wouldn't." That had been my fear in the past, with Cory, with Victor, both of whom betrayed me in every way they possibly could. But Fleming was right. Lund would never betray me. Lund would never hurt me. Lund would die to protect me.

So what was my problem?

Tequila appeared next to the house. He watched, leaning against the railing with his arms folded.

"Listen, Chandler, I don't agree with what you did, and I don't know what's possible and what's not for any of us now that you did it. But if you want to change who you are, I can guarantee there's no better time than now."

Another groan from Hammett tickled my shoulder. Not certain my voice would work, I nodded to Fleming and headed into the house. I carried my psychotic sister upstairs to one of the bedrooms. Not only did the rooms have locks on the outsides of the doors, but the closets did as well. I dumped her into one and removed the dozen storage boxes stacked inside. I was not about to underestimate Hammett.

As I locked my sister in the closet, I heard the deep *boogada boogada boogada* of a Harley engine drive up the road and turn into the farmyard. By the time I'd secured the bedroom door behind me, heavy footfalls were climbing the steps.

My pulse spiked, and I slowed my breathing, trying to regulate my heart rate. It was no use. By the time Lund reached the top of the stairs, it was thumping hard enough to break a rib.

"Hey," I said.

"I'm leaving, Chandler."

"We're all leaving."

"I know. But I'm not going with you. I just came in to say good-bye."

I shook my head. "I have to tell you something."

"There's nothing to tell. There's nothing to say."

All my thoughts, my explanations, my feelings, caught in my throat, as if too many words were trying to get out at once. "This morning…I was wrong, Lund. You and me…the farmhouse, the long showers…I want that. More than anything."

He stared at me as if I was speaking gibberish.

"I'm sorry. I need to slow down. I can explain."

"It's too late for that, Chandler."

"Too late?" He couldn't be saying this. "I know this day hasn't gone well, but—"

"Hasn't gone well? You're kidding, right?"

"This morning I made a mistake. I'm sorry."

"No, I'm sorry. This whole thing was a mistake."

"You can't mean that." I shook my head. This couldn't be happening. It had always been so easy to communicate with Lund, effortless as breathing. So how had that suddenly fallen apart?

"I can't be with you, Chandler. Not anymore."

"It's the thing with the president, isn't it?"

"The fact that you *assassinated* him?" He drew in a shuddering breath. "I have to admit, that is hard to take."

"I did it to save you."

His eyebrows dipped low. "It doesn't matter, Chandler. It wasn't the president's death. It should be, and I don't know what this says about me, but it wasn't."

I wasn't sure I wanted to ask, but I did anyway. "Then why can't you be with me?"

"The man guarding the truck. I watched you slit his throat. I saw..."

"If he saw us, he would have shot us."

"It's not that."

"Then what is it? I don't understand."

"I saw your face when you killed him." Lund narrowed his eyes on me, as if peering into my mind, my heart; and at that moment I felt more naked than Hammett lying in that closet. "There was...nothing there. Your eyes, they were flat, dead, as if killing him was nothing more to you than swatting a mosquito. You ended a man's life, and you felt nothing at all."

I opened my mouth to explain, but no words came to my tongue. No sound crossed my lips.

"Last night I thought I was falling in love with you. I thought we had something together. But..."

"I'm sorry."

"That's not enough."

"Then what is? Name it. I'll say it. I'll do it."

He shook his head. "I don't understand being able to kill like that, Chandler. I don't *want* to understand it...and I don't want to forgive it."

I closed my eyes. Of all my fears about Lund, this was it. The reason I'd pushed him away this morning. The thing I'd sensed all along but hadn't wanted to face.

He was a far better person than I was. And now he'd finally recognized it, too.

* * *

I didn't walk Lund to his truck, nor did I pine at the window waiting for the chance to watch him drive away. While I was upstairs, Tequila had carried Fleming into the house; and I could hear her rummaging around in the kitchen, packing up pieces for her chair and other supplies we could use while Lund asked if Tequila would like a ride to fetch his truck.

I wondered if Lund would tell Tequila what had gone down between us, or if he'd wait for the gymnast to ask, which would never happen. Either way, Tequila wouldn't be surprised by what Lund told me. He'd chalk up Lund's rejection as a by-product of that pesky old morality, and I suppose he had a point.

The only problem was that I knew Lund was right.

For a second, I thought about going down to the kitchen and helping Fleming pack once the men left. But I knew that was only one of the jobs that had to be done before we could disappear.

There was another.

I'd lost my Berretta to the Instructor in the cemetery, but the Skorpion would do fine. I checked the magazine and slipped it into my waistband. Then I unlocked the door to the bedroom.

Hammett was awake when I opened the closet, and peered up at me, blinking in the sudden light. "About time."

"Get up," I said.

She struggled to her feet. "Something to wear?"

"Shut up." I motioned her out of the room, down the stairs, and out the front door, avoiding the kitchen. A thick forest loomed beyond the cattle pens and a barren field. I marched Hammett straight back, barefoot and naked and wearing those ridiculous fur-lined handcuffs. And every time she stepped on a thistle or slipped past a clump of blackberry thorns, I felt a certain satisfaction.

Rain threatened. Finally we entered the woods, a mix of fresh-smelling pine and a few deciduous trees like locust and birch. Once we were deep enough to be hidden by the thick shadows, I stopped.

"Should I kneel?" Hammett said. "Make it easier for you to put one in the back of my head?"

I didn't say anything, just stared at the dark blood in her hair from the blow Lund had dealt her and listened to a bird. A cardinal, judging from the call.

"Come on, Chandler, we both know why I'm here. You're going to kill me. But are you sure that's your best move? Am I such a threat to you that you need to neutralize me immediately, or could I possibly be an asset?"

"An asset? You're the most dangerous person I've ever met."

"Thanks."

I pulled back the bolt on the machine gun.

"I know more about the Instructor than anyone," Hammett said, talking fast. "I have an idea of where he's going. I know what his plans are. You wouldn't believe me if I told you."

"Try me."

"First off, he's not the only enemy right now. He's not even the most dangerous one."

"Who else is there?"

"I tell you, you kill me. Why would I do that?"

"Maybe I'll put a few rounds through your knees first, and you'll be more forthcoming."

"Listen, Chandler, this is a lot bigger than you know. Like worldwide bigger. You don't know what killing the president has set into motion."

"I don't hear you explaining it to me, either." I was starting to lose patience. Hammett was trying to play me, that was clear, but I wasn't in a mood to be played. "You have thirty seconds."

"Like I said, this thing is big. And complicated. And I don't know all the pieces yet. But together, we can put them together. Between what you know, what I know, and what we can find out, we can take the whole thing down. And we can save our own identical little hides in the process. You can trust me."

"Bullshit."

"We have the same goal. Getting the tape and clearing our names. We're on the same side. The enemy of my enemy, and all that."

"You're wasting my time." I kicked the back of her right leg and pushed her to her knees.

"Think what you like," she said. "I should have known you wouldn't care who the Instructor's plan hurts. You don't have much feeling for anyone, do you? At least, that's the gist I picked up from your conversation with your boyfriend. Whoops, my bad—*ex*-boyfriend."

I placed the barrel against Hammett's temple.

She had the nerve to laugh. "I knew it. You're just like me, Chandler. You don't have any humanity. Not anymore. The Instructor has finally wrung it out of you."

I felt sick. I didn't want her to be right. I didn't want Lund to be right, either. But how could I argue? How could I refute the facts?

"Why are you hesitating, Chandler? Do it already."

Taking a deep breath, I did what I needed to.

Fleming

"There's a thin line between love and hate," said the Instructor. "And there are times you'll have to straddle it."

Fleming and Tequila didn't talk. There wasn't much to say.

Tequila and Lund hadn't had any trouble recovering the white SUV, a fact that made Fleming suspect the Instructor had called off his troops with some sort of plan in mind. Once Tequila had returned to the farm, it hadn't taken more than a few minutes to load their few supplies and Fleming's chair. Now all they could do was wait.

Outside it had started to rain, drops pattering against the kitchen window, and the smell of precipitation hitting sun-heated gravel filled the house. The news droned from a transistor radio they'd found in one of the rooms upstairs, an endless prattle about the presidential assassination and the resultant manhunt for those responsible. Apparently the Instructor hadn't turned over the evidence. Fleming wondered if he would, or if he'd take another shot at forcing them into his service. She suspected the latter.

She needed to figure out what action she would take when that time came.

Footsteps sounded on the front porch, the door creaked open, and Chandler walked down the hall to the kitchen.

Fleming wanted to ask her sister what had happened, but decided it best to let Chandler take the lead. However, when close to a minute had ticked by with none of them saying a word, Fleming couldn't stand it any longer and finally decided to break the silence. "Tequila said he'd help find us a car."

Chandler swung her eyes to Tequila. "Thanks."

He gave a nod.

Chandler glanced around the kitchen. "Everything packed?"

"It's all in the truck, except for the trash here." Fleming gestured to the garbage bag waiting in the center of the linoleum floor, the last signs they'd ever visited this farmhouse. "We wiped the place down. We can leave whenever you're ready."

Chandler focused on the black plastic bag. "My old clothes from yesterday, they in the trash?"

"Yup." They were dirty and torn beyond repair. Chandler had tossed them this morning, a move Fleming didn't see reason to change.

Now Chandler felt differently. She opened the bag and pulled out the black sweater and torn jeans. A wave of algae and sweat odor wafted from the clothing.

"Lund is gone," Fleming said, unwilling to steer clear of the subject any longer.

"I know."

Fleming couldn't guess exactly what had happened between her sister and the firefighter, but it was clear things hadn't gone well. "He said you went somewhere with Hammett."

"To the forest."

Fleming nodded. As soon as Lund had mentioned it, she'd figured out what Chandler had set out to do. And Fleming had to admit, she didn't feel bad about it. Not even a bit. In fact, she wanted to hear Chandler say the words. "Did you…do it?"

Chandler paused for a moment, then she gestured to the door with the wad of dirty clothes. "You need to see something."

Fleming wheeled her way to the front entrance, Tequila following behind. Chandler opened the door and stepped to the side.

Hammett stood at the bottom of the porch, completely nude and drenched from the rain, her arms handcuffed around a railing. "Hi, Crippled Sis," she said. "Looks like we're going to be working together."

Tequila looked at each of the sisters, his gaze settling on Chandler. "And now there are three."

The White House

"I, James Phillip Ratzenberger, do solemnly swear."

"I, James Phillip Ratzenberger, do solemnly swear."

"That I will faithfully execute the Office of President of the United States."

"That I will faithfully execute the Office of President of the United States."

"And will to the best of my ability, preserve, protect, and defend the Constitution of the United States."

"And will to the best of my ability, preserve, protect and defend the Constitution of the United States."

"So help you, God."

"So help me, God."

The former vice president, now president, put down his right hand and nodded solemnly for the cameras, the crowd, fighting not to smile. He'd waited his whole life for this moment, and though it came because of the death of his predecessor, he still felt like he'd earned it.

The UK missile incident and the recent assassination had plunged this country into chaos and fear. It needed a strong leader to banish the fear, and to restore this nation to its former glory. Ratzenberger knew he was that leader. And he had a plan. A colossal plan, to solidify the US's dominance as the world's only superpower, and to ensure it remained so for the next millennium.

The history of America, and the world, was about to change, and no one would be able to stop it.

The new president closed his eyes and said a solemn prayer, asking God to forgive him for the tens of millions of people who were about to die.

THE END

***Chandler, Fleming, and Hammett will return in* Three.**

CAST OF CHARACTERS

CHANDLER is an elite spy, working for an agency so secret only three people know it exists. Trained by the best of the best, she has honed her body, her instincts, and her intellect to become the perfect weapon.

FLEMING used to be a field operative like Chandler, until she was paralyzed on a mission. A genius, Fleming turned her attention to miraculous inventions and being Chandler's handler, but she's always longed to return to the field.

HAMMETT is a dangerous psychopath with all the training of Chandler and none of the moral fabric. She's a superassassin, and she loves it. Unsympathetic to her fellow human beings, she has a soft spot only for animals.

JACQUELINE "JACK" DANIELS is a Chicago cop who appears in *Shot of Tequila*, *Whiskey Sour*, *Bloody Mary*, *Rusty Nail*, *Dirty Martini*, *Fuzzy Navel*, *Cherry Bomb*, *Shaken*, and *Stirred*. *Flee*, *Spree*, and *Three* take place in the time span between *Dirty Martini* and *Fuzzy Navel*.

HARRY McGLADE runs a private investigating firm with Jack Daniels. McGlade is possibly the most offensive human being of all time.

TEQUILA ABERNATHY was an Olympic gymnast before he became an enforcer for the Chicago mob. Now semiretired, he only does favors for friends and those who can pay his rates. He is featured in the thriller *Shot of Tequila*.

DAVID LUND works as a firefighter in central Wisconsin. The picture of an everyday hero, he is incapable of turning down a person in need of help. He is featured in the thriller *Pushed Too Far*, by Ann Voss Peterson.

VAL RYKER is the police chief of the small Wisconsin town of Lake Loyal. She is featured in the thriller *Pushed Too Far*, by Ann Voss Peterson.

JAVIER ESTRADA worked with the Alphas, a badass paramilitary team who protected major drug cartels. He is featured in *Snowbound*, by Blake Crouch.

ISAIAH BROWN is a former Force Recon Marine featured in *Abandon*, by Blake Crouch.

SANTIAGO, a psychopathic sadist whose specialty is interrogation, is featured in Jack Kilborn's *Afraid*.

THE INSTRUCTOR is the man behind the top-secret Hydra superassassin program. He trained superspies Chandler, Fleming, and Hammett, as well as their now deceased sisters Ludlum, Clancy, LeCarre, and Follett.

AFTERWORD …

…in which Ann and Joe interview each other about the experience of writing* Spree*…

Joe: Wow, this was a long book. But the only way to shorten it would be to cut action, and I love the action. I think the Chandler series is loads of fun because it is so over the top. We wanted to do a contemporary female James Bond, and that meant sex, gadgets, and above all, big action scenes. But this one just kept going and going. Did we plan on *Spree* being over 100,000 words?

Ann: I think we originally planned it to be about 60,000, although once we got writing, I knew it would be 80,000. Wrong on both counts.

Joe: Hopefully it still qualifies as a quick read. And a seamless one. We both worked hard to make sure the writing was consistent, so readers couldn't tell which scenes you wrote and which scenes I wrote. What was your favorite scene to write?

Ann: Tequila riding the horse. It was fun to take a guy who is so athletic and throw him into a situation where he's over his head, at least at first.

Joe: I know you read my novel *Shot of Tequila*, which introduced him, but was it weird to write for a character you didn't create? I did a Lund section or two (one of your heroes from *Pushed Too Far*), but not to the degree you did Tequila. And you did a perfect job with him. One I never could have done, because I've never been on a horse. But you did all that professional riding…

Ann: I loved Tequila when I read him, but I was a little nervous about writing from his point of view. As it turned out, it was a lot of fun. I started riding when I was eleven years old, showed my own horse, and worked for a quarter-horse trainer in my early twenties. I had a lot to learn about men's gymnastics, though. What was your favorite scene to write, Joe?

Joe: The whole idea behind *Flee* was to have a female operative in way over her head. One of the set pieces I was excited about was blowing her out of the ninety-fifth floor of the Hancock Building in Chicago, and having her cling to the side of the building. In *Spree*, I wanted to have a big scene like that, which became the hot-air balloons and the high-tension wire.

That scene was challenging to write. I did hours and hours of research about electricity, and I'm sure I still got stuff wrong. But I like how it turned out, and really dig the idea of two women walking a high-tension tightrope, trying to kill each other.

Ann: Our setting also gave us a lot of ideas.

Joe: Right. We visited the Badger Ammo plant in Baraboo, and a cool guy named Verlyn Mueller gave us a tour. We saw the reservoir Chandler got stuck in (which is filled with a rare species of salamander) and the cannon area and the graveyard. We were so captivated by all of it, half of *Spree*'s action happens at Badger.

Ann: Oh, and the industrial grinder!

Joe: How could we not use that? It's huge and grinds up cement and metal. That was just begging to have characters fight on it.

Ann: A lot of it also takes place in the neighboring Devil's Lake State Park, a place I've visited since I was a kid.

Joe: You're from Wisconsin. I go there every year on vacation, and have been since 1973. It was nice to set a novel there. People don't normally use "Wisconsin" and "thriller" in the same sentence.

Ann: Although you set *Afraid* in Wisconsin.

Joe: I did. But that was a horror novel. That's one of the reasons I included Santiago as a bad guy—he's one of the villains in *Afraid*.

Ann: I set *Pushed Too Far* there, too. And a lot of my romantic suspense novels take place in Wisconsin.

Joe: So I guess we've overused America's Dairyland.

Ann: We'll have to take *Three* someplace else.

Joe: Any thoughts about where? And how it'll work out with Hammett on their side? Isn't she too much of a psychopath to trust?

Ann: Oh, I have a lot of thoughts. We can take this international. And I love the idea of an enemy becoming an ally. I guess it remains to be seen how Chandler and Fleming deal with Hammett.

Joe: I also gotta say thanks to our friend Blake Crouch for letting us use his characters Javier and Isaiah. Those are his villains from his books *Snowbound* and *Abandon*, and he was cool enough to let us borrow them so we didn't have to make up new characters on our own. So thanks, Blake.

Ann: Are we paying Blake anything?

Joe: Hell, no.

You did the sex scene in *Flee*, and in *Spree*, and I just added some naughty bits to them. I think, for *Three*, we each do a sex scene. I feel I'm ready to do one on my own.

Ann: Your transition to sex just gave me whiplash. But, you'll be great! When people try to guess which part you wrote and which I wrote, they're usually wrong.

Joe: They'll know for sure this time. My sex scene will take place while they're plummeting from a helicopter while on fire.

It'll be hot.

Ann: And they'll really fall for each other, right?

Joe: Ugh. You've been collaborating with me too long. People are going to think I wrote that joke for you.

Ann: You didn't?

Joe: Sadly, no.

So, is *Three* going to be it for the Codename: Chandler series? Or will there be more books with these characters?

Ann: We've written three Codename: Chandler novellas; *Exposed*, *Naughty*, and *Hit*, which all take place before *Flee*. I can't imagine the ideas will suddenly stop flowing. These are fun characters!

Joe: You're doing another Val/Lund book, right?

Ann: I'm writing at least two follow-ups to *Pushed Too Far*: *Cut Too Deep* and *Dead Too Soon*, in addition to other things. And you have about a billion books planned, don't you?

Joe: I'm doing another Kilborn horror novel called *Haunted House*, and a sequel to *Origin* called *Second Coming*, among other projects. So the only way we can squeeze in another Chandler is if she becomes a huge hit and fans want more.

Feel free to contact Ann at ann@annvosspeterson.com and demand another Chandler story.

Ann: Great idea. You can also contact Joe at—

Joe: Sorry. We're out of time.

AUTHORS' NOTE

We truly hoped you enjoyed *Spree.* While it can be read as a stand-alone thriller, this is the second part of a trilogy featuring Chandler, Hammett, and Fleming. If you like to read things in order, it is *Flee*, *Spree*, *Three.* Chandler also appears in the short novel *Exposed*, and in *Hit.* Hammett appears in the short novel *Naughty.* All of these take place prior to *Flee.*

The characters of Lund and Val appear in *Pushed Too Far*, by Ann Voss Peterson.

The characters of Jack Daniels and Harry McGlade appear in *Whiskey Sour*, *Bloody Mary*, *Rusty Nail*, *Dirty Martini*, *Fuzzy Navel*, *Cherry Bomb*, and *Shaken*, written by J. A. Konrath. They also appear in *Stirred* and *Serial Killers Uncut*, written by J. A. Konrath and Blake Crouch.

Harry McGlade also appears in *Babe On Board*, written by J. A. Konrath and Ann Voss Peterson.

The character of Javier appears in *Snowbound*, by Blake Crouch.

The character of Isaiah appears in *Abandon*, by Blake Crouch.

The character of Santiago appears in *Afraid*, by Jack Kilborn.

The character of Tequila appears in *Shot of Tequila*, by J.A. Konrath.

THE CODENAME: CHANDLER SERIES

By J. A. Konrath and Ann Voss Peterson
In chronological order

Exposed
Naughty
Hit
Flee
Spree
Three

The events in *Flee, Spree,* and *Three* occur after *Pushed Too Far* by Ann Voss Peterson, before *Afraid* by Jack Kilborn and *Abandon* and *Snowbound* by Blake Crouch, and in between *Dirty Martini* and *Fuzzy Navel* by J. A. Konrath.

Be sure to check out* Shot of Tequila, *the novel by J.A. Konrath that introduces Tequila and Jack Daniels, available for $2.99 in the Kindle Store...

A gutsy robbery—

Several million bucks, stolen from the mob...

A perfect frame—

All caught on video, with no chance of redemption...

A red-hot recipe for roaring revenge—

Now one man must single-handedly face the entire Chicago Outfit, a group of hardened Mafia enforcers, a psychotic bookie, the most dangerous hit man on earth, and Detective Jacqueline "Jack" Daniels.

His name is Tequila. And he likes those odds.

Shot of Tequila takes place in the early 1990s and is both an homage to and a reenvisioning of classic action novels by authors like Mickey Spillane, Ross Macdonald, Donald Westlake, and Elmore Leonard, but with a more modern twist. The breakneck action is intercut with scenes featuring Konrath's series hero Jack Daniels, here as a supporting character chasing the main protagonist. Edge-of-your-seat suspense, nonstop action, and dark humor punctuate this heist novel/fugitive-on-the-run thriller. Fans of Konrath's police procedurals will enjoy the slight departure from his normal writing style, while still finding familiarity in the setting and characters.

And look for **Pushed Too Far**
The first Val Ryker/David Lund thriller by Ann Voss Peterson
Introduction by Blake Crouch

Two years ago a woman was brutally murdered, her body burned until only ash and shattered bone remained. Police Sergeant Valerie Ryker solved that case, putting undisputed monster Dixon Hess in prison for life, and becoming the first female police chief of her tiny Wisconsin town.

Then the original murder victim turns up in a frozen lake, all in one piece and only recently dead, and Val must enter a race against time. In only forty-eight hours, Hess will be set free, and he's nursing one hell of a grudge. And Val, her town, and everyone she loves are at the top of his list.

But surviving Hess's vengeance is only part of her dilemma. For there's another killer in Lake Loyal. One who may be closer to Val than she thinks...

A page-turning thriller of police procedure, passion, and revenge, *Pushed Too Far* is approximately 65,000 words long.

"If you're a fan of Tess Gerritsen, James Patterson, or Kathy Reichs, don't even hesitate. Filled with nail-gnawing suspense, dark mystery, and even a dash of sexy romance, Pushed Too Far *qualifies for Thriller of the Year."* —J. A. Konrath, author of *Shaken*

J. A. Konrath/Jack Kilborn Works Available on Kindle

Jack Daniels thrillers:
Whiskey Sour
Bloody Mary
Rusty Nail
Dirty Martini
Fuzzy Navel
Cherry Bomb
Shaken
Stirred
Killers Uncut (with Blake Crouch)
Serial Killers Uncut (with Blake Crouch)
Birds of Prey (with Blake Crouch)
Shot of Tequila
Banana Hammock
Jack Daniels Stories (collected stories)
Serial Uncut (with Blake Crouch)
Killers (with Blake Crouch)
Suckers (with Jeff Strand)
Planter's Punch (with Tom Schreck)
Floaters (with Henry Perez)
Truck Stop
Symbios (writing as Joe Kimball)
Flee (with Ann Voss Peterson)
Babe on Board (with Ann Voss Peterson)

Other works:
Afraid (writing as Jack Kilborn)
Endurance (writing as Jack Kilborn)
Trapped (writing as Jack Kilborn)
Draculas (with J. A. Konrath, Jeff Strand, and F. Paul Wilson)
Origin

Disturb

65 Proof (short story omnibus)

Crime Stories (collected stories)

Horror Stories (collected stories)

Dumb Jokes & Vulgar Poems

A Newbie's Guide to Publishing

Wild Night Is Calling (with Ann Voss Peterson)

Shapeshifters Anonymous

The Screaming

Visit the author at www.jakonrath.com.

Ann Voss Peterson's Works Available on Kindle

Thrillers:
Pushed Too Far
Flee (with J.A. Konrath)
Exposed (novella) (with J.A. Konrath)

Short stories:
Babe on Board (with J. A. Konrath)
Wild Night Is Calling (with J. A. Konrath)

Romantic suspense novels:
Gypsy Magic (with Rebecca York and Patricia Rosemoor)
Claiming His Family
Incriminating Passion
Boys in Blue (with Rebecca York and Patricia Rosemoor)
Legally Binding
Desert Sons (with Rebecca York and Patricia Rosemoor)
Marital Privilege
Serial Bride (*Wedding Mission* series)
Evidence of Marriage (*Wedding Mission* series)
Vow to Protect (*Wedding Mission* series)
Critical Exposure
Special Assignment
Wyoming Manhunt
Christmas Awakening
Covert Cootchie-Cootchie-Coo
Rocky Mountain Fugitive
A Rancher's Brand of Justice
A Cop in Her Stocking
Seized by the Sheik
Secret Protector

Visit the author at annvosspeterson.com.

ABOUT THE AUTHORS

Award-winning author Ann Voss Peterson wrote her first story at seven years old and hasn't stopped since. To pursue her love of creative writing, she's worked as a bartender, horse groomer, window washer, and other odd jobs. Now known for her adrenaline-fueled thrillers and Harlequin Intrigue romances, Ann draws on her wide variety of life experiences to fill her fictional worlds with compelling energy and undeniable emotion. She lives near Madison, Wisconsin, with her family and their border collie.

J. A. Konrath broke into the writing scene with his cocktail-themed mystery series, including *Whiskey Sour*, *Bloody Mary*, and *Rusty Nail*—stories that combine uproarious humor with spine-tingling suspense. Since then, Konrath has gone on to become an award-winning and best-selling author known for thriller and horror novels. He is also a pioneer of self-publishing models and posts industry insights on his world-famous blog, *A Newbie's Guide to Publishing*. He lives in Chicago with his family and three dogs.

39909033R00224

Made in the USA
Middletown, DE
24 March 2019